Tender
Offers

By the same author

The Overachievers
High Gloss
A Controlling Interest

Tender Offers

A Novel by

Peter Engel

St. Martin's Press   New York

TENDER OFFERS. Copyright © 1983 by Peter Engel. All rights reserved. Printed in the United States of America. No part of this book may be used or reproduced in any manner whatsoever without written permission except in the case of brief quotations embodied in critical articles or reviews. For information, address St. Martin's Press, 175 Fifth Avenue, New York, N.Y. 10010.

Library of Congress Cataloging in Publication Data

Engel, Peter H.
   Tender offers.

   I. Title.
PS3555.N39T4 1983   813'.54   83-2935
ISBN 0-312-79093-7

First Edition

10 9 8 7 6 5 4 3 2 1

To Patricia, with love and trust.

Tender Offers

1

The Waldorf Astoria is no longer the most elegant of New York's hotels. Its lobby, which used to be spacious and dignified, has been cluttered with expensive boutiques until it looks more like a Galleria-style shopping center than a welcoming entranceway. And the guests, who used to be the cream of visiting dignitaries, are now mostly salesmen at conventions, all potbellies and loud laughter. But the Grand Ballroom remains the most celebrated, glittering, chandeliered of all the ballrooms in the city—and the one where inevitably the most expensive fund-raisers are held.

So it was in the Waldorf Grand Ballroom that the tycoons of the real estate industry gathered—the men resplendent in tuxedos, their wives bejeweled, gowned and thoroughly painted—to honor the mayor of New York. In the V.I.P. cocktail foyer were the great sharks of the industry, men whose names read like a map of the city's tallest buildings. Circling them like pilot fish were their aides and sycophants, fetching drinks, making small talk, currying favor.

Harry Helmsley, the tallest, toughest, biggest of all the magnates, owner of the Empire State Building and the Helmsley Palace Hotel—far more opulent than the poor old Waldorf—smiled calmly at his thronging admirers. Sometimes he held hands with his pretty wife, Leona.

Next to Helmsley stood Oliver Chapin, whose shiny pate, haloed by a fringe of white hair, above his red-cheeked cherubic face, made him look like a monk. Yet there was about him, as about Helmsley himself, a sense of power. No doubt he was the sort of monk who ran his monastery's most successful wineries.

Oliver was chortling. "I say," he insisted in his rich Boston accent, "what a wonderful necklace, my dear." About $500,000, he estimated. Behind him, Sidney Rosenberg, his most trusted lieutenant, followed his boss's glance and made an almost identical evaluation.

"Thank you." Leona Helmsley acknowledged the compliment simply. Her husband put his arm around her shoulder.

Protecting his investment, Oliver thought cynically. Very wise. "Tell me," he asked of no one in particular, "what charity are we honoring anyway? Heart, is it? Or cancer? I always get confused."

"The Greater New York Heart Fund," Rosenberg informed him.

"Is it, is it? Very good." Oliver Chapin beamed and moved away to chat with another group.

Even though special invitations were needed to enter, the throng in the V.I.P. foyer increased to rush-hour density as the dinner hour drew closer. There seemed no place left to stand.

"How're you doin'?" men called across each other, trying to remain jovial in the crush.

"Fine, fine. And you?"

"Great."

"We must get together for lunch."

"Sure. Love to. Call me anytime."

"Lovely dress, darling," women sniped. "They're very popular now."

"Oh, but you look perfect yourself. And I'm so jealous! How do you resist becoming a slave to fashion like the rest of us?"

The larger lobby, the one for all those guests who had

neither deserved nor finagled a special pass was, if possible, even more crowded. But here the atmosphere was more convivial, less brittle and bitchy than in the V.I.P. section. The junior real estate salesmen, their wives still young and pretty, seemed to be having fun talking shop with contractors more used to hard hats than dinner jackets. There was more genuine laughter; less hard, sophisticated chatter.

At eight o'clock precisely, the lights in both foyers dimmed briefly and, more to the point, the bars closed. It was time to enter the ballroom itself.

One hundred and twenty tables, twelve seats each, at a minimum of a hundred dollars a plate, Sidney Rosenberg calculated quickly as he surveyed the scene. One hundred and forty-four thousand dollars income at the least—and most guests donated more than the minimum. He himself had paid a cool three thousand to get a table for the Chapin party close to the dais. As he looked up, Sidney saw that even the two tiers of balconies were filled. Perfect place to shoot from, he thought, and flinched. He glanced over at his boss. Surely there could be no danger this evening. Still, you could never be too careful . . .

Oliver looked entirely appropriate in a tuxedo. Rolypoly and short he was, and even slightly rumpled, but his clothes nevertheless fit him as well as the feathers on a penguin. No one would have guessed by looking at him how very far he was from "to the manner born." Nor would anyone observing Oliver Chapin in this setting have even considered calling him Ollie, the name to which he had answered until well into his twenties. "Which is our table?" he now demanded of Rosenberg, his good humor suddenly evaporated. His feet hurt, he felt confined by his cummerbund, and his irritation at having to spend the next hour or more enduring speeches was mounting.

"Table four, sir." Sidney knew that military precision was the best way to deal with his boss in this mood.

"Fourth from the left, dead center, right in front of the head table."

"Thank you." The words might have been "at ease!" "And our guests?"

"The state senator and the city commissioner. They said they would be honored. You know the ones." It was force of habit for Sid to mention no names.

"At those prices, they should be honored."

Sid Rosenberg wasn't sure whether Oliver meant the price of the table or the size of the monthly payments to each man's designated recipient—a Swiss bank account for one; a small, gray-haired mother in Brooklyn for the other. He decided it wasn't important. "And a minor diplomat. Very minor."

"Who's covering me?"

"Limpet," Sid referred to a bodyguard christened Alberto LaVinci but nicknamed Limpet for his tenacity. "He has decent manners and he's reliable. He's watching the entrance, but he'll join us later."

"Very good. And the . . ." Chapin paused to emphasize his sarcasm, ". . . and the ladies?"

"The senator's wife, and a live-in who goes with the diplomat. The rest are models who work for you. I've checked that they're all reasonably safe. Anyhow, nothing's going to be said at the table."

"Lovely." Oliver was, as usual, mollified by efficiency. "So let's get on with it. Sounds boring as hell!" But secretly he was pleased that he'd be spending the evening with four pretty girls he owned. Maybe later, after he'd talked to that fellow . . .

"And where are we meeting?"

"It's all set. One of the girls, the redhead, has a room here. One floor up. She'll take you there as soon as the evening's done. Then she'll leave. No one should see you go in, but even if they do, they'll only assume you like redheads."

"Oh, but I do, I sure do," Oliver chortled away merrily. "Don't we all!"

"Then he'll join you a few minutes later by the other door. There are two rooms connected so there'd be no proof you ever met even if someone was watching the whole time."

"But . . ."

"Which they won't be," Sidney reassured quickly. "I'll see to that."

"Yes, that would be wiser." For a moment the merry eyes hardened.

Sid Rosenberg was, as always, grateful that he had prepared the plan so thoroughly. Oliver Chapin was not the sort of boss who tolerated mistakes. "I think that's it, then," he said.

"Well arranged." It was considerable praise from Chapin who usually took perfection for granted. "Oh, and by the way, perhaps it might be wise if you could send the girl back later, after I've finished."

"I've already told her to stand by."

"All of them, perhaps?" The questioning tone did nothing to hide the fact that it was an order.

"Of course."

It took half an hour of pushing, chairs scraping, minor territorial arguments about who's table it was anyway, and general confusion before all fourteen hundred guests were seated. Then, as the occupants of the head table filed in—venerable men holding themselves self-consciously erect plus the two mandatory females—everyone had to stand again for the invocation. Meaningless cant, Sid thought, and too damn long. At least at his Temple young Rabbi Yolitz tried to say something that made you think. All this fellow was doing, representing the Catholic archdiocese, was mouthing emotional slogans. Quite a real estate dealer though, Sidney thought irrelevantly. He noticed that Oliver appeared to be listening raptly to the invocation. He was nodding in benign approval.

When it was over, Oliver sat down heavily, totally the jovial friar again. "Beautiful invocation," he beamed at his guests. "Welcome everyone. Have a good time."

The waiters served the food with all the efficiency and finesse of production-line workers in an automobile factory, throwing first soup, then Beef Wellington and finally an ice cream parfait with chocolate sauce in front of the guests with brusque rudeness. The girls cringed, trying to avoid stains on their expensive gowns. Their employer had provided them, but the girls got to keep them as part of their pay.

But Oliver ignored the waiters and refused to be anything but the genial host. He chatted easily with the girls, enchanted the senator's wife by listening intently to every word she said, and acted altogether as if he had neither a care in the world nor any other motive but charity on his mind. Above all, he seemed so disarmingly gentle . . . truly a gentleman from the old school, Sid thought as he watched the performance with awe.

At one point, one of the waiters, even more brusque than the rest, almost spilled some gravy on the prettiest of the four girls, who squealed in protest.

"You have to realize, my dear, that these fellows really aren't waiters at all," Oliver explained to her with a twinkle. "They're actually retired boxers. That's why no one complains."

"Is that so," said Limpet suspiciously. He had been silent up to that moment.

"I wondered what it was." The senator, too, had taken Oliver seriously. "I thought it was that they were all unionized." His wife kicked him under the table. "Yeah, boxers." He grinned suddenly. "Maybe they're ex–football players too," he added, failing to improve the joke.

"Do you come to these events often?" the redhead next to Oliver Chapin asked him. Since she was to take him to her room later, they'd better be seen talking a little over dinner. "You seem to know everyone."

"Indeed yes, my dear, I do get around a bit." He beamed at her. What would she be like? A temper, probably, he thought. But she looked too brittle to be much fun on her own. All four would be more of a challenge.

"I bet you do." She made the innuendo quite clear. He seemed a sweet old man, not like some of them she'd been with . . .

"Waiter!" Oliver's tone of command stopped the surly old man rushing past their table.

"Yeah?"

"I'd like two more bottles of that red." He indicated several wine bottles, almost empty, on the table.

"I ain't got time right now."

"Make time." The command flashed like a blade.

"Yes sir." The waiter forgot what else he had to do and hurried off on his errand.

The redhead raised her eyebrows in surprise. Maybe he was harder than she had thought. Better be careful, my darling, she admonished herself. Instinctively, she patted her hair.

No one saw Oliver Chapin enter the room with the redhead. He glanced at his watch. "Take a drink, why don't you, stay a little, and then perhaps you'd better leave," he suggested.

"Okay," she smiled at him, understanding that this was the plan but assuming that he would like a little friendliness in the meantime since he had asked for her later. "I'll do just what you want."

He turned away from her and pulled the most comfortable chair away from the window—not that anyone could see in through the drapes, but it never hurt to be cautious—and sat down. He felt the tension, the excitement start to build. This could turn out to be the biggest deal of his life if Sid was right. Not that there wasn't a lot that could go wrong if the man was interested. He'd have to be careful. All his life Oliver had struggled to avoid risk. It's what kept him powerful—and sometimes what kept him alive. Of course, there were times when what seemed like the most dangerous path was actually the safest. He made himself more comfortable in the chair and tried to relax. Winning was often a question of having less to lose than the other guy. That, and more patience . . .

Oliver's thoughts were interrupted by the girl sitting down on the edge of his chair. A pretty little thing, he decided, but presumptuous. "Off," he said in a cold voice.

"But . . ."

"When I want you on my lap, my dear, I'll tell you."

"Oh!" She started to flounce away.

"Sit over there," he commanded, his voice as dangerous as when he had told the waiter to fetch the wine. "And do try to keep quiet."

The girl obeyed without delay. Suddenly she found herself hoping he'd never ask to see her again. She tried to keep very still. And when, five minutes later, he politely suggested she might want to leave, she went quickly and without any comment.

Oliver Chapin, looking not only small and rotund, but deceptively elderly and soft, smiled when the interconnecting door from the adjacent room opened and the man entered. "Good evening," he said. "You looked good up on that dais."

"And you at table four."

Carlos Spinosa was in total contrast to Oliver Chapin. He was lean, hard, sinewy and gray, with a hatchet face and business instincts to match.

Oliver had known of Spinosa for years and had met him once or twice. But they had never done business before. "He's really not quite my type," Oliver had explained. "I'm afraid his antecedents are rather, well, unclear." He had paused carefully. "You know, he's both Italian *and* Jewish." But times had changed.

Sid Rosenberg had given Oliver as much additional background on Carlos Spinosa as possible. There wasn't much to know, but what there was Sid had dug out.

Spinosa's main power base was in New York real estate. Indeed, as *The New York Times* and, more shrilly, the *Post* often hinted, he was involved in some of the most unsavory real estate deals in the city. Beyond that, however, Oliver knew that Spinosa had interests in companies as diversified as an entertainment conglomerate, several trucking firms, and a giant pharmaceutical company. Most recently he had heard that Spinosa was the driving force behind an attempt to corner the road-repair contracts for New York City. Altogether, Oliver Chapin had decided, here was a man who was no doubt a financial heavyweight. However, he probably couldn't command the sort of army of loyal people, willing to put themselves on the line—rather than merely faceless shareholders or employees—that Oliver Chapin could.

"Drink?" Oliver offered, checking to see whether his research was right and Spinosa would refuse.

"No thank you." Spinosa's voice was extraordinary, as impersonal as a computer. Its perfectly enunciated English accent was barely tinged with some indefinable foreignness; its timbre was as abrasive as an emery board.

Wordlessly Oliver opened a packet of Marlboros and offered one to Spinosa. I know you smoke these, you bastard, he was thinking.

Silent too, Spinosa accepted it. You have studied me, my friend, he was thinking, and we both know that. But still you know nothing of what I am, of where I come from. That is the advantage I have over you. You are a poor boy made good—although most people assume you were born with that phony Cabots and Lowells accent—but I am a dead man, come alive.

Still they studied each other, each waiting for the psychologically right moment to speak.

The cigarette was half-finished, the glass of wine Oliver had poured for himself half-drunk, before they felt they had tested each other's mettle and patience far enough. Either one could speak now, without losing face.

"You wanted?" Spinosa asked.

"Your drug company is doing well? Your pharmaceutical investments?" Oliver wanted to interest Spinosa in the scheme he and Sid Rosenberg had so laboriously developed—but without revealing too many of its details. It was bad enough that he'd had to initiate this first approach; there'd been no alternative to that. But from now on, let Spinosa come to him. Otherwise, if he wasn't careful, the son of a bitch might try to handle the whole thing without even involving Oliver. . . .

"I have several pharmaceutical interests," said Spinosa warily. "Some are doing better than others." He had no idea what Oliver wanted. But he knew the Chapin empire was powerful—and rich. He would certainly listen to anything this deceptively effete old gent had to say. The trick would be to get him to reveal what he wanted before having to commit to anything himself. It wouldn't be easy. . . .

"Some of my more distant associates, too, have some interests in the business."

"In pharmaceuticals?" Spinosa was surprised.

"A different branch of the business. The products are similar, but their supply source is not as convenient as yours."

"So?" Spinosa was starting to understand. There had always been rumors that Chapin was connected with some of the most unsavory groups of them all. The New Jersey mob was a hint one of Spinosa's researchers had picked up. Not that anything could be proven, of course; Oliver Chapin's only known interests in New Jersey were a local bank and a small chain of fish restaurants. But then the name Chapin Investments kept appearing in the strangest places. . . . But even if Chapin were involved with drugs, the question remained, what had that got to do with him? In spite of himself, Spinosa was becoming intrigued.

"My friends have reached two rather interesting conclusions," Chapin was saying.

Spinosa inclined his head to indicate he was listening, but said nothing.

"One is that the stock of that company you're connected with—that Turner something—it doesn't seem to be setting the world on fire."

"Turner-LaMott; quite static," Spinosa agreed. That much was common knowledge. No point in denying it. But the inflection in his voice remained entirely dispassionate. Even Oliver Chapin's carefully attuned ear could pick up no sense of whether Spinosa expected a change, was satisfied with his investment, or intended to sell out any day.

"Seems to us it could stand a little pushing," Oliver could not avoid making that much of his scheme clear.

"It could." The fact was that buying that much of Turner-LaMott stock had been a lousy move for Spinosa. A gamble that, although it hadn't hurt him, had taken up a large percentage of his total assets, over half, in fact. And he hadn't made a dime on the damned company. He had expected far bigger advances, particularly from their genetic engineering work. But so far nothing had come of it. He wished Oliver would tell him more. Don't be impulsive, he warned himself, as he often did. Let him come to you. . . .

Again there was a space of silence. Then, "I believe we might help with that," Oliver started.

"How?" Had he asked just a stroke too quickly? Spinosa wondered.

"We might be willing to invest."

"Money. Very important, of course," Spinosa said. "But not everything." He'd long ago learned that investments always came with a mass of strings attached, ropes frequently.

"There's also people. My friends think they've got the right people on this one." Chapin's voice had lost part of its caution, and the careful Boston drawl now seemed more clipped.

He's really excited, Spinosa realized. This must be bigger than I thought. But instead of feeling he had an advantage because the other man had revealed himself, Spinosa could feel his own excitement rising. It took an effort not to ask more questions.

Again both men stopped speaking, each waiting for some sort of advantage to suggest itself. But eventually it was Spinosa who broke the silence. "Tell you what," he said, finally losing patience, "why don't you explain the whole thing, Mr. Chapin? I'll stipulate that it's wholly your scheme, your money and your people. Then, if I like your plan, we'll be partners. If not, you go ahead alone and I'll forget we ever had this meeting or that I heard about your idea." Unless, he was thinking, it's really worth remembering. . . .

"I call that very fair, Mr. Spinosa." Oliver was pleased that he had made up at least some negotiating ground. "Okay. I'll tell you the scheme Sid Rosenberg and I figured out. If you'd care to join us, we'd be pleased. If not, we'll both forget we ever saw each other here." Unless, Oliver Chapin was thinking, you make a grab for it. In that case, Latino, you'd better walk around keeping your head way down.

2

Oliver Chapin's body jiggled as he bounced his five-year-old granddaughter on his knee. His round, monk's head bobbing on his baggy body made him look like an aging Michelin man. The little girl squealed in delight.

"Falling in the bog, turns her to a frog," her grandfather recited, blowing his cheeks out and croaking. "Falling on the grass, green stains on her—"

"That's enough, I think." His wife, a middle-aged lady of great elegance, surveyed them over her half-glasses.

Oliver laughed. "I suppose so," he agreed pleasantly. He was never upset by his wife's reprimands. Imperiousness was simply part of her heritage. He had chosen her for her social prestige and ambition, won her by offering her excitement and promising to finance her ambition—and he was perfectly satisfied with his bargain. Fun and games, he reflected contentedly, thinking briefly of last night's redhead and her friends, he could always have away from home.

"More," cried the little girl.

"Of course, of course. But we'll have to invent a different game. Grandmother says we're getting a little rowdy."

The little girl pouted but was careful not to let her grandmother see.

"I know," Oliver said cheerfully. "Let's play invent."

"What's that?" The little girl was immediately full of curiosity.

But before he could explain, the butler entered. "I beg

your pardon, sir, but there's a telephone call for you. I wouldn't have disturbed, but it's your office and they say it's urgent."

"Thank you, James. I'll take it in my study." He set his granddaughter down firmly onto the carpet. The suppressed anger in his voice was such that the little girl dared give no hint of complaint. He rose and strode out of the room.

"You will stay for dinner?" his wife called after him. She feared that this telephone call meant he would have to rush off again. How disappointed the children would be.

He didn't bother to answer.

Oliver entered his soundproofed study and slammed the door. It locked automatically. It was the only room in the house which had any connection to his work—and no one was permitted to enter. A year ago, before he had installed the lock, his granddaughter had pushed at the door and unexpectedly found it open. She had been curious—and unwise—enough to want to explore. Oliver had instinctively pulled himself back into a corner when the door started to open and had waited tensely to see who was invading his privacy. When he saw who it was he relaxed, but he kept quite still until she was fully inside the room. Then he picked her up roughly and smacked her bottom until she screamed with terror and pain.

"Don't ever come in here, little girl, not ever again," he had warned her coldly. Then he had half-thrown her out of the room, much as one might throw out a cat.

Oliver now picked up the telephone. He said nothing until he heard the click of the receiver in the kitchen being placed back on its cradle. The kitchen instrument was specially made so that it could neither be lifted nor replaced without a loud noise on his extension.

"Yes?" he asked. "What do you want?" Even in the short phrase his voice seemed menacing.

Sid Rosenberg hated calling his boss at home. He only

did so when there was an emergency. "We have a rumor that our friend Caro may be thinking of circumventing us," he said without preliminaries, using the nickname—the Italian for "dear one"—which had been bestowed upon Luigi Pollo. "He claims you don't have enough merchandise for his organization to sell. So he's letting the word out that he'd be willing to buy from your competitor." Even over the safe house phone, Sid kept his conversation ambiguous.

"We knew that before, didn't we? That's what yesterday's meeting with our friend was all about. What's different?"

"I've just received the message that the dear chicken has decided not to wait. Apparently he's planning to buy from a new source as early as next week. Says it's just business, that his masseuses need, er, oil."

"And you think we'd better stop him?"

"Well, even though Caro is emphasizing that he's only looking for the extra he needs, that he's not out to fight you . . ."

"You're right." Evidently Caro was feeling stronger than he should. Of course, it might still be bluff. But that wouldn't last long if Caro thought the Chapin group was weakening. Oliver's anger started to mount, and as it did his voice became smoother, his features, if possible, took on an even more benign cast. "Listen, my friend," he was almost purring. "You were right to call me. Something should be done about our chicken. Perhaps you should ask him to visit my office."

"I'll try, Oliver, but he doesn't like it there."

"The carpets intimidate him." Oliver chortled as if he had not a care in the world. "Well, if he won't come to Park Avenue, perhaps our Brooklyn place?"

"Tonight?"

"I think it would be best." He paused. "Oh, and perhaps later, some relaxation . . ."

* * *

On the corner of 125th Street and Lenox Avenue the addicts nodded, the garbage blew—making angry but futile little stabs into the evening air—and the hookers plied their mundane wares at less than the price of even one good fix. For every dollar they collected from their tricks—or spent with their supplier—Caro Polo collected his dime.

On Third Avenue, seventy-five blocks south, derelicts handed out leaflets for massage parlors to passersby who smirked at the pictures briefly and then tossed them into the nearest gutter to merge with the rest of the city's litter. A few, of course, secreted them about their persons for reference.... And for each of those who later sneaked into a massage parlor, Caro Polo collected his cut.

In the lobby of an elegant hotel on Park Avenue, the porter bowed his head slightly as he took a tip from a wealthy guest. It was not deference that caused him to dip his head, but the wish to see the note's denomination. Ten dollars. Good. "I think I can arrange something," the porter assured the guest. "What time would be convenient?"

"As soon as . . ." The guest was embarrassed at seeming too eager. "At about nine-thirty," he corrected himself.

"Very well. As before, slim and. . . ?"

"Yes," said the guest quickly. "And blond."

"Of course, sir." The porter assumed that Mitzi, or whatever she was calling herself these days, had an appropriate wig.

And from both the porter and the girl herself, Caro Pollo received his percentage.

In a loft office in Brooklyn, the door of which identified it as the home of both the E-Z Manufacturing Company and the A-1 Haulage Corporation, three hard-faced men, shirtsleeves rolled up, faces haggard from a long day, talked angrily.

"I told Rosenberg already it's the supplies that's killing us," one of the men whined. "I've done all right on the rest: massages is up; and the garbage business is going fine. But sales is down overall—we just ain't got the inventory. And I'm mad as hell about it."

"What did he say?"

"He just said they was working on it."

"That's easy for him to say."

"Yeah, well, what do you expect? Sid can't say nothing else. It's not up to him. Trouble is, God knows what the fucking Deacon's up to. The old man seems to spend half his time at balls and dinners, and the other half sitting in that funeral parlor he calls an office planning what company he's going to buy next. Meantime, I got about a thousand shitheads out there screaming for the stuff."

"He'd better do something pretty fucking soon," agreed the third man. "I got a worse problem than you guys. My hookers is all getting pissed off having nothing to sell but their twats." The speaker was a tough little Italian-looking man with a beaked nose, bushy eyebrows and a permanently belligerent expression.

"Ain't that what they're supposed to sell, Caro?" the first man asked. "What you got, hookers that's virgins?"

Caro snorted with laughter. "In the left ear, maybe, some of the younger ones."

"So, at least you're not out of business like I am."

"Their cunts is their own," Polo explained succinctly. "It's the shit they gets from me. If I don't supply, I lose 'em. So if fucking Ollie Chapin, or whatever he calls himself now, don't supply soon, I'm gonna have to go some place else."

"Like where?"

The man they called Caro, whose real name was Luigi, stared at his questioner. "Dunno," he growled, "but it's for fuckin' sure I ain't gonna sit back and do nothing."

* * *

The limousine that picked Oliver Chapin up from his Westchester home was a dark blue Buick. A Cadillac or Lincoln—even a Rolls Royce for which he secretly hankered—would have been too ostentatious. The chauffeur was also dressed in blue, his uniform so well-cut, however, that he seemed rather more militaristic than would be expected in an ordinary driver.

Oliver was already waiting at his front door as the car climbed the long hill of driveway and crunched to a halt on the graveled oval in front of the house. The chauffeur jumped out smartly.

"Hello, hello." Oliver beamed at him. "Good of you to give up your Sunday, Limpet."

"No problem, sir." It was a lie; his wife had needed a good smack across the chin before she'd quit whining. Broads! Never knew when they had it good. So the Deacon needed him some weekends and evenings. So what? The money was something else and the bitch surely liked that. "No problem at all," Limpet repeated.

"Fine," Oliver maneuvered himself into the car. "Then I suppose we'd better be off."

"To your office, sir?"

"No, I'm afraid we'll have to go to our Brooklyn place this evening. The normal precautions, I think."

"Very well, sir."

The head office of Chapin Investments, Inc., the main holding company of Oliver's empire, was in an elegant office skyscraper on Park Avenue. A private elevator sped him, or special visitors, up to the forty-first floor where they were enveloped in mouse gray carpeting, a slight leathery scent, and all the "white noise" of air conditioners and power. Secretaries walked almost furtively along those corridors, making no sound whatsoever; and all but the most self-assured of businessmen spoke in hushed tones. Occasionally, however, Oliver needed a more mundane venue for his meetings. Some of his business acquaintances would simply not enter his Park Avenue lair, feeling either too gauche and conspicuous or, out of their own habitat, too unsafe. For these meetings, the company kept a different sort of office in Brooklyn.

Limpet pulled the limousine into an abandoned parking lot. It was dark and the building walls surrounding it had no windows. He controlled his reflex to jump out of the car and instead made sure the light switch was off so that there would be no illumination when his boss opened the door.

With considerably greater agility than he had shown entering it, Oliver Chapin got out of the car, glanced around once to make sure no one was about, and started to walk slowly down the street, apparently an aimless elderly man. The limousine pulled quickly out of the lot and proceeded in the direction it had been going as if it had never stopped at all.

Even now, the old terror came back easily. It was irrational, of course. Hell, one flick of the beeper in his pocket and Limpet would be here within seconds. But rationality had nothing to do with this boyhood terror of the dark and of the rats that inhabited it. Oliver forced himself to walk slowly. There were no rats here, none that would dare come close, neither rodent nor human. Shit, he wished he could allow himself the relief of running, of scampering away to safety as he had done so often as an urchin on the slum streets near the Boston docks. Instead, he forced himself to slow down even more. He would not give in to this fear, any more than he had bowed before any obstacle in his entire life. And what obstacles . . .

Ollie Tchapinisky was possibly the son of a Polish dock worker and certainly of an Irish part-time maid who stretched her legitimate income—and bridged her periods of unemployment—by selling her body. "But only for a week or more at a time," she insisted. "It's consortin' I do, not hookin'. I won't just fuck anyone." She would hold her head high and righteous.

"Just anyone who pays, cunt," her main old man would tease her.

"Don't see you objectin' to the money."

"Hell, woman, what good would it do?"

"None." She would cackle with laughter. "I got no shame left. And nothin' I do is to be shamed of, I reckon, since I could never have fed the kid if I'd done different." She would cackle again, an overblown, overweight woman, far too familiar with Irish whiskey and all forms of debauchery, forlornly pretending to be still a mischievous colleen.

"Even in front of the boy, you'll do it." Stan never ceased to be shocked by his woman's openness before her son.

"Hell, he'd find out. Anyway, what's it to you?"

"He's my son."

"Maybe so, maybe not," she would shake her head. "Whose son are you, boy," she would demand of Ollie, an undersized boy of ten. "Who's your real dad, then?"

"He is," Ollie would answer sullenly. He hated her for forcing him not to be sure. His friends all had fathers—even if some of them had left home or were living with other women. How come Mom kept saying that his dad might not be his dad?

Once he tried to ask her, choking back his rage and tears and trying to remain calm and reasonable when she refused to take his question seriously. "But Mom, why can't you tell me?" he insisted.

"I don't know lad, and that's the truth."

"Of course you know who my dad is. Everyone what has a dad *knows*." He paused, quite unable to figure it out. "Hell, even Harpy down the street knows who his dad was even though he's dead and rotten his Mum says."

"Well I don't."

Ollie couldn't stand it. "Tell me," he screamed, stamping both legs in uncontrolled rage. "Tell me, tell me, tell me, tell me. . . ." His face was contorted and white, tears streaming down it. His small fists were clenched, ready to pound at his mother if she refused.

In response she merely swatted him once hard about the ears. "I don't know who your father was," she said. "And I don't much care."

Later, of course, he understood. In a sense it gave him his freedom. He could have any father he wanted. At first he would choose one of the heroes of the day. Sometimes it was Babe Ruth; at other times, Lucky Luciano . . . he could have anyone he fancied. Eventually, when he was fourteen, he made his final choice. Enough of the rats and the filth of the slums. His father was English, or maybe Irish, but aristocratic, not shanty-town Irish. And of course he was rich. A Kennedy perhaps, or a big man like the mayor. Of course his mother really knew who his dad was. But she couldn't tell him for fear of embarrassing him. After all, she still loved the man. He was probably even a Cabot.

That was when young Ollie started insisting on the name Chapin, and set about making a fortune. It hadn't been easy, especially not at the beginning, in the middle of the depression. Even after he became an accomplished thief, he found very little to steal.

But his father was a "big man," and that gave him the courage to persevere. Every day he would scrounge a newspaper and read the business reports. They fascinated him. Rockefeller was one of his idols. Perhaps his dad had been related to the family . . . or even to Commodore Vanderbilt?

Oliver's first real entry into the business world came when, at the age of fifteen, he managed to get a job as a messenger boy at one of the smaller Boston banks. Every day he carried the mail between the partners' offices; every day he wished he dared open it and see what secrets and fortunes lay hidden inside the envelopes. No moral scruples prevented him. It was only that he could think of no way to open them without getting caught. There was no time to steam them open and tearing them would be a dead giveaway.

Still, it was an honor enough to be allowed into the big boss's office. He was quite stunned the first time he saw it. Those great leather chairs. And that desk! That was where he wanted to be, in an office like that. No doubt his father had one just as big. If only there was a way to get the boss man to notice him. Maybe he could tell him that his dad was a big man too.

The idea came to him quite suddenly, and as promptly he put it into practice.

"Excuse me, sir, but you may not have realized that your shoes need a bit of a shine. It's probably from the rain, sir."

"What?" The big man was barely aware the messenger boy had said something.

"Your shoes, sir. They've got dirtied from the rain. Would you like me to shine them?"

"The shoeshine man—"

"But not till later. I can do it for you right now."

"You have the stuff?"

"Just be a second, sir." Oliver had raced out, heart pounding at his own temerity, wondering desperately where he would get a shoeshine kit. He'd know how to use it all right, having earned coppers often enough working on overflow customers at the stand near the Commons. But where to go . . .

Ollie was jumping from one foot to the other, quite panicked with indecision, when old Sam, the shoeshine man, came around the corner. Hardly thinking, Ollie rushed up to him. "Sam," he shouted, "they've been lookin' for you man. I don' know what you did, but are they *mad*."

"What?" The old black man looked dazed. Had they found out about the pencils he'd been taking all these months and having his sons sell on street corners? "Oh my," he muttered, wiping his forehead.

"You'd better go quick," Ollie pushed his advantage. "I'll look after your stuff."

"That's right kind of you," the old man was most grateful.

"The boss never received a better shine than that day," Ollie would chortle in his forties, by which time he was called Oliver or Mr. Chapin and had made quite a reputation as a retailer of food—and sometimes of many other things. "After that, I became his regular shine boy. It meant I got into his office at least once a day. And I got to *listen*. That was important."

Later still, in his fifties, Oliver Chapin never spoke of those early days at all. By that time, his dream of having a rich father and a solid Boston background had been fully authenticated, right down to the detailed, certified family tree that hung in the living room of his elegant Westchester house.

Oliver Chapin continued his slow old man's walk, refusing to give in to any demons of the dark, for three blocks before he finally reached a nondescript warehouse building. He pushed open its front door. It would have astounded any observer that, once inside, he bounded up the first flight of stairs two at a time, slammed open the door of the first-floor offices, and barged in, violent as a conqueror.

Inside, the offices of the Ace Messenger Service—for such was the name chipped on the door—were as unremarkable as their exterior. Linoleum covered the floors; the furniture was sparse and old, not antique, simply worn from years of use; the windows, gray with city dirt, were covered with ancient Venetian blinds, one half-raised with a slat hanging loose; and the lighting came from bare neon tubes set in the ceiling, one flickering. The office could accommodate fifty people. During weekdays it would be alive with telephone calls and coded messages, succinctly received, quickly forwarded and then instantly forgotten. But the only man there at this time on a Sunday night was Sid Rosenberg dressed in a black leather windbreaker.

At the far end of the room was the only private office, a cubicle really, made of metal partitions and frosted glass. Oliver strode across the main room and slammed in. Gone entirely was the appearance of a benign grandfather. His soft bulbous body seemed barrel-chested rather than plump, his twinkly eyes were hard and his jaw was set firm. Sid Rosenberg, who had been waiting just inside the front door, followed him and closed the door carefully behind them.

"Let me have the details," Oliver demanded, seating himself erect on the worn office chair behind the equally scruffy desk. As he waited for Sid's answer, he stacked the pile of papers, untidily strewn across the desk, into an orderly pile. "Why the sudden pressure?"

"I'm getting other rumors too," Sid explained. "Dissatisfaction. Pretty widespread. It's more than just Caro and his New Jersey boys. Atlantic City is up in arms, and even Harlem—which has been getting more than its fair share—is pissed off."

"About what?"

"Always the same. Supply. The same problem we've had for months. But it's getting worse. Their business is down because we can't get them enough stuff to sell." Sid always kept his reports strictly factual, his voice flat and expressionless. He rarely smiled and never laughed; and, beyond frowning, which he did most of the time, he never allowed himself to show excess worry or dissatisfaction. Categorically, he forbade himself to show fear—however terrified he might be. For that was the most involving of emotions—and for years he had survived by never participating in decisions or actions, by never being involved. He was, he prided himself, the only member of Oliver Chapin's vast organization not really dominated by the boss. Frightened, yes, often; but never *owned*.

"Now look here," Oliver started, his voice for the first time showing at least part of his anger, "you've got to find a way to fix it."

"I just report," said Rosenberg. A New York University MBA, and a CPA with a prestigious accounting firm after that, Sidney Rosenberg knew that his usefulness lay in knowing what was going on—and that his safety depended on his having no responsibility for the results. If ever he became ambitious and took on a more active role, he knew that sooner or later, someone—perhaps even the old Deacon himself—would cut his balls off, or maybe carve out his heart. . . .

"Why are you so passive?"

"Because you pay me for telling you what's going on. Not for doing it."

"Right," said Oliver, who never lost his grip on reality however angry he became. "So, go over it again. What's the problem with the supplies?"

"It's the Feds. They're clamping down all over. That, plus the goddamn president. He's acting like he never got a campaign donation from us. Perhaps next time we'll have to give him more."

"Or less." Chapin felt that if a hundred grand didn't buy a politician, nothing would.

"Yeah," Sid agreed. "Anyway, he's put political pressure on Turkey to limit production. And Mexico's got no more capacity. Nor has Colombia. On top of that, the customs boys are getting hyper. Those new computerized immigration facilities at Kennedy are a pain in the ass.

They don't have to spend as much time as they used to fussing with the tourists. So instead they hassle our people—"

"I know all that," Oliver interrupted.

"The problem is we just can't get ahead of the game," Sid continued in his precise monotone, ignoring the interruption. "As it is, your whole import organization is hustling just to keep up present supply levels. Unless you do something, you're stabilized at best."

"So how come our competitors can get it? If Caro's not lying."

"They can't. Christ, if we can't, no cheap group of Italian hoods is going to. At least, not at reasonable prices. We've always outsmarted, outbought and outsold them. But since they've got no business to speak of, they can pay high and take a loss in order to get Caro to go over to them and put a gap in your organization."

"Moreover, as you point out, it's not just Caro. If that were all, I imagine we could take care of it. He was little more than a punk, after all, when I arranged for him to get his first section to run."

"That's right. But Caro's forgotten that. He's starting to think of himself as really important. Trouble is, the others are listening."

"The poor fool always did talk too much."

"At least he's out in the open. The others are humming under their breath."

"Fine, so we understand the problem," Oliver said sarcastically. "But what are you going to do about it?"

"If I knew that," said Sidney Rosenberg, phrasing the answer very carefully, "I would be sitting where you are."

"And I won't be here long, if I don't find the answer?" Chapin demanded. "Is that what you're trying to say?" He was not in the least worried, however. Certainly there was a problem—but there had been problems before in his life. A million of them. And he'd survived them all.

He just couldn't become concerned about little Luigi Pollo—or upset by Sidney's chronic pessimism. "That's what you were thinking, right?" He wished that just once Sidney would make a useful suggestion.

"In point of fact . . ." Rosenberg had no intention of answering any question as loaded as that one, ". . . we haven't had any volume growth in the last two years. Where dollar sales are up, it's only because our selling prices have increased. But unfortunately, so have our costs." He sounded precisely the same as any other corporate financial officer. That was how he viewed himself. "Marijuana unit sales have trended up slightly. Coke is fine for now, up almost twenty percent over last year, and only half of that is price increases. The rest is volume."

"How come?"

"That was the impact of the Argentinian deal you made last year. The merchandise hit the street this year—so, as long as that lasts we're getting major sales gains."

"Trouble is, I can't repeat it. The man's dead, I'm afraid." Oliver laughed cynically. "A heart attack, apparently, which caused his car to fall off a cliff."

"Pills are down in units and even price increases have barely been able to keep dollar sales level," Sidney continued without comment. "But the biggest problem is that H is down severely. At the prices we are forced to charge fewer people are buying. Quite a number have switched to methadone which, of course, we don't supply. Others have dropped out—dead or locked up—because they just haven't been able to keep up. So even with price increases, our dollar sales are falling—and so are our profits."

"Please, my dear fellow, you sound just like a computer." Oliver's distaste showed on his face as clearly as if Sidney had been waving some rotting carcass in front of him. "But I'm still unclear what you think we should do about it."

"I'm afraid I cannot advise," Rosenberg said coldly, hating to irritate the old man, but preferring to do that than be required to take responsibility.

"Yes, I see that." Oliver Chapin's voice was soft, deep, caressing—and, to Sid Rosenberg's finely attuned ear, very dangerous indeed. "Never mind," he continued, "as Mr. Micawber was wont to say, 'something will turn up.'" He paused. "Including our friendly associate Caro Pollo?"

"He'll be here shortly. One of his henchmen called to say he had an important meeting and would be late."

"He is getting arrogant." Oliver's voice remained quiet, but Sid could sense the fury. "We'd better take care of that." The voice dropped further to a near whisper.

In spite of himself, Sidney Rosenberg felt his stomach contracting with tension. However long he worked for Oliver Chapin he would never be able to overcome it, this fear of the man. Oliver, cheerful benign Oliver most of the time, could, whenever he wanted to, exercise this power over people. Perhaps one day Sidney would be rich enough to back out. Certainly Oliver paid him enough; already Sid could gloat to himself that he had more than a million dollars squirrelled away. But no, he knew too much. In fact he was perhaps the only person except Oliver himself who had any idea how farflung the Chapin empire really was. Even Pollo's family—who were major clients—would have been astonished at its diversity, at the strength and breadth of its financial tentacles. No, Sidney would never be able to leave; he'd be there until the day he died. He smiled to himself wryly. Let the day be a long way off.

"Don't worry, I'll deal with Pollo," Oliver was saying, his jaw jutting in quite unmonklike determination. "He thinks he's an awfully big fish, but I doubt if his teeth are really as sharp as he thinks." He pronounced the word "sharp" with an even flatter Boston accent than normal, a hint of his mother's Irish accent, which he normally hid, breaking through. "Baby teeth, I should think, prickly but not all that dangerous."

It was a strange thing to say about Caro Pollo, Rosenberg decided, since he was viewed by friends and rivals alike not only as the best whore organizer on the Eastern seaboard but also as one of the toughest hit men in the business. A psychopath, who preferred to do his own killing rather than hire specialists—and who thought no more of taking a life than others thought of giving someone the finger. And a man widely proficient at killing—by gun or knife, by garrote, machete, blunt instrument, shotgun, subway train, or drowning. To Caro Pollo, inflicting death on another person was no more than a sign of his limited respect.

The door to the main office opened slowly, almost surreptitiously. For a second, there was emptiness beyond. Caro was professional; he would never leave himself exposed in an open doorway until he had seen what was inside. Instants later, reassured, little Caro Pollo strutted in.

"Luigi," said Oliver Chapin, avoiding the nickname lest it seem too much of an endearment. "How are you?"

"Good, thank you Ollie." He used the abbreviation on purpose, knowing that for years Oliver had forbidden its use wherever he could. "But not happy Ollie. Not happy at all."

"My dear fellow," Oliver beamed at him as if inspecting a particularly bouncy baby, "I'm so sorry. We must do something about that."

"That's why I want to talk to you." Caro could not help feeling uncomfortable under Oliver's scrutiny. "Here are me and my boys working out our guts, and still things ain't going good. So it's necessary we talk."

"It's other people's guts you're working out, Luigi, other people's," said Oliver very softly, his tone menacing in its intimacy.

But Pollo was not easily affected. He puffed his chest forward and started to say something. "I—"

"If they were your guts hanging out, I suspect you would be in greater pain."

Pollo remained unintimidated. "The one thing everyone says about the Pollo organization is we work together like brothers. When one of us is in trouble, we all is," he assured Oliver. "An' that's where we are right now."

"Dear, dear," was all that Oliver would reply, his cheerfulness unabated.

"'So when's it going to get better?' my men ask me," Pollo continued importantly. "And I say to them jus' one word: 'Loyalty,' I say. The time will come. And in the meantime we got to stick with our friends." He puffed his chest out again, in pride.

Watching him, Oliver decided that Caro Pollo definitely felt a damn sight too self-important. "You complain that our supplies are drying up, but you suggest nothing to help," he chided him as he would a recalcitrant child, his face now as stern as a Jesuit's.

"You are our supplier. All we want is you should supply."

Oliver realized he was trapped. His new scheme had only just begun. It would be months before it paid off; it was far too early to reveal his plans. But if he said nothing, Pollo would have every justification in buying from competitors.

He cursed himself for having waited this long before concentrating on the problem. But originally it had seemed merely a question of money—and these days there were easier ways to make money than this. He hadn't realized how important it was, or how much harm it could do him if it escalated and—God help everyone concerned—if a fight developed to decide whether he or those incompetent wops should control the supply.

"Now don't worry, Caro," Oliver started to reassure.

"That I cannot do," Caro Pollo interrupted. "You're our supplier—and you can't get us what we need. Of course I have to worry. A lot."

"I have things under control," said Oliver in an icy tone. "Within a few months you will see."

"I sure hope so." Caro Pollo made the mistake of seeming to threaten.

It was the chance Oliver had been looking for. "You sure hope so?" His voice was barely above a whisper. And suddenly, gone was all geniality, softness, warmth. In a flash he had reverted to the Boston dockside where he had started. "You sure hope so, you little son of a bitch, you fucking two-bit prick? You doubt Oliver Chapin when he gives you his promise?" Oliver's voice was rising. His face was white with fury and the vein on the right side of his neck protruded like a bluish worm. "You doubt my word? Why you undersized punk, you miserable little two-bit piece of shit, by what right do you doubt the word of Oliver Chapin even for one second?"

There was probably no other man alive, Sidney Rosenberg realized, who would dare to talk to Luigi "Caro" Pollo like that. Men had died just for sneering at him. Ever since Luigi was a little kid he had understood the power of violence. He had killed his first man when he was barely fifteen, using a handmade, superpowered BB gun. He had killed no less than one a year ever since, more than twenty men in eighteen years.

Caro reached instinctively for his gun. But then he hesitated, partly from astonishment at the risk Oliver was taking, partly from a well-honed survival instinct. He glanced quickly toward the windows to see if Oliver had backup men ready to take him out if he made his move.

"I don't need backups to take care of you," Oliver Chapin said witheringly, reading Caro's thoughts precisely. His voice, his whole demeanor, reverted to its accustomed rationality. Only the arrogance of certain power remained.

"You got no right . . ." Pollo's hand still hesitated halfway to the pistol which he always kept tucked in his trouser belt. Surely there must be reinforcements somewhere, even if he couldn't see them.

"I have every right, little Luigi Pollo. I placed you in your exalted position. I hold you there. I protect you. So you just relax and don't ever doubt the word of Oliver Chapin again." He leaned back in the office chair, making it creak, and put his feet onto the table. They barely reached and he looked so round, elderly and weak that Caro Pollo could hardly imagine how, only seconds earlier, he had seemed insurmountably dangerous.

Pollo hesitated for a moment. "Look," he said finally, seeking accord, "I realize you're angry, but—"

"I'm not angry," Oliver interrupted, his face again wreathed in a warm smile. "I just wanted to make sure we both knew where we stand."

"But you do have a plan?"

"As I said." Oliver Chapin knew that, even though he had won this battle of bluff and threat, he could not survive without a solution to the supply problem. "Just a few months."

"I'll tell my boys," said Caro. He left the inner office and walked across the outer office to the front door, swaggering to show his importance. "My boys will be real pleased," he called over his shoulder just before he left.

Sidney Rosenberg wiped the sweat from his brow.

"Close call," Oliver agreed with his henchman's thoughts, "but you can't let Pollo bully you. You're dead if you do." For all his apparent nonchalance, he was flushed with the excitement of his victory.

Sidney grunted his agreement, wondering whether he should point out that fighting Pollo could be at least as dangerous as agreeing with him. He decided to keep silent. The Deacon had won that round, hadn't he? For the moment they were both unscathed. No point in dwelling on what might have happened. Instead Sid allowed himself just one repetition of the obvious: "It just makes our plan that much more important," he said portentously.

———3

"Time for my exercise," Oliver Chapin announced, jumping up from his chair. "I'm going to the gym. Is there an instructor on duty?"

"Indeed. A new one." Salacious, vicious son of a bitch, Sidney Rosenberg thought, looking at his boss, half-admiring, half-disgusted. Would he ever slow down? Oliver's appetite seemed to increase as he got older. The "instructors" rarely lasted more than one session these days, even though Sidney picked only the toughest broads he could find.

"Good, I can use a little workout." They walked toward the door. "Hope this one's a little stronger than the last."

"I think you'll be satisfied."

"Oh, *I'll* be satisfied all right." Oliver grinned and, for a split second, looked again like a neighborhood grandfather. But a neighborhood grandfather, Sidney thought, who would love to punish all the little girls. He shuddered.

The gymnasium, as Oliver liked to refer to his retreat, was designed for private excess. To reach it, one had to leave the Ace Messenger Service, climb a second flight of stairs, and enter a flaking wooden door, ordinary in the extreme. Beyond it, however, there was a second door made of plate steel, and then a third, heavily padded. There was a second entrance at the back of the gymnasium, similarly arranged. Oliver wanted neither to be interrupted nor overheard when he was playing his private games.

Once inside the third door, Oliver entered his fantasy world. The short entrance corridor was dimly lit, just enough to illuminate the gold tapestries on the wall and the deep-pile red carpet. After a few steps the corridor opened into a large room which he called his entertainment center. Like the corridor, the floor was covered by the thick, blood red carpet, but here the carpet also climbed the walls, giving a rich backdrop to the garish tapestries which glittered under the concealed spotlights, so that their lewd scenes came alive with a hundred couples cavorting in every conceivable form of sexual congress.

In the center of the room was a small round stage, raised about two feet above the floor. Around two-thirds of it was a soft-cushioned, semicircular couch.

The rest of the room contained several casual groups of chairs, each clustered around a table with a dimly glowing lamp. Somewhere, invisible, there was a source of "black" light which gave a glow to white clothing and an extra brightness to colors. One white pinpoint spotlight illuminated the exact center of the stage.

There was only one occupant of the room as Oliver entered: a giant, muscled, swarthy man, stripped to the waist and oiled to make his skin shine. He wore a long, Turkish-looking mustache, skin-tight blue jeans and golden sandals. In one hand he carried a small black whip with a long, dangerous-looking leather thong that split at its end. In the other, he held a padded club evidently intended to strike the huge gong which hung suspended from the ceiling next to the stage.

Oliver Chapin moved briskly to the center of the room, silently acknowledged the presence of the muscled giant by a movement of his hand, and settled himself onto the sofa.

The huge man remained motionless until Oliver was seated comfortably. Then, wordlessly, with an economy of movement only available to the very strong or the very old, appearing to move in slow motion, he swung his club in a wide arc and smote the gong, which resonated with a deep, reverberating thunderclap. Although the noise was enormous, Oliver did not blink. He was proud of his ability never to be startled, never to close his eyes inadvertently. Stay alert, he had taught himself. A knife takes only an eye-blink to travel into your heart. He beamed his blessing on the giant; the show could begin.

The giant left quickly through a side door as the lights dimmed. Oliver leaned back into the soft couch in satisfaction. In front of him, against the only wall not covered with golden tapestries, a curtain gradually moved to one side. Behind was blackness.

Oliver adjusted his belly and crotch more comfortably on the sofa.

Suddenly there was a blood-curdling scream. Oliver's face took on a look of mild annoyance. Admittedly, it was a good scream, but it was fake. Why the hell couldn't they think of something original? Or, at least, why couldn't they make the scream real?

From far in the recess of the black void, a light started to glow. Gradually its power increased, broad and diffuse, a whole screen of brightness. At first it was still, cool, fluorescent, bluish, like a giant empty television screen. Then, as Oliver's impatience mounted, the light started to move, to undulate in waves of light. At last, when he was about to lose patience altogether, two figures appeared, silhouettes on the screen of flowing light. One, muscled and very male, carried a small whip, similar to the one carried by the giant, but even more lethal, with its thong split into three vicious ends. The other silhouetted figure appeared to be a young girl, nude, with pointed nipples and a slim but well-rounded body.

For an interminable moment, the couple, while immobile, seemed to undulate with the waves of light so that there was an incredible tension in their stillness. Oliver sat forward in his seat. Then the light stopped undulating and, very slowly, the two bodies broke their pose. As smoothly as honey oozing off a spoon, the girl bent forward and the man placed his foot, encased in a hobnail boot, onto her rump. He pushed, slow but hard so that the girl spun and then fell balletically onto one knee, her arms held high in the symbolic pose of fear. Very slowly, his arm still at the elbow, the man swung his whip toward her. The thong travelled too slowly to stretch it taut, more like a curved scythe than like the spoke of a wheel. It landed on her back and wrapped itself like a snake around her torso. She moved in response, but it was more like a shiver of pleasure than a jerk of pain.

Slowly the man pulled the whip back toward him. Its end snaked across her torso caressingly as it left her. Then, slightly faster, he repeated the action. And her reaction was somewhat sharper too. The stage lights were rising now, as the backlighting dimmed, showing Oliver that the girl was indeed naked, her buttocks and breasts emphatically white, and her blond hair almost silver against her golden-tanned body. The man, in contrast, was Spanish-complexioned, superbly muscled, and oiled to glisten as sleekly as an eel.

Oliver, leaning back again into the cushions, sighed with satisfaction.

By the third stroke, the whip was moving fast enough

to stretch itself to its full length. The girl shuddered more violently as the three leather tips bit into her, and she let out her breath in a tiny mew of pain.

Oliver Chapin's teeth showed in his taut smile.

Each stroke thereafter increased in power until, by the time a dozen strokes had been administered, the whip's cord was as rigid as a long steel rapier, the three thongs at the end thin, raping erections. The whip now whistled under the man's swirling attack, and the girl cried out in pain as, at each stroke, the three thongs clawed at her, leaving an inflamed fleur-de-lis of lacerated skin. Her body shuddered with pain.

Suddenly the girl forsook her passive role. With a shrill scream of anguish and anger she turned from beaten waif to vicious Amazon. Her hands arched themselves into talons, each finger tipped with a razor-sharp nail. With a banshee wail she launched herself up from the ground like a vicious cat leaping, slashing with those nails at his face, his stomach, his balls.

Gracefully he evaded her. She eviscerated only the air, while the man, part ballet dancer, part toreador, swirled his whip through the air with whistling precision, cutting, time and again, into the soft flesh of her naked body.

With hysterical screams of pain and anger, the girl launched herself again and again at the man. Her feet left the ground and she flew at him, an eagle with deadly talons. But each time he side-stepped, as smoothly slow as ever. Finally, with a great scream of anguish, she leaped even more aggressively and, missing her elusive target once more, crashed down on all fours beside the stage, out of the spotlight, panting, humiliated, defeated.

Oliver was now totally absorbed, staring at the girl with quite incredible anger and hatred. But there was no explanatory circumstance, no hint of justification for the anger. The girl had not provoked or antagonized him. So, since there was no reason or cause for his rage, it was pure, almost pristine, a violence that fed only on itself and seemed to grow on the feeding to a dimension that was terrifying. The girl, who up to that moment thought she had seen everything, observed his anger and started to fear that, after all, this was one client she would not be able to control. Her fear gave her strength. As rapidly as a crab scurrying toward the ocean, still on all fours, she scuttled sideways from her landing place back onto the stage. She paused there, clinging to the edge of the stage, her flanks heaving, glistening with sweat. The welts over her back and sides were as red as burns.

She struggled to her feet until she stood, facing her attacker, and at right angles to Oliver. The muscled man started to raise the whip to punish her further, but there was a new power in her; she seemed taller, and her talons were held low and lethal in front of her like the knife of an experienced street fighter. This was not part of the act they had rehearsed. The man fell back a pace, afraid. When he did crack his whip again, he lashed at her with less certainty.

His hesitation was his undoing. Quick as a lizard's tongue her arm flashed out so that the thongs of the whip entangled themselves around her arm. Then, with a sudden twist of her whole body—a lurching pirouette halfway between a balletic twirl and a desperate wrench for freedom—she threw the whole weight of her body against the whip. The man, taken entirely by surprise, tried to hold on but lost his grip on the handle. It landed at her feet and like a flash she had it. In the same instant, she untangled herself from the thongs. Crouching low, infinitely vicious, she had become the attacker.

Her first blow hit him across the bridge of the nose and drew three lines of blood. They were as thin as razor slashes at first, but then they swelled, as the blood oozed out, and became as wide as smears of brilliant lipstick.

The second blow caught his cheek. Before the third he was already fleeing from the stage.

Slowly the girl turned toward Oliver, now sitting bolt upright on the sofa below her. As she did so, distantly but insistently, the beat of hard punk rock music started. At home Oliver was scathing about the music his elder grandchildren loved to play; now his fingers began to beat in time with its rhythm.

On the stage, the girl's feet moved very slightly to the beat. Her legs were astride now and Oliver could see that she had shaved her pubic hair into a thin line covering only her slit. The rest of her body shone with sweat. The welts from the whip, which covered her back like a grid, touched her front only where the encircling thong tips had left sharp triple points like the footsteps of clawed birds. In her hand she carried the whip that had punished her.

One moment she was victorious Amazon, barely moving, queenly on the stage. The next, she was coquettish temptress, holding the whip by its thong, swinging it in front of Oliver, taunting him.

Oliver's lips pulled back over his teeth into a snarl so tight that they drained of blood and became white rims around the edge of his mouth. The skin of his temples was pulled back so taut that it was stretched in tiny diagonal lines from his ears to his hairline, giving his normally round face the feral look of a wolf. There was a horizontal band of sweat, about an inch high, glistening across his forehead. From deep in his throat came a keening wail that seemed both the ultimate expression of his anger and a mourning dirge lamenting the pain, the mutilation, perhaps the death that alone would assuage it. The girl was now deeply afraid that the death might be her own. She had no intention of relinquishing her weapon to him. That might be what they had originally intended, but this whole thing was out of hand, far beyond the rehearsed part she had agreed to play. The son of a bitch below her was mad, those crazy eyes . . .

Oliver Chapin grabbed for the whip. She tried to snatch it away, but such was the power of his anger that it physically slowed her, as a snake will paralyze a bird. To her dismay, he had it firmly in his hand before she had even started to move. Trying to jerk it away from him was useless—almost at once she lost her grip entirely.

"Bitch," he shouted, taking a grip on the handle. "Fucking bitch." His lips were wet with saliva.

"Hit me then, mister," she yelled back at him in a harsh Southern accent, trying to match his rage. "See if you can tame me." But her bravado lacked conviction. She felt more terror than anger.

"I'll tame you." He brought the whip down onto her shoulders with a stinging crack. The girl's feet never moved, but her head tossed back and, her mouth grimacing with pain, she let forth a string of obscenities that seemed to fill the air with pus.

The whip whistled again in Oliver's hand and cracked like a shot as it struck her. Then again and again as, demented, he slashed at her with considerable skill and every ounce of his strength.

After only seconds the girl could stand it no more. She was desperate. If she didn't do something to save herself, he would whip her to death. Her face now covered in tears, her voice hoarse with the screams which emanated uncontrolled from her throat, she threw herself off the stage at Oliver.

At the instant she would have collided with him, he stepped smartly to one side and, in the same surprisingly athletic movement, wrapped the whip cord tightly around her body, forcing her arms to her sides. First once, then again, he curled the cord around her, a fat spider tightly binding his prey.

For a moment they stood immobile, then fell back onto the couch, Oliver half on top of his victim. Immediately, the girl changed her tactics. Her struggles lessened and then, as if in spite of herself, changed their import. No longer was she struggling to be free, but now her body was straining to accommodate her mounting desire. Her screams of rage seemed to change to moans of lust. Her acting was superb. Gradually Oliver allowed the whip cord around her arms to loosen to accommodate her writhing. Then he let it go entirely, and with a wrench she was able to tear herself free. She started to claw at Oliver's clothes. Pretending not to be angry now, but passionate with desire, she ripped at them with her long nails.

For minutes the struggle continued, with Oliver still lying half on top of her while she was sunk deep into the cushions of the sofa. His shirt was ripped now, the length of his chest, and his pants were unzipped. His belly protruded over his underpants. He was panting and seemed older and more vulnerable.

The girl, tiring, and assuming he must be too, became gentler, more caressing. She was still very frightened of this old man who was as tough as anyone she had ever serviced. But she was attracted to him too, in spite of herself. His power, invincibility almost, was tremendously exciting. He could kill people, she realized, or, if he wanted, build them large fortunes, lend them part of his power.... Perhaps, if she could just get him to complete the act, he might help her. Sure the pain was stinging and the welts would take days to heal. But being Oliver's girl would be incredible. Worth almost any pain—and she'd always half enjoyed the whips.... If only...

But she made the mistake of being too gentle. Suddenly Oliver sensed her antagonism waning. "Bitch," he said softly. Grabbing a handful of her hair, he gave a great tug to pull her half-upright. Then, bracing himself against the back of the couch, he used his legs to throw her violently onto the floor.

She was back at him again in an instant, trying to hurt him, to redeem her mistake. But her effort lacked brutality. He slapped her face once, hard, knocking her backward. Then he struggled to his feet and pulled up his trousers.

The girl was half-crouching before him, abject. The tears were again streaming down her cheeks, partly from the terror of what he might do, partly from anger at herself for her stupidity.

For a moment they stood, regarding each other, master and slave, waiting. For another second she felt a surge of hope. If only he would make a move toward her, even to punish her. Then, disgustedly, Oliver turned and walked toward one of the doors leading out of the room. "You're pathetic," he said to the girl, "not worth my time." He left the room, closing the door firmly behind him. He picked up the phone in the small dressing room he had entered.

"Yes, sir?" Sid Rosenberg's voice sounded immediately.

"Hopeless, I'm afraid," Oliver explained, sounding more tired than angry. "A sad creature, but I did her no harm."

"I'm sorry."

"Try to get one that's a little tougher next time," Oliver dismissed the subject. "Which still leaves us with our dear friend to deal with. I think he'll be a little tougher than the whore. Wouldn't it be nice just to be rid of him? But, as we said, that probably wouldn't stop the others." Oliver was musing rather than making any points they had not discussed previously.

"Right," Sid agreed unenthusiastically.

"So first we have to really do something to improve those damned supplies. After that, he's no problem. We can do what we want with him. No one would even bother to notice."

"Absolutely."

"Do stop agreeing with me," Oliver said irritably, "you're sounding like nothing but a yes-man."

"Only when you're correct." Sid Rosenberg made his voice sound belligerent. But he grinned to himself. This was the only sort of argument he liked having with Oliver—where he could sound as tough as he wanted without any risk. "What do you want, then? I should tell you you're wrong when you're right?"

"Okay, okay," Oliver growled, pleased in spite of himself, as Sid knew he would be. "You'll be seeing the man again tomorrow?"

"Right. To go over more of the details."

"My only concern is, does he really have the contacts and know-how? We would have millions involved, tens of millions, maybe more."

"I'm sure he does."

"Remember it's only partly my money—the others will follow, but they'll hold me responsible."

"I know." Later, Sidney Rosenberg realized that he should have said nothing more. But the project was so sound, so exciting, so necessary. Against all his own convictions he continued. "I'm sure he's the right man," he said.

"Then you think we should proceed?"

"Yes," Sidney answered, "I do." Suddenly he realized what he had done. But it was too late. He was committed. For the first time since he had worked for Oliver Chapin, he had recommended action, taken responsibility. What if he were wrong? Already, he could feel his skin crawling. If only . . . But what was said was said. There was no reversal. He'd just have to make sure the scheme worked. Fortunately, he was sure it would.

"Is the first step underway?"

"Sure is," Sidney assured him. "They're on the track. Apparently they have a candidate, a pigeon, already being plumped up. Their first interview with him will take place in a few days, they say."

"Very good. And the candidate will not be aware of the plan?"

"Absolutely not. They promise he won't even know he's been hit."

"Good, good." Oliver Chapin was back to being the friendly friar, his voice as fruity as ever, his face as cherubic. "Well, I'd better be getting back home," he said. "Give Limpet a call for me, would you?"

Slowly he walked down the stairs and into the street. "Millions," he muttered to himself as he walked slowly away. "In fact, hundreds of millions."

4

Morgan J. Galsworthy, president of the renowned executive recruiting firm of Galsworthy & Merit, was a silver-haired, smooth, soft-spoken, impeccable gentleman. At sixty-five he had twenty years of experience as a headhunter. He knew everyone—had placed senior executives in most of the world's major corporations. His every conversation was filled with the names of the famous in business, as if they were the luscious chips of the really superb chocolate chip cookie that was his life.

Morgan Galsworthy never spoke too emphatically or allowed any harsh tones in his voice to affect his flawless appearance. He liked any extraneous noise in his office to be muted by the gentle strains of Mozart chamber music played softly. His office, high in New York's General

Motors Building, was arranged with two entrances so that applicants coming in at the front door might never be embarrassed by meeting those leaving from the back. From his desk he could gaze at Central Park through one wall of windows and across the fountain square to the venerable Plaza Hotel through the other.

Leaning back on his tufted leather chair, his hands clasped behind his neck, a tapered, manicured hand occasionally smoothing his perfect hair, Morgan Galsworthy surveyed the applicant before him. Between them, his vast mahogany desk glowed with the patina of a thousand polishings. It was empty but for an oversized Lalique ashtray. On the wall facing him—and thus behind his visitor—was a large mirror in which Galsworthy could observe the back of his guest's head or view himself, as he preferred. Observing an applicant in the round, he always felt, gave him an advantage; observing himself gave him pleasure.

Simon Bagnew, sitting hunched in the chair opposite, reminded Galsworthy of a rather sad toad, or perhaps of a basset hound with short legs and drooping eyes. In any case, he stank of losing.

Four years earlier, at fifty-two, Bagnew had been fired from his position as president and chief operating officer of an important, although not enormous, pharmaceutical company. His boss, the sole owner of the company, had strolled into his office one Friday afternoon. He had been dressed in golfing gear, Bagnew remembered, and he looked tanned, relaxed, self-satisfied. "Good afternoon, Bagnew." The owner had sounded bland and friendly.

"Good afternoon." Although Bagnew had no suspicion of the impending bombshell, he felt nervous—he always did in the owner's presence.

"I have decided to bring my son into the business. He's thirty years old now and it's time."

"Yes. Very good idea. He will do well."

"I think so." There was no inflection in the owner's tone. "That is why I've decided he will become chief operating officer effective Monday morning."

Bagnew looked at him uncomprehendingly. "But . . ."

"So, obviously, I no longer need your services. You are therefore fired effective immediately."

Bagnew had been too amazed to utter a word.

"Your contract says that I have to pay you one year's salary, but I'm only going to give you six months. You can of course sue me, if you want—but I wouldn't if I were you." The owner smiled his warm, almost gentle smile at Bagnew, who stared back at him stunned and wordless. "Have a good weekend," the owner had said as he left the room. Incredibly, he had appeared to mean it.

That was the third time in less than ten years that Simon Bagnew had lost his job. The first time had been an unfortunate but nontraumatic experience. The company at which he had worked for many years, gradually moving up from junior accountant to chief financial officer, had been acquired by a larger corporation. After a three-month take-over period the acquirers had decided they wanted their own man in that job. They made a fair settlement with Simon Bagnew and helped him considerably in finding another job.

The job he had found, after three months of searching, had been at best a step sideways: his new title, executive vice president, pharmaceuticals, was lower, but at least the company, a large multinational, was more important. His salary was about the same. Nevertheless, he was delighted to have the job. Then, only six months later, he enjoyed a stroke of what seemed at the time to be pure good fortune: his supervisor, the divisional president, died of a heart attack—leaving Bagnew to become president and chief operating officer of the division. Although he felt guilty about gloating over his boss's death, he couldn't help himself. At last, fate had handed him his chance.

Bagnew later rationalized that what had happened thereafter was fate punishing him for his callous pleasure in another man's death. He had certainly faced, almost from the first day on his new job, a series of insuperable calamaties. First, there was a major strike; then a competitor broke into the marketplace with a superior product and, before Bagnew could react, cut the market share of his biggest brand in half; and finally a group of his senior marketing and sales executives banded together and quit en masse to join that same competitor.

Bagnew tried to fight back, but lack of experience plus a tendency to indecisiveness led him to talk more vigorously than he acted. Sales fell; profits plunged. Try as he would, Simon Bagnew could not stop the erosion. After less than a year, the management of the parent became fed up. He was asked to resign, and his settlement was less than generous. No one believed the public announcement that he was "pursuing private interests."

This time Bagnew remained "on the street" for almost a year. At first his wounded self-esteem made it difficult for him to fight for a job. He spent the whole of that first summer painting his house. At last, however, as the weather cooled in fall, he gathered his strength and reentered the job market with inner terror but outward determination. What he lacked in charisma, and where he was impeded by his tarnished reputation, he compensated with dogged thoroughness and stubborn energy. He left no lead unfollowed, no letter unwritten, no contact untapped. He refused to give way to his discouragement. And his wife, Janet, a solid lady, invariably outfitted in "walking shoes" and a "sensible" tweed skirt, stood behind him, a rock of trust, faith, and support. Whenever he was too dejected to continue, she sympathized—but without any implication that his depression was justified. How amazing that you haven't found the right job yet, her manner implied. She never, by word or deed, gave the slightest hint that there might be no right job out there, or that not finding it was in any way his fault or worse than a nuisance.

His daughter, Susan, as pretty as her mother was ordinary, provided Simon with his other pillar of strength. Although only sixteen at the time, she had inherited much of her mother's common sense. Instead of using the energy of her age to rebel against her parents—as she saw so many of her friends doing—she used it to develop first a friendship with Simon and then a rare father-daughter relationship. The two of them became companions in all sorts of adventure, camping together or visiting museums. They laughed a great deal. And, whether it was about business or Beethoven or how to handle boys, he showed unflagging patience in teaching her everything he knew. As a result of the conscious and unconscious efforts of both mother and daughter, Simon never lost his sense of self-worth, not even at the gloomiest periods. He remained, basically, a happy man.

Eventually his perseverance—and their faith in him—paid off, and to his immense relief he became president of the privately-owned pharmaceutical company. He spent two successful years there converting the owner's flights of brilliance into practical plans. He was able to capitalize upon the spurts of energy that emanated from the owner like lightning flashes and administer them effectively to achieve rapid but steady growth. His financial experience and big-business training proved invaluable. Everything was going fine until that fateful Friday afternoon.

"It's happened to us before," Janet reassured him. "You pulled it off the last time."

"But I'm older and it's one more nail in my coffin."

"Nonsense." But this time she couldn't quite give her voice enough conviction to convince him.

"You're frightened too," he accused.

"I have great faith in you."

"More than I can say for myself," he replied bitterly, and poured himself a drink.

As the months passed he had become ever more terrified. Interview after interview, rejection after rejection. He made the rounds assiduously, ate the luncheons, played the golf games, visited the bankers, wrote the letters to his friends, acquaintances, even his enemies. He tried to keep cheerful, as he gradually sold one possession after another; tried to maintain his sense of self-worth as his wife went out to work; wrote cheerful letters to Susan, who was now in college in San Francisco, pretending that he was enjoying his enforced vacation; tried . . .

But gradually the terror had turned to despair. After two years there were not even any more interviews. He weeded the garden, lectured occasionally to alternative education classes at the local business college, endeavored to write a book.

He had not been interviewed once in the past six months. There was no money left in the family bank account. The stocks they had once owned had long been sold, and, except for a simple gold wedding band, Janet had no jewelry left. They still lived in Greenwich, one of the affluent suburbs of New York, to keep up appearances, but there was a second mortgage on the house. That had kept them going for a few months. Now the house was on the market. The asking price was two hundred twenty thousand dollars, but he would settle for anything over two hundred thousand dollars—and probably for less if he had to. The first and second mortgages added up to one hundred seventy thousand dollars. The realtor's fee, at six percent, would be twelve thousand dollars, and lawyers would eat up another two or three. He'd be lucky to walk away with fifteen thousand dollars—not even enough to finance Susan for the rest of her time in college. But at least the drain of the upkeep would stop. They'd move into a small apartment. "We got fed up keeping the garden going. Better to travel and be free and easy," he would try to bluff his friends. No one would believe him.

The one thought that recurred quite often now was the final solution. At first he had barely allowed himself to glance at the thought, but later he had investigated it more and more thoroughly. The final solution. The insurance was over a quarter of a million dollars. It would finance everything. Janet could live on it for years; Susan could finish college, even go to graduate school if she wanted to.

As the months passed, the thought became more frequent. Gradually, he got used to it, so that eventually the idea became comforting, the only port of safety in his ocean of worry. When things went particularly wrong, when bills could not be paid, when yet another distant hope vanished, the thought would sustain him. It *was* a solution, after all. Perhaps not an ideal one, but still . . .

Only when he thought of the practicalities of implementing his final solution did Simon Bagnew's anguish master him again. What if he just couldn't do it, couldn't find the courage? What if that way out were blocked off, too, by his own incompetence?

When Simon couldn't sustain his courage with daydreams about his final solution, he drank instead. Only then would Janet turn her back on him, partly realizing that admonition would not help, partly to hide her fear.

"Why don' you have a drink with me?" Simon would demand thickly. "Too refined, are you?"

If she answered, there would be an argument. She had tried that at first, before realizing it was hopeless. Now she would try to walk away. But it wasn't easy.

"Can't stand me?" Simon would demand. "Is that it? Not that I blame you," he would add, letting the whiskey make him maudlin. "Can't say I can stand myself much these days."

"Don't be stupid. Of course it's not that," she would storm back at him, unable sometimes to avoid being sucked into his self-pity. "I just can't see what purpose is served by your trying to drown yourself."

"Purpose? Purpose? What purpose is there in any of it? Why are we put here? Why am I here? To paint the house? Hell, it's got three layers on it already. And I've pulled out the weeds so often, they've quit trying! All I *do* is attack weeds. They don't have any more chance than I do. Purpose, you say?" Tears would well up in his eyes and he would stagger over to the bar to get another drink.

The whole performance would so fill Janet with frustration she could have shaken him, hit him even, just to make him snap out of that awful whining. There was just *no* excuse for it, as far as she was concerned. None. One did what one had to do, shopped at the discount counter at the supermarket hoping no one would see, and held one's head proudly if they did. When you were a Daughter of the American Revolution, you always kept up appearances, good times or bad. *Always.* Sometimes, when he let her down like that, she could almost hate him.

Fortunately, there were other times. The times when he could laugh at their misfortunes. On her days off, usually Fridays, if he had no appointments, no one he could even hope to see, they would walk in the country, holding hands and watching the birds. Between them, they had spotted fifty-one different varieties.

"I wonder if I could become a professional birdwatcher," Simon would muse. "Do you think they have executive recruiters for birdwatchers?"

"Of course." Janet would smile at him. "With binoculars, peering from behind rocks—or probably from under them." They were fully united in their dislike of headhunters.

"And no doubt deciding who's overqualified and who's 'development material.'"

"What does a birdwatcher develop to?" Janet wanted to know.

"A full-fledged ecologist?"

"A double-breasted lobbyist?" They would laugh together, savoring their affection for each other.

If only he could get a job, Janet would think, late at night, when they were both pretending to sleep. It was so unfair that he should be dumped like this, useless as flotsam. For he was really an admirable man, she felt, and basically strong in his adversity, at least most of the time. It was astonishing, really, how resilient he was, how hard he was trying, even now, to find a job. Many men would have given up by now. If only the drinking didn't get him. He would stop if he got a job, she knew. But if not . . . she dared not think.

Simon watched Morgan Galsworthy as a hiding rabbit would watch a fox. Manfully he tried to control his nervousness. But with all the disappointments, all the despair he lived with, it was hard. He had dressed carefully for this occasion. It was, after all, his first interview in months. The white shirt was entirely appropriate. He had many of them left from better days and they never really went out of style. But the suit was too heavy for this time of year, a winter suit, even though it was barely September and still hot outside. It was well-cut, hiding his little potbelly and making him seem taller than his five feet eight inches, the only really good suit he had left. The others either looked rumpled with age, or were just too out-of-style. Nevertheless, overall he made a good impression—conservative, prepossessing. If only he could keep his hands from shaking as he lit one cigarette after another.

"So you were president of Skidder and Rowe," Galsworthy was saying genially. "Jim Skidder's a good friend of mine. Known him for years."

"A dynamic man," Bagnew said noncommittally. "I understand his son is still working with him."

"Young Horace. So they say." It was Galsworthy's turn to be noncommittal. It was widely rumored that young Horace Skidder was unusually ineffective, even in comparison to other ineffective business scions. On the other hand, it would hardly be tactful for Morgan Galsworthy, in his position of father-confessor, friend, contact to everyone, to mention this. He preferred to say nothing. "How long were you president there?" He knew the answer perfectly well.

"As my résumé says, for something over two years."

"And then?"

"I retired for a while." Bagnew tried to make it sound plausible.

"How long?"

"Well, I played golf for two years. Watched birds. Thought I might retire for the rest of my life. Then I started getting itchy so I taught a university course for a while." Perhaps Galsworthy would not question too closely which university—Underwood College was hardly a center of academe. "Thought I owed it to the next generation to pass on some of the experience I'd gained," he continued quickly. "But after a while, even that palled." He coughed to clear his throat. "One shouldn't ease around too long, you know. After all, a man in his fifties has too much energy to do nothing—however much money he has." There, he'd managed to get the subject of his age into the conversation before Galsworthy asked him.

"Latter fifties, isn't it?"

"Fifty-six." Bagnew hesitated. "Got a few good years in me yet," he added, trying to make it sound casual. He failed. Damn, he should have left it at a simple statement of fact. You're pushing too hard, he warned himself. But he knew that was almost impossible to avoid. If only he had some alternatives.

"Out of work for four years, then," Galsworthy interrupted his thoughts.

"Yes, indeed, time to start looking for something new."

"Fifty-six years old and broke." All semblance of friendliness had evaporated from Morgan Galsworthy's face. He sounded glacial.

Bagnew remained silent. He simply had no strength left to keep up any pretense.

"I may have a job for you."

"Oh God." Simon almost broke. With a great effort, he fought to recover. "I'd certainly consider it. But of course it would have to tempt me."

"Anything I offered would do that."

Stung, Bagnew tried to retaliate. "I can assure you that is not—"

Galsworthy was totally unimpressed. "You know Turner-LaMott, of course," he interrupted rudely, referring to the large international pharmaceutical and medical appliance company.

"Yes."

"Well, they're looking for a president."

"Oh I see," said Bagnew dully. His heart sank. President of a company the size of Turner-LaMott? Ridiculous! Obviously, Galsworthy was only using him as a straw man—someone to include in the list of candidates to make the others look better. Goddamn the man anyway. Simon's bitterness and disappointment flashed to anger. "You're wasting my time, Mr. Galsworthy," he said coldly. "Of course I would be interested. But we both know I'm not a serious contender, don't we?" He started to rise. His normally slightly receding chin jutted forward in anger. His face mottled red. "I think it's time I was leaving."

"Sit down."

Simon Bagnew hesitated a second. Then, although he knew he should simply continue with his exit, he gave in. Perhaps there *was* some tiny chance. And, after all, there was no point in offending a man as powerful as Morgan Galsworthy. Slowly, he sank back into his chair.

"You may find yourself unworthy for the position, Mr. Bagnew," Morgan Galsworthy said. "And it may well be that you are justified in that belief. Nevertheless, for reasons of my own, I intend to recommend you for the job."

Simon Bagnew left the offices of Galsworthy & Merit and walked slowly down Park Avenue. His shoulders slumped as if the heat of the day, aggravated by the weight of his suit, were pressing down on him, a physical burden almost too much to bear. On his left, set back behind its reflecting pool and fountain, rose the Seagram's Building, towering and majestic in its deep metalic brown. Just ahead of him was a less imposing skyscraper, and beyond that, in total contrast, St. Bartholomew's Cathedral, as elaborate as a wedding cake. And to his right, across the broad boulevard with its artificial-looking flowers—natural only in the sense that they had been manufactured horticulturally rather than chemically—the green-glass Lever Brothers building. Further south, the inevitable banks and then ITT, where he could remember students holding protests back in the days when students cared . . . back in the days, he thought bitterly, when he could walk this street with pride.

Why? Simon asked himself angrily—as he had a thousand times before—why couldn't he be satisfied to run the local post office like his father before him? Who said he had to be a corporate president? Wasn't it a curse, this ambition, like a disease. . . ? If it was a disease, he decided bitterly, it was certainly incurable. Even now, after all his disappointments, he wanted a top job back more than he wanted anything else on earth. That was why men like Galsworthy were so despicable. They knew what drove him and how hard, and they trifled with the desire, took advantage of it, made their own mockery of his ambition, and degraded him.

In earlier days, when he could stride down this avenue with his head high—or be chauffeured down it—he had not thought his ambition excessive, nor felt the atmosphere in which he lived to be too rarefied. Had he not achieved his position entirely through his own efforts? Was he therefore not entitled? Would it not last forever? Not for a moment had he cared to admit that he had reached his pinnacle partly by luck; nor considered that his luck might not hold. Most certainly he had never stopped to pinpoint the reason for his everpresent, vague uneasiness. And under no circumstances had he allowed himself to consider, let alone to plan for, the possibility of his own downfall.

Simon Bagnew had lived at the top of the mountain of business success for so long that, body and soul, he had totally adjusted to that stratosphere. Now he could no more be satisfied at the altitude of ordinary men than could a surface fish swim to the ocean's bottom. Like the fish, he would collapse under the pressure of living again near the bottom.

He could feel the pressure now, pressing in on him. There was no hope. Whatever that son-of-a-bitch headhunter might claim, it was perfectly obvious that he would never get the Turner-LaMott job. No job would ever come his way. Perhaps he could start a business of his own, raise money on Wall Street, buy a franchise. . . ? Unrealistic, all of it pipedreams. He had followed them up early in his unemployment, but nothing had been possible. "Very interesting proposition. But not right for us. Why don't you try . . ." He had tried them all. He had failed more times than he could remember. Even Janet, who at first had gone to work only as a stopgap measure, was now talking of her job as a "career," which gained in importance and permanence each time he tried and again failed. Failed and failed . . .

The heat pressed down on him so heavily that he started to feel giddy, as if the buildings were circling around him and mocking. He staggered slightly and leaned against a wall. In the old days, he had commanded buildings like this; now, he could use them only for support.

He'd have to get to somewhere cool, or he really would faint, fall down in the street. He couldn't allow that. Too embarrassing, too demeaning.

With a great effort Simon Bagnew forced himself to walk another block past the cathedral. In the middle of the next block, he turned into the Waldorf, up the steps and into the main lobby of the hotel. Staggering dangerously now, he found a chair and slumped into it. It was marvelously cool in the hotel. The air, like cool liquid, flowed over his hot, damp body. He let out a sigh of relief as he felt his strength returning. Perhaps there was a chance after all, he thought. Galsworthy had said he would recommend him. He didn't really believe it could happen, not after all the rejections, all the disappointments. Still, it would be fantastic. He allowed himself a brief daydream.

And if not? Well, he decided, struggling to his feet, the time was approaching when he would have to act. If he didn't make it this time, he'd have to really get down to it in detail, figure it out, plan and put into action his ultimate solution.

5

"Shit!" Morgan Galsworthy spat out the word as the dice came to rest. Seven and four showing, and the croupier expertly swept the piles of chips away from the losers and toward the winners. Galsworthy was a heavy loser.

Expensive casinos in Las Vegas normally discourage swearing or, for that matter, any other vulgarity or excess. You can pump your arm full of anything you want—but only *under* your rolled-down sleeve. You can screw whomever you like and say whatever comes to mind, but only where no one—except someone paid to eavesdrop, of course—can see or hear. But, at least for the moment, the croupier decided Galsworthy should be forgiven. After all, he was down almost twenty thousand dollars in the last hour. So he limited himself to a stern look in Galsworthy's direction.

Hunched over the end of the craps table, Morgan Galsworthy was almost unrecognizable as the smooth, honeyed persona of the executive recruitment office. Here, his face showed such intensity, and its skin pulled so tight that the tip of his nose whitened and his mouth stretched, as in a rigid scream, across the lower half of his face. His normal aloofness was replaced by an addict's desperate concentration.

Royal Command Casino, the newest in Las Vegas, was also the most opulent. A thousand people, casually dressed but beautiful, swirled through its mirrored halls. The lighting was designed to make a man's five-o'clock shadow look like a suntan, and to erase the lines around a woman's eyes. The carpets were so soft they turned a tired walk into a bounce. The mirrors covering every surface expanded the room to eternity, but kept it ever full with excited people. The velour stools, like exotic mushrooms, stood in front of the shimmering bars placed strategically throughout the room—lest anyone ever face a thirst with more than thirty steps needed to quench it—and recalled an 1890s bordello. And the women, mostly blond and magnificent, clad in anything from low-cut cocktail dresses to trendy T-shirts (Mickey Mouse or sequins or both) added sexual immediacy. Everyone was hustling; everyone on the make. Money and glamour and sex merged into an electric passion, no less intense for being wholly artificial.

Galsworthy, shirt open to his navel, face glistening with sweat, white hair rumpled, observed nothing of these surroundings. When he gambled he could hear, see, smell, feel nothing but the dice in front of him. Nothing would stop him now until he was up to his limit in debt, until the house, as tactfully as possible, eased him from the tables.

Since he was one of the Royal Command's best customers, the management went to great pains to keep Galsworthy satisfied—and coming back. Free lodging was the least of the privileges automatically accorded to any high roller. Much more important was the need to keep the dream, the compulsion, alive. This was done by the canny operators in a thousand ways. The girls admired Morgan more here than elsewhere. In other casinos they wanted money; in the Royal Command they wanted only him.

"What's in it for you, then?" he would ask, cynical and no fool, as a new girl clung to his arm.

"I don't blame you for thinking that." Her eyes would fill with tears. "And you're right, sometimes I do it for what I can get."

"So. . . ?"

"It's not like that, not this evening. I feel special with you."

An academy-award-winning performance, he would decide. But he would be flattered nevertheless—and in those awful moments when he realized how much he'd blown (and the risks he'd have to take to recoup), even simulated love was important.

Morgan pushed his last pile of chips onto the table and neatly placed them in the special diagonal pattern that was supposed to assure him victory. It was a highly complicated series of bets that had been worked out on a computer by a brilliant young systems expert. But it wasn't working tonight. "Goddamn luck," he muttered. "Dice are cold."

The man next to him, a caricature of a Texan, tall, ruddy-faced, sweating his excitement, pushed his belly over the rim of the table. He blew on the dice with a snort and shook them hard. "Baby needs new shoes," he chanted the old gambler's prayer. "Seven for heaven." He flung the dice down the table. "Two fives," called the croupier unemotionally.

"Fuck!" Morgan Galsworthy violated the house rules again.

"Don't worry," the Texan drawled. "I specialize in ten the hard way."

The croupier pushed the dice back to the Texan who blew on them again, even harder than before, and then hurled them to the end of the table. They hit so hard against the green baize backboard that they bounced halfway back.

"Snake eyes," said the croupier impassively and swept away Galsworthy's chips.

Galsworthy's face drew tighter still. "Another marker?" he asked.

The croupier nodded. He had his orders.

"Okay. I'll take ten thousand more."

Again the croupier nodded. He pushed a pile of chips wordlessly toward Galsworthy. With his other hand, he made a practically invisible sign to the watching floor manager, who slid up beside Galsworthy and handed him a promissory note on a rhinestone-framed tablet. On the top of the tablet, clipped in place, was a gold pen. Hardly looking at the note, Galsworthy scribbled his signature.

"Here, honey." The Texan pulled the girl next to him forward to the table. "I know you-all's hot."

Her teeth, her hair, her sequined top, everything about her glittered. As she tossed her smile at her escort, she reflected light as if she were another of the mirrors that lined the room.

The floor manager slid away into the crowd, barely brushing his arm against the croupier. The signal was enough for the croupier to understand. "No limits," he announced. "This is the last player. After her, the table closes."

"Oh no," said Galsworthy in horror.

"We're just getting hot," the Texan argued. "The other tables aren't closing yet. Why is this the only one?"

"Sorry, sir," said the croupier. "Union rules. I've no choice. But, as you say, there are other tables."

"Don't worry, honey," the girl reassured them. "It's still my turn, and I ain't giving up the dice so quick."

Galsworthy pushed half his chips, five thousand dollars worth, into his pattern. Then the girl, her beautifully manicured fingers digging into the flesh of her palms, squeezed the dice and rolled them gently to the end of the table. They barely hit the backboard before settling down. "Seven," called the croupier.

"That's my girl," bellowed the Texan, his face even more florid than before. "And again."

Galsworthy collected his winnings. Together with his investment of five thousand dollars, and the other five he had not bet, he now had chips worth twenty-seven thousand all in neat piles perched on the ledge in front of him. Breathing hard, he distributed the whole amount onto the table, leaving only a single hundred-dollar marker in front of him.

"Do it again, honey, do it again," the Texan implored.

The girl picked up the dice, and her whole body seemed to go rigid with the pressure she placed on them. Again she rolled them so slowly that they seemed to float down the table, barely touching the backdrop, and then settling into place in slow motion.

"Seven," called the croupier again. As the Texan whooped, the croupier pushed an immense pile of chips toward both the girl and Galsworthy.

Galsworthy's face was gray with his suppressed excitement. Still leaving only the hundred-dollar chip in front of him, he again arranged the whole of the rest of his chips, over a hundred thousand dollars in all, into the pattern.

There was dead silence around the table as every eye watched the girl repeat her act of concentration. Viewers from other tables, hearing there was a hot streak, had hurried over to watch. The girl, with a toss of that golden hair, threw the dice once more.

"Eight," said the croupier.

"Do it, honey, do it, do it, do it," the Texan was chanting. "Son of a bitch. Do it!"

Every eye was on the girl as she once more pressed the dice into the palm of her hand. Her arm muscles were rigid with the strain. Her fingernails left red indentations on the flesh of her hand. She threw the dice. They seemed to travel for an eternity before they hit the green backboard; they seemed to stand on their edges for an eternity before they finally settled flat onto the tabletop.

"Seven," said the croupier in a flat voice. He swept all of Galsworthy's chips toward him. "Table's closed."

Galsworthy wiped a weary hand across his face. Its muscles seemed to sag. He looked like an old man. With one final effort he tossed his last remaining hundred-dollar chip toward the croupier. "Thanks." The croupier sounded almost sad.

The crowd drifted off to the other tables. The Texan, with one look of disgust at the blonde, stomped off toward the nearest bar.

The girl turned toward Morgan Galsworthy. "I'm sorry, honey," she said. "I did my best."

"Yes." His shoulders slumped. "I know."

"I'll walk you home," she said with a bright smile.

"Yeah. Okay."

"You handled that well," the floor manager said to the croupier. "The normal bonus, of course."

"Thanks." The croupier smiled cynically. "It was nothing, really." He handed the floor manager the set of special dice he had in his pocket. "Any time." He closed the office door behind him, and left the casino by the rear entrance, pleased with the five thousand dollars he had earned for an easy evening's work. Better than hustling extra aces at poker with hoods who'd as soon kill you as give you the time of day. Strange, though, he thought briefly of Morgan Galsworthy, that they'd have it in for just one man like that. Poor bastard. Still, better forget it. The less you know, the better.

Back in his office, the floor manager picked up the phone. Before dialing he glanced automatically across the room to make sure the door was shut tight. Then he dialed quickly. "Job's done," he said. "Like you said—he owes us about thirty grand."

"Great."

Morgan Galsworthy had not become fully addicted to

gambling until his middle forties—a time of many crises in his life. He had been a successful account executive in a large advertising agency when it started. Up to then his life had been satisfying, pleasant, sometimes a little boring perhaps, but acceptable. He had enjoyed the good food and the theater evenings when he entertained clients. Nor had he objected to having to provide an occasional girl—or to letting the client win at golf. He had been a competent account excecutive who worked hard to understand his clients' businesses. His Princeton and navy manners, his dignified look and already prematurely gray hair, gave him a certain status, and considerable credibility.

His major account had been a tooth paste called Action. The advertising slogan "For folks who want Action," used in conjunction with mildly suggestive scenes of men and women propositioning one another, had ranked with Clairol's "Does she or doesn't she?" as one of the most effective double-entendre slogans of the 1960s. Action's sales had risen steadily, carrying Morgan's career—and salary—into orbit. But then several new fluoride toothpastes had come in. Proctor and Gamble's Crest and Colgate's Colgate Dental Cream had attacked each other with massive advertising, and every other brand, desperate for survival, had flung itself into the fray. Tens of millions of dollars went into television; hundreds of millions of coupons were sent to consumers' homes; and Action, with no fluoride, had gradually dropped out of the running, its share whittled away, until eventually it could no longer afford to compete at all. One gray Thursday afternoon Morgan Galsworthy had been informed by the client that they were going to cancel all further advertising.

"We'll milk the damn thing; see what money we can get squeezed out before it stops selling entirely," the company's advertising manager had explained. He had only joined the company a few months before and had no attachment to the brand. To him it felt like a loser—along with this fellow Galsworthy and the whole damn agency for that matter. He wanted no part of it, or them.

"But we could build our share back up," Morgan had insisted, trying not to let his desperation show."

"Not likely. Anyhow, we're basically a household products company. I'd prefer to gamble our money on a new detergent."

"Then perhaps we could be helpful to you in that area," Morgan had said, still smoothly. "After all, the agency has had a long, successful run with Action, and our expertise within your company is such that—"

"Sorry. But all our brands are assigned already," the advertising manager had said coldly. "I'm afraid I can't do anything about that."

"But—"

"Let's have lunch on it after a while. I'll be out for a couple of weeks, but after that we should get together." The advertising manager had ended the conversation abruptly. He was not especially cruel, but he'd made up his mind, and he hated to see an account executive cringe.

The next few weeks had proven to Morgan Galsworthy that even the best-established career is tenuous. The moment the agency realized that billings on Action had ceased, Galsworthy found himself out of a job. Worse, there was a recession on, and Morgan's career was closely aligned with a single brand, one which had fallen on evil days. He knew he would be out of work for a long time. Thank heaven his wife had some money.

But an astonishingly short time after he lost the Action account, Morgan Galsworthy had also found himself deserted by his wife. Precisely one week after the advertising manager had fired his agency, she told him, cooly and calmly, that she wanted to discontinue their marriage.

"But why, honey? What is the problem?"

"I want out. That's all. The children are old enough to look after themselves most of the time. And I'm fed up with them, with my life, with you."

"But I just lost my job."

"That has nothing to do with me. I won't need any alimony. So there's no problem. We're through."

Morgan Galsworthy was so stunned that he was left feeling nothing at all. It was a time of emptiness, he recalled. He was a man walking through a vacuum, although the outward calm, the smooth, careful appearance he had cultivated for so long, remained.

It had taken him many months to renew the structure of his life. Eventually he found a job with a firm of executive recruiters—"headhunters" as they were universally known. But he had been forced to take a big salary cut—and, even so, it was made clear to him that he was hired merely for his contacts. If he could bring in new business, he would stay; if not . . . He ignored that alternative and turned instead to the most careful and assiduous cultivation of all the friends and acquaintances he had made during his years in advertising.

After a while, when it became too empty, he sold the house in which he had lived for eighteen years, the home in which he had presided all that time, husband and father, over his wife and two children—and moved instead to an adequate but drab apartment in New York. Slowly he started to have some success in obtaining clients. Evenings he spent either entertaining them or interviewing potential candidates for the jobs he sought to fill. On a few occasions he dined with an appropriate young lady; on even fewer occasions he spent a night with one.

But there was no meaning in his life, and still no feeling. He was a good-looking, fairly effective, reasonably successful shell.

Then one evening, as he dined with a potential client at

Christ Cella's steak restaurant, his life had changed drastically. It was a change that would give him the incentive for his enormous future success, and be the cause of his greatest problems.

"Good steak," Morgan had said politely to his dinner partner.

"They serve the best."

"You come here often?"

"Maybe once a month. Otherwise I go down to Pen and Pencil."

"Oh, really? How interesting."

"Not very."

"They are all really the same, aren't they?"

"I guess."

"So what else do you do when you're not working?"

"I . . ."

"Screw around, eh?" said Morgan Galsworthy, acting through his role as a man's man. "You're divorced too, aren't you?"

"Sure, I do a little of that, but I prefer . . ."

"Prefer what?" Morgan's interest was piqued.

"I play. Not play around, if you know what I mean."

"Play?"

"Yeah. Blackjack, craps, poker."

"In New York?"

"There's lots of private games here. Or in New Jersey. I go to Vegas sometimes, but really the New York games are hotter."

"I've heard of them, but I've never been."

"I'll take you sometime."

"Great," said Galsworthy, his interest really aroused for the first time in days. "When?"

"When we're finished here, if you want. Do you know how to play poker?"

"Not well enough to play, but I'd love to watch."

"How about craps?"

"Yeah, I know how that goes. One of my kids taught me. But I've never played in a major game."

"Hell, there's nothing to it. I'll show you in two minutes."

Morgan Galsworthy's first experience with craps had been enough to addict him for the rest of his life.

The room to which his client took him was smoke-filled and as rank as a locker room, hardly a fitting locale for Galsworthy to rediscover his zest for living. Potbellied men knocked back bourbon and puffed on cigars, bantered with one another good-naturedly, and sweated profusely. But under all that locker-room camaraderie there was a tension which hit Morgan Galsworthy with the power of a blow to the solar plexus. It left him breathless and with a cramped pain of excitement that simply had to be alleviated.

The makeshift craps board was on the floor in the middle of the room. The players knelt around it chanting their superstitious rhymes, blowing on the dice, throwing them with strange rituals, as their convictions about luck moved them.

"You wanna try?"

"Sure." Morgan could remember to this day the beat of the blood in his ear drums as he picked up the dice. "Sure, I'll give it a try."

That evening Morgan had won almost a thousand dollars. The next night he had won twelve hundred more. By the end of the week, however, Morgan Galsworthy was five thousand dollars in the hole; exhausted from playing with barely three hours sleep a night; and quietly desperate about how to pay his next month's expenses.

"No, you can't have a raise, for Christ's sake," Howard Merit, head of the executive recruiting firm, had said. "What the hell have you done to deserve one?"

"I need the money, is all. I'll bring in more business."

"Okay." Merit had inclined his head in saintly acquiescence. "You bring in the business and I'll give you the raise."

"Then let's make it a percentage."

"Instead of a salary, not in addition."

Morgan had no choice. "All right," he had been forced to agree. "A straight ten percent of everything I bring in."

"Fair enough."

They had signed a paper on it the same day.

"Best deal I ever made," Howard Merit would boast in later years. "Soon as I give him the ten percent, that son of a bitch went out and got more business in the next four weeks than I did. Hell, he got more business in the next four weeks than I had in the previous six months!"

Morgan Galsworthy himself often wondered how he had been able to achieve such success. Clients seemed to fall into his lap. He was never quite sure what the magic ingredient was. But, at his most introspective, he tended to think that it was his need for money that had created a vulnerability in him that, together with his unquestioned competence, made him enormously trustworthy. He impressed but did not threaten potential clients. He was desperate for their business, but the years of training in an advertising agency allowed him to avoid the patheticness of desperation—and transform it to look instead like great dedication to the job.

Within six months, Morgan Galsworthy was earning more money than he had ever dreamed possible. Within a year he was a junior partner of Howard Merit's firm. Three years after that, the name of the company was changed to Merit & Galsworthy. Now, of course, Howard Merit was long retired. For the last ten years, it had been Galsworthy & Merit—the second name kept on the letterhead merely to add to the company's prestige.

But, as fast as the money flowed in, Galsworthy poured

it out, initially onto the craps tables, and later into poker, blackjack, horses, every lousy-risk gamble ever invented by a Mafia hood or an Atlantic City real estate operator. Private games or public ones, in New York, Las Vegas, San Juan—or on the planes he took to fly to places—Morgan Galsworthy was known at all of them. The gambler's mania was in his blood. Often he would promise himself to give it up. Sometimes he even managed to for a few weeks or a few months. But his life became gray and meaningless. Gambling was his only passion. He couldn't get away. He didn't even really want to.

Morgan Galsworthy often won thousands, occasionally tens of thousands of dollars in one night. But, of course, he lost even more. The giant gambling institutions all set their odds so that he was bound to lose more than he gained. Their lavish but relatively inexpensive hotels, huge staffs—not to mention the cost of the money they poured into these establishments, and their greed for profits—all made it certain that Morgan Galsworthy and his like had to lose in the end.

Most of the time, Morgan's considerable earnings were enough to cover his losses. But occasionally, when it suited their purposes, the powerful men who ran most of the places at which he gambled were willing to manipulate the odds. It was not primarily that they wanted him to lose more than he would have done on his own, but rather that they lumped these losses together and arranged for them to come at times most convenient to them. Then they had him. His debt would mount beyond his means. And, as the ground of his financial solidity fell away from him, he would become desperate enough to do anything to save himself. Nowadays he was used to what he had to do. But he could still shudder when he recalled that first time. Even though it was fifteen years ago, he could see it as if it were yesterday....

Except for the fact that the man who had entered his

office had no appointment, he seemed quite ordinary. "I'm afraid I must insist," he had started without preliminaries as he seated himself facing Galsworthy. "Yes, I'm afraid I must insist," he had repeated, his tone as reasonable as a professor's.

"What are you doing here?" Morgan had demanded. "Insist on what?"

"You owe my employers fifteen thousand eight hundred and twenty dollars." The voice was cultured, unemotional, matter-of-fact. "I have your IOUs. They are demand notes. If you doubt my word, I'll give you photostats."

"I don't doubt your word." Morgan knew the sum was accurate. He had worried about it unceasingly for the last three days. He had barely slept. "And, of course, I shall pay you."

"Before I leave."

"But I can't."

The man seemed so relaxed—as if he were enjoying himself. It was unnerving. The whole situation was even more sinister because of the obvious affluence of the man. The five-hundred-dollar suit with the white cuffs neatly protruding from under it, and the highly polished shoes, suggested a senior business executive. The tan bespoke success. Only the small monogram on the tie and the slight extra decoration on his shoes hinted that this was not just another senior job applicant. "I don't think you understand, Morgan my friend," he said, his voice smooth and low. "You owe them money and you have to pay. It's not a question of whether you can or you can't. You must."

"I know. I will, I will." Morgan had felt acute fear for the first time in his life: the terror of physical pain. Nonsense, he tried to reassure himself, these people wouldn't attack him physically. This was his office, after all. "I'll pay in five days," he promised with renewed assurance.

"No!" The man smacked his fist onto the arm of his chair and exploded the word into the room. "You will pay *now!*" His fist smacked down again. Then repeating himself softly, with venom in his voice: "Now."

"But I can't." Galsworthy's face set into a frightened and stubborn mold. "Whatever you do, I can't. I haven't got the money."

The well-clad stranger leaned forward. He seemed ready to strike. Instinctively, Galsworthy recoiled. At any second he would see the knife. He was literally quivering with his fear, his hands vibrating against the desk top. He couldn't control them.

"You will pay."

"I said I would. Just not immediately; I can't immediately."

There was a protracted silence in the room. The visitor remained leaning forward, ready to spring, but for the moment entirely immobile. Morgan, leaning backwards, away from the stranger, tried to control his shaking. It was a tableau of domination and submission.

"Very well," the man said at last, his voice still soft and menacing, but with some of the harshness gone, "then we'll have to make some other arrangement."

"What arrangement? What. . . ? I'll do whatever you want, anything that's possible."

"We have a small assignment for you, Mr. Galsworthy."

"What assignment?"

"A small headhunting assignment. We want you to place a particular man in one of the jobs you are presently retained to fill."

"But it depends on the man . . ."

"Of course it does." The stranger had seemed sympathetic. "Of course we wouldn't want you to propose a man to your client who was not right for the position. Fortunately, we know that our particular candidate is perfect." The man paused. "So all you have to do is to make sure that your client sees it that way too. I'm sure you understand."

Galsworthy had understood perfectly. Within a few days the man had been hired.

That had been the first of several placements over the years that Morgan Galsworthy had made for what he thought of as his hidden partners. In some cases, clients had been reluctant at first. But eventually they had been persuaded. After all, Galsworthy had an impeccable reputation—one of the leaders in his field. If he recommended someone strongly, surely the man must be suitable. And, to Morgan's great relief, in every case the recommended employee had proven to be highly qualified and dedicated, anxious to find out not only all about his own job but equally eager to learn about all aspects of the business in which he had been placed. Admittedly, these placements tended to be somewhat short-lived. Still, quitting after a year was not unheard of—and, as for those one or two who quit in six months, well, they were rapidly replaced by Morgan Galsworthy with even better candidates at no additional expense to the client.

As the years progressed, such "specials," as Morgan classified them, became rarer but at a higher level. They had to be handled with the utmost circumspection. For now his reputation had risen to the point where he could place almost any candidate with any client. Even though his need for money was sometimes enormous—thirty thousand dollars lost in one night of craziness represented more than a month's hard slogging even at Morgan's exorbitant fees—he would deal only with those representatives of his hidden partners he could really trust. And then only if they were willing to pay, in thoroughly washed cash, the exorbitant sums it now took to buy Morgan's highly respected reputation.

Morgan Galsworthy, back in his office the next morning, was again as smooth as cream. Hidden entirely was the obsessive gambler of the previous night. He was dictating to his middle-aged secretary, Miss Larsen, his mellifluous voice rising and falling like the gentle swell of a calm ocean. Miss Larsen had been in his employ for twenty years. She was perfectly put together, rigidly coiffed and made up, trim, efficient. Her pencil flew over the dictation pad. Between sentences, she had plenty of time to gaze at her boss with total approbation.

Galsworthy concluded his dictation. "That will, I think, be all, Miss Larsen. Except that I am expecting a visitor of some importance and I would appreciate your bringing him in the moment he arrives: a Mr. Spinosa."

"Of course."

"And perhaps you would be kind enough to hold my calls."

"Yes, Mr. Galsworthy."

Miss Larsen smoothed her wrinkle-free skirt over her diet-controlled hips, rose gracefully and eased out of the room.

For a moment, Galsworthy leaned back in his chair and allowed his face to change from its public blandness to its private worry. His mouth drooped and lines of pain and sadness appeared around his eyes. Why did it always hurt so? The doctors said it was tension, but what did they know? Everyone else said he was the most relaxed man in the world. Probably a strained tendon or something. What the hell . . . He shook his head clear of his ruminations, bent forward in his chair and reached for a pad of paper. He was starting to make a list of his next day's activities when there was a gentle knock on his door.

"Come in."

Miss Larsen pushed the door open. "Mr. Spinosa to see you, sir."

Spinosa entered the room rapidly. "Afternoon." He did not smile. Halting in the center of the office, he waited for the door to close. As soon as he heard its click, he threw himself into the chair opposite Galsworthy. The headhunter, who was just rising to greet him, was forced to sit down again. "I'm pleased you've made progress," Spinosa said. He fell silent, evidently waiting for Morgan to give him a complete report. Although he sat absolutely still, he exuded vitality.

"Yes, fine progress, considering you only gave me the brief a short while ago." Galsworthy paused, trying to think of a way to prolong the discussion. Giving a quick summary of what he had done was most undesirable, he had learned over the years. Clients always underrated the work and expertise you expended for them if you made it sound too simple.

Spinosa waited.

"I understand your take-over bid of Amalgamated Road Haulage was successful." Galsworthy wanted to demonstrate his knowledge of Spinosa's business.

Spinosa inclined his head a fraction of an inch. He said not a word.

"You're the controlling shareholder." Instead of sounding knowledgeable, Galsworthy appeared merely gossipy.

Again, Spinosa indicated he had heard only by the tiniest movement of his head. He still made no sound.

"We have made considerable progress on your assignment," Galsworthy said, annoyed that Spinosa's silence was forcing him to move faster than he wanted. "As I told you, I believe we've found precisely the right man."

"Good." Spinosa's eyes stared unblinkingly at Galsworthy. He moved not a muscle.

It was not for nothing that Spinosa was known as one of the most successful of corporate negotiators, Galsworthy thought ruefully. The man always managed to keep you off balance. "Not only does my man have the right credentials," he continued, "but I'm certain we can control him."

"Will he understand the patents?"

"Not the technology. No, I've looked into that. He does have a degree in chemistry, but it's only an undergraduate one and it's been a long time. Of course, he'll see their potential. Anyone would. After all, to get him in, he's got to have something going for him, the right credentials and reasonable experience. But the fellow I have in mind wouldn't be able to tell whether the patents are technically sound or not."

"He sounds suitable."

"I'm sure he is. I searched diligently to find precisely the right man." Galsworthy was annoyed with himself at feeling such relief at Spinosa's approval.

Spinosa made no further comment.

"Simon Bagnew is ideal in that respect," Morgan Galsworthy insisted, as if his judgment were being challenged. "He's been president of three different companies, so no one can object on that score. In fact, he's simply perfect." Damn, Morgan thought, I'm practically blabbering. He tried to control his nervousness. "Simply perfect," he repeated, failing to tone down his anxiousness. "He'll take advice on the patents with no problem, or on anything else for that matter. A toady with a potbelly and a second chin."

"He'll get good advice." Spinosa allowed the tiniest shadow of a smile to crease his eyes.

Again, Morgan Galsworthy felt the wave of relief, almost of pleasure, as he noted Spinosa's approval. "In fact," he concluded frivolously, "he even looks like a toad."

6

Foster Harrison, chairman and chief executive officer of Turner-LaMott, looked the part: avuncular, confident, impressive. He sported a Savile Row suit, a suntan and a politician's shock of perfectly combed gray hair. He exuded conservatism and wisdom. He could easily have been sent over from Central Casting to play the part. The board room in which he now greeted the corporation's other directors, with its dark green leather chairs, long shiny mahogany table, and portraits of earlier chief executives honoring its walls, seemed like an extension of himself. It had a solidity—an everlastingness, it seemed—which would have enormously reassured any shareholder lucky enough to be invited there.

In fact, however, the benign exterior of the man and the solid respectability of the room belied a major struggle that had been going on for some months among the board members. Each of them knew that it was to erupt today in a final confrontation between the two most powerful factions of the executive suite.

"Please be seated, gentlemen." Harrison smiled kindly at the other directors.

Quickly the group of middle-aged men and one woman found their seats. Three were executives from within the company—the heads of the finance and legal departments, and a figurehead vice-chairman. The rest were outside directors, each of whom had behind him a brilliantly successful business career, a powerful position in his own corporation, and enough money to last him lavishly at least for the rest of his life. While they differed in appearance and background, each evidenced a sense of complacent power that comes only after years of controlling the lives of thousands, sometimes tens of thousands of others. Each was a dictator who, whether superficially benign or ruthless, flexible or stubborn, ultimately demanded his own way, compromised not one millimeter if he could help it, and would have fought tooth, nail, wealth and life to maintain his power.

Even in this group of the immensely strong and rich, Carlos Spinosa stood out. He was not a director of the Turner-LaMott Company because he was any friend of Foster Harrison. In fact, the chairman detested him. The reason that he was a director, and a most powerful one at that, was simple: he owned about two percent of the outstanding shares of the company. A small percentage, perhaps, but it made him the corporation's largest single shareholder. At the current market price of about twenty dollars a share, his shares were worth about thirty million dollars. The whole company, at current market, was worth one and a half billion dollars.

As chairman of the board and chief executive officer, Foster Harrison seated himself at the head of the table in front of a charmingly old-fashioned wooden easel and blackboard. Carlos Spinosa, wordlessly, sat down at the other end.

Over the years in which Spinosa had clawed his way up in the business world, successfully negotiating deal after deal—frequently from a position of weakness—he had learned that silence was one of the most powerful of all the bargaining tools. Often, he would sit through entire business meetings still as a bird of prey. But, as with such a bird, there was nothing of repose in his silence. The Hawk, he was nicknamed by his allies; The Vulture, by his enemies.

"I call the meeting to order," Foster Harrison commenced the board meeting as he had a hundred times before. "With your concurrence I shall waive the reading of the previous minutes."

No one even bothered to state the formal motion. It was recorded automatically, assented to by one or two slightly inclined heads. "So we might as well jump right into the basic question," Harrison said, his voice easy. "I know you'll all be terribly sad to see me go, but the fact of the matter is that I've reached sixty-five and it's time for me to retire. Matter of fact, I gotta," he smiled. "My wife's already planned what color I'm to paint the living room and where the new rose bushes are going."

There were some smiles around the table. They all knew that, even though the old man was forced to retire by company rules, he would not do so graciously. He liked the power. For all his casually understated manner, he had no intention of putting himself out to seed. "So the only real question," Harrison continued, "is who should be my successor."

It might be a simple enough question but, as the directors encircling the table knew, agreeing to the answer involved a battle that had already raged for months.

"We have with us today Mr. Morgan Galsworthy, whom you all know," Harrison continued. "Hell, you should, he put most of you in your jobs." There were nods of recognition and a few chuckles around the table. As everyone noted, two of the men chuckling easily had, indeed, been placed in their positions by Galsworthy. No doubt it was largely their influence that had caused the board to choose Galsworthy & Merit to help resolve the conflict about the next president.

"Thank you," said Morgan Galsworthy in his smooth way. "I believe my firm may be able to bring some experience to bear in helping you to choose the right man."

"Let us hope," Carlos Spinosa interrupted, his voice filled with gravel.

The men around the table looked at Spinosa with surprise. He rarely volunteered a comment. Clearly he was signaling a point of view, not talking idly.

Foster Harrison ignored the interruption. "As you all know, I am in favor of promoting Mr. Jim Lester, who has, for many years, been my second in command. His background, age at forty-five, his personal character, his strength, his dedication to the company—"

"And his dedication to you." The interruption came from Mrs. Millicent Carpenter-Smith, the only female director. A wily, gray-haired lady, she had made her initial success when much younger, by being sponsored, as she called it, by a senior banker on Wall Street. Mrs. Smith was full of euphemisms. Under this banker's sponsorship, Mrs. Smith had enjoyed a series of rapid (but circumspect) promotions. With the reputation she had gained through this rapid rise—and with her solid grasp of the banking business—she had landed the presidency of a small Long Island bank. This she had built to high profitability, not so much by attracting women depositors as by attracting the type of women who could persuade rich males to use her bank. Sometimes, of course, she did the attracting. One of her earliest depositors had been Foster Harrison.

Mrs. Smith had met with no success whatsoever in the case of Jim Lester. He was such a straight arrow, so dedicated to his pretty wife and young family. None of her employees or contacts had been able to, as she liked to describe it, "influence" him. As a result, she really did not like him much. Surely there must be a better choice for the presidency of Turner-LaMott. In earlier days one word to Fossey would have been enough. But he was old now—insisted that she call him Foster, and wouldn't do one damn thing she wanted any more. Too old for the techniques she used to employ to have much impact. Or was it only she who was too old? She'd seen him look at her speculatively every now and then, wondering whether he could get her off the board. Not if she could help it. No sir! She liked the prestige of sitting on this board, and she'd fight to stay. Perhaps the old goat had a new protégé . . . some bimbo with an MBA, no doubt. What the hell, Mrs. Carpenter-Smith decided, she'd attained the position she wanted. She was secure in it—and with money in the bank. No point in really fighting against Jim Lester. Still, if someone else were nominated and needed her vote, he could have it. The main reason was that, with Jim in the job, old Fossey would be hanging onto his power. Retire he might, but he would continue to call the shots.

"Personal loyalty is, of course, a desirable characteristic," Harrison agreed blandly.

Why couldn't he say "good thing?" Mrs. Smith wondered. Why was he so unalterably pompous? She almost interrupted, but decided at the last moment she shouldn't. Teasing was an admission of more intimacy than he cared to admit had ever existed between them. And it was an inviolate part of her code not to use such intimacy to embarrass an old friend. At least not without first giving him fair warning.

For his part, Foster Harrison would willingly have throttled the lady. "However, fortunately," he continued, "we can all be fully assured that Jim puts—and will always put—company loyalty above all personal considerations." He looked directly at Mrs. Carpenter-Smith. "I don't believe that anything could seduce him away from that."

Dangerous old bugger, Mrs. Smith thought. She returned his smile—and decided to leave the argument alone. The old coot might still win before the day was done.

"If you will forgive me," the company lawyer interrupted, "I believe that the internal members of this board, who will be working for whichever chief executive is ultimately elected, should be excused." He was a large-stomached man—portly—with an exaggerated sense of his own importance. "Although there is no legal requirement for us to withdraw, it might be wiser."

"Agreed, agreed," said Harrison. "We wouldn't let you vote anyway. So what the hell, you might as well do some work while we're arguing." Pity, he was thinking, they would certainly have favored Jim Lester.

There was considerable shuffling as the three internal directors left the room. But, once the door had been firmly closed, an uncomfortable silence descended. Harrison had made his point; now it was up to Spinosa.

For over a minute Carlos Spinosa remained silent, allowing the tension to build. Finally, speaking in his most computerized voice, Spinosa made his statement. He used the fewest words possible. "I disagree. Lester is competent, but lacks stature." His mouth stopped moving; the robot had been switched off.

"If we were to look at potential candidates' résumés, we'd be pleased to get one as good as Jim Lester's," Harrison jumped to the defense. "Perhaps it is only your familiarity with Jim that makes you think he lacks stature. That view doesn't hold on the outside. I've talked to bankers who—"

"I also know a few," Spinosa interrupted Harrison in midsentence. "They say only what they think I want to hear."

"Nevertheless," Harrison continued, sounding a shade flustered, "Jim's reputation outside is good."

"But not powerful."

Harrison did not bother to answer. Clearly there would be no changing Spinosa's mind. The question was, could he muster the boardroom votes to beat the man? He calculated shrewdly. Nine people around the table. Three were his cronies—with his own vote that made four.

But Spinosa controlled two directors, holding major interests in their companies. And Millie, damn her, seemed to be leaning toward the Spinosa faction. So they had four votes too. And the swing vote? Harrison looked at Harold O. Johnstone sitting sleepily halfway down the table. He was an elderly, taciturn, stupid man who held his board position because he had inherited a large number of Turner-LaMott shares. After Spinosa, he was the largest shareholder in the room. But he offered neither the company nor the board anything of value. For years Harrison had wondered how to get rid of him. But there had been no easy way and no obvious need. Damn! He wished he had made the move when his instincts first warned him. The trouble with Johnstone was you had no idea how he'd vote on any issue. Probably he didn't either—made up his mind at the last moment on the basis of whatever argument he'd managed to comprehend. Thank God, Foster Harrison was thinking, he'd agreed to bring in Morgan Galsworthy—just the sort of man to convince Johnstone. And hadn't he just observed some flash of distaste between Galsworthy and Spinosa?

"And I do want to make certain you are equally fully reimbursed, whether we ask you to find someone on the outside, or you convince us that Lester is the right man," Harrison had assured Morgan Galsworthy when he appointed him. That meant that, if he recommended Jim, the headhunter would get his full fee without doing a stroke of work. "Furthermore," Harrison had continued, "both Jim Lester and I agree that your services are so valuable to Turner-LaMott we plan to use them for a long time to come."

"We always stand ready to find you the right people," Galsworthy had responded, with just the right mixture of obsequiousness and self-confidence.

"Since there seems to be some difference of opinion,"

Harrison now continued pompously, "I feel we should call upon Mr. Morgan Galsworthy, whom we have retained as an expert in the field of executive placement, to provide us with his independent view."

"We should hear his views," Spinosa agreed. It was quite clear that he was not committing himself to agree with them.

"As always in these important succession matters"—Galsworthy commenced, his tone weighty. His composed face, impeccable hair, superb suit, distinguished him totally from the fanatic of the gaming tables—"we at Galsworthy and Merit have investigated this matter with the greatest possible care. We've probed into Mr. Lester's career, talked to executives inside and outside the company, and investigated many alternate candidates.

"As a result, we have presented you with a short list of four excellent executives: Each would be suitable as president and chief executive officer of the Turner-LaMott Company. One of them is, of course, Jim Lester."

Harrison stifled a yawn.

"The first question we asked ourselves about each candidate," Galsworthy was continuing, "was whether he is technically competent. We have no doubt that all four men are. I trust you will accept my word on this score." He looked around the room sternly to see whether anyone had the temerity to question his judgment. "So that leads to the more difficult question: Does the man have the needed stature?"

Harrison was ruminating about plans for the next three years, which he would implement through the strong right arm of Jim Lester. First there was the new products program. Now that the patents were almost ready, that area would have to get into high gear.

". . . I believe each of the three outsiders and Mr. Lester have the stature we are seeking."

No problem with Galsworthy, Harrison congratulated himself. Just as he had anticipated, the man wanted the money without the effort.

"There is, of course, a third point," Galsworthy was concluding his peroration, "namely, what will the investment community think of the company under its new leadership?" He paused for effect. "That's the most difficult problem of all."

Harrison became suddenly alert.

"As you all know, the shares of Turner-LaMott have not been as, um, let us say, buoyant as they might have been."

"Right." The word from Spinosa was like the crack of a rifle.

"Yet, the quality of the company is unquestioned."

"It's the idiots who run Wall Street," Harrison started to remonstrate repeating long-held, fervent views. "They—"

"Do not view the company as sufficiently progressive," Galsworthy took over smoothly. "I believe we need a change of face to change their minds."

"Yes." Spinosa agreed promptly.

Too late, Harrison realized the trap. Already there was a babble of discussion around the table. "He makes a good point." "Could do with a rise in the stock." Harrison heard the comments with mounting anger. Ungrateful bastards. Just because Turner-LaMott stock hadn't risen in the last year or two. When he started ten years ago it was hardly more than half . . .

"Thus, I am forced to the conclusion," Galsworthy was saying, "that we should choose a new man to run Turner-LaMott. A good man, of course, but one who would seem to the investment community to bring in some new blood. Jim Lester is a good man, as we all agree. But, by definition, he's part of the current regime—he can't pretend to be a new broom!"

Harrison's anger flared. "I do not buy your point," he said loudly. "Wall Street is so unpredictable that no one can possibly tell what would happen to the stock whether a new man or Lester were elected. But the company would be better under Lester. And in the end that's what counts, even on the stock market." Harrison could see only blank faces around him. He was making no progress. "That's how I've been able to double the stock price in the past ten years," he insisted.

"We've a better chance to see the stock rise with a new man than with Jim," Galsworthy said, sounding patient. "Therefore, after careful consideration, we at Galsworthy and Merit recommend seeking a new chief executive from outside the company."

"So move." The voice of Carlos Spinosa cut through all other conversation.

"Second," said Johnstone.

His was the key swing vote, Foster Harrison knew. Christ! But why had the fool decided against Lester? Foster had no idea . . . how could you predict what a fool would do? He shook his head, knowing that he had to proceed. "All those in favor please raise your hands," he said, managing to keep the disappointment out of his voice. He'd lost before, hadn't he, and bounced back? Well somehow he'd do it again.

Harrison decided to be generous. "And may I add my own vote to the affirmative," he said pompously. Perhaps he could hold some of his influence if he could avoid seeming to have lost too badly. "I have made my views clear. But since Mr. Galsworthy has more experience in these matters, I must also respect his. And I believe that, in personnel questions like this, the board should be unanimous." He noted the relief on the faces of the three hold-out directors as they quickly raised their hands.

"Very well then. Now we face the decision as to which of the three other candidates we should choose." Harrison, seething with disappointment and anger, was sure of one thing: Even though he'd lost Jim Lester, he was going to make damn sure he'd stop *them* from electing some wet-behind-the-ears son of a bitch who'd run roughshod over everything he'd built over the years. He just wouldn't stand for that! With a great effort he kept all emotion out of his tone. "Notwithstanding Mr. Galsworthy's persuasive views," he said reasonably, "I believe we should not choose someone who might rock our boat so much that it starts to, er, ship water." Even in a cliché, it was unthinkable to refer to the boat as sinking.

"We need action," Spinosa said. "Not recklessness, but action. And a new face." The directors looked at him with surprise. It was a long speech by Carlos Spinosa's standards.

"Indeed not recklessness, as you so rightly say," Harrison's voice carried an edge; he would not be bested twice.

Again, it was Morgan Galsworthy who intervened. "I believe we need a candidate who would provide Turner-LaMott with the presence it needs on Wall Street, while also ensuring that all corporate improvements he undertakes would be commensurate with this company's traditional values...."

Harrison wished fervently that he had never heard of Morgan Galsworthy. The man was a goddamn snake! Now what the hell was he talking about?

". . . and so I believe that one candidate of our three is ideal: I suggest that you offer the job of president of Turner-LaMott to Mr. Simon Bagnew."

Harrison almost allowed his relief to show. He covered himself only by a simulated coughing attack. Perfect, he was thinking, trying to keep his face noncommittal. If there was ever a nonactive president, Simon Bagnew would be it. In fact, with Bagnew, Harrison could stay firmly in the driver's seat after all.

"He hasn't the dynamism," Carlos Spinosa stated flatly.

"I'm not sure I agree with that," Harrison said carefully. "He's certainly had the experience. He'd probably give exactly the right impression to Wall Street."

"He's weak," Spinosa said.

"Perhaps we should have a formal motion whether to accept or reject him?"

Spinosa hesitated, his eye glancing over the other members of the board.

This time Harrison was quite sure of his ground. This vote he'd win. No one would risk appointing a new chief executive opposed by the retiring one. He could force Bagnew in if necessary.

Evidently, Spinosa reached the same conclusion. "I don't think that will be necessary," he said, his voice full of gravel, as impersonal as ever. "Foster, if you and Galsworthy think he's right, then okay." It was Spinosa at his most gracious.

"Then, so it is agreed," Foster Harrison proclaimed. "Mr. Simon Bagnew will become the next president and chief executive officer of Turner-LaMott."

It was a job, Foster Harrison decided with pleasure, that, without his help, poor Simon Bagnew would surely fuck up.

———7

When Simon Bagnew answered the phone these days, he did so without enthusiasm. It was usually a bill collector or, at best, someone trying to sell him something he couldn't afford. The very fact that he was the only one home to answer the phone reminded him constantly that his wife had to go out to work because he was unemployed.

He reached the kitchen extension by the fourth ring. "Simon Bagnew speaking," he answered, trying to make his voice sound cheerful or at least positive, relaxed too, like a man taking a vacation, perhaps.

"Ah, Simon. Morgan Galsworthy here." The mellifluous voice oozed into his ear. "I'm so pleased I managed to catch you at home." The sarcasm, while muted, was entirely intentional.

"I normally only teach in the evenings. Leaves me free to write—and relax if I feel like it—during the day."

"Quite. We both realize you have nothing to do."

Bagnew was instantly incensed at the rudeness. Should he simply slam down the phone? His instincts cried out that he should—how could the son of a bitch treat him like that? His hand, white-knuckled against the receiver, started to move. But just as he had made up his mind, his eye fell on the portrait of his wife half-visible through the kitchen door in its place of honor over the dining room table, and he stopped moving. She looked so calm and beautiful, as she had been twenty or more years ago. How lovely. Just like Susan looked now. And how deeply in love with her he had fallen. He still didn't quite know why she had accepted him, a serious, slightly plump youth with nothing to offer except ambition. But she had, and with just as strong a love as his. And he had promised to make her life wonderful.

"I didn't call to argue with you," Galsworthy was proceeding, "but to give you some news that will, no doubt, elate you."

Bagnew suddenly felt physically weak; his knees seemed to be turning to jelly. He pulled up one of the high kitchen bar chairs next to the counter and perched himself on it. "Yes?" he asked, trying to keep his voice from quavering. "What news?"

"The board of directors of the Turner-LaMott Company today voted unanimously to appoint you president and chief executive officer of that concern."

Simon Bagnew heard the words but could not apply real understanding to them. "Huh?" He was as confused as if he were just regaining consciousness after being knocked out. "They did what?"

Galsworthy's voice changed not one inflection as he repeated the sentence.

"I—I'm—very—"

"I can well understand your astonishment." Suddenly Morgan Galsworthy's voice was cold, harder than Bagnew had ever heard it. It shocked Simon into full attention to the headhunter's next words. "We both know you don't deserve the job. That is why I arranged for you to be given it. The point is, that certain key members of the board, working through me, intend to exercise control over the company. Obviously, you are indebted to us for giving you a job—and you will continue to be indebted to us for being allowed to keep it. You certainly won't be able to on your own. And you obviously realize that if you lose this job, you'll never get another. So we assume that you will honor your debt."

A miracle had occurred, that was all that Simon Bagnew could think. He was almost paralyzed with astonishment. Employed at last! Just to be able to say that to Janet and Susan. To himself! And not just in some mediocre job—he would have accepted anything of course—but brilliantly employed, at the top of a giant international corporation. The concept was overwhelming. No wonder he was only just starting to grasp it.

And, yet, at the same time, even as he was beginning to comprehend, to *feel*, what it would mean, the miracle was about to be snatched away from him again, leaving him as disappointed, as desperate as ever.

"I trust you will agree to our proposition?"

Simon Bagnew heard himself answering as if from a

great distance. "I am honored that you have chosen me," he heard his voice saying. How dignified I sound, he thought. "Of course I will recognize that those members of the board who were influential in obtaining the position for me, will be duly served." He was rather proud that he had managed to answer without saying anything.

"I don't know what that means."

Simon sighed unsteadily. It was as involuntary as the gasps that used to shake him as a child after a crying fit. This was too difficult. Still looking at himself as if from a great distance, he felt a great surge of sympathy for the stranger sitting in his own body at the kitchen counter. He wondered whether that poor, defeated Simon Bagnew down there could possibly find the strength to hold onto any of his integrity at all. Objectively, he doubted it. "I assume the policies of your group are in the best interests of Turner-LaMott?" he heard his voice continue. It sounded quite unruffled. But he felt so weak he worried that he might fall off the bar stool on which he was perched ever more precariously.

"Of course."

"Then clearly I would have no difficulty in agreeing with them."

"It goes beyond that," Galsworthy said roughly. "You're getting the job only because we're giving it to you." He paused. "So we want your obedience."

Suddenly Simon was back in his own body, knowing that now was the moment he would have to decide—and knowing too that he would have to live with his decision for the rest of his life. It would be so easy to agree. "Of course I'll do what I'm told" was all he had to say to be sure of the job. One sentence and he'd be secure, not only for himself but for his whole family. "Of course I'll do what you want," he started, then forced himself to add, "provided it's not against the best interests of the company."

Morgan Galsworthy waited. Did he want to push

harder? Bagnew was not caving in quite as readily as he should have.

The pause continued until Simon could not stand it any longer. Already he had taken a breath to speak. "Anything, anything," he was ready to say. "I'll do anything you want. Just give me the job."

But before Simon could utter his capitulation, Morgan Galsworthy had made his own decision. Thirty thousand dollars he owed those sharks in Vegas. They would not take lightly to a further delay. The money was his now, but not if he turned down Bagnew at the eleventh hour. Worse, what would Spinosa say? Moreover, even if Bagnew wouldn't say all the right words, you could practically hear the nervous sweat dripping off him. Anyone with real balls would have slammed down the phone long ago. "Very well," Morgan Galsworthy said, "as long as you understand who pulls the ropes. Report to work in two weeks. You know the address. Go straight to Foster Harrison's office." Then, his voice dripping with sarcasm, he ended the conversation: "Congratulations, Mr. President."

Simon Bagnew returned the silent receiver to its cradle very gently. Then he allowed his hand to fall onto the surface of the kitchen counter. It rested there, a white inanimate object, as soft and vulnerable as a hermit crab without its shell. For many minutes he didn't move. The turmoil inside him was too powerful to leave any energy for bodily motion. Simon's mind was thrashing with relief, but also with terror about the way he'd been given the position and then, with something close to ecstasy, at having been reborn.

Janet Bagnew didn't return until five that evening—three hours after Galsworthy's fateful call. By that time Simon had buried his doubts. All that remained was undiluted elation. Alone, he had opened a bottle of champagne and drunk most of it so that the dizziness of his achievement was compounded by effervescent tipsiness from the champagne. His mind and his body were both bubbling.

Janet Bagnew staggered into the house under a load of groceries, one large brown paper bag in each arm. Her face was grim with the discomfort of carrying the packages, but she was quite satisfied. Pork chops had been a bargain today, and she'd found some excellent oranges in the overripe pile at the supermarket. They were so good, she actually thought someone had made a mistake putting them there—and twenty cents less per pound. She'd had to do without beef again this week, but she'd had enough money left over to splurge on the coffeecake Simon adored on a Sunday morning.

"I did it, I did it, I did it!" Simon shouted as soon as he heard her fumbling with the front door. "I did it, Janet, I did it." He was jumping up and down, uncontrolled as a school boy, beside himself with the pride of being able to tell her.

"What?" she asked, totally bewildered. "You did what? What are you talking about?"

Instantly a wave of annoyance swept over him. Why couldn't she just accept his pleasure, take his word for it? Why did she have to ask?

With a great effort he forced himself to be calm. "Janet, I got a job," he started to explain. "A real job. A fantastic job. I did it!" His voice started to rise again.

Slowly her face, set grim when she had entered the house, started to soften. "You did, darling? You mean you're interviewing for a job."

"Not *interviewing*. I've *got* the job." He was instantly angry again. "That's right, dammit, I got it. I tell you I got a job."

"What sort of job?" She could hardly believe what he was saying.

"President." He exploded his bombshell. But she looked

bemused, uncomprehending. "Don't you understand," he said, his aggravation flashing higher. "I'm president."

"Of what?"

"Of Turner-LaMott." He shouted the words as if he were an old-fashioned butler introducing the duke of something-or-other, or an emcee announcing the lead act. "President of Turner-LaMott."

"The pharmaceutical company? You're president?" She couldn't keep the disbelief out of her voice.

"God dammit, yes, I'm president."

"Of the whole of the American company?"

"Of the whole of the world," he shouted. "The world! I'm president of the world." For a moment he wondered if he should tell her all the circumstances. No, why force her to share his concerns? He'd won, hadn't he? "They were looking for somebody and I fit the bill, that's all," he added more quietly. "I gather they'd been searching for a long time, and last week they said they'd honed it down to four people. Earlier today they had a board meeting and selected me." He smiled at her and then added cynically, "I was probably the compromise candidate."

"Oh no, darling. That's not true," she reassured him, appreciating just how shaken he was to have the job. "I'm sure they chose you on your merits."

"Morgan Galsworthy was the headhunter," Simon said, expansive again. "Called me in early September and we talked. He's an unpleasant man—slimy and insincere—and I didn't think anything would come of it. That's why I didn't mention it. A few days after that I met this fellow Harrison, he's the chairman who's retiring next year. Polite, but dreadfully pompous. Said he'd call me, but he never did. Just one call from his secretary last week. So I just decided to forget about the whole thing. Then today—just three hours ago—Galsworthy called." Simon's voice cracked. "President! Don't you understand?"

"Yes," Janet replied fervently, "indeed I do. I know just

what it means to us. It's not only that the scrimping will die down. Or even that we'll be able to be straight with Susie. It's you I'm most pleased about." She looked at her husband fondly. He was a good man. That was the first thought that always came to her mind when she looked at him. A really good man. "Above all, darling, I understand what it means to you."

Yes, he thought, it means I can live. For a fleeting moment he thought again of his final solution, his only real comfort these last months. He could banish that now. He felt its weight falling from his chest. He had a better solution, he told himself delightedly, a really perfect solution. At least, so he hoped.

8

Carlos Spinosa, a man of strange contrasts, obtained almost orgasmic pleasure from grand opera. He would sit entranced, night after night, at the Metropolitan Opera, letting the voices of the singers wash over and through him. Tearful at the death of Mimi in *La Bohème*, or with his face wreathed in smiles—which his business acquaintances would have found utterly astonishing—during the comic arias of *Figaro*, he would lose himself entirely in the music. He could hum a hundred arias, forcing his flat voice into a parody of the music while in his head he heard Gigli's marvelous tenor or the superb basso profundo of Chaliapin.

Spinosa had not heard a note of opera, or any other classical music for that matter, until he was sixteen and already a successful entrepreneur in the back streets of São Paulo, selling visiting businessmen sex and fantasy in a heady mixture. His main beat in those days had encompassed the sidewalk outside the São Paulo Hilton—the only American-style hotel then in the city—and the street between there and the infamous brothel-cum-night club, La Fontaine. He had been as talkative in his youth, brash and appealing, as he was taciturn in adulthood.

"What you want, mister?" he would accost a strolling businessman. "I make your dreams come true."

Inevitably the businessman, intrigued by the street boy's fluent English and unique approach, would stop to listen. Spinosa had learned the value of knowing the language very early, and had studied it assiduously ever since he was a little kid. He had a musical ear and a fine memory, so while his English was still thickly Brazilian, he could talk easily with an unusual selection of words which made his sentences precocious and interesting.

"You can make my dreams come true, eh?"

"Sure, mister. Any dream. My customer yesterday very pleased with the young twins, seventeen, beautiful girls what danced for him. . . . Or like I give my gentlemen from New York, sometimes a much younger girl. . . . And what about this girl in the rubber suit? She is diver, you know, but what she dives for I wouldn't know." Young Carlos would amuse his quarry with quick descriptions of excess, all the time watching him like a hawk. "The golden shower I can arrange for you, or a Greek goddess . . ." Watching, he would usually see a sudden movement in his hearer, a guilty start, an unconscious thrust forward of a hip, a hand rubbing the back of his neck. Then he would know where to concentrate his sales pitch.

Sometimes the reaction was more immediate: "Twins dancing? What are they like? Black or white?"

"For you mister, one each color," Carlos would tease. "Which you prefer?"

"Well, I'm not—"

"Here, I show." The boy would pull a large book of photographs from inside his jacket. Without its bulk, he looked even more emaciated. He would riffle through its pages with concentration until he found the photo of a girl he thought would appeal. "Here. This is picture of one of the girls. You like? The other is same, only a little tinier. But she dance better, faster. Her sister, she can lift her many ways when they dance. You get good views."

"How much?" The clients always wanted to know that early in the discussion. But young Carlos had learned not to answer too soon. First hook the mark; then fix the place; and only after that get around to the price. "That way you're dealing with a guy whose prick has bought already," Carlos would advise the apprentices he retained to sell cheaper girls in the poorer parts of town. "A lousy bargaining tool, the prick."

"You dance too, mister," Carlos would continue. "Sometimes with the smaller twin, sometimes with the stronger." Still he would be watching his buyer's eyes, searching for that special flicker of response to a word he said. "She's very strong, the bigger girl. And the little one can be real dangerous. When you dance, you better watch out they don't bang into you like two tough little wrestlers and—"

"Listen, my room's on the same floor as—"

"Don't worry, boss. Carlos fix everything. You have fine room with the twins where they stay. Better place than the Hilton. No one hear if the girls get excited, cry out . . ." Again, the involuntary flicker and Carlos would home in on that new idea too. "They can be noisy, those two, when they get excited by a big American. Sometimes they scream."

"Okay. Where is it, this place?"

"Mister, you could throw a stone at it. That entrance, over there. Tell you what we do. We go to this bar. Carlos order you a drink. My friend in the bar give it to you very cheap—Brazil price, not American. And by the time you finished, I be back with arrangements . . . take you to the suite." Carlos would emphasize the word suite. He sometimes thought his income had doubled the day he learned that word from a visiting businessman who liked small white boys and big black mamas doing strange things to each other.

"You still haven't said how much."

"Don't worry. Brazil price also for Carlos's twins. One hundert twenny—for everything. The two girls *and* the suite. For as long as it takes."

"Takes for what?"

"Ah, mister. A hundert and twenny for as long as it takes till the girls are satisfied and you are satisfied . . . but I don't know about all that. Me, I'm just a kid."

Young Carlos figured he closed over fifty percent of the sales pitches he started. Then all that remained was to deliver the goods. That was the easy part—a telephone call to Big Maria. "Two girls, one a little bigger, the other smaller. Youngish, say about seventeen."

"Okay."

"And he went for page thirty-two." Carlos would add, referring to the book of photos to give Maria an idea of the physical type the mark would be expecting. "Oh, and they're supposed to be twins."

"Twins?"

"Not to worry. Just so they look a bit alike." Young Carlos would continue with the specifications. "What he wants is a little dance, a little discipline and to scream a bit."

"How much?"

"He's paying one-twenty U.S." Carlos was always scrupulously honest. "We split like always, sixty each."

"But I got to provide two girls." Big Maria would occasionally try to argue.

"You don't *have* to provide any girls. There are many sources." Carlos's voice would become glacial.

"Okay, okay. Fifty-fifty. I was only explaining about costs." Big Maria could not afford to lose Carlos as a salesman. Even though his percentage was higher than her others, he usually sold the girls for more money so she came out the same. And even though he was her youngest salesman, he was by far her biggest producer.

The girls liked Carlos well enough and shared their favors with him. Ever since a young whore with nothing better to do had seduced him when he was barely fourteen and only just old enough to be interested, Carlos had enjoyed all the sex he could possibly want. It was pleasant but routine. The fantasies of excess he wove for his clients were more exciting to him than the mundane realities he experienced himself.

Then, Carlos's life was changed a few weeks before his seventeenth birthday by Margaret, an American. He could remember only rather general details about her now, recalling that she had a boxy, mannish figure, liked to wear well-cut suits and had short brown bangs. But he had long forgotten all intimate facts about her, like whether she had tiny golden hairs on her inner thighs, like Bella, the woman he lived with now, or perhaps a tiny scar under her lip like the nun who was his only surviving sibling.

It had been late on a typical evening of young Carlos's business life. Sales that day had been even better than usual and the young man was well pleased. He was also hungry because he'd had no time to eat. He'd get himself some supper, he decided, some meat. Already he was earning enough money to be able to afford the best of food—and even at that age he was treating his body as a valuable resource to be pampered. He had a horror of letting it run down or become ill—and thus interfere with his white-hot ambition to be rich.

Carlos entered his favorite chiaroscuro restaurant with a swagger, already salivating from the slightly acrid smell of the meat broiling over the giant charcoal grill. He greeted his friend, the headwaiter, and waited a moment to see which table would be free.

"Hello, young man."

He heard her, presumably addressing him since he was the only male standing there, before he observed who she was.

"You," she commanded, "come over here and join me."

He saw her then, alone and staring at him intently from a table in the alcove where only the most important guests were placed. Immediately he was intrigued. It was rare for a woman to dine alone in Brazil, let alone an American, as her accent said she was. And even rarer for that particular table to be given to a single person, and a gringo at that. She must be very influential—or tip lavishly. Either way, young Carlos was interested.

"You speak English," she asked, "or do I have to struggle in my lousy Portuguese?"

"I speak English good," he said proudly.

"You speak English *well*," she corrected, "or you speak good English. If you say you speak it good, you speak it lousy."

He was instantly offended. "How well," he asked, emphasizing the word, "you speak my language?"

"I speak Portuguese lousy," she laughed. "Don't be angry. I love to teach."

Carlos was slightly mollified. "Okay. Now you tell me what you want. I make all your dreams come true."

"You will, will you? First let's eat. You want a steak or what?"

"Sure a steak. Is what I always have here." He was anxious to prove that he too was important. "Best steak in São Paulo. I tried all the good places. I know."

"Selling dreams must be profitable."

"Sure. Make some money. Not too much because my dreams are Brazil prices, not American."

"You're quite a promoter."

"Oh, sure."

"After we eat, maybe we can make some dreams come true for each other, make beautiful music together." She laughed, as if at some private joke.

"Make music?" He was not sure what she meant.

"Beautiful music, you and I. Maybe I'll be able to teach you something after all."

"Maybe," he said, doubting it.

They ate together, laughing and friendly. She told him she was a singer, but he hardly believed her. He knew about singers. They were sexy young women mostly, or at least they tried to look it, who vamped with their microphones in the nightclubs he sometimes worked. Or they were old women in the market place, singing their sad, dirgelike songs of sailors and love lost to the sea. But they were never important American women like this one, slightly overweight and not very pretty. Still, he wasn't about to argue as long as she was paying for his meal.

After dinner they walked back to her hotel, not the Hilton as it turned out, but a traditional Brazilian hotel, old-fashioned but luxurious. The Palace d'Oro, so named after the gilt that emblazoned the curlicues covering the ceiling, pillars and doors of the entire lobby.

Carlos had never dared enter this hotel before. The Hilton was different. That was for Americans, for business. There he knew all the bellboys—two of them worked for him part-time, fingering likely candidates for him to approach. But a traditional Brazilian hotel like this was different. They would never let people like him in here.

"It's beautiful," he said, and then instantly regretted this show of naïveté. "I mean, it's like another hotel I sometimes stay."

"Yes. I like it for that reason, and also because they give me a room where I can practice to my heart's content without disturbing anyone."

"Practice?"

"Singing, my dear boy. Don't you believe I'm a singer?"

"Oh, sure."

Then she took Carlos up to her room. It was huge, by far the largest bedroom he had ever seen. In the corner, lid already raised, was a grand piano. He knew upright pianos, of course, from the many bars which had them. But he had never before seen an instrument of this size.

"Listen," she said and sat down on the bench in front of the keyboard.

As Carlos stood beside her, bemused with surprise, her fingers started to stroke the keyboard and a gentle melody seemed to float into the room. Then in a voice as high and delicate as a lark's, she started to trill her song.

Carlos stood entranced as her operatic soprano moved up and down the scales of her vocal range, sometimes following the tune her fingers were cajoling out of the piano, sometimes in counterpoint to it.

When she beckoned him to sit next to her, he almost threw himself to her side, snuggling up to her like a puppy. Still she sang to him, soft songs full of love and melody. Then, gradually, her music became harsher, more demanding and young Carlos could feel the excitement rising in his loins. She stopped playing with one hand and started to unbutton her suit jacket. To his amazement, she wore nothing underneath and within only seconds her breasts, large and pendulous, were swinging free.

Still she sang to him, but now her voice had dropped to a lower register. In a full contralto, she was singing the powerful, commanding music of Wagner.

At last he summoned up the courage to suck on one of her nipples. He could feel the resonance of her voice on his tongue.

Suddenly her hands crashed onto the piano in a final mighty chord. Then, holding his head firmly to her breast, she picked him up like a baby and carried him to her bed. There she lay him down and, before he could move, stripped the clothes off his lean body, tearing his shirt off in her hurry. Before he could protest at all, she was out of her own clothes too and sitting astride him with his penis deep inside her, writhing on top of him, bearing down so hard that he was immobilized, powerless, overwhelmed, dominated.

It took only seconds for her to reach her climax, which she did with a great melodic shriek of her giant voice. It was a tidal wave of ecstatic sound and it brought Carlos instantly to his own orgasm, a more violent one than he had ever experienced. To this day the memory of that shriek and Margaret's orgasm filled him with the most potent desire. He remembered every detail—and to this day became instantly erect every time he heard those great crescendoing arias of Wagner.

Carlos Spinosa stayed with Margaret for six months. In that time she taught him to love opera, to speak grammatically perfect English, and to tell the difference between good wines and poor. They stayed most of the time in São Paulo, where she had a semipermanent place in the local opera company, but they also visited New York briefly and spent three weeks in Europe.

Carlos was astonished and delighted at all he saw; and constantly reaffirmed in his conviction that he needed to be rich. He loved the life he saw in Europe. More importantly, he was utterly determined to escape forever from even the remotest possibility that he might slide back into the awful, bastard poverty of his earlier childhood.

Carlos left Margaret in Italy when she made the error of taking him to La Scala. Hearing a great singer perform a part from Margaret's own repertoire, Carlos instantly recognized his mentor's mediocrity. He would not stay with any second-rater, he decided. And anyhow he was bored with her by now. So the next morning he walked out without a word of good-bye or apology. He took all Margaret's loose money and one valuable diamond with him; but he left behind her other jewelry and her checkbook, credit cards and other valuables as too easily traceable. The diamond, a two-carat stone, valuable but without distinguishing characteristics, he pried out of its setting and sold the same day.

The money he stole, as well as that he got for the diamond, he deposited quite openly in an international bank account. Even if she decided to make a fuss, which she wouldn't, she could never prove the money wasn't his. After all, he'd had a nice savings account before he met her. And since they'd been together, except when they traveled, his earnings had continued—while all the time she'd taken care of his expenses. In any case, this was Italy, and first she'd have to find him, which wouldn't be easy. He left that same afternoon on a train for Rome.

Carlos Spinosa had never seen Margaret since that day, almost thirty-six years ago. But his fanaticism for opera had remained. His whole apartment was built around it. Half the living room was filled with the ultimate in stereo components, capable of reproducing every tone and nuance of the Metropolitan Opera, and at any decibel level he wanted. And in every other room there were enormous subsidiary speakers able to duplicate the main sound system with virtually perfect fidelity.

Much had changed for Carlos Spinosa in those years. Many other women had come and gone. Many compromises had been necessary. He had experienced the most awful deprivation, had almost given up and died. . . . But he was a rich man now, able to indulge his every whim. And some things had not changed: he still refused to settle for mediocrity; he still exhibited neither gratitude nor any other sign of what he considered weakness; and he still pampered his body, treating it to only the best food, and that in moderation, exercising it regularly, having it massaged. . . . He was proud of the body, which he viewed objectively as a thing apart from himself, as something he owned, like a wonderfully expensive car, and which he took care of so that it would continue to give him good service.

Carlos lay in his luxurious bath now, warming the body and soothing its skin with the scented oil that floated thickly on the water's surface. The oil was specially prepared for him by a well-known cosmetic house in which he had a financial interest. Occasionally, he reached out with his foot to change the temperature of the water flowing gently into the bath from the gold taps at its foot. They were fitted with the extended handles found in the preparation areas of operating rooms. Surgeons could turn them on and off with their elbows without unsterilizing their hands; Carlos could move his with his toes without having to disturb the layering of hot and cold water in his bath.

He felt relaxed and satisfied. The Turner-LaMott deal was progressing precisely on schedule. He had been hesitant at the start knowing that Oliver Chapin, for all his soft appearance, false Anglo-Boston accent and pretenses to Brahmin status, could get excessively rough if things went wrong. But then he had decided that there was very little chance of that happening. And he'd been right. Poor Harrison had first been tricked out of Lester and then into accepting Simon Bagnew with almost suspicious ease. But no, there was nothing to be suspicious about, Carlos reassured himself. And Bagnew himself could hardly be improved upon. Galsworthy had earned his keep on that one.

Carlos considered the various angles yet again. He'd have to watch Oliver Chapin very closely, of course. But then Chapin had approached him on this proposition, not the other way round, *and* put up all the front money. So they were allies, and Carlos could see no way and no motive for Chapin to double-cross him. No, everything seemed clear. He'd be careful, but at present it was safe to proceed to the next step.

He stretched himself out to his full length in the bath and turned off the taps. Enough for today, he decided, enough hot water. He didn't want to get waterlogged, or be too hot when he went out into the New York chill later. Under no circumstances could he afford to catch a cold. And he wanted to stop thinking about that damn deal. Your brain could get waterlogged too with excessive thinking about one subject. You could give yourself an ulcer; many bad things . . . Anyway Bella would be back soon. His body looked forward to her. He watched with pleasure as his penis stiffened under the bath water.

He rose, slipped on a terrycloth robe, placed his still stiff penis against his stomach, and tied the robe's belt around himself to keep it in place. Then he entered the bedroom. He was delighted to see Bella just entering by the other door.

Simon Bagnew's first day at the office had been nerve-wracking. It had taken him ten minutes to decide which tie to wear with the new suit he had bought over the weekend. They'd altered it for him on the spot, but he couldn't make up his mind whether the pants were actually the right length. Finally, he chosen a simple maroon tie—only to discover, when he was already on the commuter train into the city, that it had a stain on it. He wasn't sure whether it was noticeable enough to warrant buying another one at Grand Central Station. Doing so would mean that he would be late since the stores didn't open till nine.

Deciding against a new tie, Simon arrived at the office at ten minutes before nine and found his way up to the main reception area. The receptionist hadn't arrived. When she did turn up, at five past nine, he gave his name and asked for Mr. Harrison.

The girl frowned, dialed the number and waited.

"There's no answer," she said. "He doesn't usually get in until half past." Her voice sounded annoyed, as if surely he should have known such an obvious fact.

Foster Harrison hurried in at twenty after nine, glanced at Bagnew sitting in the corner, but failed to recognize him. "Has a Mr. Bagnew come yet?" he called to the receptionist.

Embarrassed, Simon jumped to his feet. "Er, Mr. Harrison, er, Foster, I'm here. . . ."

"Ah Bagnew. Hiding in the corner! Never saw you." If the chairman shared Simon's embarrassment, he certainly didn't show it. "Come on into my office. And welcome aboard. Miss Toblansky," he added heartily, turning to the receptionist, "Mr. Bagnew here is our new president."

"Oh, very nice." The girl showed little interest.

"Nice to meet you."

"Yeah."

"Come on, then, I'll show you around." Harrison set off at such a fast pace that Simon practically had to trot to keep up with him.

The next hours were spent in Harrison's office. The chairman gave Simon a typewritten list of the key executives. Then each of them was summoned in turn. After each introduction, Harrison allowed a few moments of stilted conversation before requesting the executive to give a brief résumé of his department's function and his own background. "Go ahead and tell Simon what you did before you got here," he would insist. "If you get to know each other right at the start, there'll be fewer misunderstandings later."

"Well, I've been here for twenty years, and . . ." the man would start hesitantly.

"Then I'm sure your experience will be of enormous help to me." Simon would try to accelerate the conversation. "Tell me—"

"What did you do before that?" Harrison would interrupt, and the unfortunate executive would be forced to delve even further into his past.

Even worse, Harrison would then demand that Simon summarize his own background for the executive. "Turnabout's fair play," he repeated in a precisely similar hearty tone with each of the eight executives they saw during the morning. And eight separate times Simon was forced to summarize his career, more as if he were applying for a rather junior job than taking over as the new chief executive.

By noon, Simon was more than uncomfortable. His head ached, he was getting hotter by the second, and he had already sweated so much in the overheated room that he dared not shed his jacket for fear his smell would permeate the office. On top of that, the final meeting of the morning boded to be the most difficult of all.

"Well, I've kept the best for last," Harrison announced, his coat off, his joviality unabated. "Jim Lester will be up in a moment. You'll like him a lot, I'm sure. I do. He's been my right-hand man for years. Would have been president, in fact, if the board and I hadn't decided that we needed a bit of a new image to make our stock perform a little better on the street." He paused. "Not that Saturday's announcement that you joined us has done anything to this morning's prices." For the first time that morning, he looked positively stern. "I just checked. They're unchanged from Friday's close."

"I suppose it will depend on the degree of change I initiate," Simon said, trying not to sound defensive. "In my experience, the Street never reacts quickly to personnel moves. Investors first want to see how the new man performs."

Harrison looked at Bagnew speculatively. "You won't want to make too many changes too quickly, will you?" It seemed more like an order than a question.

"Far too early to make any decisions," Simon was quickly reassuring. "It will take me quite a while before I know the business well enough."

"Quite so." Harrison nodded his head. "Quite so. Too early to rock the boat." He was uncomfortably aware that Bagnew had not actually agreed with him. Perhaps the little man wasn't quite as much of a pushover as he seemed. Still, Foster Harrison reassured himself, he was certainly no tiger. He'd been reticent all morning, to put it mildly, and the impression he'd made on the key executives certainly hadn't been especially favorable. Perhaps, after a while, he could even be pushed out altogether. That would be ideal. At worse, he could be kicked upstairs to vice-chairman with Jim getting the presidency after all. Foster Harrison sighed with some satisfaction. He'd as much as hinted that plan to Jim when he'd been forced to tell him that the board had appointed Bagnew. No, he'd lost the first round, but the damage wasn't irreparable.

Suddenly, Harrison realized that Bagnew was staring at him speculatively, a frown contracting his forehead. What was the little bugger thinking? Was he maybe planning to try to throw his weight about, make changes all over the place? Well, let him just try! He'd soon be wondering who'd cut his legs off at the knees. "Well, well," said Harrison, sounding just as pompous but less jovial, "I believe I hear Jim coming now."

In fact, Simon was thinking about the need for change. But the chairman ascribed those thoughts to a wholly wrong motive. For Simon could fully sympathize with the chairman's desire to avoid rocking the boat. He had no desire to do that. Quite the contrary, he'd have enough enemies at Turner-LaMott—including the chairman himself, probably, and certainly this Jim Lester—without further antagonizing everyone by moving too fast. Let the dust settle; let them accept him. Some of them might even learn to like him, he thought, without much optimism. Above all, let the old man's retirement last a while—for now, he still wielded far too much power. Then there would be time enough for Simon to start making modifications—if he really felt any were needed. After all, it wasn't as if the company were in any particular trouble. No, Simon's stomach was contracting into a knot of worry for a different reason: What if Galsworthy and his friends wanted fast changes made? He felt suddenly battered by a wave of worry. Then he'd be caught right in the middle. Christ, what if they insisted, and Harrison refused. . . ?

Before he could finish the thought, Jim Lester entered. He was younger than Bagnew, a trim, good-looking man wearing a conservative suit and a dark blue tie with small sailing-ship emblems woven into it in a subdued pattern.

"Hello, I'm Jim Lester," he said, walking easily toward Simon, hand outstretched, a wide smile on his open, slightly boyish face. "Welcome to Turner-LaMott," he continued as Simon struggled to his feet. "You can count on me to do anything I can to help." He smoothed back his unruly, sandy hair, slightly thinning on top but still refusing to lie down neatly.

"Nicely said, nicely said." Harrison beamed, a proud parent admiring his eldest son.

"Thank you." In spite of his recognition that Jim Lester was a potential enemy, Simon felt an immediate liking for this personable younger man. "I look forward to working closely with you, and I shall be relying on you a great deal. In fact, I hope we can organize the 'office of the president' so that we apportion responsibilities between us and share in running the company." Simon was pleased to see Jim smile warmly. Perhaps, if he continued to play his cards right, this man could become an ally, even a friend. Simon only hoped that his instinctive trust of Lester was not misplaced.

Gina Belladonna—for that was her real name, although few people knew it and she never used it professionally—looked at Carlos Spinosa with a mixture of resignation and pleasure. She recognized his expression, was excited by what it portended, but also realized that it meant she would miss at least three appointments this afternoon. And then, dammit, she'd have to go through the whole boring routine of getting herself dressed, made up, coiffed all over again—for at thirty-five she was far too old to dare to go out unprepared. On balance, she decided with rising annoyance, she should never have come here this afternoon. Still, there was nothing she could do about it, now that his blood was up . . . might as well lie back and enjoy . . .

Carlos looked at the woman he called only Gina or Bella, with great pride of ownership. She was superb—and she was his, even though he would not acknowledge her publicly. If he did, half her usefulness would be gone. She was his for many reasons: because he'd scooped her up when she'd slid pretty near the bottom and placed her at the head of one of New York's fastest-growing fashion model agencies; because, with just another flick of his wrist, he could destroy the agency, and her too; but mostly because, whenever he wanted to, even against her wishes, he could arouse in her a sexual need so powerful that it permeated every fiber of her tense, bitchy body and mind.

Yes, Carlos acknowledged, he was delighted with his property. Thin to the point of gauntness, raven-haired, with a slash of red lipstick highlighting a pale oval face so full of character that one almost forgot its beauty, she seemed both cooly untouchable and explosively sexual. She never failed to excite him.

"Come here," he commanded, standing in the center of the room, feeling himself become even stiffer against his belly.

"Sure," she mocked, making no move to obey.

"Bitch."

She took a tentative step toward him. "I can't stay. I have work to do."

"Come *here*."

"No!"

He merely smiled at her, coldly superior. "I said, come here, bitch," he repeated, sarcastically patient. "You have no choice."

In spite of herself, she felt both desire and anger starting to mount. Astonishing how quickly he could make her *feel*, this arrogant man. He was the only one who could. With all the rest she knew how to remain distant, cool, untouched. It was they who became angry, lustful, jealous, even violent. Only Carlos, of all her men, could arouse in her that passion, equidistant between love and hate, that made her both shake with anger and pulse with desire.

He started toward her and she backed away. "No," she repeated, "leave me alone. I'm all dressed."

"I'm not."

"That's your problem."

"I intend to take care of it." He continued to advance toward her. "I want you now." His harsh voice never lost its menace for her.

"Why do I have to put up with this nonsense?" she cried. She could feel herself get wet for him. "It's midafternoon. I have people to meet."

Still he advanced on her. Now he was loosening his robe. As she saw the physical evidence of his desire, she became incensed, the more angry because she could feel the rush of response in her own loins. Refusing to accede to her desire, she tried to circle the room to get away from him. But he was too quick. Tricky as a boxer full of ring craft, he maneuvered her inexorably into the corner of the room near the bed, easily cutting off her attempts to escape.

"Carlos, for Christ's sake!" She was tense as a cat in her exasperation. "Leave me *alone*."

He had her fully backed into the corner now. She held her hands up, the sinews of her wrists rigid, her red fingernails extended. Her eyes were wild and her face gaunt with rage.

Suddenly he pounced at her. Grabbing both her arms, he pushed his belly violently against her.

"Carlos! Don't," she screamed, struggling to loosen his grip, trying to kick at him.

But his hands were far too powerful. Slowly he bent her arms back, forcing her gradually down the length of his body, buckling her knees under her.

As her hose became excessively stretched over her knees she could feel a giant ladder rip down one leg. "Shit!" she spat the word at him. He was going too far. She would not give in to the bastard. Let him rape her if he would. It wouldn't be the first time some bastard had violated her. But she wouldn't respond.... "Carlos, you fucking bastard, didn't you hear me?" she screamed. "I said no, and I meant it." God, how she wanted him!

"I heard. But I say yes." He swung her onto the bed, almost gently, but inexorably, so that she knew that struggling was utterly useless. With one stride he was next to her. Then, holding her down with a powerful hand on her chest, he unbuttoned her blouse and unhooked her skirt. She still struggled, but whether with anger or lust, to get away or get closer, she could no longer tell. All she did know, as he systematically undressed her, as unemotional as an automaton, was that his complete remoteness was driving her crazy. She was so aroused now that her hips were bucking involuntarily and her whole body was inflamed for him. She still hated him and burned with fury that by not caring he should so debase her. But she burned with desire too, wanting him more than she could possibly resist.

When he entered her, still cool, distant, controlled, her passion was so intense that her orgasm came almost instantly. It seemed to last an eternity, continuing to rise as he pumped rhythmically, harder and harder.

"Stop," she screamed at him. "For God's sake stop, Carlos. I can't stand it." She started to struggle again, truly desperate to get away. Only then, finally, did Carlos reach his own release. With one sharp cry he was done, still. Quickly he withdrew. "What a fuss, my dear," he said. "What a noise!" He chided her as if she were a child and very spoiled.

"Justified," she smiled, feeling thoroughly content. Sex with Carlos was superb—no other man had ever roused such passion in her, or induced such satisfaction. "I feel marvelous."

"Good," he said and smiled fleetingly. It was the first sign he had given that he was even mildly interested. Then, almost at once, he dismissed the subject. "Now, let me tell you about a little job I have for you."

"What job?" She was instantly suspicious.

"Don't worry. It's something you'll do very well."

"What is it?"

"All I want you to do is to drive someone a little mad."

9

Simon Bagnew took over his new job with a display of extraordinary pomposity. As if to boost his own frail self-esteem, he pontificated to his managers, talked too much in meetings, plagued his financial department for more and more reports and summaries of reports—and managed to create in his new staff the sense that he was more windbag than decisive chief executive.

Each week he took it upon himself to investigate a different department of the company. He tackled sales first, because he knew it to be an area of great importance, but one which made him generally uneasy. He was never comfortable in the presence of salesmen. They were too ebullient for his conservative nature, too enthusiastic to seem trustworthy.

"I'd like to spend two days working in the field," Simon instructed the sales manager, a large gentleman with a florid face, a booming voice and a fatherly manner, given to wearing bedroom slippers in the office because his feet hurt. "Please make sure it's typical work. In my experience, the chief executive is shown only the easy accounts. Don't give me one of those milk runs."

"Hell no. Of course not." The sales manager, who had been christened Samuel Peter Pestalotski, but who preferred to be called Sam Peters, intended to make quite certain that an easy trip was exactly what Bagnew got. No point at all in having the new boss see one of his weaker men, or be exposed to problems. "How about starting out either in the Connecticut area or in New Jersey?" he suggested, knowing that those were poor territories for him and anticipating that Bagnew would turn down whatever he mentioned first.

"No. I'd like to work New York itself the first day," Bagnew disagreed, on cue. "Maybe Chicago the second."

"Fine by me. Only Chicago's another big city: the same problems as New York." Plus lousy distribution, Sam was thinking.

"Okay. How about Cincinnati or Indianapolis? Somewhere in the Midwest?"

"As you prefer. Those are both pretty typical, Cinci's a little poorer for us than Indy." The reverse was true.

"Then I'll take Cincinnati. The tougher the better. It's been my experience—"

"Fine," the sales manager allowed himself to interrupt. "I'll set it up right away." This fellow was going to be a piece of cake. "When would you like to go?" He needed very little time to set up some friendly buyers.

"We'll start this afternoon in New York," Simon threw his first curve. "I assume you know how to find your man around lunch time? I'll meet him wherever his route list starts this afternoon."

"Well, that might not be so easy for you. . . ." Having Bagnew arrive without any warning was not what he wanted. "You see . . ."

"You mean you *don't* know where your man is?"

Sam Peters, a highly political manager generally adept at manipulating his superiors, revised somewhat his opinion of his new boss. Bagnew had trapped him neatly on this one. He wasn't going to be quite so easy after all. "Of course I can find him," he admitted reluctantly. If he pretended he couldn't, it would look as if people wandered through their day's work uncontrolled. This was quite untrue—for Sam, a stickler for route lists and discipline, prided himself on knowing where every man was at every moment. The trouble was, Sam happened to know that his New York salesman was working some of the rougher independent drugstores of Brooklyn this week. He hated for Bagnew to see that.

"Well?"

Sam Peters bowed to the inevitable. "I'll tell him to meet us in Sheepshead Bay at two-thirty."

"Where's that? I'm afraid I've never worked that territory. I thought I'd seen them all, but . . ."

"Out by Coney Island. No reason for you to know. Lousy part of the city, most of it, although the bay itself is pretty. You sure that's where you want to go?"

"I'm sure."

"We'll leave here at one-thirty then."

"I'll go alone thanks, Sam. Just tell your man to look for my limo. After that, I'll go in his car."

"But—"

"No need for you to disturb yourself," Simon said firmly, brooking no further argument.

When Simon reached Sheepshead Bay, the salesman was dutifully waiting for him. "Afternoon, sir," he said briskly. "I understand you're planning to go in my car. Shall we meet your limousine back here later?"

"Where do you live yourself?"

"Out near Kennedy airport. Practically on the runway."

"Fine. Then you can drop me at the airport and I'll take a taxi into town. I'll be staying in tonight anyway." He turned to the driver, who had been waiting patiently for his instructions. "You can take the rest of the day off," he instructed. "At least for one night I won't have to keep you working late."

What was the idiot talking about, his driver wondered? He hadn't worked late one night this week. "Thank you very much, sir."

"Now," said Simon, turning to the salesman. "What's your first call? May I see your route list?"

The salesman's heart sank. This was precisely what he had wanted to avoid. His normal first call this afternoon would be on old Pa Colibri, a vitriolic old bastard who owned a drugstore on a busy corner just where a white and a black area merged. Never had a kind word for anyone, old Colibri, and a foul mouth into the bargain.

"Tough account?" Simon guessed.

"Yeah."

"Good. That way I'll see for myself what you fellows are up against. In my experience . . ."

Decent fellow, this new boss, the salesman decided. But pompous. Still, what could you expect?

"'Bout fuckin' time you bothered to come see me," were Pa's first words as they walked into the store. "Ain't I good enough for your goddamn mighty company any more?"

"Come on Mr. Colibri, I was here just five weeks ago. It's right here in my book. You bought a whole bunch of drugs from us."

"Yeah? And damn slow they were getting delivered." Colibri was in no way chastened. "I don't need nothing today, that's for damn sure."

"Very well," said the salesman, noncommittally, "so let me just show you the specials for your interest."

Grudgingly, the old man walked over to where the salesman was opening his book of brochures. "What you got?" he demanded, surly and suspicious. "I don't need nothing."

"First, we have a discount on our cough line. You'll need that for the fall."

"I told you, young fellow, I don't need a fucking thing. So don't you go telling me what I need and what I don't."

"I only thought—"

"Well, don't. I ain't interested in your lousy company."

"Now look here," Simon Bagnew started to intervene.

"And who may you be?" the druggist turned on him. "The fucking president or what?"

"As a matter of fact that is exactly who I am." Simon pulled himself up to his full height. "And I don't think—"

"That's good," the druggist interrupted, cackling. "He don't and you do. See young fellow, if you don't think, you can be president too some day." He cackled some more.

Simon, feeling thoroughly foolish, wasn't sure what to do next. He was just wondering whether to cut his losses and tell the salesman that they were leaving, when the salesman himself resolved the problem.

"So you don't want any cough and cold remedies then?" he asked.

"Of course I do." The old man examined the selling sheet. "Give me one unit."

"The display unit?" The salesman was not sure what the druggist meant. That was a far larger quantity than the store should have.

"Of course. What else?"

"Okay." The salesman wasn't about to argue. If the old goat wanted to show off in front of the president by over-buying, that was just fine. "And what else? How about this deal on Sleep-Aide. . . ."

By the time the call was finished, Colibri had bought five times as much as ever before.

"That was great," the salesman said enthusiastically as they returned to his car.

"In my experience—" Bagnew commenced.

"It always helps when they feel they have the upper hand," the salesman was too excited to stop himself talking. "You sure were a big help in there, sir."

The meeting with the financial department was very

much easier for Simon Bagnew. He felt far more at home with the impersonal objectivity of figures, and the unemotionalism of the people who spent their lives with them.

"Would you request Mr. Hendrick to join me in my office," Simon asked his secretary, referring to the company's chief financial officer.

"Yes, sir." The lady looked at him dourly, as if his request were vaguely distasteful. "Now?" She seemed hardly able to believe it.

"Now."

"Very well." She had been assigned to him, a problem employee, highly qualified, but thoroughly unappealing. In twenty years with the company she had not made a single friend among its employees. Simon wondered how long he would have to put up with her before he would demand a somewhat pleasanter, perhaps even a somewhat prettier person.

"And ask him to bring the latest financial statements with him."

"The latest financial statements?"

"Yes, Miss Caruthers, that is what I said."

He was pleased to see Hendrick, a small, bespectacled man whose face never lost its look of utter seriousness. "Please come in and sit down. Make yourself comfortable."

"Thank you, Mr. Bagnew."

"Please call me Simon. It makes me feel about a hundred to be called 'mister.'"

"Very well, Simon. And my name is Arthur."

Fleetingly, Simon wondered whether this sincere little man had ever been called "Art." Never, he decided. Quite impossible, even when he was a little boy.

"I understand you wished to go over the financial statements. I have brought the audited versions with me, the last three years and the quarterlies. Of course, we have monthly statements as well, issued on the tenth of each month. You could study those too, but of course they are unaudited."

"Quite."

"I have also taken the liberty of bringing the annual forecasts. . . ."

For a congenial two hours, closeted undisturbed in the large quiet office, the two men pored over the figures of the Turner-LaMott Company. Everything seemed perfect. Profits were unspectacular, perhaps, but they had grown steadily over the years. Sales, too, had risen a consistent, sensible eight to ten percent in each of the past five years. Investments seemed sound. The ratio of current assets to liabilities was a conservative three to one.

"You seem to have everything in excellent shape," Bagnew concluded as the meeting drew to a close. "Are there any problems you have not mentioned?"

The accountant considered the question with the same care he had shown throughout the meeting. "I think not," he concluded finally.

"Excellent, excellent," Bagnew agreed heartily. "I too see no problem. Everything seems in apple-pie order."

"Thank you, Simon," Arthur Hendrick said meekly as he arose to leave. "And may I say," he added, suddenly looking embarrassed and stumbling over his words, "that it will be a pleasure to report to someone who understands about conservative financing, and who knows what the figures mean." He blushed and hurried away.

"But I don't understand, do I?" Simon muttered after the door had closed. "Not one bit." If everything was in such excellent shape, why had they wanted him? Who were Galsworthy's real clients anyway? He wiped his hand over his brow, his head suddenly aching. "Christ," he exclaimed, wanting to reassure himself by being hard and angry. "It's over two months already. When the hell's the other shoe going to drop?" But his voice was muted by the deep pile carpet and all the soft, plush furniture. Even to his own ears, he sounded merely peevish and ineffectual.

"God, am I relieved Dad finally has a job." Susan Bagnew was home for the spring vacation. "It must have been awful!"

"It was bad," her Mother agreed, busying herself with putting the kettle on.

"How can America just put people on the *shelf* like that? It's um . . ." She searched for a word strong enough to express her outrage. ". . . It's *disgusting*."

"I didn't realize you knew. I mean, about how hard it was for Dad."

"Of course. I could tell from his letters, even though you were both being so *cheerful*. But I could hardly say anything to you, could I?"

Janet Bagnew looked at her tall, slender, blond daughter with astonishment. "In more ways than one you've become quite a swan, my love," she said obtusely, as much to herself as to Susan.

But her daughter understood at once. "And you and Dad the ducks? Nonsense. You're great parents. I've compared notes about you a lot with other kids, especially these last few months. You're okay."

"We are? Well, that's a relief." Janet Bagnew chose irony to hide her pleasure at the compliment. Her upbringing had taught her that self-deprecation was essential.

"No, I mean it," Susan insisted. "Dad is such a *good* man."

That was a compliment Janet Bagnew could accept easily. "Yes, he is," she agreed. "I've always thought that." She looked at her daughter with wide eyes. "How very adult you have become," she said with wonder.

"I'm twenty and a senior in college, you know Mum."
"I didn't mean like that. I realized a while back that you'd grown up, but . . ."
"When you let me share a room with Pete?" Susan teased.
"Long before." Janet Bagnew dismissed the subject quickly; even now sex was not an area she could discuss. The less said the better. "But that's not what I mean." She hesitated, trying to puzzle it out for herself. When had the girl become so aware? Only yesterday she still viewed herself as the center of the universe. Now, suddenly, she was sympathetic, caring. "It's . . . you've become womanly, darling." It was still not quite what Janet meant. At last she found the phrase, a cliché, but apt. "Womanly wise."
"No longer a girl? Mother, what a nice thing to say."
Mother and daughter smiled at each other. How wonderful, each felt, to have such a friend. Suddenly, with the same spontaneous gesture, they threw their arms around each other. The slim California blonde and the dumpy, proud New England mother formed a Norman Rockwell contrast. But, for that moment at least, their love and understanding—their admiration of each other—was complete. Then the kettle started to whistle.
There was an awkward pause. Neither woman was used to showing emotion.
"I was going to tell you—"
"What are you going—"
They burst out together. Then they laughed and were again at ease.
"I was going to tell you what I'm thinking of doing when I graduate," Susan started again.
"I thought you'd hoped to go on to business school."
"Later. Sure. I'd like to go to Harvard B School if I can get in. But all I've studied so far is science and a little

economics. I've no business experience at all. Anyhow, they rarely take anyone nowadays without at least one or two years of practical achievement."

"But will you want to go back, then, once you're away from the academic track?"

"Don't know. Lots of kids do. But I don't have much choice. There's no point in going to a second-rate business school. Anyhow, after four years of lectures and labs I'm going nuts to be *doing* something! Mom, you've no idea how boring your last year in college can be. I feel as if I've done it all." She grinned at her mother, teasing her again. "Even Pete's boring!"

"So you want to go to work. It's ironic. . . ."

"Because now I don't have to?"

"That's right. Six months ago, we couldn't see any way to send you to graduate school. We weren't even sure how to finance this year."

"Oh, I knew that." Susan Bagnew was scornful. "It wouldn't have been so tough. I was all set to declare myself an independent and get a loan for part of it. And the rest I would have earned part-time."

"Now stop it."

Susan looked at her mother in surprise.

"We weren't entirely destitute, you know." Janet Bagnew stood stiffly erect, D.A.R stamped all over her suddenly craggy features.

"Of course not, Mom." Susan quickly corrected herself. "I only meant I would have been proud to help the family. I was planning on it. It's part of *being* a family, isn't it, participating I mean?"

Janet Bagnew unbent slightly. "Possibly," she said, not willing to accede much. "In any case, that's over. So what are you going to do now, dear?"

"Well, that's what I wanted to discuss with you." Susan paused, hesitant about how to proceed. She had carefully rehearsed her speech, but it was easier alone in her room than now. "Well, I was thinking . . ." she started again. "Do you think Dad would mind if I applied for a job at Turner-LaMott? I mean, would it embarrass him or anything?" Why should she be so nervous, she wondered? There was nothing wrong with what she wanted to say. "You see," she started to explain, "I've been away at college for almost four years now and . . ." All at once, instead of the careful explanation she had rehearsed, the words came tumbling out, full of pain and loss. ". . . and all that time Dad's been going through hell, hasn't he? I've seen him fight it. He's brave and everything. But it was getting to him. Last time it happened, I was home. But this time, even though I've visited fairly often, basically I wasn't here. So I couldn't even help. And he's aged a lot, you know. His head kept getting lower there for a while. As if he had this great weight he had to carry. Well, he did too, I guess. But now he's holding it high again. And his skin isn't gray like it was. He's up again and he deserves it more than most. That's what I think, anyway. He's really a good man, and I admire his guts tremendously. And, well, I'd just really like to be, I mean for a while, sort of *near* him." She paused for breath finally. "You know what I mean?" She searched for her mother's reassurance.

"Yes, my daughter, I do know what you mean," Janet Bagnew said, her voice hoarse. "And your father will be very happy and very proud when you tell him." Her eyes glistened and her throat almost choked with her effort at control. "Now you must excuse me," she said most politely, and hurried out. How foolish I am, she kept thinking, what a foolish old woman. But she could not help herself.

Alone, and terribly grateful for the privacy, Janet Bagnew, descendant of one of America's oldest and most prestigious families, wife of a past and future captain of industry, mother, she had just decided, of the most wonderful daughter in the world, broke down for the first time in her adult life, and sobbed her heart out. Great gasps of departing pain wracked her body—and for the first time in years she allowed herself to feel secure and, at length, even happy.

10

The beer hall in which Caro Pollo had chosen to call the meeting had the merit of being very private. It also had entrances at the back and at both sides that made unobserved arrivals and departures easier. From the upstairs windows, an excellent view in all directions ruled out surprise visits from competitors or the police. In all other respects, however, the place was run-down, dirty, depressing. Part of the floor was covered with greasy carpeting, too filthy for individual stains to be still distinguishable; the rest with worn linoleum. The chipped plastic tables sported tin ashtrays, mostly full and filthy. All the chairs were rickety.

Caro's listeners sat around a table in the back of the room listening to his harangue with sullen expressions. The few patrons who had been there when Pollo and his cronies arrived had left. And the bartender was busying himself being deaf.

Caro himself was the only one of the group not seated. He was strutting around the table, an angry, dangerous bantam rooster, crowing at his flock, partly to convince them, partly, it seemed, to keep up his own courage. "Listen you fuckers," he said, "I'm making a point to you." He smacked his fist onto the table to emphasize the importance of what he was saying. The glasses of beer in front of the men danced and spilled.

"Listen, you fuckers," he repeated, enjoying the power of being able to insult these men without retribution, "how long are you goin' to wait, for Chrissakes? What's he done, tell me that?" There was no response. "Well, I'll tell you. Fuck all, that's what. He ain't done one goddamn thing since he personally promised me he'd fix it. An' it's been close to six fucking months. Or maybe you think he has? So where's the stuff? Every one of my broads is hollering and I don't got no supplies. No more than I had before. How about you?" he demanded belligerently.

"A little better, but not much," one of the men agreed. The others nodded their assent.

"Well, I'm sayin' again we gotta do somethin'," Caro continued loudly. "Otherwise, we're all up shit's creek with no paddle and no hope of gettin' none."

"Fine, Caro," said another man, a little older than the rest. "But what you planning to do? It wouldn't be easy. I agree the Deacon ain't done much. But don't ever get no idea he's a pushover."

"Listen Ricardo, I'm not saying we should do anything against old Ollie himself." Pollo's voice turned to a nasal whine, the sound of a bellboy trying to ingratiate himself for the tip. "All I'm saying is we can't sit around on our arses forever."

"So what do you suggest? I hear tell you were back to thinking of getting the stuff from the competition. That's what you said last year."

"I thought of that," Caro Pollo admitted. "But it don' make no sense when you get down to it. What have they got to offer up here that we don't? Sure, they're strong in Miami and places. But they wouldn't let us in there. So who needs them?"

"Okay. So what's the alternative?" another man chimed in.

"First off, I suggest we start doin' a little importing ourselves. We know the exporters—and the customs people here—as well as anyone. Hell, Ricardo, you probably collect more imported stuff for Oliver every month than he allocates back to you every six. So why not pick up some on the side direct for us? We can pay more than the Deacon's payin' now and still get it cheaper for ourselves."

"He wouldn't like it. He got real rough when those guys down in New Jersey tried it. How are you goin' to avoid that?"

"Hell, that was years ago," Caro sneered at the idea. "He was a lot younger." He was glad Ricardo had asked that question. It was what he'd been waiting for. Now he'd show them that he had brains too, as good a brain as Oliver Chapin any day. Better maybe. And he was part of the family, a real man, not some damn Park Avenue phoney who spent more time on three-martini lunches with fucking bankers than on real business.

"Hell, Chapin ain't so tough any more," he reassured them. "For one thing, where's his backup? No loyalties, see. All he ever was was a trader. And he ain't doin' so good in that department these days." Pollo stopped to survey his audience. Yes, he decided, they were getting themselves convinced. Good. He'd show 'em. He, Luigi Pollo, head of the whole Pollo family, would show them what a real man could do, a specialist. For one thing, think of all those men he'd killed, and never been caught. The cops hadn't even got close. "An' who you think fixed that thing in New Jersey for our Mister Oliver fuckin' Chapin?" he sneered triumphantly. "Heh?"

"Who?"

"Me. That's who. Me! That was that Brazilian mob that snuck in. The Cruz brothers, some dumb name like that. And they got a little too big for themselves. Decided to go into competition. So the old man wanted them stopped but he couldn't handle it himself. So he asked me. An' I did. No problem." He looked straight at Ricardo. "But now things is different," he said softly, "because I'm the one that wants to get in the extra supplies. An' on top of that," he added, hitting the table another solid smack, "we Pollo's ain't no bunch of damn Brazilians."

"All I said was that he'd be mad. That's all. I didn't say he could necessarily do much about it. Still—"

"Still, it couldn't hurt to be careful," a tall black man interrupted.

"Right." Caro Pollo thumped at the table once more, agreeing vigorously. "Who said we wouldn't be careful?" He regarded them craftily. "Let me tell you, we're gonna be real careful. An' you know what else? We ain't gonna do the old Deacon one bit of harm. We're not out to hurt him, just to protect our rightful interests." He paused at the head of the table, making sure he had his listeners' full attention. "But if the old man don' like it," he said, posturing theatrically, "then let me tell you somethin' else: He'll be the one that had better be taking it nice an' easy."

Caro Pollo rubbed the inside of his thigh where the tiny gun he always carried was strapped. He often carried other weapons too, but he was never without his tiny "comforter," as he called it. The gesture was quite unconscious—in the same way one of his pimps might adjust his crotch, or his accountant his glasses—but its meaning was very clear to his listeners nevertheless. "Yeah," Caro repeated softly, "I'm tellin' you, Ollie Chapin's the one that needs to watch out and take care."

Gradually, systematically, department by department Simon Bagnew investigated and learned about the Turner-LaMott Company. He visited the American factories—all five, flying in the company plane, first to Grand Rapids and then, in a tiring week, in a giant circle to Cedar Falls, Sacramento, San Antonio, Atlanta and back to New York. He met with both the company's advertising agencies and listened to their hyperbole with barely concealed distaste.

"In my experience," he pontificated, "one tends to spend too much money on advertising gimmicks. Take your Calmex commercials, for instance. The basic ones are pretty good. They tell you honestly what the product is and what it does. 'Helps calm you down and let you sleep.' Very clear. But those other commercials, with the kids running around keeping the Mother awake . . . they seem way off the subject to me."

"Yes, sir, I tend to agree." The agency's account supervisor, an unusually charming gentleman of military bearing, looked at Bagnew with new respect. He was a pompous windbag, no doubt, but Jim Lester had said much the same thing about the commercials. And Jim knew his stuff. Moreover, hadn't he himself told the creative department that campaign was too complicated? The agency man felt sure he had, he'd certainly intended to. "Absolutely. Your exec, Jim Lester, made much the same comment. So we're downplaying them."

"What does that mean?"

"Running them less frequently."

"Why run them at all?"

Why indeed, the agency man wondered? But if he agreed to pull the campaign entirely, the creatives would get incensed. Particularly that tough new woman, the one who kept using words like "nifty" and who kept her hair styled to look like a younger version of Mary Wells. She'd have a hemorrhage.

The account supervisor hesitated. "Well . . ."

"Think about it." Simon relented and took him off the hook graciously. No point in embarrassing the man. He needed all the allies he could get, not angry advertising agents snapping at his heel. "All in all, the advertising is excellent," Simon reassured everyone. "You've done a fine job."

When Simon had seen all the plants in the U.S. and visited most of the departments in the head office, he visited the company's international headquarters in Brussels. Taking an overnight flight to avoid losing a whole day of business—and to make the point to all his subordinates—he arrived in Brussels airport with swollen ankles, bleary eyes and heartburn. The head of the European division was waiting at the gate to greet him, and they made uncomfortable small talk while the bags were being packed into the limousine.

Even after a shower and a shave at the Amico Hotel—a wonderfully kept palace, full of priceless Oriental carpets and self-important American visitors—Simon felt terrible. "Well, shall we get started?" He forced himself to sound cheery as he joined his patiently waiting European vice-president in the lobby. "Sorry to keep you waiting."

"Not at all. I hope you feel better. Very tiring those night flights. Are you sure you wouldn't prefer a few hours off?" The vice-president would have been happy to delay.

"Thank you, but I feel fine. We can get started."

"Cup of coffee, then?"

"Love one," said Simon, meaning it. "As soon as we get to the office."

During all these visits, whether in America or overseas, Simon knew he had to fight the subtle distancing, the delay, the carefully misleading statement, the informal conspiracy to keep him isolated in his ivory tower so that the managers and underlings could continue to do their own thing without interference. Wearing, oh so wearing. Fortunately, he was used to this game of isolation. He had not sat in the president's office twice before for nothing. They had been smaller companies, but he'd experienced the same employee instincts to serve warm pap instead of facts, reassurances and bland promises instead of tough warnings.

What few of these people realized, of course, was that he had not only sat in two offices of the president before—but had been fired from each of them. Not one person at Turner-LaMott could know the terror he had experienced. In comparison, the frustration of their petty procrastinations was nothing. He, who had waited through four years of unmanliness, could certainly find the patience to probe slowly, methodically into his new job. Sooner or later, he would find out all about it—including the secret things, even the shameful things, that had been covered up and that he might, or might not, wish to expose. For clearly, there must be something, some dark secret which needed either a permanent impenetrable cover, or perhaps full exposure. Maybe there would even have to be a scapegoat. That too might become his lot. Oh yes, there must be some hidden, festering sore. Otherwise why did they need him? Jim Lester, whom he was getting to know better, and to like more all the time, would otherwise have been entirely competent as Harrison's replacement. So the question that haunted Simon day and night, which he could never forget for more than a few hours at a time, was when and how he would discover where the cancer lay—or be told about it in the long-delayed but still inevitable message from Galsworthy.

"We plan to start by giving you a brief overview," the European vice-president was saying. "Then . . ."

Simon realized with a start that he had been daydreaming. He must pay attention. Even though he had had no sleep, he must stay alert. Otherwise he might miss a clue, overlook a sign. And it was important, vital, that he find the problem before Galsworthy told him. If he knew in advance, he just might be able to protect himself. At least it was something to hope for. Today might be the day.

* * *

Carlos Spinosa's main office was furnished like an elegant drawing room at the palace of Versailles. The ornate gilded desk and tables, light blue silk chairs, heavy damask drapes and enormous paintings constituted one of the finest collections of Louis XIV furniture in private hands—and perhaps the only one that was used as working furniture. Spinosa himself, slender, silent and gray, seemed the perfect occupant of this room. Even in modern dress, he exuded the mystery and subtlety of a Talleyrand. And the comparison was apt, for, just as Talleyrand had plotted successfully to hold power for post-Napoleonic France, so in this room Spinosa plotted to increase the power of his empire.

For hours on end, barely moving, Spinosa would ponder his plans. If they were important, he would think about them for days with the intense concentration of a chess champion, double-checking any weak point—and then, if at all possible, he would delay the start of them for a week or two while he concentrated on something different. Returning to his strategy, his mind fresh, he could reevaluate it thoroughly. Only then, if the plans still seemed sound, would he start them in motion. It was not Carlos's natural inclination to act this slowly. Quite the contrary, by nature he was impulsive. But it was the safe method which he had arduously taught himself, just as he had taught himself to curb the glibness of his tongue. These were two lessons he had learned the hard way, many years previously. . . .

Oh, he had been such a clever, chattering, impulsive boy. And by the time he was twenty years old his precocious charm, tremendous "street smarts," wiry good looks, unending energy—all had combined to make him one of the most successful young villains in São Paolo. He had so enjoyed his women, his horses, the high life of the city. He had loved the excitement of cocaine smuggling, the power of running a hundred or more gorgeous girls, forcing them to do precisely what he ordered. He had reveled in his extravagant life, in the ease with which he moved within Brazil's upper crust.

There were many young men like him, suave, polished, with money to burn and gorgeous females attending their every whim. They might live anywhere in the sprawling, accelerating city. Sometimes their exotically luxurious houses grew up right in the center of a slum, like gorgeous toadstools pushing up through the cobblestones of a muddy farm yard. Wealth in Brazil was such a recent phenomenon for all but a few Portuguese settler families, that both its genesis and its flowering were haphazard. The city itself was growing so fast that it had almost no pattern: it was estimated that a hundred houses, a hundred kilometers of new roads and at least two major apartment buildings were completed in the city every single day.

So no one asked how Carlos was rich. It sufficed that his car was a Mercedes 300 SL, his women stunning, his suits from Paris and his tips lavish. He understood wine and operatic music, didn't he? What better proof of a fine family heritage? No one cared that his taxes were unpaid, or that last week three of his girls had been severely beaten because he had leased them to men more brutal than even he had anticipated. No one cared either that one of the girls would never walk easily again, even if she lived. And certainly no one asked or cared why he paid all his bills in cash, peeling off the notes as if they were the thick outer leaves of a cash onion, so bulky that he had to have a pocket for it specially tailored into each of his suits. Just as long as he *did* pay, that was all that mattered.

Carlos's life was exciting; he was rich, popular, invincible. His name was not Carlos Spinosa then, of course.

That came with his second life. He was Carlos Battistros—an upper-crust, man about town. Forgotten—or at least buried—were the days of his childhood when his family had lived in a slum, forever enveloped in the sickly sweet, revolting stink of the sewer. Forbidden also were the childish memories of his father, drunk and vicious, beating his poor mother until she screamed and shook her head so hard in terror and anguish that the gray, lank wisps of her hair tangled themselves into an ugly mat. Avoided, too, was the memory of hunger that had been part of his everyday existence from the time he was four until about his twelfth birthday.

Although his mother later confirmed that his father had started drinking seriously when Carlos was four, the boy had actually known it for himself. Even now, fifty years later and with a different name, a different language, a different life, he could still remember—feel—his uncomprehending horror at seeing his father drunk for the first time.

"What's wrong with Papa?" he had cried to his mother.

"Hush, darling. He's not well. Very tired."

"Rubbish, woman, I'm not tired. Stupid bitch. Think I'm drunk, don't you. Well, I'm fine, you hear. Great. Magnifico!" He had slapped her hard across the face. "Don't you mouth your rubbish at me, woman, make me look like a fool in front of my son!"

His father had continued drinking, more and more heavily. Gradually he had dropped himself and his wife and young children from the decent poverty of the still proud working man into the abject destitution and filth of the lowest slums.

His father had finally drunk himself to death when Carlos was twelve, leaving his mother too battered to be fully human. By then she had started drinking too, and Carlos and his older sister were left alone by her, ignored to hunt for their own food and clothing. It was only a few weeks before his sister decided to become a novice in a nunnery. It was the one thing, she told him, that could ever give her the feeling of safety. For that she would make any sacrifice.

Forced by his father's death, his mother's drinking and his sister's defection to fend for himself—and hating the sight and smell of the old crone who had been his mother—he left home for good only days after his sister did. It was exactly one month after they had taken the corpse of his father away.

From the first day, when he found a wallet sticking invitingly out of the back pocket of a tipsy businessman, his luck changed. Unhesitatingly, he appropriated the wallet—and found a fortune inside: over two hundred American dollars, enough to live on for months.

After that, he never left the area where the businessmen and the Americans congregated. At first he begged and stole for a living. Then he got smarter and started to sell things, tourist gifts and dirty postcards. Finally, seeing the postcards sold far better than anything else in his collection—and having understood the facts of life early and thoroughly—he graduated to selling not only the photographs, but the women depicted in them.

It took young Carlos only a dozen years to become rich, adding drugs of all sorts to his inventory of women, and blackmail to his sales of dope. And it took only two months, and two mistakes back-to-back for him to find himself in a foul stinking Brazilian jail, stripped of money, clothes, power, dignity and almost life itself.

Impulsively, thoughtlessly, he had recruited a particularly beautiful girl he had met one day in a park. She was very stupid, almost moronic, but so beautiful, so friendly and fresh, that he had thought her worth adding to his string. Casually he seduced her, accepting her gift of virgin love as no more than his due, and made sure she became pregnant. When, utterly horrified, she told him, assuming he would do the honorable thing and marry her, he arranged for an abortion instead. Then he made her sign a full confession. With that confession, and dire threats of what he would do if she disobeyed him or told anyone about him, he forced her to obey his commands and become one of his girls. She started working at La Fontaine only four months after he first met her. Even though she was stupid and miserable, her looks were so remarkable that she soon became one of his better producers.

Everything went well for Carlos until, some months later, the girl's father, who had lost all trace of his daughter, happened to accompany a business associate from New York to La Fontaine to gawk. There, to his amazed horror, he found his daughter. Unbeknown to Carlos, the girl came from a powerful family, one which now became determined to seek their revenge on whoever had caused their daughter's downfall.

The family rescued the girl and incarcerated her in a nursing home. There, unrelentingly, they cross-examined her. But for weeks she refused to tell her story. Even though she now hated Carlos—and he dared not contact her—the memory of his threats so terrified her that she would not reveal anything. Moreover, Carlos had given her only his first name, common enough in Brazil, and she was not nearly bright enough to piece the bits of her knowledge about him together into a picture clear enough to pinpoint him. For a while, Carlos assumed he had survived with nothing worse than a bad fright.

The smart thing to have done, as Carlos later berated himself a hundred times, would have been to leave São Paulo, and preferably Brazil, at once. He had other choices, after all, with money in the bank, an excellent command of English, and health and youth on his side. He could easily have started afresh. But, arrogant in his self-confidence, he decided to stay. And, indeed, he would have got away with his first mistake had he not committed a second foolish act. It was the combination of the two that caused his downfall and subjected him to the most awful punishment.

Driving home to his luxurious apartment down a little-used shortcut late one night, he had seen an expensive car, evidently stalled, at the dark end of a narrow street. The driver, a well-dressed, middle-aged gentleman, was peering agitatedly at the car's wheels.

Carlos stopped, sensing an opportunity. "What's the matter. Can I help?"

"Something with my steering. Damn car suddenly developed a wheel judder. Thought it was a flat, but the tires look fine." He bent over to examine them again and Carlos could see the wallet—just like the first one he had ever taken—sticking out of his pocket. Impulsively, for old times' sake really, Carlos had grabbed it. But either the man had been suspicious, or Carlos's skill as a pickpocket had declined, for before Carlos could hide the wallet, the man had swiveled and was pulling a gun from his waistband.

Carlos hit him then, realizing it was his only chance after having been caught red-handed by an armed man. Although the blow was solid and true, the man did not go down. Instead he lunged back, his fists pounding like sledge hammers. The man almost won. But at the last moment, Carlos lashed out with his foot at his opponent's groin and, by luck, connected. The man collapsed and Carlos was able to disarm him, knock him unconscious and get away. He forgot to take the wallet with him.

The next day, to Carlos's horror, there were headline stories about the incident in every newspaper. The man Carlos had beaten was an army general of great prestige, part of the main power structure of Brazil. Worse, Carlos had apparently dropped a tiny amulet he had been wearing around his neck. It was silver, in the shape of a highly ornate heart with a big initial *C* intertwined among the filligree work. The newspapers had a field day picturing close-ups of the only clue.

The heart had been a gift from the girl he had seduced, the first of her gifts to him, given in celebration of the flower of her love. When he had refused to marry her, she had demanded it back. But he, rather liking it, had laughed at her and kept it.

Somehow, in the girl's simple mind, that little heart amulet had become the focus of all the bad things Carlos had done to her. When she saw it in the newspaper, her anger overwhelmed her and, regardless of the consequences, she told her father all about the bad man who had ruined her. Her father, far more intelligent than his daughter, had no difficulty in piecing the clues together.

Carlos was trying to charter a plane for his getaway when they caught him. He remained in prison for two years without trial. Political prisoners did not require due process of law, and attacking an army general—however unknowing of his status—was a political crime. The general and the girl's family cooperated to make sure of that. The authorities also confiscated all Carlos's assets, broke up his legal and illegal businesses, and washed his name and history out of the record books. Carlos was alive, but legally nonexistent, doomed to remain in prison at the will of his enemies—and their will was to leave him there for the rest of his days.

Ironically, it was the fact that he didn't exist legally that saved Carlos. During two years of gruesome deprivation, he managed to remain well-behaved and cheerful enough to endear himself to the guards who were more accustomed to insults and violence from their maximum security prisoners. As a result, he was eventually allowed to work in the prison's laundry. From there, after the most careful thinking and rethinking of a plan, he intended to escape.

Before his plan was completed, however, Carlos became severely ill. First he caught a cold, possibly from moving constantly between the steamy heat of the laundry room and the damp cold of São Paulo's winter. It quickly worsened to laryngitis and then to pneumonia. Fortunately, the prison hospital had been quarantined as a result of an outbreak of typhoid. So Carlos had to be transferred to a civilian hospital. By this time he was so weak that they expected him to die anyway. It would be more convenient, the warden felt, if that could happen outside his jurisdiction. Fewer forms to fill out . . .

By the time Carlos reached the hospital, he was delirious, so close to death that the authorities did not even bother to place a guard at his door. He remained in the balance between living and dying for three days. Then he started to recover. But he pretended not to, warming the thermometer on the radiator when the nurse was out of the room, and pretending to be still delirious when she was there.

On the fifth day, he overheard one of the doctors talking to the nurse. "Surprising that his condition doesn't change," the doctor sounded puzzled. "He should either be dead or improving."

That afternoon, Carlos stole a coat from the closet in the room next to his, took some shoes from the orderlies' dressing room—and walked out of the hospital. He found fifty cruzeros in the pocket of the coat he had stolen and used it to take a taxi due north.

"Take me toward Campinas until your meter shows forty cruzeros," he instructed the taxi driver. "Then let me off. I shall give you the fifty I have with me—and you will forget you ever saw me. Agreed?"

"Fine by me. I don't care who you are," the driver agreed readily. "But that much won't get you far."

"As far as I need."

The taxi driver shrugged his shoulders, drove to the edge of town, showed Carlos that his money was up—and deposited him at the side of the road.

Desperately weak, his throat terribly sore again from the rapidly worsening laryngitis, Carlos half staggered, half crawled part way up the hill beside the road. There he found a tumbledown abandoned hut and crawled inside before he lapsed into unconsciousness.

Carlos Spinosa survived partly by luck, partly by an unusually strong constitution—but mostly because of the depth of his anger at his own stupidity. He would *not* allow himself to die for such foolishness. He would survive, to prove to himself that he was more than a moronic petty crook fit only to be caught and dropped in jail.

For days he stayed in his tiny hut, alternately shivering and burning with fever. When he recovered slightly, he would lick rain water from an indentation in the wall, a sort of tar paper receptacle. The rest of the time he lay on the ground, terrified by nightmares, clutching his throat to try to ease the awful pain, but never giving up his implacable determination to live so that he could vindicate himself.

After four days he started to feel better. On the fifth he was weak, dirty, exhausted—but, for the first time since he became ill, hungry. He knew he had to eat soon if he were to survive. Knowing that, he lay for an hour summoning all his reserves of energy, pulling them together for one great effort. Then he crawled out of the hut into the watery sunlight.

The nearest sign of habitation, he saw, was several hundred yards up the hill, a cluster of huts of tar paper and corrugated tin, almost as poor as the one he had just left. Clinging to the steep slope, they were typical of the shanty towns that surrounded São Paulo—and, for that matter, every other major city in Latin America. He wondered if he had any chance of reaching them, and if the inhabitants would share their scant food with him if he did. But he knew he had no choice but to try.

The effort of will which allowed Carlos to reach the nearest hut and survive his incredible pain and fatigue always astonished him when he remembered it. But reach it he did, many hours after he had started his ascent.

"Holy Maria!" said the woman inside as Carlos crawled through the door and collapsed. She crossed herself quickly, frightened of the filthy apparition before her. Perhaps it was the devil.

Carlos knew he must somehow convince her that to let him die would be unholy. "Praise Maria indeed," he cried out, raising his face, which looked almost dead already, so white was it and so bedraggled, with days of irregular stubble covering his chin. "Bless this woman, oh Goddess on high, bless her that she may succor your holy servant." The pain in his throat was awful, and he barely knew what he was saying. "Blessed is the holy man, blessed because he will bring good things on her who succors him." That was all. He subsided, unconscious. But it was enough. She fed him soup, by drops, all that night. And then for weeks, against the advice of her neighbors and the protests of the man who occasionally visited her to sire yet another of her children, nursed him back to health.

"I think he has holiness in him," the woman insisted. "I think he will bring me good fortune." She would not budge from her view.

In the end she was proved right. For Carlos recovered completely, all except his voice, which remained hoarse and restricted to a virtual monotone. He left her home and managed to steal enough money to buy a new passport. That was when he changed his name to Carlos Spinosa—all trace of his previous name and persona having been wiped away. He chose the second name from the one he had found in the very first wallet he had stolen after leaving home. It had been lucky for him then, perhaps it would be again. He left for Italy, an entirely new man, three months after he had walked out of the hospital.

Some years later, when he was already on his way to great wealth, he sent the woman who saved him five thousand American dollars. "From the holy man, with gratitude," the accompanying note read. It was more money than the woman had ever seen—and the only charitable act of Carlos's entire life.

Carlos Spinosa stretched his legs, pushing back into the smooth silk of the armchair, lifted his arm over his head, pulled in on the muscles of his stomach and sucked in a deep lungful of air. He felt alive, challenged, excited. The Chapin plan, which he had put out of his mind a week ago, seemed as good now as ever. Better the more he reconsidered it. Sidney Rosenberg had suggested the general outline. But he, Carlos Spinosa, had filled in the details, eliminated the obstacles, perfected it. That was why Oliver Chapin would split the profits with him fifty-fifty. Enormous profits.

Carefully, painstakingly, Spinosa went over every detail, checking and rechecking his assumptions. He sipped on a chilled Moselle wine, a Spätlese from the Himmelreicher Domthal, savoring its sweet, flowery, multilayered taste—as complicated as the scheme itself. It was an incredible scheme, huge . . . but, hard though he searched, he could see no risk. Already the groundwork was laid. Bagnew was in place. Chapin, under pressure from that little runt Pollo, wouldn't back out. The patents and the new technology had been ripe for exploitation for some time. "Flawless," he announced at last. Finally he could let himself be enthusiastic. Now he was sure.

"Hundreds of millions!" He spoke with awe. Even in his flat, damaged voice, the words carried momentous impact.

11

Sidney Rosenberg was even more worried than usual. It wasn't only that Caro Pollo was getting more aggressive by the day. That was bad enough. What was far worse was that Oliver wasn't pulling the plug on him. For some reason, he seemed absolutely unwilling to do anything about the damned punk.

"The little bastard's threatening to import the stuff on his own. Holding meetings with his hoods down at that bar where they think they're so secret. Ricardo told us the whole thing. At least he's loyal."

"Maybe."

"Well, he told us, didn't he?"

"Sure, Sid. But why? To start with, he was there, wasn't he? I wouldn't describe that as overly loyal."

"Do you want to put out the word on Pollo? I'm sure I could arrange something appropriate." Sidney made the statement merely factual.

"No, Sid," Oliver insisted, "we're not ready yet."

"Why not?" Sidney Rosenberg remonstrated uncharacteristically. "You may be taking a considerable risk leaving Pollo out there. Particularly as you haven't decided whether to go ahead with the scheme or not. After all, most of the Chapin group investments are either tied directly to your trade with Pollo and the others, or at least are financed from it. I hate to think what would happen to your housing developments in Arizona, for instance, or to the condo project in Atlanta, if you lose that cash flow." Sidney was incensed and far more involved than he wanted to be. "If Pollo does start importing, the others would go along with him. And you're risking it all. Good God, Oliver, you personally must be worth twenty or thirty million bucks at least, not to talk of the hundreds of millions the others have put under your control. How can you jeopardize—"

"Enough!" The word stopped Sidney like a karate chop. "Too much talking's no good."

"I'm sorry, sir." It was rare for Sidney to have to apologize. He seldom committed himself far enough to make a mistake. But he had this time, of that there was no doubt. It was that damn Spinosa plan that was getting to him. Even if the Deacon didn't go ahead, Sidney would be probably held somehow to blame that the supply situation was getting worse. That's what you get, Sidney Rosenberg thought bitterly, for ever recommending anything. Nothing but responsibility and blame. The worst part was that it wasn't even clear who was doing the delaying. Spinosa was being just as cautious as Oliver. The whole plan had been fully prepared, with the right man and all the other pieces in place, since January. And still the two men procrastinated. Spinosa claimed to be thinking about it. Well, what the hell, Sidney had thought about it already. It was flawless. And immensely profitable. Most important, it would solve this damn supply problem—and with it, the Pollo problem—once and for all. And Oliver wasn't pushing at all. But why not? Perhaps, after all, he was getting old. Could it be that he was intimidated by the Pollo clan. . . ?

"The problems fit together. One into the other." Oliver interrupted Sidney's thoughts so germanely it startled him. "It's punks like Pollo that do our dirty work—so you can't expect them to be good boys." He snorted with derision. "At least we always know what our little Luigi's up to. He couldn't keep his foolish mouth shut if it cost him his life . . . and it probably will! But before anything can be done about him, we first have to take care of his gripe. I think I've actually made the point before." Oliver sounded as bored as a professor before a freshman class. "If we ask Limpet to deal with him now, before we fix the problem, they'll all be against us. I agree I'm pretty powerful—at least compared to where we were say ten years ago. But we're not ready to do without these soldiers, mobsters like Pollo and his friends. The only reason the rest of them listen to a punk like Luigi is because he's got a point. So first we'll fix his point. Then we'll fix him. Oh, and when we do, it'll have to be dramatic—so no one forgets."

Sidney had never heard Oliver Chapin explain his thinking in such detail. Normally he kept his own counsel, issued orders, and that was that. It worried Sidney. Did it mean that Oliver was trusting him—or just that the old man was getting garrulous? He wasn't sure which was worse. Being trusted meant that he would be expected to take responsibility all round. And that meant his head would be on the line whenever *anything* went wrong. Dammit, Sid thought, that would be *awful*. But then, if the old man were just getting chatty in his old age—senile—God, there was no one to take over. Which meant there'd be some battle among the jackals. What would happen to Sidney, who knew too much for everyone's comfort, didn't even bear thinking about.

"Which is where your Spinosa scheme comes in. Right?"

My scheme! Yes it was. Sid Rosenberg felt his stomach contract with fear, but he also felt a surge of pride. It *was* his scheme, and an incredible one at that. A man had the right to at least some feelings of pride.

"That's where we need the action!" Suddenly Oliver had raised his voice. He was angry, Sidney realized, and incredibly, he was showing it not by dropping his voice to his typical dulcet whisper, but by virtually shouting. "So where is it?" Suddenly his voice was quiet again, and truly dangerous. "Why is there no advance on our scheme?"

"Well, I thought you didn't want—"

"It's your job to make this one work," Oliver interrupted, his voice now as gentle as a child's. "You proposed this scheme. It's up to you to get it going."

"Yes, sir." There it was, Sidney realized, the very worst he had feared, out in the open. But he wanted to sleep nights, not worry. "Oliver," he started to remonstrate, "really, I don't feel qualified to decide—"

"Then you'd better become qualified." Oliver Chapin had no intention of letting his accountant off the hook. For years Sidney's lack of involvement had bothered him. How could you control a man who had no commitment, no passion? Half the secret of Oliver's success was to play on other people's desires, to use the momentum of their own needs to keep them rushing forward in the direction he, Oliver Chapin, born Ollie Tchapinisky, wanted. Although he'd never formulated that thought very clearly, it was part of his basic credo. Sid had been the holdout. Wanting nothing except the money to which he was entitled—that silly million he thought Oliver didn't know about—desperate for nothing and therefore with nothing much to fear, Sid Rosenberg had remained a free man all these years. Now, at last, Sid was caught up in something. He was proud of his Spinosa scheme, justifiably so. Therefore he felt responsible, committed—and, for the first time in his life, truly under Oliver Chapin's thumb.

"Very well," Sidney agreed, finally accepting the inevitable. "I'll push our friend to get it started."

12

Susan Bagnew left her parents' home for her first day of work as an administrative assistant at Turner-LaMott's advanced research center in Wilton, Connecticut, only two days after she finished her final exams. She was both nervous and elated. It had been surprisingly difficult to get the job in the first place, and she was determined to make a success of it.

The first interview, the one on campus, had been easy and she had been pleased but not surprised to be invited to visit the company itself. As a straight-A student, a vice-president of the student body, a reasonably accomplished tennis player who was attractive and personable as well, she was used to getting what she set out for. Of course, at that time they hadn't realized who her daddy was. She had used her mother's maiden name of Lodge.

It was halfway through the pleasant enough interview with Dr. Turner, the head of Turner-LaMott's research and development department, an administrative scientist with a paunch that seemed out of place on his small frame, a large mustache and a rather pompous manner that seemed to suggest that neither science nor scientists should ever be taken lightly, that she had decided to explain her position.

"No relation to the company, I'm afraid," Dr. Turner was answering her question. "Just a hard-working fellow who got into science and never got out." He was feeling expansive, so Susan knew the interview must be going well.

"I'm afraid I am, though," Susan interrupted. "A relation, I mean. A daughter."

"Oh really? What was your name again?" Dr. Turner adjusted his glasses to search the application form.

"I'm afraid I lied on the application. You see, I wanted you to accept me for myself, not my father." She managed to sound apologetic but not contrite.

"What's your real name then?"

"Bagnew. I'm Susan Bagnew."

"Oh, dear." The remark was unintentional, a thoroughly human reaction to the little doctor's surprise and disappointment. She seemed such a competent young woman. He would certainly have hired her. But the new president's daughter, well . . . "We do have policies against . . ." He hesitated, not sure how to say it tactfully.

"Nepotism?"

"That's a bit pejorative."

"I'm on my own, Dr. Turner. I told Dad I'd be applying and you know what he said? He said, 'Don't use my name, that's all.' Of course, he probably didn't mean it literally." She laughed somewhat embarrassed. "And I don't plan to—except in the technical sense. If you decide to hire me, it's because of my school record and of what you feel I can contribute. And if you don't, then that's fine. In either case, I won't go running to Daddy."

"Nevertheless, it does make you special, doesn't it? You surely recognize that you'd be different from an ordinary undergraduate coming in here."

"I suppose," she had to admit.

"Why Turner-LaMott then? There are other companies."

She had, of course, been reflecting on the question, had thought about it deeply. But, try as she might, she had not been able to come up with a clear answer. She just wanted to . . . but why, exactly, she found it almost impossible to explain.

"Well, it's a good company," she started lamely, "and . . ."

Dr. Turner watched her stumble to a halt. Bright girl, he thought, and clean-cut all the way through. He wished his own daughter was half as . . . how could he describe the quality? . . . half as wholesome, as *decent* as this one, instead of running around with greasy youths, ingesting god knows what drugs and trying so hard to destroy her life. Where had he gone wrong, he asked himself for the millionth time? With an effort Dr. Turner brought his mind back to the young woman before him. "Perhaps you just want to be near your dad?" He hazarded the guess more from his own sense of emptiness than from real insight, but he touched the right nerve.

"That's it, I guess." Susan was astonished by the simplicity of the explanation. It was why she wanted to live at home, after all. "You're right," she mused, "I do. I want to be part of what Dad's doing. Somehow before, when he was out of work, I couldn't share. Now I can." She suddenly realized how indiscreet she had been. "I mean when he'd decided to retire and . . ."

"It's none of my business, you know," Dr. Turner assured her gently. "And I'm quite able to keep confidences."

"Thank you." She felt very close to this over-blown little man who had suddenly become so kind and who looked so sad. She wished it were appropriate to ask him if there were anything she could do to help.

"Well then, I guess we'd better find a way to get you in here." Dr. Turner had paused. "Perhaps the best place to start would be at TULIPS. They don't care who you are or where you're from."

"Tulips?"

"Oh yes. You wouldn't know about that, of course. It's the nickname for our pure research center in Wilton, Connecticut, the Turner-LaMott Institute for Pure Science . . . TULIPS for short."

"What do they do?"

"A sort of think tank. They experiment and debate, they do what they want, really. We give them a budget at the beginning of the year, and at the end they describe what they've done with it. Other than that, they're free."

"It sounds . . ." Susan hesitated.

"Weird?" Dr. Turner had a knack for filling in her thoughts.

"Well, yes," she laughed. "But I was looking for a more polite word."

"It is a bit. But they're brilliant. And fun."

"I imagine."

"More important, they're looking for a really bright person who can help out as a lab assistant and who can also do some of the administration that's needed." He smiled. "They're not great administrators out there, it's fair to say."

Susan grinned back at Dr. Turner. "Oh, I'd love to do that."

"You'd fit in beautifully . . ." He hesitated.

"And be out of the way?" It was Susan's turn to complete a difficult thought.

Dr. Turner chuckled. "You wouldn't have to stay there too long, just until people got used to the concept of the president's daughter."

"Truly, I'd love it," she repeated. "And you're quite right, it's a perfect place for me to start." She paused and then asked simply but intensely, "May I please have the job?"

Dr. Turner hesitated only a second longer. "Very well," he said briskly.

Susan looked directly at her interviewer.

"I do appreciate what you're doing, Dr. Turner," she said. "Thank you. I'm very grateful."

Wilton, Connecticut, in the late spring and early summer is superb: bulbs and late-blooming azaleas, pink and white dogwoods, bright red clusters of rhododendrons all contrasting with a background of endless leaves each shimmering its individual dance in a gentle, clean breeze that never even heard of pollution; a hopelessly overstated blue sky; and, to top it off, snow white clouds, specially manufactured of ultrafluffy polyester.

It was still only eight-thirty when Susan reached the driveway of the technical center. And already she'd dawdled as much as she could. Well, no harm in being a little early her first day. She pressed the accelerator of her secondhand VW beetle. What a good feeling to have her very own car. How generous of Dad to lend her the money; she'd repay it in no time. Goodness, but she felt ready to accept any challenge this morning, in spite of the butterflies in her stomach.

With a conscious effort, she put her nervousness to one side. By God, she was going to make a success of this—and make her Dad as proud of her as she was of him.

Knowing that Susan had started to work at TULIPS only a month earlier, Simon Bagnew left his investigating of that part of the business to the very end of his review process. In any case, it seemed less important than the other areas. As far as he could see from the records, they had contributed very little to the company. Still, he would wait and see. Susan had certainly been impressed by the people she had met there. Particularly one young man, what was his name again, yes, David Fellows, had been reviewed most favorably.

As his limousine drove up the driveway to TULIPS, through the hundred-acre forest preserve, full of spring-fed streams, bird song and grazing deer, Simon felt as happy as he could recall being in a long time. The center itself, as it came into view over the crest of a hill, was small and half-hidden by the trees. Simon knew that it housed only two dozen scientists—but that each was brilliant, a creative authority who had already made a name for himself before he joined Turner-LaMott. He was looking forward to learning what they actually were doing here. Quite correctly, Susan had not wanted to discuss it with him except to hint that some of the work was, in her term, mind-boggling.

Simon had, of course, already visited the regular research and development facility near Princeton, New Jersey. That was where practical new products were developed, competitive activities monitored and often copied, and cost reductions pursued. Standard R&D, an important part of the company, Simon felt, worked efficiently under Turner.

"Been in the field ever since I was a kid," Dr. Turner had answered Simon's question. "Always loved chemistry. They used to call me Winnie the Pooh even back in junior high. I assume because I liked chemistry experiments so much."

"Quite," Simon couldn't help noticing the physical similarity between the roly-poly head of R & D and that charming bear. Pity Dr. Turner exhibited little of the same gentle charm. "And now you have a large, important staff. In my experience—"

"One hundred and nineteen professionals supported by two hundred and forty-three technicians." Dr. Turner liked to be precise. "And a budget this year of eleven point eight million. That doesn't include quality control at the factories, or TULIPS."

"Yes, I know a little about them."

"Most of their work is so advanced it gets closer to philosophy than science. Brilliant stuff, some of it, but not too practical. I read one of their papers recently by a very young fellow who's working at the cutting edge of genetic engineering. It really opened my eyes to whole vistas of new scientific opportunity."

"Like what?" Simon suspected that Dr. Turner, sound

administrator though he probably was, didn't really understand what they were doing at the institute.

"Nothing immediate, of course. But the things that could develop eventually—astonishing. You know that General Electric has already patented a microorganism they claim can eat up an oil slick spilled onto the ocean and convert it into harmless protein? And I'm sure you've read of the spectacular rise in the share prices of those new companies specializing in genetics."

"Of course."

"Well, our boys up there are thinking along lines like that. But years ahead, to where we can *grow* machines, robots really, but not mechanical ones, organic ones. They're actually imagining machine-animals."

"Sounds like nonsense," said Simon, partly to see how Dr. Turner would respond.

"You said it, I didn't," Turner growled. Then he smiled trying to turn his remark into a joke; he succeeded only in sounding both jealous and angry.

"Perhaps not all nonsense?" Simon probed.

"Perhaps not all nonsense."

Simon Bagnew would remember that remark often. "Perhaps not all nonsense." What an understatement it turned out to be!

"Well, of course, much of what they do is useless," Foster Harrison had agreed when Simon had later asked him his view about the institute. "That's what Turner down at R and D thinks. But, frankly, I suspect he's just jealous. My feeling is that, overall, they serve a useful purpose."

"Have they actually developed anything that we've been able to use?"

"Not really. But they build our reputation in the scientific community. That means that many of the better universities bring us practical new processes that they don't want to develop themselves. Also, I do believe that some of that genetic development they're working on has unusual promise. I haven't seen it lately, but it sounded exciting a few months ago when I investigated . . . before you came on board."

"So then is it worthwhile?"

"It wouldn't be there if I didn't think so." Harrison was acerbic. "Besides," he added more gently. "its budget is only a million dollars a year after taxes. And over the last five years, the real estate has appreciated about eight million dollars."

Its wheels crunching on the gravel driveway, Simon's limousine pulled up in front of the TULIPS building. It looked more like an old farmhouse than a research building, except that there was a space-age, glass and steel structure built out as one wing of the old house. As Simon alighted, the sunlight filtered through the leaves of a huge maple, dappling his charcoal business suit into a golden brocade. "I should be a couple of hours," he instructed his driver. "I imagine they'll give you a cup of coffee. I'll find you when I'm ready to leave."

Simon entered the building, feeling as if he were playing hookey. "I'm Simon Bagnew," he told the young receptionist sitting in the living room–like entrance hall.

"Hullo, Simon," she said, startling him by using his first name. "I'm Sheela. We've been expecting you. David Fellows and Lee Carrello are waiting for you inside. It's just through there." She pointed to a heavy oak door but made no move to accompany him. After a moment's hesitation, Simon pushed open the door and entered a large study where a young man in jeans with long hair and an older one in corduroys and a tartan shirt were arguing heatedly.

". . . Chromosomes be damned," the young man was insisting. "The question is not whether they can be synthesized, activated, rejuvenated—hell, you can fry them up with toast and make them into a bread pudding for all

I care. The real question is, what will it do in the long run to the gene pool as we understand it? Of course, everything is possible, at least eventually." His English-accented voice was passionate. "Surely we've proven that with the work we've done already. But is it *desirable?*"

"Do we have a choice?" The older man puffed on his pipe. "Isn't knowledge the only ultimate inevitability . . ."

Simon coughed politely to draw attention to himself.

"Oh, hello. Sorry we didn't see you." The younger man was all smiles. "You must be Simon Bagnew. I'm Dave Fellows. I've been looking forward to meeting you. If you're Susan's father, you can't be all bad." He laughed with real friendship. "She's terrific. On the other hand," he gestured toward the other man, "this old fellow here, the ignorant one, is my partner in crime, Dr. Leandro Carrello—Lee to his friends, only he hasn't any."

"Welcome to TULIPS." Lee Carello held out his hand. "Most people think we're unnecessary, by the way. So you'll forgive my Limey colleague here for pretending it's true. Actually under the hair and the strange accent, he's quite bright."

The two men laughed delightedly together, old friends who enjoyed their banter and were willing to allow this visitor to share their enjoyment.

"Would you like a cup of tea, Simon?" David Fellows asked.

"Alternatively, we can also be civilized and offer you coffee," said Lee Carrello firmly.

Simon laughed nervously, intrigued by these two men, but out of his depth. "Coffee," he said tentatively.

"There, you see," Carrello turned victoriously toward his friend. "I told you the great ones prefer a man's drink."

"Oh dear," Fellows said plaintively, "another colonial."

An hour of pleasant chatter had passed, some of it almost childish, some enormously erudite. Simon had met six of the other researchers. Each was as friendly as David and Lee, each a character, idiosyncratic in clothing and outlook. Susan walked past and waved at her father shyly and then disappeared. Simon noticed that David Fellows's eyes followed her all the way until she left.

"The other fellows and Harriet aren't in today, I'm afraid," Lee explained. "Harriet's depressed, I happen to know, so she'll be at home with the covers over her head."

Simon looked startled.

"Oh not to worry," David chimed in. "It's hard on her, of course, but she does some of her best work like that. She'll be back in a few days, full of beans and with new insights."

"And the others?"

"Not really sure." David had appointed himself Simon's guide. "I know two of them are down in Peru staring through a telescope."

"What are they working on?" Simon wanted to know. "How do telescopes have anything to do with Turner-LaMott?"

Immediately there was a silence in the room. It was as if Simon had committed some awful social gaffe.

"I have no idea," David Fellows said formally. "It is not a question with which I concern myself."

"Nor I," Lee Carrello added, his tone glacial.

No one else said a word.

Eventually, acutely embarrassed, Simon was forced to break the silence. "Look," he said, hoping he was not digging himself in deeper, "I realize I have offended you by mentioning Turner-LaMott, but I don't understand why. Perhaps you'd explain. After all, the company does provide this facility and you do all work here."

The tension eased somewhat. "We like Turner-LaMott," Dave Fellows explained. "But we're concerned that the company not encroach on our academic freedom."

"Fine. But how was I doing that?"

"You were implying that our work should be evaluated against its applicability to the parent," Carrello replied.

"And you feel that is wrong?"

"Not wrong exactly," Fellows interrupted. "Only dangerous—because applicability can't be defined."

"Against what criteria *do* you measure yourselves then," Simon asked, intrigued.

There was a babble of disagreement. Everyone expressed his own view. Philosophies of rational understanding competed with altruistic principles. One youth—hardly old enough to shave, Simon thought—even suggested that commercial gain might be a measurement criterion. That was seen by his peers to be the most radical concept of them all.

"Apparently, you have differing views of what constitutes success," Simon said drily as the discussion abated. "Is there a concensus, then, about any successes you have had?"

"Certainly," said David Fellows.

"None at all," said Lee Carrello in the same breath.

Everyone except David laughed. "But you all agreed that the new bug Harriet and I worked on was a success," he insisted.

"All except you," Carrello teased. "You've been worrying about God ever since you developed it!"

"What new bug?" Simon interjected before they could launch themselves into another argument. He guessed that this was the subject they had been debating when he had first entered.

"Dave and Harriet have done some breakthrough genetic engineering work," Carrello explained. "You know that General Electric developed—"

"Yes, I've heard of it."

"Well, starting from a slightly different point and using the nonpatented part of the G.E. process, David and Harriet have developed a whole new family of microorganisms."

"New?"

"Oh yes, new all right. They do things backwards."

"How do you mean?" Simon was confused.

"Basically the same as the G.E. organisms, but going the other way."

"You mean you feed them protein and they make oil slicks?" Simon asked, intending the question facetiously.

"That's precisely right. Go to the head of your class." David grinned broadly.

"What sort of proteins?" Simon had to ask the question twice to make himself heard above the laughter.

"Well, it's not protein as such," David explained. "You see, it's actually a two-stage process—two interlocking microorganisms, so to speak, which thrive in sequence."

"Sequential civilizations is how he described them originally," Carrello interjected, sounding like a proud father.

"We called the first group Grecococcus, and the second Romacoccus," David laughed.

"Greek and Roman?"

"Precisely. The Grecococcus are really unicellular herbivores. They sort of graze on hay or woodmeal—anything high in cellulose, even paper. In doing that, they fatten themselves up into something approaching standard protein. They also transmute into a related but different strain—the Romacoccus. They're the carnivores—tough little buggers that devour protein. They'll convert the Grecococcus—and any other form of protein—into animal oil. What's really frightening about it is the parallel to sequential human civilizations. You see, the second organism really emerges from the first—and destroys it—"

"I'm sure I'm missing something here," Simon interrupted quickly, wanting to avoid another philosophical debate. "Because what I'm understanding is that you've developed a way to make paper or hay or wood and turn it into oil. Is that right?"

"That's it," said David Fellows cheerfully. "You've got it."

"Waste paper, for example?"

"Ah yes, any old garbage. Actually, regular household garbage is fine because most of it is either cellulose or protein in the first place. So either the Greeks or the Romans will get it. We've tried it on small piles of garbage. Actually, you could do huge garbage dumps in no time. There'd be nothing left except meal, glass and a few old tires!"

The enormous potential of the concept was only just seeping into Simon's mind. It couldn't be, could it? Surely there must be something important he had missed. "I can hardly believe such a theory would work in practice."

"Oh, it's no theory," David Fellows answered him. "We've tried it several times. It works fine."

"What stops the bacteria—they are bacteria, aren't they?"

"Not really. But that will do."

"Well, what stops them? Why don't they just eat everything around them? Why don't they eat me, for example?"

"Living protein is self-protecting—it's stronger than the Romacoccus itself. All living protein is, except for the Grecococcus, of course. It's a rather complicated factor that has to do with genetic chemistry. Certain DNA isomers—"

"Never mind, then. But why can't the Romans keep eating dead protein?"

"Well they can—as long as there's any left—and the organism is still active. But after a while the batch would be gone, wouldn't it? Then they'd become static and—"

"And we have our oil slick," Carrello interrupted.

"That's it."

"I must say, it sounds dangerous to me," Simon said doubtfully. "For example, what would happen if they get into the sea? Isn't the plankton largely dead—and full of protein? Could they destroy all that food?"

David Fellows looked at Simon as if he had asked a truly witless question. "There's no risk of that sort at all," he said, clearly remaining patient only with considerable effort. "Protein-conversion organisms like Romacoccus can't survive longer than a few hours because they can't reproduce themselves. That's why they don't exist in the natural state. They can only be grown by a mutation of the Grecococcus. And once there are enough of the Romans, they eat up all the Greeks and that's the end of the cycle."

"Otherwise the whole world would be one vast oil slick," Carrello added. "And presumably we'd all be Arabs."

Once again everyone laughed.

"What happens is that the Greeks multiply like mad for about an hour. Then they start their mutation and the first Romans emerge. The Greeks continue to multiply—but the conversion to Romans accelerates and after about two hours the Romans have gobbled up all the Greeks. Then they last about another hour. So after about three hours, varying slightly with exterior conditions, the cycle has finished. The only way you can start it again is to introduce some new, laboratory-grown Grecococcus."

"Fascinating!" Simon's mind was spinning with the implications of what he was hearing.

"Theoretically, one whole cycle would convert about one ton of cellulose to protein, and that to oil," David Fellows was continuing to explain. "But in practice, there would be all sorts of interruptions in the synthesis, so it would be much less. So even if the worst happened, and you applied fresh Grecococcus into the sea, I doubt you'd lose more than a few hundred pounds of plankton from any one event."

"But you could convert more garbage than that?"

"Of course. For one thing, we would eliminate more variables." David Fellows was becoming bored with this simplistic explanation. "But even when the Romans have died off, we can always generate more Greeks and send in an army of fresh recruits." He ended with a sigh. "I say," he added with far more enthusiasm, "isn't it time for lunch?"

"That is mind-boggling." Simon, totally uninterested in the food in front of him, couldn't hold down his enthusiasm.

"What is?" Lee Carrello asked, intent on his steak. "Oh, you mean David's bugs. Yeah, I guess so. First-class genetic work—you'd never think he had it in him." He grinned across the table at his friend. "I think it's Harriet mostly," he added.

"Absolutely," David agreed immediately. "But I'm invaluable to her . . . I shovel the garbage for her experiments." He looked slyly at Simon. "Except I have a rather talented assistant now, so she gets to do some of that instead."

"Do her good, no doubt," Simon said drily. "Probably a spoiled brat from some Greenwich family who's never done a day's garbage carting in her life."

This time the laughter was entirely with Simon. From now on, he realized, they would trust him easily. Still, he thought carefully before asking his next question. "Have you thought of the implications of this discovery?"

"Absolutely!" Suddenly Fellows was full of enthusiasm again. "They are truly astonishing. You see, if Grecococcus can convert cellulose to protein, it follows that what we have known about the chemistry of protein up to now has to be rethought, even—"

"I don't think that is what Simon meant," Lee Carrello interrupted. "I think he was wondering about garbage disposal."

"Oh. Yes, that too. But—"

"Does anyone know about your discovery?" Simon risked interrupting Fellows. "I mean outside TULIPS?"

"Shouldn't think so. Except for some of the preliminary work, which we got patents on a year or more ago. But we've come a long way since then. And we haven't applied for any patents on that new work, so there's been no need to tell anyone." He considered for a moment. "Oh yes, I did mention some of the new theory to Dr. Turner." David Fellows emphasized the "doctor" enough to make it sound absurd. "But he didn't seem to get it."

"And other than him?"

"Don't think so."

"Would it be asking too much to request you to keep it confidential?"

"Not necessarily." Fellows sounded suspicious. "Why?"

"Because if it gets out," said Simon, wondering whether he was using the right approach, "the next thing you'll know is that G.E. will have patented it!"

"Christ, you're right!" David was truly shocked. "I'd never thought of that." His face paled. "That would be awful. They'd probably stop Harriet and me from continuing to work on it."

"It's time we had lunch together," Galsworthy informed Simon Bagnew, by telephone. "I understand you have finally completed your review of the company. It's certainly high time."

So the other shoe was about to drop. Simon felt almost relieved. The tension had been getting unbearable. Far better finally to know where he stood. "Love to," he said, trying to pretend he had not a care in the world. "I'm a little busy, of course, but—"

"Today."

"Oh, I'm afraid that's not possible. I've got a previous—"

"One o'clock at my office," Galsworthy continued as if Simon had not spoken. "We won't be interrupted here." He hung up the phone, not even considering the possibility that Simon would not appear. Miserable little toad, he thought, no guts at all.

For his part, Simon sat quite still at his desk. "Bastard," he muttered angrily. For a few moments he wondered whether he dared refuse to go. He did have a lunch date, after all. Simon's memory of those years out of work was far too potent, his bank account still far too small.

He lowered his head into his hands and sat entirely still for several minutes, the picture of dejection. What would Galsworthy demand—and how far would Simon be prepared to go? Was there anything he would not do to hold his job? Anything at all? Oh, how different it had been when he was young.

What an idealistic fool he had been in his youth, never doubting that America really was the land of the free and the home of the brave. That was what they had taught him at school, wasn't it? And why should he doubt what his parents and his teachers all insisted was true. Moreover, he could prove it for himself easily enough. Hadn't America licked Mr. Hitler, trounced him but good, because he was a vicious tyrant and America had the strength of God and freedom on her side? And wasn't it true also, as Johnny Webb said—and he should know because he'd actually been wounded in the Pacific fighting the Japs—that America was winning against those little yellow devils too. She had to win, didn't she, because she was right.

Centralia, Illinois, "Center of the Nation," the city called itself, claiming to be geographically situated precisely at the midpoint of the great U.S. of A. And home of the Hollywood Candy Company, where Simon's dad worked as a foreman. Most of Simon's friends' fathers—except a few who had gone away to war—worked there too.

Most of his friends were idealistic, like him. But like his, their ideals were limited, pragmatic, small-minded. All these boys wanted for their country and themselves—and probably in reverse order at that—was to win the war, and make a fortune. Perhaps he'd become a big landowner someday, Simon dreamed, or own a factory, like Mr. Marticcho who had founded the Hollywood Candy Company back in Chicago, on a shoestring, and who had become a millionaire with his own horses and everything.

That was what America could do for you. Make you proud—and rich. Even if you were only a little Italian man like Mr. Marticcho.

Then, maybe, you could go into politics and help to run things, become a state senator even, with influence in Chicago. And make sure that there would never be another war like this one, and that both the Germans and the Japs were kept in their place—so that America could stay free and powerful, and you with her, an important person in God's country.

But first he had to go to college. The excitement of the thought! He just knew he'd manage it. The University of Illinois in Urbana had an excellent reputation, and as a resident of Illinois it wouldn't cost him much at all. He'd already asked Mr. Drury, the owner of the drug store who'd graduated as a registered pharmacist from there, what it was like.

"You'll do fine, Simon. Great. I loved my time there. You just couldn't do better," Mr. Drury had assured him.

Excitedly, Simon had written off for the prospectus and entrance forms. When they arrived, shiny and impressive, he was so pleased he hurried off to see his faculty advisor to show him.

"I will be able to get in, won't I, Mr. Garcia?"

"Of course." Garcia was a swarthy young man who had lived in Centralia for only three years. He had come from New York because his wife had grown up in Centralia and had become homesick. "But I don't think you're shooting high enough."

"What do you mean?"

"With your record, you don't have to go to the state university. There's nothing wrong with it, mind you. But there are better."

"Like what?"

"Well, like Harvard, for one."

"Harvard!" It was a fantastic thought to Simon Bagnew. Harvard was the very pinnacle of learning. "But I wouldn't be able to get in there, would I?"

"Well, it's a reach, I admit. But you've done exceptionally well at school here. *We're* proud of you. If you apply, Harvard might accept you. You never know. It depends, really, on who else they have to choose from. So why not send them an application? It wouldn't hurt. I'd be pleased to help you fill it out."

Simon hadn't told his parents a word about his applying to Harvard. He would never get accepted anyhow, and if anyone heard about it, they'd die laughing. He made Mr. Garcia promise not to mention it either. But for all that, when the application forms arrived, he worked hard at filling them in. And when they were done, he had to admit his record looked pretty good—certainly a lot more impressive than Simon thought himself to be. For one thing, there was his academic record, straight A's three years in a row. Of course, that wasn't as hard as it sounded; nearly ten percent of students at his high school managed that. Still, it looked good on paper.

For another thing, he had some fine-sounding extracurricular titles: secretary of his graduating class, chosen because everybody agreed that young Simon Bagnew was always reliable; manager of the football team, because he was too small to play but was willing to devote himself tirelessly and, more importantly, self-effacingly to the task; stage manager for the school's major theatrical performance two years in a row, because he was willing to sweep the stage, take care of the props, lock up after everyone else was already having a ball at the cast party.

Everything taken together, Simon realized, his application looked like quite a career. Only *he* knew that his achievements weren't particularly significant, not when you looked at what they really meant.

The waiting was a small torture. He was accepted right away at the University of Illinois, but that seemed second best now, and for weeks Harvard did not reply. Even though he never expected Harvard to take him, he couldn't help hoping. Just maybe . . . So every day he would visit Mr. Garcia's house on his way home from school to see whether the letter had arrived. That was the return address he had put on his application; he didn't want his family asking questions about the rejection letter he'd anticipated. Finally, when he had given up hoping that they would even reply, the letter arrived.

> We are pleased to offer you a position as a freshman in the Arts and Science Faculty of Harvard College, starting in September 1946 . . .

Simon didn't stop to read the rest of the formal note. Whooping with delight he raced home to tell his mother. "Harvard. I've been accepted at Harvard," he shouted as he rushed into the house.

"That's lovely dear," his mother said calmly. "I didn't know you'd even applied. Would you want to go?"

"Would I want to? It's Harvard, Mom. Do you know what that *means?*"

"Of course. It means your dad will have to work even harder than he does now to afford it."

The heavens fell. Somehow, in the challenge of applying, he'd never really considered the money question. But of course his mom was right. Even with the money he'd saved working in the summers, he wouldn't be able to afford it. And it certainly wasn't fair to ask his dad. He was utterly dejected.

"It's quite an honor though, isn't it?" his mother took pity on him. "Your dad will be very proud. We'll talk it over with him this evening and see what he has to say."

"Sure, Mom. Thanks. But I wouldn't want to go if it made things too hard on you and Dad."

Simon slouched morosely off to his room. All those hopes. How stupid he'd been not even to consider the money. And selfish too. What could he have been thinking of? He took the letter out of his pocket with a leaden heart. It was quite short, the most impressive thing about it the seal of the university in the corner of the paper. ". . . September 1946." For the first time Simon read the rest of the note.

> We also wish you to know [the second paragraph read] that your academic and extracurricular achievements are such that you are eligible for full scholarship assistance. By applying . . .

"Mom!" He yelled so loudly as he bounced down the stairs that in fright she dropped the dish of apple pie she was holding. "Mom, they say I can have a scholarship!"

For the first time he could ever remember, his mother left her kitchen a mess. "I'll get it later," she explained. "Let's go and tell your dad."

* * *

Simon lifted his head from his hands. Stupid daydream. Childishness. This was the 1980s. You couldn't mention God in school anymore. The Hollywood Candy Factory had been sold to some giant conglomerate, as impersonal as Turner-LaMott, no doubt. And he, Simon Bagnew, had become successful. His daughter had graduated with honors from Stanford. Not as good as Harvard, he would tease, but okay. All in all, he was fortunate enough. So what if there was a price he had to pay. That was reality.

He picked up his phone and buzzed for his secretary.

"Yes?" She sounded as sour as ever.

"Please call my lunch date and apologize that I cannot make it today. I have to meet with Mr. Galsworthy."

Morgan Galsworthy evidenced neither surprise nor gratitude when Simon Bagnew arrived. "Sit down," was all he said, and his tone was both pompous and impatient.

"What did you want to see me about?" There was no point in beating about the bush, Simon decided. He felt sufficiently humiliated by Galsworthy's behavior—and by his own weak-kneed response to it—to want to complete the conversation as fast as possible. "I assume you have some specific instructions you want me to consider."

"To act upon, not consider."

"What are they?"

"Perhaps we should have some lunch first." Galsworthy decided the conversation was moving too rapidly and that Bagnew was too much in charge.

"Thank you, I already ate." Simon enjoyed a moment of pleasure as he voiced the lie. But it was short-lived.

"My dear fellow!" Galsworthy seemed quite unconcerned. "Then I'll eat alone." He signaled on a special buzzer and sat back as a waiter, fully attired in appropriate uniform, wheeled in a luncheon trolley with pâté, smoked salmon, a beautiful salad, two halves of a cold roast Cornish hen and, to top it off, a chilled bottle of wine. "I'm so sorry you have already eaten," Galsworthy said, clearly disbelieving Simon. "Mr. Bagnew will not be dining," he added to the waiter. "Please clear his place."

As the waiter swiftly removed the second place setting, the headhunter poured himself a glass of wine, served himself some smoked salmon, and began to eat with gusto. He uttered not a word to his guest, even after the waiter had left.

"I'm afraid I'm in rather a hurry," Simon said eventually, trying hard not to let his annoyance show. "So perhaps if you could proceed with whatever you wish to say."

"Of course," Galsworthy tasted another mouthful. "It's not too complicated, as a matter of fact." He interrupted himself to swirl his wine around the glass in the time-honored motion of the expert taster and then bury his nose deep into the glass. "Ah," he said, lifting his head and exhaling appreciatively, "excellent!"

Bagnew waited silently. One more minute, he promised himself. Just one more and he'd walk out.

"What we want you to do"—to Simon's relief, Galsworthy spoke before the minute was up—"is related to the new technology on which TULIPS, as they call it, is working."

"Yes?"

"I am referring to work in the field of genetics. I understand you have already reviewed it."

Christ, they were well-informed. How the hell did they even know—and was it just a general awareness or did they know the specifics? Fellows had said no one but Winthrop Turner had heard of it. Could Turner be Galsworthy's man too? He seemed such a straightforward, unimaginative type.

"Well, have you?"

"Yes. I've been to Wilton," Simon tried to sound noncommittal.

"Then you realize how important these developments could be if they prove practical."

"Indeed." Simon refused to indicate that David Fellows had assured him they already were. "But it remains to be seen whether they will be." They evidently didn't have the whole story. "In my experience—"

"Nevertheless," Galsworthy interrupted, "my associates feel the time has come to announce to the world that we have this technology." He took another sip of the wine and rolled it around his mouth with a great show of enjoyment. "That is your simple task."

"You want me to announce that we own valuable new technology—even though we're not sure the technology is sound? Is that right?" This was too good to be true. Evidently, they didn't realize how far along the scientists were. Simon felt elated; Galsworthy was about to force him to do something he'd be perfectly willing to do without being forced. What a massive stroke of luck! With a great effort he managed to continue to look worried and morose.

For a long moment, Morgan Galsworthy stared at Simon. "Yes," he said coldly. "You are to make the announcement Friday week. That is in just under two weeks from today. We want a major public statement."

"And if I refuse?"

"Why should you refuse? There's no point. The company's chief chemist will assure you that the technology is entirely feasible."

"But not proven." Bagnew was anxious to confirm Galsworthy didn't know.

"Not fully, I admit. But nevertheless the announcement will be made." The headhunter paused ominously. "If not by you, my dear fellow, then certainly by your successor." Galsworthy smiled benignly. But for all his calm appearance, he was agitated. Bagnew should have been a hell of a lot more amenable than this. By now, he should have agreed and be enjoying a congratulatory glass of wine. Instead, he was sitting there with a sour look on his face, evidently deciding whether to proceed or not. God help them both, Galsworthy was thinking, if the toad decided not to do what he was told. Sure, Simon would be out of a job, but he, Morgan Galsworthy, would also be in deep trouble. He had promised that Bagnew could be controlled, and he'd been quite firm about it. If he was wrong . . . well, neither of the men involved forgave mistakes lightly. He shuddered at the very possibility. Suddenly he could feel a cold sweat prickle at his back under his expensive, handmade shirt.

For his part, Simon had to pinch his knee under the table to stop himself from grinning. Maybe he was free after all.

The silence in the room stretched until it became almost unbearable for Galsworthy. And still it continued . . .

Finally, Simon broke the silence. "I shall investigate the technology before I make a decision," he stalled.

"And then you will do what you are told."

"Perhaps."

"For Christ's sake, not perhaps." Galsworthy was starting to get angry. "Otherwise—"

"You have made it quite clear what happens otherwise. As I have said, first I'll investigate, then I'll decide." Simon arose. "Is that all?"

"For today," Galsworthy forced a smile. "But God help you if you double-cross us."

Simon Bagnew pulled himself to full height. "I shall let you know my decision in the morning, Morgan," he said, trying to look like a man facing a struggle with his conscience. How wonderful to be able to give in under pressure without having to give in at all . . . for once it would be so easy to do the right thing.

Briefly Simon wondered what their scheme was—not that it was so hard to guess. They wanted him to announce the new technology so Turner-LaMott's stock would go up. Then they would sell their stock at the high price. Later, when the stock reached its peak, they would no doubt sell more than they had, sell short, in other words, for future delivery. Once they'd done that, they'd have him break the news a few months from now that the technology wasn't sound after all, or at least not practical. That would push the price down so that they could fulfill their obligations to deliver the stock by buying at a much lower price. Simple. An illegal stock manipulation with no risk to Galsworthy and his cronies. And they'd make a fortune, no, two fortunes consecutively.

The only trouble with their scheme was that the technology *was* sound. There was really no way they could announce that it wasn't if it was; they would be found out far too quickly. For one thing, he'd make it a point to make certain that Jim Lester knew all about the new technology. That way, if Galsworthy did try to force him to say it was no good, there would be a witness—and a courageous one who wouldn't be muzzled—who'd say publicly how it was. So the price of the stock never would collapse—more likely it would rise further. He dearly hoped they'd lose their shirts!

But the best part of all was that he, Simon Bagnew, couldn't be blamed by them later. He'd have done exactly what they ordered. All he had to do now was to convince Morgan Galsworthy how hard he was struggling with his conscience. If he agreed too readily, Morgan might sense something amiss. "I'll call you tomorrow, Morgan," he repeated, and turned for the door.

As he left the room, Simon was assailed by a far less

pleasing thought. What would he have done, he wondered, if the technology had not been sound? Where would his bravery have been then?

He pushed the thought to one side. He hadn't been forced to make that moral choice, had he? So why worry about it?

13

Simon Bagnew had taken to spending first two and sometimes three nights a week in the Turner-LaMott apartment in New York. He was working so hard that he felt justified in not fighting the hour-long commute out to Greenwich each evening. Moreover, when he did get home, his wife, with what he felt was incredibly little understanding of the burdens of his office, would pester him with household details.

"You wouldn't believe what happened today," she had complained only yesterday. "The dryer pilot flame went out—and it just wouldn't stay lit even though I tried everything, *including* kicking the miserable thing."

"Why don't you buy a new one, like I said?"

"That makes seven times the damned man has come." She refused to deal with his suggestion. "Seven times! And it's still not working."

"So, why not—"

"Anyway, it *is* new."

"Oh come on. It's five years if it's a day."

"No more than three. And do you have any idea what they cost?"

"So don't get a new dryer. What do I care?" The moment she mentioned money he became incensed. "We've got the money we need now," he insisted angrily. "That's what I'm working my tail off for, isn't it? Don't bitch at me." Or did she still think he couldn't hold the job, didn't deserve it? "Look, do whatever the hell you want. But honestly, Janet, do I have to listen to this crap every evening?"

"And another thing that happened—I'm telling you, you wouldn't *believe* my day—I'd just finished cleaning when the dog got sick all over the rug and I—"

"Dammit," he exploded, more enraged than he ever dared show at the office, "I don't give a damn." He found himself yelling at her uncontrollably—except that, somewhere in the recesses of his mind, he knew it wasn't really uncontrollable. It was a release more than genuine rage, a letting off of the steam of his tensions. He rather enjoyed it. "I just don't care," he bellowed. "I don't want to hear."

Janet looked at him with hurt eyes. What right had he to shout at her like that? Hadn't she been through the same four years of his being out of work, the same deprivations, the same small humiliations by her friends? "Oh, darling, do let me pick up the check," they would say when they went out to lunch together. "I know how much of a struggle it is for you." Were they actually gloating, or was she getting paranoid about it? How painful it had been. In the end, she had simply stopped seeing most of her friends altogether.

"There's no need to yell, you know."

"I'm sorry." His apology was automatic; she knew he wasn't really apologizing at all. "It's just that your problems are so *unnecessary*. Every month now you're getting about ten thousand dollars. And that's net—after taxes and everything. On top of that, there'll be a bonus at the end of the year to build back our savings. Surely ten thousand a month ought to let us afford one lousy dryer." He loved rolling the sound of the money over his tongue. "Ten thousand dollars a month!" It was a higher salary than he'd ever earned in his life. Actually, it was fifteen before deductions. One hundred and eighty thou a year. He revelled in it.

"And the dog—"

"God damn the dog. Fuck the dog. Do whatever you want with the dog. Get a servant if you want. Get two."

But Janet Bagnew, sensible and frugal, was not convinced. She preferred to hoard the family finances against the possibility of another rainy day. There had been quite a few in the past. "I think maybe we should be a little conservative for a while," she said tactfully.

"You really don't believe I've got what it takes, do you?" This accusation, whether spoken or silent, was at the heart of every one of their arguments. "But you'll see, this time nothing can stop me." Not even Galsworthy and his friends, he wanted to add. I've got their number too.

"I understand," she said.

But of course she didn't. She knew nothing about how he'd gotten the job in the first place. Women like Janet never understood the realities, Simon thought. Hell, she just assumed someone called and gave you a job for a hundred and eighty grand. Just like that, with no compromises attached. How naïve could you get? But he'd beaten them, hadn't he? He could almost hear the relief in Galsworthy's voice when he'd called the next day and agreed to make the announcement.

"I'm glad you've made the right decision," Galsworthy had said. "It has to be a powerful convincing announcement, remember."

"Very well." Simon tried to sound guilt-wrenched.

"My colleagues feel strongly about that." Galsworthy had been just a shade too insistent.

He's losing his cool, Simon gloated. I'm getting the better of him. "I imagine you will be pleased," he replied.

There was nothing more Galsworthy could say, but Simon sensed that the headhunter had remained dissatisfied. Good! Keep the prick off balance.

"Look," he explained to Janet patiently, "I know you have a lot to do. But you're doing more than necessary. You can give up your job now, anytime you want."

"The moment you're employed? And have everyone think that the only reason I took it was because we needed—"

"Hush. It's been over three months. And you can always say you're quitting because you have to entertain for me."

"I guess." But Janet preferred to continue working a little longer. At least up to Christmas, she decided. It would make her feel better about all the money that Simon would undoubtedly spend on Christmas presents—especially for Susie. Not that the girl really wanted much. She liked clothes, of course, but not excessively fashionable things. And with her salary, she could afford anything she really wanted. What a good daughter she had turned out to be, Janet reflected. And how happy she seemed at her job. How much did that have to do with that David Fellows Susie seemed to talk about all the time? Perhaps he would turn out to be the right man for her. How wonderful, Janet thought. She hoped fervently that her daughter would find someone as good as Simon. Anyhow, Janet thought, switching the subject of her thoughts again, why not work? Simon was away half the time, either traveling or working late and staying in the city.

From Simon's point of view, it made sense to stay in New York. So often there were late meetings and business dinners to attend. Oh, and so many charity functions! Tonight, for example, the National Cancer Society was holding a big formal fund-raiser. Turner-LaMott, involved with medicine at many levels, always contributed substantially to cancer research. Arthur Hendrick, who had to approve all charitable donations, always clucked about them.

"I'm afraid we have no choice," Dr. Turner would argue. "It's the dues we have to pay to maintain our standing within the medical community."

Simon noted that Turner liked that argument. He wondered what that "standing" actually did for the company—or was it only Turner himself who benefited? Still, they'd always contributed to the cancer fund; it seemed right to continue.

"How much did we give last year?" Simon asked.

"Ten thousand, all told. But in three installments," Hendrick said fussily.

"Very well. Then let's give them five thousand for the dinner."

"That's rather generous." Hendrick was so shocked he made the mistake of interrupting his superior. "It makes us a 'sponsor.' Last year we only gave three thousand, enough to be a 'donor.'"

"Nevertheless"—Simon hated to be contradicted, particularly when there were others to hear—"better to give five thousand and get some recognition, than three and be left in the cold."

"Very well, sir."

With a donation of that size, and as president of Turner-LaMott, Simon had inevitably been invited to sit at the head table. That meant, of course, that there was no point in Janet's coming since they would not be able to sit together. Anyway, she hated these evenings, since she always worried so about what to wear that it drove them both to distraction.

When the invitation arrived, Simon complained. "I suppose I'll have to go," he told Turner with a great show of reluctance—and equally great secret pleasure.

"I could deputize for you if you prefer."

"Thank you, Winthrop. Most generous. But I really couldn't ask that of you."

Simon turned to the man standing just behind him as the procession to the head table formed. "One has to do this, doesn't one," he said conspiratorially.

"I rather enjoy it." The response amazed him. So crass! Simon hoped the man would not be his neighbor all through dinner—or at least that he would turn out to be more important than his superficial remark, naïve really, suggested.

"Ladies and gentlemen, would you please follow your leader onto the stage, and then remain standing behind your chairs for the invocation," the master of ceremonies instructed.

Suddenly, a small commotion. "Phew, only just made it!" A young woman excused her way down the line of waiting dignitaries. "Are you number four?" she asked Simon.

"Yes. Fourth in line."

"Ah, good. I'm five. I'm Sandra Maguire."

"Welcome," said Simon, trying not to stare. She was quite beautiful. "Pleased to have you as a dinner partner."

"Hello, Sandra." His naïve neighbor evidently knew her.

"Tony. How nice."

"We must stop meeting like this," he said facetiously. "Tongues will wag."

"My dear Tony, how flattered I would be to have tongues wagging about us," she responded flirtatiously.

What rotten luck, Simon was thinking. Against all the odds, he found himself placed next to a beautiful woman for dinner—only to find that she was old friends with his idiot neighbor. For she was indeed stunning. Her hair, falling with brilliantly coiffured casualness onto her shoulders; her pouting mouth, painted a startling red; and her evening gown, conservative but nevertheless, full of implications—all combined to make her breathtaking. She was surprisingly young too, Simon estimated, no more than thirty-two or -three. If only he could think of something quick-witted to say. He wracked his brain but remained tongue-tied. Damn, why couldn't he think of something smart as well as fitting. How he'd always admired men who could. Even in school, he'd been so envious of his friends' knack for making wisecracks—and using them to pick up girls. They made it seem so easy. Hell, he'd been a virgin until Janet took pity on him, and that only after they were engaged.

The line was moving. Simon pulled back his shoulders, mounted the stage and walked the length of the table. He found his place and turned to face the audience. On his right, he noticed, was a clergyman. How boring. Then Sandra glided up to stand on his left. She smiled at him, making it seem a private communication, as if the whole evening's performance were some sort of a joke only they shared. They stood quietly until the invocation was concluded.

"Please be seated, ladies and gentlemen," the dinner chairman invited. "Enjoy your food. Later, in retribution, we'll make you listen to speeches." There was a wave of laughter followed by what looked like total confusion on the floor of the ballroom as a thousand people moved back their chairs to be seated. Simon turned to Sandra to help her with hers only to find that the naïve Tony was already doing it.

"It's nice to relax," he said as soon as they were seated. Damn, he thought, that's not only boring but sounds neurotic too. "Meetings with everyone from unions to bankers," he tried to recover.

"Oh, don't I know it. I only wish I could put my feet up."

Simon pointed to the sea of guests below the head table. "I fear the pit would misunderstand."

His companion laughed. "Not what Mother would call appropriate," she agreed and smoothed her skirt more closely around her legs.

"Oh, I didn't mean . . ." Simon blushed and hated himself.

"Listen," she said, ignoring his discomfort, "I'm sure I know you from somewhere, but I've forgotten your name. How stupid of me. Do remind me what you do, and then I'll remember like a flash."

"No, not at all. I'm sure we've never met. I'd certainly remember you."

"How nice of you."

"I'm Simon Bagnew. I'm president of Turner-LaMott. The new president."

"Oh, but of course." She was immediately fascinated. "I read about your appointment. Oh maybe three months ago."

"Just about. You have an excellent memory."

"Thank you. What an interesting job. Such responsibility."

"It's a fair bit of work."

"And the best you can do for an evening off is to go to a charity dinner?" she teased. "Is that what you call relaxing?"

"One has to, doesn't one? But what about you? Surely this isn't your ideal either."

"Hardly."

"What do you do the rest of the time? I mean when you don't have your feet up."

"Oh, I run a little business," she said self-deprecatingly. "But it's nothing like Turner-LaMott. How many employees do you have?"

"Thirty thousand or so, around the world." Simon could feel his pride surge. "It *is* quite an undertaking."

"I know you sell Calmex. But . . ."

"Do you use it?"

"No." She smiled at him ambiguously. "I find there are better ways to get to sleep." She made the statement in such a flat voice that Simon wasn't sure what she meant. He didn't dare ask. There was a moment's pause. "What other products do you make?"

"Are you really interested?"

"Absolutely. Business is fascinating. It affects every part of our lives, doesn't it? It helps us live better, healthier. I hate the hypocrites who say they're against business, but live off it anyway."

"The biggest complainers about 'materialism' are the ones serving martinis from silver shakers."

"The two things I hate most," she said, mimicking an excessively refined accent, "are materialism and servants who won't clean the pool."

"Exactly," he laughed delightedly. What an enchanting woman! Gorgeous and sexy, yet intelligent and full of common sense, quite captivating. What a contrast to poor Janet, with her narrow experience, her unnecessary worries about money.

Dinner flew past. He had no idea what food they were eating until she commented on the rubber chicken.

"I think they're factory made," he replied. "An advanced form of genetic engineering." He felt most knowledgeable.

"But not yet perfected, it seems."

When dinner was over, they listened dutifully to the speeches, very conscious that, being at the head table, they were on display, with the audience able to observe their every expression. The whole time Simon was more aware of her perfume than of what was being said. She had invaded his nostrils, his eyes, his mind—he cared to perceive nothing but her.

Then the speeches were over. "Thank you all for attending this evening," the dinner chairman said. "And may I thank all those who so generously helped . . ."

"I hope you will let me give you a lift," Simon whispered. He was suddenly in a panic that her neighbor would offer her a lift before he could. "My car will be waiting downstairs."

"Of course," she whispered back. "I'd really appreciate it."

Sandra Maguire, mink casually draped, jewels glittering on bosom and fingers, was the sort of woman Simon Bagnew had always dreamed about but had never known. Bystanders gazed as she swept past. And when she entered into *his* limousine, and he hurriedly behind her, they stared at him with such obvious envy that he glowed. Let them eat their hearts out!

"Ahh," she let out a long sigh and leaned back into the cushions. "This is the life. I wish I had a limousine any time I wanted it." Their shoulders touched as the car accelerated, but she didn't move.

"Feel free to call on mine," he smiled at her. Very tentatively, as if by accident, he let his hand graze her knuckle.

"I will if you're not careful," she said, playfully catching his fingers. "And let you take the subway."

All too soon the car reached her apartment building. Gracefully she alighted. Simon pushed himself out of the car after her.

"Thank you so much for the ride," she said, looking up at him. "And for a far better evening than I ever anticipated." Then, to his unutterable delight, she kissed him quickly on the lips. For just a split second, he felt her body pressed against him. The building's doorman tactfully turned away. Then, before Simon really knew what had happened, she was gone. Reluctantly, he reentered his limousine. "We'd better go back to my apartment," he told his driver.

"Yes, sir."

All the way back, Simon had to fight not to grin like a schoolboy. What a girl! Of one thing he was damn sure, he told himself gleefully over and over, he'd sure see more of that one. A helluva lot more!

Sandra's apartment was filled with the sound of the final aria from *La Bohème*.

"Where've you been, Bella?" Spinosa called over the music without stopping his passionate conducting.

She walked over and kissed his neck. "Hooking a toad, my love," she said with a look of mild distaste.

14

"Dammit, I see no need for such an undignified arrangement." For once, Oliver Chapin's exasperation was uncontrolled. "There must be a better place to meet than in a taxi." He was seated behind his gleaming mahogany partner's desk—circa 1830. It was immense but, even so, barely large enough for the enormous office. "Why can't he come here? Up the private elevator; and you arrange for the corridors to be empty." Oliver was at his most military.

"Too much risk, sir. You just can't afford to be seen together," Sidney Rosenberg explained. "We'll be sailing close to the wind on the stock market regulations issue as it is. So they'll be looking for trouble. If there's even a breath of suspicion that you and Spinosa are associated, the whole scheme would smash, and they'd have you in jail. I'm sorry, sir, I know it would be more comfortable, but I'm afraid the meeting just can't be here."

"Very practical," Oliver agreed, but with the distaste of a saint forced to witness the sins of the world. "So why not the New York safe house?"

"It's possible. But quite a waste for just one meeting. It took a lot of organization to make it safe—lots of middlemen, false deeds, shell companies so that it can't be traced back. Pity to blow it if we don't have to. And once Spinosa knows about it, we might as well put your name on the door."

Oliver grunted. "Very well," he agreed reluctantly. "I'll approve the taxi scheme."

"I'm afraid you'll be a little squashed on the floor," Sidney started tentatively. He was rather enjoying the thought of the Deacon being forced into such an undignified position. Still, he made a mental note, he'd better make damn sure the floor was perfectly clean, polished.

"Why me, not him?"

That was the crux, of course. Neither man would be pleased to lie at the other's feet. "The first one in has to lie down," Rosenberg explained, "so that the second one seems to be riding alone."

"Obviously."

"But to risk having you riding around alone in a taxi doesn't seem like a good idea. It's not very likely that anyone would see you. But if one of Pollo's boys did happen to—and most of them would recognize you right away—he might start to wonder. After all, it's not your normal pattern. So, on general principles, he'd probably try to follow the car. Of course, most likely we'd spot him. Still, some of them are pretty good and if we didn't he might be there when the other man got out of the cab—"

"Enough," Oliver stopped his lieutenant. "My boy," he said magnanimously, "I should have known you'd have all the answers." It was as close as Oliver Chapin ever came to a compliment. Sidney Rosenberg was delighted.

The taxi—one of a New York fleet owned by a Chapin-controlled transportation and parking garage firm—picked Oliver up quite casually in an empty midtown street. Although the pickup was by prearrangement, no observer would have realized that, for Oliver seemed to be hailing a cab in the normal way. Then, when the driver was quite sure no other car was in sight, and no pedestrian even casually observing, Oliver lowered himself laboriously onto the floor of the cab and the driver switched his meter off and his off-duty sign on. As far as anyone could see from the outside, the cab was empty and on its way home.

The taxi driver switched his off-duty sign off again as he turned east onto Eighty-second Street—but only after making sure there were no pedestrians who might want to flag him down. Thus, when half a block later Spinosa flagged the cab down, no one could have guessed he was doing so for any extraordinary purpose. Sid had used the arrangement before. On this occasion, as on the previous ones, it worked perfectly.

Carlos Spinosa seated himself comfortably in the taxi without even glancing down. He was thoroughly enjoying the incongruity of having the powerful Oliver Chapin at his feet. He said not a word until the cab was well underway and there could be no chance of his being observed.

"Good evening," he said at length, his tone as formal as if they were virtual strangers meeting in, say, a bank. The pointed politeness of the greeting, the tacit assumption that this situation was quite normal for Oliver, was so subtle a slight that Oliver could sense the barb without being able to pinpoint it. Spinosa leaned back more comfortably and lit up one of his Brazilian cheroots, perhaps the only habit he had carried over from his previous life.

From his ludicrous position on the floor of the taxi, Oliver Chapin had no opportunity for the subtleties of negotiation. How had he ever let Rosenberg convince him this was a good idea? Absurd. How could a man possibly win a debate like this? "Look here, Spinosa, we'd better make this fast. I'm damned uncomfortable here, and I'm not anxious to draw this meeting out."

"Very well." Spinosa was quite enjoying himself.

"It seems we're making very little progress." The car lurched to the left, pushing Oliver's head against the door. "Damn," he said to no one in particular. "The point is," he added, "I don't see much happening."

"But it is," Spinosa drew on his cigar, noting that they were just pulling onto the upper level of the Fifty-ninth Street Bridge. Evidently, the driver was being especially careful: there would be no pedestrians here to peer into the taxi, and at this time of day not much traffic either. Fine by him, Spinosa decided. You could never be too careful. He shifted his feet, bumping Oliver. "Oh, I do beg your pardon," he apologized. "I keep forgetting you're at my feet, so to speak."

If the remark was intended to annoy Oliver, it did. But the effect was entirely different than Spinosa had anticipated. Instead of the older man becoming angrier and less in control of himself—thereby providing Spinosa with a bargaining edge—he became icily calm.

"What progress?" he demanded, his voice soft.

"I've explained to you about the technology."

"Yes."

"It's the key, of course."

"I know."

"And we have our man, Simon Bagnew, in place."

"You've tested him?"

"Indeed. Your headhunter gave him his first assignment. He accepted it readily."

Oliver merely grunted.

"You're unconvinced?"

"Depends. The fact that Bagnew did one thing you asked doesn't mean much. What do we have on him, to make sure he stays in line?" Oliver had learned very young to hedge his bets. Always have a way to force a man if you have to. The best thing was if you could threaten him with disgrace; that was how they'd had Galsworthy all these years. Disgrace was neat and tidy, no need to wipe up any traces afterwards. More effective than violence, although more difficult to arrange. The only thing better was threatening a man's loved ones. The only trouble was that these days you never quite knew who they were, with all this living together and trial marriage . . .

Spinosa interrupted his thoughts. "He's weak. Frightened of losing his job."

Oliver considered. Would this fellow Bagnew think losing his job was a disgrace? Stupid. But he might. Oliver couldn't be sure. And if he wasn't sure, then it wasn't good enough. "Not enough," he summarized his thoughts.

"The headhunter assures us—"

"Assures us? A gambler like Galsworthy? And if one day he assures us differently?"

"I agree." Spinosa was impressed by Chapin's cynical intuition. Not many people impressed him these days—a good thing Chapin was on his side. One wouldn't want this cherubic little man with the white horseshoe of hair surrounding a pink pate as an enemy. "I agree," he said again. "So I've added a second string."

"Yes?"

"The toad's falling in love with one of my people."

"Is that what you call him, toad? That's good," Oliver chortled. It was an entirely incongruous sound emanating from the floor of a taxi cruising through Queens. Spinosa, who saw nothing funny in the world, glanced down at the rippling belly of Oliver Chapin and tried to understand why he was laughing. He failed. "Man or woman?" Oliver asked.

"Huh? Oh, woman. Bagnew's not gay."

"I wasn't sure."

Spinosa didn't reply.

"It's a start," Oliver conceded. He still wished they had more on Bagnew. Perhaps if he really fell in love with Spinosa's operative, they could use her. They could send the toad—what a lovely name—one of her nipples as a warning if he didn't cooperate. That would probably impress him. Oliver wondered whether Spinosa would object. If he did, they could always send her other one to him. This time Oliver chuckled very softly to himself at the thought. "Well then, that's good enough," Oliver agreed. "You know what I want?" he demanded, suddenly changing the subject. "I mean from the whole deal?"

"Of course."

"So tell me again. I don't want any misunderstandings." Oliver loved repetition. It reassured him, made things seem safe. He always insisted that his assistants repeat what he had told them. Even Rosenberg had to go through the drill. They all hated it, of course . . . it made them feel like children again. No doubt, Spinosa would resent it too. "So tell me again," Oliver repeated.

Spinosa hesitated. Should he accept this rather demeaning demand and appear obsequious—or refuse and risk seeming rude, or worse, petulant? He certainly didn't want to back out of the deal. It was much too good: using only the Chapin group's money—but with the profits, enormous profits, split equally. Only a fool would turn it down. So Spinosa would humor the older man at his feet, but not too far. Once you let Oliver Chapin think you were owned by him, he'd kill you. Carlos Spinosa decided to compromise.

"Control," he said, answering Oliver's question. A one-word answer could hardly be construed as too accommodating, but nevertheless it was clear.

"Right, my friend." Oliver's voice was at its most ecclesiastic. *Benedictus, benedicat per* Oliver Chapin . . . very dangerous indeed. "That's exactly what I want: control. I don't give a damn about their technology, or their real estate, or any of the rest of it. All I want is to do what *I* want to do, without interference. I'm sure you understand."

Carlos Spinosa looked down at his partner on the floor. "I've understood that all along," he said. His voice sounded so superior that the driver, a long-time employee of Oliver's, was worried that his boss might blow. It only happened occasionally, but when it did, the explosion was immense. The muscles at the back of the driver's neck tensed and his hand started to move to where he always kept a gun.

"Good, good. That's good," Oliver said, still blessing the multitude.

The driver relaxed.

"I'd hate there to be any misunderstanding, you know."

Spinosa remained silent.

"You see, as I told you, one of my associates is in the pharmaceutical business too. We're more specialized than your Turner-LaMott people, but some of our stuff is similar to your Calmex. Except ours is purer." He chortled pleasantly. "I imagine you never thought of that," he said, pleased with his point. "The government says your stuff can't be above a certain strength, whereas ours is virtually undiluted."

"Interesting point."

"But we do have a few supply difficulties," Oliver continued. "So if we get control, as we discussed, there'll be fewer problems all around."

"I'm aware of your interest in a takeover," Spinosa said

coolly, "at the right price and with control. That's what we're working on."

"Then you'd better know I am very keen on it. Very keen indeed."

"I know that too. And you're willing to pay a lot of money."

"If the price is right . . . a hundred million dollars to start."

"But that's only to start," Carlos interjected quickly. He didn't want to leave Chapin under any illusions. "It'll cost a lot more later. At least another three or four hundred million on top of that. But, of course, you'll get it back."

"For control, my friend," said Oliver Chapin softly. "For control of the right company—without the Feds looking over my shoulder every ten seconds—for control of a worldwide pharmaceutical company like Turner-LaMott, Mr. Spinosa, we'll put in whatever money it takes."

Susan Bagnew was bursting with laughter watching David Fellows, whom she was learning to admire more every day, trying to rig up a new experiment.

"Oh for goodness sake, you look as if you're trying to get bacon rind into a bird feeder! Here, let me do it." Deftly she rigged the appliance together. "How can you be so brilliant and so impractical at the same time?" She smiled at him warmly. "You do need looking after."

"Yes, I imagine so," David's mind was far away. "If this works, do you realize we shall have found a way to catalyze their metabolism to double its norm?"

"They'll eat garbage twice as fast?"

"Yes, but what's important to us is . . ."

But Susan already thought she knew what was really important to them. And it had nothing to do with garbage. Genetic engineering? Maybe. She smiled to herself.

She could feel herself becoming excited. Soon she would explain it quite clearly to David, she decided.

Mrs. Chapin had arranged for the cook to prepare beef Wellington tonight. It was Oliver's favorite, particularly when it was very rare. She had left word at his office to that effect. Maybe it would entice him home—it sometimes worked, more often than anything else. And if not, why, the cook made excellent Wellington and she would certainly enjoy it herself.

Sidney Rosenberg had found a new "instructor" for the gymnasium. Oliver wanted to try her out this evening. He only hoped she'd stand up better than the last girl; Sid didn't need two fiascos back-to-back. Still, if he were lucky, the boss mightn't go after all. Sid had just received a coded message for him. "Wellington tonight," it said. Sidney Rosenberg resented not being told what it meant.

Janet Bagnew had finally decided to buy a dryer. This business of the old one not working was getting to be too much. Now it was a question of which replacement machine would be the best value. She wondered whether the repair shop would give her a special deal. They should, considering the trouble they'd put her to. She was looking forward to Simon coming home. He'd be pleased she'd made the decision, proud of himself that they could afford it.

Briefly she wondered why she was still having such trouble accepting that he'd keep the job. There was something about him that bothered her, something he hadn't confided in her perhaps. She couldn't put her finger on it, but the uneasiness remained. "Better forget it, girl," she admonished herself out loud. "If you love him enough, it will work out okay." That's what all the romances she read insisted. And she chose to accept their view. "And I do," she assured the old dryer before hurrying out to find its replacement.

In the Turner-LaMott Corporation, business was as usual. Secretaries typed memoranda in triplicate ordering the purchase of raw materials; the purchasing department bought what was ordered from hundreds of suppliers from Istanbul to Tokyo; factories synthesized and refined pills and powders, and then bottled them faster than the eye could follow; and giant trucks delivered the merchandise at top speed, either directly to customer's warehouses, or to airports from which it would be flown to the far corners of the earth. And on none of these transactions did Oliver Chapin as yet make a penny.

But if he and Carlos Spinosa and Sidney Rosenberg had their way, that would all change before very long.

"Join me for a sandwich?" Simon asked. Jim Lester and he were alone together in Simon's office, Jim on the couch surrounded by piles of papers and computer printouts, Simon in shirt sleeves behind his desk.

"I'd better. I'll starve to death before I extricate myself. Thanks." Jim's grin was open and friendly. "At least we seem to be making progress." He pointed to the papers. "I'm glad you insisted we delve a bit. Good for the soul. There are parts of the growth plan I think I really understand for the first time."

"And some that won't work?"

Jim Lester hesitated. Was Simon attacking? No, he decided, his new boss was not a devious man. It was a fair question. "Oh sure," he agreed. "The new-products program for one. It looks way overstated. Not that the figures don't make sense. That's why I've not really been aware of the problem before. They seem fine. But when you dig underneath like this, I'm not sure the support is there. What new products are we actually talking about three years out?"

Simon Bagnew smiled at his executive V.P. with the greatest pleasure. That was just the question he'd been waiting for. "Well, there I disagree," he said with full emphasis.

"Really?" Jim Lester was surprised. His boss was rarely so emphatic. "Why?"

"Because the new technology on the garbage-to-oil conversion they have out at TULIPS is stunning."

"But is it practical?"

"Ah, that's the question," Simon agreed. "I think it is. But I would really appreciate it if you would look at it for yourself and draw your own conclusion. I'd like corroboration."

"Fine." Jim Lester was flattered by the request. "I'll get to it right away."

"What would you like?"

"Huh? Oh, the sandwich. I thought you were still on new products. Can I have a pastrami on rye? Or would dear Agatha think that was too déclassé?"

Simon laughed. "Probably. My secretary has clearly defined views on the appropriate. I think I'll join you—then we can really watch her puff disapproval!"

"Puff?"

"Oh yes. Like an annoyed pouter pigeon. Terribly dignified, feathers all puffed out, head high, clucking. It's rather comical—and very annoying!"

"We'll have to get you someone new."

"I've tried. No one wants Agatha, even though she's efficient enough. And I haven't the heart to let her go. She must predate LaMott!"

Jim smiled at Simon. He really was a decent man, he reflected again. Most new CEOs coming in wouldn't think twice about firing a secretary. And once you got under the pomposity, Simon wasn't bad at his job either.

"It's just that he's so *boring*," Jim had complained to his wife. "I'll never be able to stand it."

"I know, love," Mary Lester sympathized deeply. After twenty years with the company—and five in the top spot under Fossey—*he* should have been president instead of some ugly little fellow like Bagnew. "It's just not fair."

"I know it's not Simon's fault that the board decided to go for an outsider. It's just . . ." Jim Lester hated his own feeling of pique and refused to put it into words; jealousy was such a petty feeling.

"Why not try it a while longer?" Mary not only understood, she shared both this disappointment and his envy. He *should* have had the job . . . and she the prestige that went with being the president's wife. Okay, so that wasn't a very worthy emotion to have, she admitted to herself. But she was human, they both were, and she felt jealous as hell. On the other hand—her careful Maine upbringing asserted itself—there was no point in being hasty. "After all, if you stay a year you won't have lost anything," she advised. "And there has to be a good chance Simon Bagnew won't stay."

"What ever makes you think that?" Jim had asked sharply. "Why wouldn't he?"

"I don't know. It's just that I still don't quite understand how he got chosen. . . . I still think there must be something we don't know."

"Maybe."

It had been good advice, Jim now reflected as he ate his sandwich and politely pretended to listen as Simon started into one of his sermons.

"In my experience . . ."

Those words were a clear warning for Jim to tune out and fantasize about something else.

". . . there is always a valid potential . . ."

In spite of Simon's verbosity, Jim decided, he was basically likeable and sound.

". . . develop a base-line capability schedule . . ."

Still, Mary was right, nothing he had learned about Simon Bagnew explained why or how he had actually got the job.

15

"It is an honor to present to you the Turner-LaMott story." Simon Bagnew was at the speaker's rostrum, before him the members of one of the most prestigious business clubs in New York. "We have some exciting news to announce today."

Senior reporters, men and women representing such publications as the *Wall Street Journal, The London Financial Times,* and *The New York Times,* were invited to the club's activities only on special occasions. This was one. There was an expectant rustle in the room. Pencils were at the ready.

Firmly in control of his audience, Simon was enjoying himself immensely. What a sense of power to have them hanging on his every word. He poured himself a glass of water to extend the suspense.

"Our announcement is," he recommenced, watching the reporter from the *Journal* quite literally move forward to the edge of his chair, "that the Turner-LaMott Company is in the final stages of developing breakthrough technology that, if it is successful, will have considerable long-term impact on both energy supply *and* on solid waste pollution control." Simon glanced at Morgan Galsworthy who had come to make sure today's performance went as ordered. "Thus, the new technology should most favorably impact the fortunes of our company."

The pencils flew. Morgan Galsworthy, Simon noted, grinned.

"I do not wish to overstate the case, however," Simon continued. He was pleased to see the smile evaporate from Galsworthy's face. "It is, of course, possible that the technology we have developed will not turn out to be practical, that our system cannot be made to work. But I believe that we have a very good chance of success."

Galsworthy's smile returned. "As you know, Turner-LaMott is a conservative company." Simon was reveling in the sensation he was causing, but even more because he knew what he was saying was the complete truth. If he had harbored even the slightest doubt, it had been dispelled by Susan who, now that she knew that Simon was aware of the new technology, would not stop talking about it—or about David Fellows either. "Moreover," Simon continued, "those of you who know me personally will realize that I share that conservatism. Thus, you will appreciate that, although we are not certain of success, I would not be talking to you today were I not sanguine about the prospects."

Simon noted that Morgan Galsworthy was sitting back in his chair now, entirely relaxed. For a moment, Simon wished he had had reason to defy the man. But there was none. . . . Oh, but what if it hadn't been the truth? Would he have had the guts to defy Galsworthy then? He had tried hard to convince himself he would. There were more important things than just having a job, weren't there? Of course he'd be tempted, but in the end he'd do the right thing. Wouldn't he. . . ? In his heart, he had doubted it.

"The new technology on which we are working is a genetically engineered microorganism which can convert cellulose to protein—and, as part of the same process, protein to oil." There was a rustle of astonishment from the audience. Several reporters started to move toward the door, anxious to be close to the nearest telephone.

"Wait, there is more." Bagnew stopped then. "Let me ask you to consider the garbage you put out of your house this morning."

There was another rustle of questions from the audience. What was the man talking about?

"That garbage consists largely of paper and other forms of cellulose; and of waste foodstuffs, largely fats and proteins. Those components represent the heart of all our nation's solid waste. The only other substantial components of garbage are plastic, metal and glass. But if the cellulose and protein in our dumps could be converted to oil—and of course be combined with the fats and oils already in the garbage—then the remaining solid materials could easily be filtered out—and, at least the metal, could be economically reclaimed." Simon Bagnew paused to give his next sentence the maximum impact. "At Turner-LaMott," he said, "we believe we know how to make oil from garbage...."

Instantly there was pandemonium in the audience. Reporters knocked over chairs in their eagerness to rush to the telephones. The noise level rose to a roar. Within minutes the news would be on the ticker tapes. By tomorrow morning it would be headlined in every newspaper in America and the world. Simon Bagnew glowed with triumph. "Thank you, ladies and gentlemen. Thank you all for coming." He had to shout into the microphone to make himself heard.

Still exalted from the sensation he had made—a perfectly justified sensation, as he kept repeating to himself ecstatically—Simon stepped down from the rostrum.

From the corner of his eye he noticed Carlos Spinosa heading in his direction. Good. No doubt even that rather sinister and frightening man would be pleased today.

Carlos reached him moving very fast. Expectantly, Simon smiled. But Carlos continued to move, pulling Simon roughly to one side. His face, Simon suddenly realized, was contorted with anger. The applause was still continuing. "What are you, some sort of fucking loudmouth?" Spinosa demanded. "Who told you to brag about our technology?"

Simon, who had been feeling truly confident for the first time in years, could only gape at him in astonishment. His whole world seemed to be crashing again—and at the very moment of his greatest success. "But, I thought . . ."

"Don't think, little man. Just do as you're told." Spinosa started to turn away.

"But I *was* told—"

"I'll call you later," Spinosa overrode him furiously. "Don't do anything till then. But you'd better be ready to put this mess right."

"But Morgan Galsworthy—"

"Listen, Bagnew, Galsworthy works for me. I know goddamn well what he told you, you double-crossing little bastard. Don't you lie to me."

As rapidly as he had approached, Spinosa was gone. Bagnew, his head awhirl, his stomach churning, was left mechanically to accept the congratulations of the dozens of well-wishers, to try to answer the questions of the reporters who, having filed their main stories, were anxious for further elucidation.

How he managed to get out of the room and back to his office, Simon could not later remember. He did recall that, riddled with astonishment and panic, he almost fainted on the way. What had he done wrong, he kept asking himself? How could he have so misunderstood? And what should he do now?

He slumped in his office chair, head down, feeling as exhausted as if he had just completed a marathon. But when the telephone rang, such was his anxiety that he snatched at it immediately, jumping to his feet as he did so.

"Morgan Galsworthy here," the headhunter said, his voice full of syrup. "You do realize, don't you, that it is Carlos Spinosa, not Foster Harrison, who controls Turner-LaMott?"

"Yes, of course," Simon said weakly. "But I did exactly what you told me."

"Come now, little man," Galsworthy's voice was dripping with condescension and sarcasm. "That won't work. Who do you think will believe such a foolish lie? Why would I tell you to do just the opposite of what Carlos told me to tell you? After all, I work for the man."

"But . . ."

"But nothing. You have one more chance. Otherwise you'll be on the bread line for the rest of your life. And for good measure, I doubt whether dear Susan would keep her job much longer either. And then, of course, there is the question of Janet's so-called career at the bank. That might become a little rocky too. Or didn't you know that Spinosa is its single biggest depositor?"

Completely confused, overwhelmed, utterly demoralized, Simon capitulated. "Of course I'll do anything Mr. Spinosa tells me," he said weakly, wondering whether he was losing his mind.

"Mr. Spinosa wishes you to retract."

"I'm not sure I can. We would lose enormous credibility . . . probably be subject to government investigation . . ."

"Obviously, you are to do so in such a way that the retraction is plausible."

"But . . ."

"Mr. Spinosa insists," Galsworthy said, his voice icy. "You have only a few weeks." He hung up.

Simon Bagnew couldn't bear the thought of going home and listening to Janet's recital of the day's problems. That would be just too much. He couldn't stay in town either; it was Friday evening and Janet would expect him home. Compromising, he decided that, even though it was already eight, he'd stop off at Grand Central Station to have a couple of drinks. They turned to four. By the time he arrived home it was eleven, his clothes were disheveled and he had vomited up his guts. By that time, too, he was quite desperate.

"I'm drunk," were his first words. "And partly sober again. And I've got to talk to you."

Janet Bagnew had suspected that Simon was drinking when it had become later and later without his calling. But when he turned to her with such anguish written into every line of his face, she knew that the weight she had sensed on him all along was now close to crushing him.

"First sit down," she said sensibly. "Take your shoes off. I'll make coffee. Then you'd better tell me all about it."

"Yes," he agreed, "I'd better tell you. But it's too late. Too late." The words slurred and she was afraid he would break down and weep.

"Rubbish."

"You'll see."

"First coffee," she insisted. "Go into the living room and try to relax."

Thank God, Susan would probably not be home tonight. The last thing Janet wanted was for her to see Dad in this state.

"He doesn't know it yet, Mother," Susan had confided earlier in the evening, "but David's right on the point of falling for me!" She had been quite gleeful. "And tonight's the night I've decided he's going to find out!" She had hugged herself, quite glowing in her excitement. "So don't wait up for me. I probably won't be home till the middle of the weekend. We're going camping! I haven't done that in years, but he loves it. Oh, and there's going to be a full moon." She giggled.

At the time, Janet had been shocked, not by the facts of Susan's decision—surely at twenty-two no one could expect her to be celibate, let alone a virgin—but by the quite outrageous sexuality she beamed out. Now Janet was merely thankful Susan was away.

It took at least an hour for Simon—sipping coffee and sobering rapidly—to tell the story. Talking disjointedly at first, and then with greater and greater lucidity, he explained. Occasionally, when she wasn't quite sure of a nuance, or he hadn't recounted a conversation clearly enough, she would ask him to repeat. The rest of the time she nodded her head and made occasional sounds of sympathy and comprehension.

It was well after midnight when the story was done. Simon, still disheveled, was sober again. He sat with Janet on their living room sofa. Each had an arm around the other, for both physical and emotional comfort and support. They had each other, their pose suggested, but that was all they had. For all the world, they looked like a middle-aged version of Hansel and Gretel lost in the woods. Around them was the wicked forest full of dangerous beasts ready to devour.

Janet took hold of herself first. What Simon had said was catastrophic, of course. But, as she thought about it, there was still something missing.

"I'm afraid I still don't fully understand," she started.

"Well, I've told you—"

"No, I understand what you've said," she explained more firmly now. "I just don't understand why Spinosa doesn't want you to boost the company stock. That's exactly what he should want for a few months, even if later he wants to push it down again."

"Well, he doesn't," said Bagnew, suddenly angry in his utter frustration—angry at her, of course, since no other target could possibly exist.

"What can you do?" she asked gently, understanding him fully and taking no offense.

"How the hell do I know?"

"Do you have to do anything for the moment?"

"I suppose not. Galsworthy said make a retraction. But he's led me wrong before. And Spinosa said to do nothing till I hear from him."

"And then?"

"I'll have to talk to Spinosa. I can't retract. Maybe a press release, that my speech was exaggerated. But there's no way I could back down entirely without the SEC investigating us—and Spinosa and the directors—five ways from Sunday."

"So you'll have to tell him that retraction's impossible."

"I know that, oh, don't I know. But that's not what Spinosa wants to hear. He's angrier than you could imagine that I made the announcement. And he's the one that controls the company." He paused, looking at Janet pleadingly, plaintively. "He controls my job. And Susan's. Even yours. Don't you understand? He controls our *lives*. I just *can't* let him fire us all."

———16

In a thousand stockbrokers' offices all over the world the ticker-tape machines recorded and transmitted a constant stream of transactions in Turner-LaMott shares. It was the most active stock on the New York Stock Exchange the day after Simon Bagnew's speech. Within half an hour of opening, the stock had jumped from twenty dollars a share—the value at which it had been embedded for the past two years—to thirty. By eleven, over four million shares had been traded. Brokers were burning up the telephone wires to their favorite customers, advising them and suggesting they jump onto the band wagon.

On the floor of the New York Stock Exchange itself the specialist in TLM, the stock market's code for the company's shares, was more than earning his keep trying to keep the stock orderly. In the offices of the big institutional investors—the insurance companies, investment funds, larger pension groups—young hotshots were either congratulating themselves on having got in early or quickly inventing excuses why they had not.

Quite by coincidence, one of the new investors—but not one of the earliest—was Caro Pollo. His broker reached him shortly before noon. "Turner-LaMott looks hot. It's at twenty-eight, up from twenty. I'd suggest we buy heavy."

"Why the fuck didn't you get me in at twenty?" Pollo demanded, as usual, violent about missing any opportunity.

"Been trying to get hold of you all morning." It was an exaggeration, but true that he had called once shortly after ten. "Now if I had discretionary authority . . ." It was an old debate between them: but even after doing business with him for ten years, Pollo would never let the broker make an investment without first checking. "But, of course, I understand. Funds aren't always, er, free." His tone was purposely condescending. He knew from experience how to goad his man into a large purchase.

"Shit, man," Pollo drawled importantly, "that's not the problem. I just don't want no one fuckin' with my money." He paused impressively. "Buy twenty grands' worth," he said and hung up.

The customer's man smiled as he placed the order. The commission on that was easily worth risking a few insults.

For a while longer, Turner-LaMott gave all signs of being one of those runaway stocks that the administrators of the Stock Exchange worry about and that a phalanx of Securities and Exchange Commission lawyers, charged with avoiding illegal stock manipulation, view with undiluted suspicion. But in spite of the continuing huge demand for TLM stock, most surprisingly the price surge seemed to hit a ceiling at slightly above thirty dollars.

During the afternoon, the transactions on TLM continued fast-paced. But its price now only inched ahead. By the end of the day, about ten million shares had been traded at an average price of about thirty-two dollars. The closing price was almost exactly on the average. Thus, investors from all over the world had bought over three hundred million dollars of TLM stock that day and, of course, other investors had sold as much.

In order to become a member of the Beaver Brook Country Club in Westchester County, you required no sponsor, no official introduction, and no other form of social entree. All you had to do was to be acceptable to the manager (and, strangely, men who weren't rarely thought to apply), post a ten thousand dollar bond, and pay annual dues of half that much promptly. Any payment delay caused automatic and immediate expulsion. And expulsion was enforced by some very fierce guards stationed around the walled perimeter of the club day and night—and reinforced rather effectively on the midnight-to-seven shift by even fiercer guard dogs. The club's policy appealed only to certain groups of potential members, those who cared more about privacy than expense; but to them it appealed a great deal.

In all other respects, except one, however, the club was

a standard affluent golf club complete with deep pile rugs, an overstocked bar, expensive, imitation antique furniture finished in steel-hard synthetic wood, and a luxurious dining room dotted with ship's lamps and ornate planters. That one exception was that both the grounds and the club itself had as many secret entrances as a rabbit warren. One, a secret passage, led from the back room of a local Italian restaurant—a room which, in turn, was reached through a passage that led past the characteristic odor of the men's room and through a door marked Strictly Private. Keep Out. Another was through an ivy-covered door in the club's perimeter wall and thence up a narrow, thickly hedged path. Yet a third came directly from a quadrangle on the roof which was marked in white circles for helicopters and walled in against observation. Each of these entrances led to one or another private meeting room equipped, as necessity required, with boardroom table, bar, bed or any combination thereof.

It was in such a room, this one furnished with a small round conference table and a fully equipped bar, that three contrasting men were gathered. By common consent, they ignored the table and instead sat in three arm chairs pulled close together in one corner of the room. One man, tall, lean and unusually handsome, was dressed in light flannels and a superbly tailored blazer. Next to him, dumped into his chair like a duffel bag and looking very serious, a cherubic-faced elderly man sat, attired in an old gray pullover. He looked as if he would be more at home on a religious retreat or perhaps a convention of Unitarian ministers discussing values' clarification. The third, somehow the most incongruous of all, was dressed in a business suit, white shirt and tie. Each had arrived by a different entrance, had poured himself a drink, and was ready for a concentrated wrap-up of the day's events. It was nine in the evening and each planned to leave no later than ten-thirty.

"I am satisfied with our transactions," Carlos Spinosa started the meeting's business, adjusting an invisible crease in his blazer. His voice was as gravelly and mechanized as ever, but there could be no doubt of his inner excitement.

"If you say so, Carlos," Oliver Chapin slumped farther into his seat. He had a fairly good idea of the dimension of his profit from Sid Rosenberg's estimate earlier in the day. But he was waiting, cautious as usual, for the full facts before expressing any view at all.

"I say so." Spinosa seemed supremely confident.

"What are the facts, then?" Sid Rosenberg leaned forward in his chair.

"We've been buying TLM slowly but steadily for three months as you know."

"I know." Oliver's voice was unusually acerbic. "It cost me close to two hundred million." He savored the amount on his tongue as a connoisseur might savor an unusually fine and valuable wine.

"There was a great deal of depth to the stock, and of course we bought carefully, all over the world."

"Your assignment was to do just that." Oliver was not willing to allow Spinosa any credit for what had previously been agreed. No point in allowing him leeway to reopen negotiations. The deal had been made.

"As a result, we managed to buy about ten million shares," Spinosa continued as if Oliver had not interrupted at all, "at an average price of about twenty dollars. Today, with the huge buying surge, we were able to sell almost the entire amount at about thirty."

"Good." It was an almost involuntary sigh of relief from Rosenberg.

Oliver looked at him blandly. "You seem as satisfied as Carlos," he said, and Sid realized with a shock that he was being reprimanded for allowing his feelings to show. No player of bluffs or poker, no major deal-worker, should ever allow himself that luxury, he knew. And Oliver was nowhere if not in the major leagues of deal-making . . . but the profit *was* colossal.

"Ten dollars a share profit," Carlos was continuing. He paused to let the drama heighten. "In all," he said in his grating monotone, "Chapin Investments cleared a profit of over ninety-five million dollars today." He didn't bother to add that he had sold out his own investments in Turner-LaMott at the same time and thus also reaped a pleasant fifteen-million-dollar profit for himself.

"Obviously a nice performance, old man," Oliver Chapin agreed graciously. "But I feel I must remind you that our interest is to get control. Of course we appreciate a profit, Carlos. And we're pleased to pay your commission. Ten percent, I believe I said: nine point five million. Plus, of course, the profit you made on your own earlier investment, which wasn't going anywhere. Another fifteen, perhaps?" He smiled benignly. "No, no," he said, as if someone were disagreeing with him, "I don't begrudge you a penny of that." He paused. "But we mustn't lose sight of our objective." So admonishing and school-marmish was his tone that Sidney half expected him to wag his finger at Carlos Spinosa. "We mustn't forget that we want control . . . and, so far, it seems to me, between us we no longer own a single share."

"Indeed, indeed." The fact that Carlos Spinosa repeated a word was as sure a sign of his continuing excitement as anything could possibly have been. "But you know the plan. This is only the first step."

"I have heard it," Oliver Chapin acknowledged. "But I have yet to see it." He sat so far back in his armchair that his feet were barely able to reach the ground. "You see Carlos, you invested over two hundred million in the stock market and made what is, I believe, called a killing. Now, no doubt you had that all preplanned. I was impressed by that because I don't like anything that smacks of speculation. We leave that sort of thing to fellows like that Galsworthy." He beamed at Spinosa. "Gambling is not for Chapin Investments."

Spinosa's patience reached its end. "Look," he said evenly, without any change in inflection, but for all that venomously, "you made almost a hundred million dollars profit. Now, when the toad makes his retraction, as we agreed, the price of the stock will fall. That's when I'll want the original two hundred million, plus your profits, plus more than that to buy back TLM shares. Don't worry, it's going as I planned."

Oliver Chapin's smile became as broad and warm as if he were christening a newborn. "Oh no," he said, sounding quite shocked at the very suggestion, "I don't worry at all . . ."

Neither Carlos Spinosa nor Sidney Rosenberg failed to understand that the completion of that sentence, had it been necessary to utter it, would have been ". . . but you'd better."

Beaver Brook, from which the country club borrowed its name, originated from a spring located in a valley some ten miles distant, as the crow flies, from the club itself. The valley was a nature preserve and so isolated that few people knew about it. Even the campsite, which was open to the public all summer, rarely had more than one or two campers. And it was quite large enough to provide privacy, isolation even, to those few who did camp there. Apart from the brook itself there was no other connection with the country club, and certainly on this wonderful summer evening no greater distance could be imagined than between the suspicious greed of the three men gathered in their secret club room and the generous sharing of the two young people pitching their tent in an enchanting copse at the edge of the valley.

"How did you find this place?" Susan Bagnew asked, as

she sat cross-legged, struggling to hammer a tent peg into the rocky ground.

"It's lovely isn't it?" David Fellows agreed. He was still in a daze that this beautiful girl was with him at all.

"By geologic survey, I assume!"

"Oh the rocks. Sorry . . ."

"It is beautiful," she agreed. "And who cares if our tent falls down."

"I do," he said promptly. Then, regarding her with renewed amazement, he said, "How come you're here?"

"You didn't want to go camping all alone, did you?"

"I didn't know I wanted to go camping at all!"

Susan looked up laughing at him, and promptly hit her thumb with the hammer. "Ouch. Damn. Also more than that."

Immediately, David was kneeling, at her side. "You all right?"

"No." She smiled up at him, her thumb forgotten as her arms reached around his neck. "I'm deprived."

They kissed slowly, exploring each other's mouths with their tongues. His hand stroked her breasts as she leaned slightly backwards into his arms. "God, you kiss beautifully," she said at last, her whole body already feeling full of him. Even though he had first kissed her only a few hours ago—after an awful lot of hinting on her part had finally broken down his resistance—she felt as if they were already lovers.

"I want you an awful lot," he said, his voice hoarse.

"Umm. Me too." She giggled again. "Why do you think I'm brutalizing myself just to get this silly tent up?"

David Fellows joined her laughter. "You could have knocked me for six when you suggested you wanted to go camping." He moved away to tighten some ropes.

"Well your bed didn't look all that appealing." She took the hammer again and smacked it at the peg, which slipped into the ground as smoothly as into butter. "A monk's cot seemed somehow inappropriate."

"It proves I was saving myself for you."

"No wonder Harriet's depressed."

"Oh no, she'd be more interested in you than in me," David laughed. "Hey, haven't you finished that yet?"

"Almost."

"Good, this side's up. And I've got the sleeping bag and stuff all set inside."

"Look at the moon coming up. It's beautiful," she said in a soft voice. "And I think I can hear a nightingale."

"Ornithology notwithstanding, I think you're right! Would you like some supper?"

"No darling," she said soberly. "I don't think I would." She rose and walked over to him. "I think" she said shyly, putting her arms around his waist, "that I'd like you to make love to me."

She raised her head up from the pillow, straining to see the flat, muscled curvature of his front as it approached and receded from her, never quite touching her except at that one point of deep, utmost fulfillment. The veins in her neck were taut, partly with the strain, mostly with the anguish of his beauty and her love of him. "Let me look at you," she insisted, craning her neck to see where he was embedded into her. "Let me *look!*"

Gently, smoothly, feeling tremendously powerful, David continued to move up and down on her. He could feel the glistening warmth of the inside of her body, clenching to him with such incredibly gentle insistence. Above all, he could smell her musk . . . perfume, sweat, love-scent, pheremones. "Oh, my God, how good we smell together," he said, "how *rude!*"

In out, in out. How in control he felt, how masculine . . . how athletic! Good God, he thought suddenly, push-ups! How he had hated them in school; probably because he never had been able to do more than ten at a time. Of course, now his knees were on the ground, between her legs spread as wide as a harbor. . . .

"You're smiling," she said, not quite accusing because the twilight in the tent made it hard to see. "God that feels fantastic, you've got a right to grin."

He faltered, embarrassed at the irrelevance of his thought. Instantly he could feel his erection start to falter.

"No don't *stop.*" Her words, half command, half desperate cry, made him rock hard again within less than a single stroke. Now he wanted more, harder, rougher.

David moved his head a foot to her right so that he lay on top of her at a slight angle, his hardness pressed sideways against her slit. As he moved steadily in and out of her, he used the leverage of the twist of his hips to rub longer and harder. Still he was fully in control as she cried and shook beneath him.

"Oh, so good," she cried, "so wonderful, so wonderful."

Gradually he started to lose control as with each wonderful, groaning thrust—each responded to by her with a wild mew of pleasure—he moved nearer to his orgasm and brought her closer too.

"Oh man, oh man, oh man," she cried out as he speeded up, a chant of ecstasy that kept rhythm with him. Deeper and deeper, she could feel him filling her every cranny with gentle but giant insistence, pushing, pushing at the very center of her womb. "My God, how I adore you," she whispered. "Oh darling, you're so big, so beautiful." Her whole body ached to receive each of his thrusts. "So beautiful . . ." She pushed her body away from the ground until her weight was resting only on her shoulders and the soles of her feet. Her arms steadied her as her pelvis thrust out toward him in the classic presentation pose, which left her totally female and vulnerable, him superbly masculine and in command.

"Oh my God," he yelled now quite beside himself, completely beyond any sort of control. "Oh, I'm coming, I'm coming. Oh, darling, my darling. *Feel. . . !*"

"Oh yes," she cried back to him. "Oh yes. Come!" And she cried, laughed, shrieked as, vibrating, she soared over the top and shuddered in an orgasm that filled her, and lasted, lasted . . .

"Yes!" he shouted. "Oh yes!" and he groaned as he inundated her, clutching her to him with both his hands. "Oh darling," he cried again and again. "Oh, my darling."

Slowly she lowered herself, very sure that he remained with her, until at last she was lying relaxed with him, warm, panting, wet, all on top of her. "Don't move," she warned, "if you leave me I'll expire."

"I already did," he grinned. "Expire, I mean. That was incredible. Just incredible."

"Yes," she agreed, "I never had anything like that happen to me before."

"Nor I."

"What does it mean, then?"

"It's my greatest discovery to date," he said seriously.

"What is?"

"That I love you."

"Yes," she agreed, her eyes showing how much she meant it, "yes, I love you too."

17

Simon fantasized about Sandra Maguire from the moment he met her, imagining what she would be like nude, excited—and he, of course, equally nude and fully rampant. In his imagination, he had only to call her to have her come running. The memory of her lips grazing his became the start of a passionate affair. But after the speech, and Spinosa's incredible reaction to it, these fantasies increased drastically in frequency, variety and intensity: gradually Sandra became close to an obsession. The memory of her garish beauty would come to him at even the most inopportune moments, and never fail to stir his loins. Not since he had been a teenager, desperately enamored of a succession of hopelessly distant prom queens and cheerleaders attached to his team's sports heroes, had he sprung so often or so readily erect. Sandra had become for him a symbol of the power he craved and felt he deserved—but that he was in such imminent danger of losing.

Yet, for all his desire, he never actually found the courage to make the call. In some cases, by the time he had finally nerved himself to do it, it had become inappropriately late. In others, just as the hour seemed perfect, there were too many likely interruptions. Yet again, when both time and place could hardly be improved—once, for instance, when he found himself alone in an out-of-town hotel with nothing to do for the rest of the evening but process a few papers and watch a video movie on a scratchy television screen—he realized he had forgotten to bring her unlisted phone number. Once he did call but, the phone having rung three times, hung up assuring himself that no one was home. And several times, especially more recently, knowing that there was no reason not to call her, he had simply lost his nerve and, cursing himself for still being as cowardly as in his youth, had retired to bed disillusioned and morose.

Looming through all of his hesitancy, of course, was the question of Janet. She was a good wife and tremendously loyal. All the things she had done for him—all the faith she had had. And he loved her, as he always had, solidly, comfortably. Not that an occasional roll in the hay when he was away on a business trip was unheard of. Everyone did that, didn't they? Nothing wrong—as long as one didn't bring home herpes or the clap, a thought that worried him deeply on the rare occasions when he had transgressed. But Sandra was different: A man could too easily get serious about her.

Tonight, Simon was in a black mood. It was only seven and he was already at the company's New York apartment. This afternoon there'd been a message that Carlos Spinosa would be calling early in the evening to get together. God, Simon had thought, sweating because he still hadn't developed any plans for how to reverse his announcement. It just wasn't right. Janet had seen that as clearly as he. And, beyond that, he didn't even see a way it could be done without the SEC and the Stock Exchange launching a full-scale investigation into stock manipulation. Surely no one wanted that. Simon had phoned Janet but she wasn't in, so he'd simply left the message that he'd be staying in town. Then, at six, Carlos's office had called to cancel. Simon couldn't decide whether he was more relieved at the reprieve or disappointed that the problem still hung over him. In any case, by then it had been too late to go home. Janet would probably have made other plans for the evening. So here he was, at loose ends. It was raining outside.

Surely this was as good a time as any to phone Sandra. What the hell, she could only refuse. His hand reached for the phone. No, first he would pour himself a drink; anyhow, it was a shade early yet. She probably wouldn't be home before seven-thirty. . . .

The phone rang, making him jump

"Hello?" He was half annoyed at the interruption, half relieved at again having an excuse to procrastinate.

"Simon?" Her voice was everything he remembered.

"Why yes. How—"

"It's Sandra. Sandra Maguire." There was a tentative, almost questioning quality.

"Of course. I recognized—"

"We met at—oh you did?" She interrupted herself, obviously delighted.

"Certainly."

"How very flattering." She laughed. "Or how very quick of you. And that's just as flattering."

"No. I did recognize you," he wanted to reassure her. "In fact, I was just thinking about you." He realized that the comment sounded thin, too obviously a come-on.

"Really?" She sounded justifiably skeptical.

"Really. I know it sounds unlikely, but I was literally just thinking of calling you. In fact," he added, determined to add authenticity to the truth, "I had decided that all I would do was pour myself a drink and then call."

"That does make me feel better." She sounded convinced. "I was surprised you hadn't called. It's been a while—"

"Terribly busy," he answered quickly. "You know how it is, spirit willing, flesh weak and all that."

"Not your flesh, surely," she laughed. God, how pompous he was! And how easy to con. She could almost hear him puffing himself up. And yet, she had to admit, he hadn't called her as she'd anticipated. Surprising, really, considering his reaction that evening. She only hoped he wouldn't be one of those loyal husband types. How boring they could be . . . even though they always succumbed in the end.

"Well, I . . ." He harrumphed with pleasure and confusion.

"Listen," she said, "I really shouldn't be calling you this late, but a friend of mind who's putting on *Garibaldi*—you know, that new musical that's getting all the raves—well, he just sent over a couple of tickets, just this minute mind you, and said I *must* see it"—she hesitated—"and so I called on the off chance that you might be free. Of course, I know it's awfully late," she rushed on, "but I called earlier at your office and they said you were in a meeting and then when I called back you'd already left." She sounded exactly as flustered as the occasion required. I'm really quite good at this, she congratulated herself, not that poor Toady needs much skill to catch.

"Of course. How very nice of you to think of me. Now I'm the one who's flattered. And I'd love to go."

"Wonderful." Simon could hear her relief. "But we'll have to hurry, it starts at eight."

"Oh, I'm afraid my car—"

"Never mind." She was annoyed at his evident expectation that a car would impress her. Silly little man! "Mine's standing by. I'll pick you up in twenty minutes."

"You know. . . ?"

"I know where you are," she assured him. When he thought about that he would be even more complacent.

She held his hand, gracefully cupping the flame, as he lit her cigarette during intermission.

"Are you enjoying it?"

"Very much. And you?" She removed an imaginary feather from his lapel.

"Indeed, it's most original."

The bell rang for the second act and she slipped her arm through his to walk back to their seats. "Very," she agreed, her smile dazzling.

"I do hope you'll join me for dinner afterwards. The Four Seasons has a little after-theater dinner—"

"I'd love to." She squeezed his arm against her side so that he could feel the hardness of her rib-cage through the delicate material of her dress, and, just above, the softening of her breast.

It had stopped raining by the time they left the theater. Just as well since her car was nowhere in sight.

"How annoying!" Sandra was incensed. "Why isn't he here?" she demanded of no one.

"Something may have gone wrong with the car," Simon suggested. "Is your man normally reliable?"

"Absolutely. And very loyal." She didn't bother to mention that his loyalty lay not with her but with his real employer—who'd undoubtedly whistled him over to some other assignment. Bastard! To leave her with the toad and, for all he knew, in the pouring rain.

"I'll get us a taxi."

"No. Don't bother." Sandra repressed her rage with an effort. "It's turned into a pleasant night for a stroll. We can walk at least to Broadway. It's only a block." She felt like stamping her feet. It was typical Carlos, totally without consideration. Here she was, working for him, fucking up a perfectly pleasant evening . . . "The *prick!*" She realized she had said it half-aloud.

"What was that?" Simon bent towards her.

"Nothing. I was just muttering."

"You often talk to yourself?" he teased. "Or only when you're mad at your driver."

"There are other times," she said archly. "Come on, there'll be plenty of cabs on the corner."

Supper at Four Seasons was, as always, delightful.

"It's one of the very few restaurants where one can really have a conversation," Simon explained. "The tables are far enough apart that you don't feel there are half a dozen strangers listening in."

"It is nice to have privacy," she agreed. Didn't he know that all this was about as dull as the weather? Did he really go through it all every time he came here? "And there's a calmness about the room," she said, "with the pool in the center . . ."

"And those shimmering metal drapes . . ."

"That makes it so relaxing."

Suddenly Simon laughed. "Do we sound as if we're talking about the weather?"

She was taken by surprise. "A little," she admitted.

"It's nervousness. Humans always sink to clichés when they're not sure what to say. When Germans go out to lunch and see someone they've been working with all morning, they'll bellow *'Mahlzeit!'* at each other. 'Mealtime!'"

"Better than what they used to bellow."

"Surely," he agreed laughing. "Do you know what Victor Borge used to claim was the only difference between a dog and a Nazi?"

"Tell me."

"A dog lifts his leg while a Nazi lifts his arm."

She laughed, surprised that he could be amusing. "Do you like jokes? I can never remember punch lines. I think it's a shortcoming with most women."

"I can't either," he said. "But it's individual, I think. My daughter, Susan, was telling me about a book of insulting jokes put together by a woman called Blanche Knott. . . ."

"That's pretty funny right there!"

"Marvelous name, isn't it," he agreed. "Probably made up to protect someone called something terribly ordinary. Anyhow, apparently this lady's found every really great, dreadful, ethnic joke."

"You have to be kidding. There's still a market for 'kike,' 'spic' and 'nigger' jokes?"

"I heard Milton Berle do an hour of them at an Anti-Defamation League luncheon."

"Incredible, his nerve!"

"It was awful, as a matter of fact. But no one seemed to think so."

"Like Don Rickles? People only feel insulted if he leaves them out. Do you know any tasteless jokes?"

"Susie told me a couple. Wait a second . . ." How nice, Sandra was thinking, that he thinks enough about his girl to bring her naturally into the conversation.

"I've got it. Do you know the difference between garbage and a girl from New Jersey?"

"Go on."

"Oh my God. Don't tell me you're from New Jersey."

"Well, actually . . ." She laughed, enjoying herself.

"I'll have to make up a whole new line."

"What were you going to say?"

Simon thought quickly. "For insulting a girl called Maguire . . ."

"Oh, you're not going to try for a limerick. It had better be good. Can you do them that fast?"

"Shucks. I don't know."

"Well . . ."

"Whose soul for New Jersey's afire."

"Barely adequate."

"While at the Four Seasons . . ." He hesitated.

"For various reasons," she added, supportively. "Now over to you for the punch line. It's all or nothing, kid. Go for it!"

"Her escort was forced to expire!"

"Very good." She clapped her hands. "As a pinch hit, it's terrific. Now tell me the difference between the girl from New Jersey and garbage."

"Garbage gets picked up." Simon hooted with laughter. "You asked for it."

They held hands leaving the restaurant. It was starting to drizzle again and together they scampered for a taxi. Amazingly for New York, it was practically brand new. "Not a single spring to goose me." Sandra patted the seat and moved closer to him. "Central Park West and Eighty-third," she instructed the driver. "And take it nice and easy."

"Okay, lady." The driver grinned at the beautiful woman. If that little fellow can get a broad like that, he thought, he's either gotta be goddamn rich or there's hope for us all. Either alternative seemed pleasant enough, and he drove off, carefully avoiding the potholes.

Simon put his arm around her. "What a lovely evening. I'm so glad you called."

"So am I." She was astonished by how much she had enjoyed the evening. Really, it was a shame to have so tricked him. The poor darling was so naïve. Oh, what the hell, she thought, it's all in a day's work. She leaned over to kiss him.

He pulled her closer still and as her lips touched his, marveled at their softness. "God you taste good," he whispered, "and so soft."

"Shssh." She kissed him again, this time with her hand on his cheek and the tip of her tongue wickedly probing his mouth. Don't go too fast, she warned herself, you don't want him to think you're a loose woman. She smiled at the anachronism and the foolishness of it with respect to herself. Was there anything she hadn't done. . . ?

"Anything wrong?" he asked, sensing her attention wandering.

"Nothing. Nothing at all." He was making a habit of surprising her. Earlier he had shown humor, now sensitivity. "I've had a lovely time," she hesitated. She should seduce him now, she realized. That's what Carlos wanted. Invite him up for a drink. All so very easy. Hell, he wouldn't even start to guess. Men were all the same—well, all but Carlos—once you screwed them they just assumed you'd love 'em forever. "I'd love to invite you in for a drink . . ." She could see his face light up. So ready! But no, dammit. She wouldn't. It wasn't fair to the toad. And anyway, that bastard upstairs hadn't even let her keep the car. "But I've got to get up real early and—"

"Oh, of course. I understand." (Why was he so blasted reasonable?)

"But I hope it won't be so long. . ." She mustn't lose him.

"Before the next time? No. No, it won't," he promised quickly. "I'd really like to. . ." He paused, astonished at his own daring. "I'd really like to see you again soon. And next time, perhaps it will be earlier, so we can, er, have that drink."

"Yes, darling." She kissed him one more time as the cab pulled up to her door. "Next time. I promise."

"I'll call . . ."

"In less than four weeks . . ."

"Tomorrow."

Upstairs Sandra first thought she might go into her own apartment instead of his. But no, there was no point in playing. For one thing, she'd long suspected that Carlos had some way of observing her bedroom. So she'd have to admit the toad hadn't come upstairs . . . might as well get it over with now. She entered Carlos Spinosa's door.

"Back early, Bella. No toad?" His voice, as always without inflection, was no less menacing for that. "Why not?"

"Why did you take my car?" she demanded, trying to find grounds to attack.

He didn't answer, merely raising his eyebrows.

"Oh hell," she answered his question, "Toady's mine for the taking. Any time and for anything you want. It just wasn't worth wasting my time tonight when I've got him exactly where you want him. He's such a nice little man."

"You like him?" Carlos asked incredulously.

"He's all right," she said noncommittally, suddenly frightened that she had gone too far in both disobeying her old man and in showing some fondness for a mark. "If you like to be bored to death."

"You bitch," he said it quietly, but now there was absolutely no mistaking his anger. "You actually think you can get away with that?" With one step he was at her and, before she even realized what was happening, had grabbed her hair. She could feel the sudden, excruciating pain as he hurled her off her feet and onto the sofa. Violently, he slapped her cheek. The stinging sensation was like a silent, physical scream.

Sandra Maguire—Gina Belladonna again now—flared with anger. "Fuck you," she snarled back at him, willing to kill. But at the same time she knew that she had indeed defied his will, so that her punishment was justified. Unlike any other man she had known, he was powerful, implacable, at all times to be obeyed. He was her man and, in the tradition of her mother and all of the womenfolk from whom she was descended, she knew she belonged fully to him—and was thereby honored.

"You need a lesson," he snarled, starting systematically to rip her clothes off her back and ignoring entirely her attempts to scratch at him. "Tomorrow, you'll screw the toad until he thinks he's the greatest stud since Flynn." He ripped her panties off her in one vicious yank. And gradually, in spite of herself, she could feel the flood start deep inside her, feel her rage turn inevitably into equally uncontrollable lust.

Susan Bagnew held David Fellows's hand and giggled

as she had not done since she was fifteen. She felt like skipping down the path. As soft as a doe, she wanted to nibble the green sprouts off the bushes or sip at the brook's water.

"It's babbling," she pointed at the stream. "I never heard one do that before."

"Idiot!" He grinned at her with delight. "Trouble is, I hear it too."

"What's it saying?"

"Hard to follow, I'm afraid. Keeps repeating itself. Brooks do run on rather, you know."

"Oh David, that's awful."

"I know, I know. Will you forgive me?"

She looked at him flirtatiously. "Only if you do penance."

"What do you suggest. . . ? Oh no, not again. God, but you're insatiable."

Simon reached for the phone by reflex every twenty minutes or so, wondering whether it was time yet to call Sandra. The last two nights had been incredible, like nothing he had imagined before. . . . Everything, they had done everything together he had ever dreamed of. . . .

"Call me, if you happen to think of me," she had suggested as she left his apartment this morning. "I'll be in later in the afternoon, sixish."

Think of her! He could think of nothing but her. She permeated his thoughts with beautiful, salacious images. . . .

Sandra, stretching, amidst rumpled sheets, feline and languid, so that her ribs became slender, elongated fingers clasping her chest, and her breasts, as softly delicate as birds nesting, perched on their latticework. Then her nipples, erect and haloed with pink, became so precious to Simon that he could not bear to be parted from them and had to throw himself back onto the bed to touch and touch and suck . . .

Sandra's lips, so incredibly soft, encircling his shaft and bringing him to a second orgasm when he had already had all semblance of his normal businessman's restraint destroyed in the unbearably tender violence of the first one.

Sandra, laughing at his reluctance to go lower on her. "Silly," she teased him, "how can you object to my peachfish?"

"Your what?" He was glad to delay.

"That's what Tom Robbins calls it in one of his books: 'half shellfish, half peach,' or 'peachfish' for short. Now touch me." She spread her legs and held her labia apart with two delicately manicured fingers so that Simon, who had never heard of Tom Robbins or seen such an incredibly arousing sight before, could see her inner lips glistening. Suddenly her peachfish became the most wonderful thing in his world, no longer dirty or crude, but infinitely desirable, and he buried his mouth in her, adoring the taste, while her hips writhed as if he were the most accomplished lover in the world.

But each time his hand reached for the phone, he had to control his impatience.

"I'll be moving around, meetings and everything," she had explained. "But I'll be back by six or so, you know, when the day's work is over."

"Can I see you then?"

"Oh, I wish," she lied. "But I have to go to a business dinner at eight."

"Of course. I understand."

"And between six and eight, I'll have to get ready." She was touched by his disappointment. "But I'll be thinking of you, darling," she had promised.

God, why wasn't it six yet? And what was she doing all afternoon, anyhow? All she would say when he asked her was "meetings."

"About what? With whom?"

"Oh, clients and things. About my business. But it's all very unimportant compared to Turner-LaMott. All I do is sell pretty boys' and girls' pictures to ad agencies and photographers. You run a really big business."

"I do," he had said, trying to sound realistic and neither falsely modest nor boastful—and succeeding in sounding only pompous. "But that doesn't mean I lack interest in what the rest of the world does. Especially you."

"Of course not. It's just that you're really under a lot of pressure."

Simon Bagnew sat in his office waiting for the chief financial officer to bring up the latest set of figures. His fingers twitched toward the phone again, his eyes glanced at the clock. Only four-thirty. No point in calling yet. Anyway, Agatha would wonder why he was making his own phone calls instead of having her connect him. Suspicious bitch. Yes, Sandra was right about the pressures, but not in the way she meant. It was simply that he knew every working moment that, sooner or later, Carlos Spinosa would call again. It had been two weeks now, but . . . Simon tried to wrench his mind away from the subject but it bounced back, as inevitably as one of those tennis balls attached to a long rubber band that return faster the harder you bat them away. Perhaps, now that the stock was up to thirty-two dollars, Carlos would be mollified. Perhaps Carlos would drop the matter after all.

Simon got as close to praying as he knew how. But what god was there? The one described by that foolish and often drunk priest in Centralia High who prayed to the Lord for a win at football? Or the one postulated by the ascetic cleric at Harvard who preached the virtue of celibacy, denial and Jesuit self-control and then reached for Simon's knee? Or, worse yet, the God who, all those months and years, had left him out in the cold to be the forgotten man? Bullshit. But still, dear God, if only Carlos would forget and let me get on with the job. If only . . . Perhaps . . .

But Simon knew there would be no response to his cynical nonbeliever's prayer. Any day now. Any day, he'd hear what he had to do. . . . No, dammit, he would *not* think about it. Sandra. That was better. She was worth the thinking. What would they do when she was available again?

Simon started to plan meticulously. Carefully selecting a piece of paper from a silver paper holder on his desk, he started to make a list. It was an activity he enjoyed. Listing what he would do always gave him the satisfaction of achievement without the discomfort of having to make final decisions. The piece of paper he had selected gave him a feeling of importance and pride: it was embossed with the words "From the Office of the President."

"Four Seasons," he wrote down in his precise hand. "Table by pool." She would expect nothing else. Six people had waved to her. Thank goodness he had at least been welcomed by the owner. That had at least partly compensated for the absence of anyone else to recognize him. None of his friends had been there that evening. His friends? Had he any? No, he would not pursue that path either. He forced his mind back to the evening. A play after supper? Yes. "To theater." That made sense even though it meant they'd have to eat early which Sandra didn't like. Too bad, he decided with bravado. He wasn't able to wait to eat until after the theater. It meant they wouldn't get back to her place until after midnight. Such an interminable delay . . . Unless she really couldn't make it earlier, of course.

He buzzed Agatha. "I need a table for two at Four Seasons for tomorrow night," he said energetically. "Early enough to make the theater on time. Also, two seats at . . ." He hesitated. What would Sandra like? He wished he was more up on the latest plays. His secretary seemed to know every play on and off Broadway. "What's it called?" he bluffed. "That latest comedy hit that just got all the raves. I forget . . ."

She named a play.

"That's it," he recognized the name with relief. "Two tickets in the front two or three rows," he commanded, adding grandly, "I don't care what they cost."

"Yes, sir." She left the room feeling somehow revenged that her boss should be so ignorant. They were all the same, these men for whom she had worked for the last thirty years: dominant males with the style of command stamped all over them but with shriveled little souls inside. How she despised them . . . although she had to admit that this latest fellow was a little different. For all his bluster and pomp, he seemed more human beneath, softer somehow, less assured and aggressively masculine than the others. Oh well, he was still bad enough. She shrugged her shoulders and dialed Harry Cohen, the scalper who made a fortune out of Turner-LaMott and always rewarded her with a free ticket to the show of her choice. "Hello Harry. I need two tickets to—"

"Let me guess!"

"Of course," she interrupted him. "What else opened this week and is all sold out. But money's no object."

"Three for the price of two?"

"That would be nice."

"You've got 'em. Dates?"

"Two for tomorrow. For the boss and his girl. The third on Saturday night."

"Classier?"

"You got it," she mimicked his tone and laughed.

Simon, back at his desk, was continuing to plan. Afterwards, we'll go to her place. "3. Home." Instantly he felt himself stirring and was inundated with an image of her standing tiptoe next to the bed on which he lay, her arms stretched up so that her body seemed to arch backward and present him with such ultimate femaleness. . . .

The buzzer startled him back to reality. "Mr. Hendrick to see you," his secretary said, her voice without inflection but, to Simon's sensitized ear, nevertheless somehow accusatory.

"Send him in." Simon tried to sound busy, peremptory, as if the matters he was about to discuss were vitally important, very difficult, greatly tiring. But it wasn't so! The profit figures would all be satisfactory, the accounting practices conservative, the papers presented to him meticulously accurate. Indeed, he was looking forward to the meeting, which would flow smoothly and end up being reassuring.

Simon thought of Sandra Maguire only once during his discussion with Arthur Hendrick. Even then he dismissed her instantly from his mind. Serious men reviewing the performance of one of the largest companies on earth, could not distract themselves with romantic and foolish yearnings.

Eventually, the two men were done. "Very valuable meeting," Simon said happily. "I think we're making fine progress."

"Thank you, sir. I believe so too. And I appreciate your . . ." He hesitated, wondering how far he dared go. ". . . your professionalism. I must say, it is quite a change." He felt himself blush at his imagined temerity.

"Good." Simon felt enormously pleased. Yet he was experienced enough to remain noncommittal. However flattered he might be, he couldn't afford to allow an employee to make critical comments about previous management. Better not encourage him and risk having to cut him down later.

"Yes. Good night. And, again, a fine job." Simon accompanied him to the door, shook hands formally, and beamed after him as he bustled away.

"Will that be all, sir?" his secretary demanded.

"Oh my goodness. You are still here? It's almost six."

"Indeed," she smiled sourly, pleased to make him feel guilty. "You were in conference and you did not indicate whether you would need me further."

"I'm sorry. Of course you must leave."

She glanced at her watch. Yes, it was just about time now. Her mother had said to meet her at the Plaza at six-fifteen. There would have been no point in departing earlier. "Very well." She started to throw her things together, as if in a great hurry. "I hope they'll wait," she muttered, making sure Simon heard. Then she rushed out, a tiny triumphant smile curling downward at the corners of her mouth so that it looked as if she were frowning at her very pleasure.

But now Simon didn't care. It was six at last. Sandra would be back in her hotel undressing, bathing, powdering . . . Oh, he could almost smell her, and he was rigid with desire. Rigid . . . His hand trembled as he dialed.

If only she could guess how excited I am. His heart pounded as the phone rang. How foolish to feel like this at my age! He felt half amused at himself, half foolish. And then, in a flash, the follow-up thought: How inexpressibly sad that he had never felt this way before.

"Hello?" Her voice was so cultured. It evoked for him immediately her whole sophisticated being.

"Sandra! Oh, how good you sound. I've been waiting all day to talk to you." He was shocked by how needy he seemed, like a lovesick schoolboy. How could he be so juvenile?

For a moment Sandra could not place the voice. There were so many with just that tone. Decent men, usually, infatuated by her and unable to imagine that she felt less for them. "Oh, darling!" she was appropriately flirtatious, noncommittal.

"I've been planning our evening out tomorrow," he said more pragmatically, trying to cover his intense emotional rush. "How does an early dinner at Four Seasons and then the theater sound? We have tickets to that latest hit."

"Oh, lovely," she said, realizing it was only the toad. "I'll look forward to . . ." She paused. "To all of it. I'd love to. The only thing is," she continued reluctantly, "I'm not sure I can make it before theater time."

"Oh can't you. . . ?" He couldn't hide his disappointment.

Poor toad, she thought, so transparent! Wants to rush home after the theater and fuck all evening long. Silly man. Can't keep it up for more than minutes at a time. "No, I'm afraid we'll have to eat afterwards." Who does he think he is? She was suddenly annoyed.

"I quite understand." He tried to believe she really was busy. But if not, he couldn't blame her. Why should such a lovely young woman want to make love to him at all, let alone all evening? Perhaps she wouldn't even let him come home with her.

But, professional that she was, Sandra sensed the depth of his concern and decided it would be unwise to let it build. "But we could eat at my place after the theatre," she relented. He was infatuated but no fool, this toad, even though he was frightened and his shoulder sagged and his cheeks were jowly. If he ever realized that she was just using him, she would lose her grip on him. That she certainly couldn't risk. Carlos would kill her. "That way, we'd have the whole night to ourselves."

"Wonderful! That would be really wonderful." Simon's voice cracked. "Wonderful," he repeated, transported with relief. "I'll bring caviar and champagne," he added, filled with enthusiasm but trying to sound calm.

"And I'll do the rest."

"Oh," he said, suddenly unable to contain his exuberance, "that's *super!*"

"Good," she laughed. Then, before his embarrassment could set in, she added, "And how are things at the office?"

"Oh you know, the usual thing. Profits up, stock price the highest in years. More brilliant deals . . ."

"You're doing well." She was serious. This was not the time to play one of the toad's silly games. She had her own agenda just now.

"I think so," he said, diffident about accepting a compliment.

"And your board?" she asked. "You said some of them were acting up."

"I have that under control," he lied, feeling the knot form, a giant fist in his stomach. "I'm fine with my board," he boasted, trying to boost his courage. Thank God she couldn't see him! She'd know in a second that he was lying. "Carlos Spinosa is the real power, you know."

"I've heard of him," Sandra said softly.

"Yes, a very powerful man," Simon repeated. "But rational. We understand each other and . . ." His sentence staggered under the weight of his lie.

"And what?" Sandra probed to see how far he would go.

"And I think we sort of *recognize* each other," Simon said, trying to make himself believe it.

"I'm sure he recognizes you," Sandra Maguire agreed, her voice soft and gentle. Poor toad! If Carlos recognized him it must be like the tire of a car might recognize a toad prior to running him over.

"Even when we have a difference of opinion, it's no problem." Like a man picking compulsively at a sore, Simon could not stop. "Spinosa says what he means; I respond as I see fit. In the end, it works out." Christ, if only it would!

"You don't let him influence you then?"

"Of course I do. If he's right. But I have to make up my own mind." Simon was full of bombast.

"For instance?"

"Carlos felt that at our last press conference I overstated the case on our new technology. I'm not sure I did. I'm wondering whether I can go along with him and retract or not." Oh God, he thought, if it were that simple. If ever I could summon up the courage to do what is right. Or if they would just leave me alone. It had been three weeks. He had heard nothing. And Turner-LaMott's stock was still edging upwards. Perhaps, just conceivably, Carlos had relented.

"Does it really matter?" Sandra asked innocently. "Won't the value of the technology prove itself one way or the other whatever you say?"

"I suppose it will. But . . ." He paused, desperate for reassurance. "Oh, I wish you were here," he said lamely, obviously quite unable to voice what he really wanted to say. "Such a waste to have you all alone and so far away."

"So why not do what Spinosa wants?" Now it was Sandra who wouldn't let the subject drop. "Whom will it hurt?"

"I'll consider it." If only he could tell her the whole story . . . confide in her. Who else would be able to help, would even care . . . other than Janet, of course? But how could someone like Janet, with no business experience and no imagination, hope to comprehend the hell he was going through? "It's partly a matter of ethics and convictions," he added importantly. "One has to be sure of one's stand."

"Of course," she agreed, flattering him shamelessly. "That's what I admire about you, you really do care about what's right." Funny, she thought, that happens to be true. It might have been the first thing she'd ever told the toad that was! "But I've found that in the end the most powerful men usually take the easiest routes. They don't have to climb mountains to prove something. They already know they can."

Simon stared at the telephone with something close to adoration. "That's incredibly perceptive," he said at last. Perhaps it was just the rationalization he was looking for. If so, maybe he could find a legal way to make the retraction. If only he could convince himself, when Spinosa finally called, that what Sandra had said about powerful men actually applied to him. Was he a powerful man—or only poor Simon Bagnew of Centralia, Illinois, Harvard, big business and, more recently, of the sad ranks of the unemployed?

———18

The summons, when it finally came, was peremptory but anticlimactic. Instead of Carlos Spinosa's steel-wool rasp, the voice had been Galsworthy's, as mellifluous and oily as the concentrated sulfuric acid kept in the security cabinet in the Harvard lab in which Simon had spent much of his first two years at college. "Get over to my office," Galsworthy had said. "You have a problem."

Simon had bitten back the desire to ask questions. It was bad enough that his palms sweated; he couldn't control that. But he could control what he said, and he simply would not give his tormentor the added satisfaction of hearing him uselessly beg for answers. He knew none would be forthcoming. "I'll drop round tomorrow at two," he answered evenly.

"Today."

"No!" Simon's anger suddenly boiled. For almost four weeks they had let him stew, suffer heartburn, jump at shadows—just as a kidnapper makes no ransom demands until his victims are thoroughly terrorized. Now they wanted him to jump on the instant. Well, two could play that game. They might fire him in the end, and God knew what would become of him then. But for right now they needed him to make whatever announcement they wanted. "No," he repeated. "I'll be there at two tomorrow. I'm tied up until then."

"Mr. Spinosa says . . ." In spite of himself, Galsworthy couldn't quite avoid a trickle of anxiety from polluting the purity of his voice. The toad was being tough when, by all rights, after four weeks, he should be practically blubbering with worry. Did he wait too long before making the contact, he wondered? Perhaps he should have called before that last trip to Atlantic City. But no, he'd only been gone three days. God, how he hoped he hadn't misjudged Bagnew. They would hold him fully accountable if something went wrong. "Mr. Spinosa insists," he started again.

"Possibly," Simon interrupted. "Nevertheless, if you wish to see me, I can't make it earlier than two tomorrow." His heart pounded at his own gall. If Galsworthy repeated his demand one more time, he wouldn't be able to resist.

"Very well," Galsworthy capitulated.

"Your office at two," Simon confirmed, keeping his voice steady and matter-of-fact only with enormous effort.

Galsworthy merely growled and abruptly hung up.

As Simon slowly replaced the receiver, his tension relaxed so suddenly that his whole body felt limp. His hand shook and his knees became so weak that, had someone entered, he could not have risen to greet them if his life had depended on the act. His head felt so light that it seemed to float inches above his neck, unconnected and free. "Christ," he muttered and caught his head in his hands, feeling its weight back on his shoulders. "Oh Christ!"

For only the third time in the year since he had first heard of Galsworthy & Merit, Simon was now sitting in Morgan Galsworthy's corner office. He looked and felt just as desperate now as he had on that first occasion, yet the reasons now were less obvious. Then he was out of work and hopeless; now he was apparently on top of the world, but actually terrorized by fear of the demands being made of him. He still stank of losing.

Galsworthy, on the other hand, had changed considerably. His pose, elbows perched on the polished table, fingertips deliberately touching as if in prayer, was habitual. But now he was concentrating entirely on his visitor instead of spending half his time admiring his own reflection in the mirror behind Simon's head. His face, even though apparently in repose, seemed haggard. A close observer might, too, have observed a tiny nervous twitch in the very corner of his left eye. It bothered Galsworthy enormously that he was quite unable to control or even influence it.

Galsworthy broke the silence, which had lasted a few minutes already. "My principals want an explanation."

"But I *have* explained." Simon's voice was close to pleading. "You say that Mr. Spinosa is concerned that we do not have enough reserves for bad debts. But it isn't so. We have two percent. And last year, as far as I recall—"

"As far as you recall?" The utterance dripped of sarcasm. "Don't you know?"

"Approximately, yes . . . But then I was not expecting—"

"What *were* you expecting?"

"I thought that the announcement . . ." Simon faded to silence, looking miserable.

"The trouble is, little man, that you think too damned much," Galsworthy said coldly. "Your job is very simple: you're paid purely and simply to do what Mr. Spinosa wants." Galsworthy's voice rose until, quite uncharacteristically, it was as harsh and forbidding as an angry dog's bark. "You hear? Just do what you're told!"

But the effect of his anger on Bagnew was not what Galsworthy had intended. Instead of further softening his victim, it seemed to instill backbone in him. "Don't you listen to me?" Bagnew asked. "I *am* willing—"

"You are willing to do whatever I tell you," Galsworthy tried to hold his advantage.

"I am not." The words were softly spoken, but with a core of steel that Galsworthy had never heard before. "I will do everything reasonable that you request. But some things I can't do. Our bad debts last year ran below one percent. Practically everyone to whom we sold paid us. This year, to be conservative, I have placed the reserve figure at two percent. If I do more, the tax people won't buy it. The IRS has rules, you know, which neither you nor I can circumvent. And my bad debt reserves are as high as those rules permit."

As he proceeded with the explanation, Simon's anger abated. And with it, he could feel his courage, a limited and vulnerable commodity at best, ebbing steadily away. "I would do what Mr. Spinosa wants if I could," he ended lamely. "But sometimes I just can't."

Thank God, Galsworthy was thinking. It was not toughness after all that had fueled the toad's momentary rebellion, but desperation. He wanted to do what he was told—he just couldn't. Poor toad—what a relief! "Mr. Spinosa feels you're overstating the company's profits." Galsworthy decided to change the subject to the more general. "Mr. Spinosa feels that, for some reason, you are trying to force up the company's stock price. Probably just to make yourself look good."

"But—"

"And he doesn't like it," Galsworthy interrupted ominously. "He doesn't like that sort of attempt to mislead our investors one bit." He separated his fingertips and tightened one hand into a fist. "Not one bit!" His fist slammed onto the table.

"But we are highly conservative financially," Simon tried to remonstrate. His voice shook, however, and he could not prevent the explanation from sounding like an excuse. "We try our best to keep every profit forecast to a minimum and every expense estimate as high as possible. We try . . ."

"Then you'd better try harder," Galsworthy said rudely, delighted to see the beads of sweat on Bagnew's brow. "You'd better try a lot harder." The twitch at the corner of his eye had disappeared entirely. It always did, Galsworthy noticed, even at the poker table, when he was winning.

Simon was so shaken by his interview with Galsworthy, and so shocked by the risk he had taken in defying him even briefly, that he left Galsworthy & Merit in shock. Blindly he reached the elevator and then found his way below street level and into the Autopub. It was a large dark drinking place populated in equal parts by tourists attracted to the romance of the phony 1920s railroad-carriage decor, and by businessmen pleased with the walled-off booths where their dalliances with secretaries would be shielded from public view.

"Scotch," Simon ordered. "Double."

The bartender looked him over carefully. He seemed

sober enough. And there were no rules against serving people in a daze—only if they were drunk. "Coming right up," he said cheerfully.

Simon downed the drink at a gulp. "Another," he ordered.

"Coming right up." The bartender's response was a recording—an accurate repeat.

Did he repeat "Coming right up" with every order? Simon wondered irrelevantly. And why hadn't Galsworthy even mentioned the announcement? Four weeks . . . and not a whisper of a follow-up to Spinosa's command. Why. . . ? He drank his second Scotch slowly. "I think I'll have another," he said to the bartender. "But make it a single."

"Coming right up."

This time Simon couldn't help smiling. Oh well, he thought, the General Motors building was probably the logical place to install New York's first bartending robot. Anything was possible—even converting garbage dumps to oil. But why hadn't Spinosa called? And why had Galsworthy confined himself to some foolishness about bad debts? Simon just couldn't understand. Yet there must be a reason. He sipped slowly on his whisky, feeling it start to numb his fingers. He remembered he'd had no lunch. What the hell, whisky had enough calories. And he could stand to lose some weight. He hated his belly, which seemed to protrude more each year no matter what he did about dieting and exercise. Thank God Sandra didn't mind.

"It's a sign of maturity," she had told him quite seriously when he had apologized for it. "Like the extra thick mane on the king of the lion pack."

Simon hadn't believed her, of course, but it was a relief to know that she wanted him anyhow. King of the lions! What nonsense. Still, it was obviously true that it was his power, not his good looks, that attracted her. Never before had a woman like that so much as looked at him twice. Oh, if only he could hold onto it. And that depended on Spinosa. Simon's mind could not stay away from its central concern. Why had Spinosa been so irate after the speech and then not said a word since? Had he perhaps found out something about the technology that Simon had missed?

Simon finished his drink. "I'll have a check, please," he called to the barman.

"Coming right up," the barman repeated, proving Simon's theory.

"Thanks," Simon said, amused; but his mind remained on his problem. That must be it, he decided: Spinosa must know something he had missed. Well, there was only one thing to do. He'd meet with everyone concerned to find out everything there was to know. "Can you change this?" he asked the bartender, laying a fifty-dollar-bill onto the table. He only hoped that the meetings would unearth some explanation. I've just got to find out what the game is. But can I?

Later, he could not remember whether it was the bartender or he himself who had answered with inevitable robot cheerfulness: "Coming right up."

The meeting between Bagnew, Jim Lester, the company's executive vice-president, Dr. Winthrop Turner, head of its research and development department, and David Fellows, who, although he held a double-doctorate, insisted on being called simply Dave, took place at Hanratty's bar on Madison Avenue and Ninety-eighth Street. It was an extraordinary venue for three senior businessmen and a near-genius scientist to meet: a pleasant Irish pub with a plank floor, rough tables and the sweet, slightly fermented smell typical of a thousand such New York beer and hamburger establishments. But the waitresses were pretty and helpful, and the food was wholesome and correctly cooked so that Dave Fellows liked it. Since his research involved a great deal of contact with the Mount Sinai Medical Center, a facility covering the three blocks just north of the restaurant, he had become a regular at Hanratty's. The meeting had been set there entirely to accommodate Dave.

"I would like to set up a meeting with you, Doctor Turner and Jim Lester," Simon had explained to Dave Fellows after Agatha, totally outraged, had explained that Fellows claimed he couldn't make it for several weeks. "I wondered if we could find a time."

Fellows had been charm itself. "Doubt it," he had explained. "That bloody partner of mine has the idea we're making some progress on the alpha project and he's holding my head to the grindstone. Shouldn't really be talking to you as it is."

Simon had been too admiring of the total independence of the man to even feel annoyed. What had his daughter called Fellows? A "corporate primitive." "But I'm afraid I've got to insist," Simon had said gently.

"Oh, you do?" Dave had been genuinely interested. "Why?"

"Well, I don't want to waste your time with a lot of explanations now, but it is important that I understand more about your garbage-to-oil project."

"Oh that." Fellows sounded disappointed. "But we've completed that."

"You mean it works?"

"Of course." He sounded puzzled. "I thought we'd explained."

"Well, yes. But I need to know more." Simon was starting to be thoroughly confused. "I mean, what is actually happening."

"Well, nothing really. I think we've learned all we want to know. That's why we've moved on to alpha—"

"But, we can't just drop it. It's potentially . . ." Simon

searched for a word sufficiently dramatic to explain its importance. ". . . It's *new*," he ended. It sounded lame, he realized, even though to him the word was full of meaning, incorporating a whole lifetime of practically never encountering things that were genuinely original. He succeeded only in sounding anguished, but genuinely so, as if he had just learned that a library of rare books had burned to the ground. "Dave, this is *important*."

"You really care, don't you?" Dave Fellows was surprised. "This means more to you than just a business opportunity." He was full of sympathy. "Why didn't you say something before?"

"Well . . ."

"Of course, we'll get together in that case. Although personally I think we'd do better to talk about alpha, which is a really interesting theory. And nothing to do with garbage." He laughed. "Still, I'm not sure it means much . . . mostly just mathematics." He chuckled. "Garbage is much more trouble! So when shall we get together? How about tomorrow? I've got to meet old Dick at Sinai anyway. He's a bit of an egghead, between you and me. But a wonderful endocrinologist, even if he isn't very practical."

"Yes, I suppose . . ."

"Make it Hanratty's at two-thirty, if you like. I'll buy you a cheeseburger. They're the best in town. Okay?" he asked cheerfully. "Good show," he answered himself before Simon could say a word. "See you there then." He hung up.

"Where the hell is Hanratty's?" Simon demanded of Agatha.

"I don't know, sir." She had sniffed disapprovingly. "But I'll do my best to find out." Her tone implied that it would be hard since she knew of no one who would frequent such an obviously déclassé place.

"You look worried," Fellows said sympathetically the

moment he saw Simon. "Come on in and have a beer. They've given us the window table so we can relax and chat. And I've told Carello, that dour old nagging partner of mine, that he can stuff himself all afternoon because I'll be tied up with you. Do him good anyway; forces him to concentrate when he's alone instead of chin-wagging all day when I'm there to listen. He'll probably win a Nobel by the time I get back."

Simon couldn't help laughing. "*Him* chin-wagging?" he teased.

Fellows looked at him sharply. "See what you mean," he said and grinned like a schoolboy caught playing truant.

Simon smiled back at him. He liked this brilliant, ingenuous young man who, under his naïvete, was rather wiser than he pretended. He could quite understand why his daughter had so completely fallen for him. He wasn't sure how far that would go in the end, of course, but judging by the look that passed between Susan and her mother when he had asked, there seemed a pretty good chance that David would be a son-in-law before too long. He hoped so . . . What clever grandchildren he would have! "The others will be here shortly," Simon said, pulling himself back to business. "Jim Lester is coming in another car. And Turner."

"Lovely," Dave Fellows said absently. "Super."

At just that moment both other men hurried in. Dave looked them over appraisingly and, glancing at Simon, with gentle sarcasm repeated "Super" under his breath.

"Welcome to Hanratty's," Simon greeted them, equally amused by Dave's comment and by the look of disbelief on Dr. Turner's face. "One of my favorite haunts." He turned half away from the two newcomers and winked at Fellows. "Come on in."

"Now what I want to know," Simon continued when everyone was seated and served with beer, "is precisely where we stand on this new technology to convert garbage to oil."

"It's not really technology," Dave Fellows interrupted seriously. "That's a somewhat dated term that seems to cover more of the traditional technical arts, whereas here we're talking more about genetics, literally the genesis of new microorganisms."

"Good God?" Simon asked blandly.

As the others looked at him in surprise, Dave Fellows brayed with laughter. "Well, I wouldn't go quite that far," he said. "But the point's taken."

"And does it work?"

"Oh, of course. Edible oil from garbage every time. All it needs is a little filtration and purification and it's ready to eat, drive a diesel engine or lubricate your squeaky door. No problem at all."

Simon's jaw set grimly as he forced himself to remember why he was here in this ridiculous setting. "Have we actually produced any?" he asked, determined to squelch the general optimism. "I mean in reasonably large batches?" He made his voice as disbelieving as he possibly could. "Surely it's one thing on paper, or even in a pilot run, but quite another in a full-sized batch." Simon felt guilty trying to trap David. But no ultimate harm would come to him, he rationalized. After all, if the process did work, the facts would indeed speak for themselves sooner or later. That was the point Sandra had made and she was quite right. But if Spinosa insisted on the retraction, then Simon would need some sort of reason for it. "Do we have a pilot plant? Have we tested in the pilot? Are there varieties of garbage on which it doesn't work? It seems to me there are a thousand questions yet to be answered. How many have even been asked?"

Simon noted with satisfaction that Dave Fellows was looking bemused. "And then there is the question of cost," Simon continued, following up on his advantage.

"Do we know that the whole process is economically feasible?" He leaned back in his chair. "I'm not saying this new, er, method is not brilliant, Dave," he continued. "I'm just wondering how far along its development path it has already progressed."

"Well, I must admit . . ." Dave started hesitantly.

But before he could continue, Jim Lester, who, apart from greetings at the start of the meeting, had remained quiet, interrupted. "I'm quite certain it works. And not only in theory but in practice. As you suggested a while back, I've investigated the matter in some detail, both with Dave and his colleagues at TULIPS, and with Dr. Turner here and his staff at R and D. Also, I've had a full cost analysis done, which turned out to be more favorable than the first assumptions. So I'm happy to be able to confirm, Simon, that there is little doubt the process will become a reality. I am quite convinced—"

"And yet . . ." Simon interrupted, not sure what he would say, but realizing that if Lester continued in this vein, he would be painting himself—and all of them—into an unretractable position. "And yet," he started again, "there must be some doubt." He tried to sound judicious. "After all, one can never be sure of such new, er, methods. They take time. Unexpected pitfalls are encountered. Things go wrong . . ." Even to himself he sounded unrelievedly pompous.

"Of course, nothing is certain," Lester said, clearly meaning this was an exception, "but—"

"That's precisely what I mean," Simon interrupted before the other man could complete his thought. "Nothing is certain, and anything as new as this is especially liable to develop bugs." He was getting desperate. Obviously, the process worked. Lester was convinced—and convincing. How the hell could Simon justify a major public announcement stating the opposite? And try to defend such an indefensible position? But, given Spinosa's probable demands, how could he not? "All I'm saying is that we cannot overplay our hand. We must be conservative, careful. Perhaps I was overly optimistic in making the earlier announcement."

Jim Lester was puzzled. For the first time he realized that Simon was troubled by something that didn't appear on the surface. But what? He had no idea. "When you announced publicly that we had the patents you were obviously convinced that they would be highly valuable," he pointed out. "Now you are less sure." Perhaps, he thought, Simon was afraid of not getting enough support inside the company if questions arose. At least he could reassure him in that respect. "All investigations indicate that you were fully justified," he emphasized. "That's a position I would be willing to defend publicly and strongly. Indeed, I'd feel duty-bound to reinforce your statements if any questions arose."

"Mr. Spinosa feels the patents may not be as valuable as we had first thought."

"Not valuable?" Lester exploded. "Making oil out of garbage not valuable?"

"There are so many practical problems left with the process," Simon argued weakly. "Perhaps we should make it clear publicly how far away we are from solving them."

"You mean you are considering making a public retraction of your statement?" Lester couldn't believe his ears. "That's out of the question." He was shocked enough to forget his normal defferential politeness. "Simon, you couldn't retract now. For one thing, it wouldn't be right to the shareholders or to all the people working on this project. And for another, it would get you in serious trouble with the Securities and Exchange Commission."

"Oh come on," Simon could not afford to agree with Jim Lester's view, however right it was. "With all due respect to Dave and the others, maybe we'll turn out to be right and we'll be converting garbage to salad oil before the year's out. But you must admit," he tried to look at no one in particular as he made the statement, "that there's also a darn good chance that something unknown and unexplained could go wrong and that we'll never get out our first commercial ounce of oil."

"Not much chance," Dave Fellows disagreed gently. He bent down and rummaged in his bookbag at his feet. "Here," he said, taking out a bottle. "Open it. Pure oil . . . or about one bag full of ordinary household garbage."

Simon unscrewed the cap to reveal a yellowish liquid.

"Quite edible," Fellows said, and leaned over to dip his finger into the bottle. He licked it clean. "See?"

Simon hesitantly dipped in his own finger.

"Go ahead," Dave encouraged. "The worst things in it are the germs from my finger."

"Okay." Simon licked his finger and pushed the bottle halfway between Lester and Turner. "Here," he said, careful not to address either one of them directly. "You try some. It's virtually tasteless. I wonder why I expected something more fishy?"

"Loaves and fishes?" Jim Lester asked, dipping in his own finger and pushing the jar over to Turner who remained hesitant. "It's a comparable miracle."

"Perhaps that is why I'm so hesitant about letting the announcement stand. It's too miraculous. Something's bound to go wrong. Are you willing to guarantee it will work?"

Dr. Turner, having made a career out of remaining uncommitted, was not about to guarantee anything. "Of course, what we have here looks highly promising," he explained wisely. "Such early experiments often do." He sat back in his chair as if miracles like this were his daily bread. "And I have every confidence that this technique will eventually lead to something. I *feel* that," he said with carefully muted enthusiasm. "But logically I know that most new endeavors break down somewhere along the line. The statistics are always against success." He paused as if about to make a major pronouncement. "So you see," he concluded decisively, "I cannot guarantee success. Indeed, I would have to *bet* against it. But I am, nevertheless, cautiously optimistic." He smiled broadly almost as if he had said something.

"And you, Dave? You see any obstacles? Do you think it will work?" Jim Lester asked the question too quickly for Simon to stop him.

"Of course it will work," said Dave Fellows with utter certainty. "Now if you asked me about alpha, I wouldn't be so sure. But this," he looked at the bottle with evident disinterest. "I've no idea what it will cost. But of course it will work. It already has."

"Yes," Lester agreed, "I fully agree."

There it was then, Simon thought. If Spinosa insisted on a retraction, Turner would go along, and Fellows probably wouldn't care one way or the other. He might never even hear about it, stuck away in the woods working on alpha, whatever that was. But Jim Lester would allow no retraction. He knew the process worked and he would not permit a public statement to the contrary. It was hollow consolation now, but that was exactly as Simon had planned it when he'd involved Jim in the first place. The only difference was that, back then, he hadn't realized just how vindictive Spinosa would be if Simon didn't—or couldn't—make the retraction.

Given Jim's knowledge, there was simply no way that, if Spinosa insisted, Simon could deliver. Which meant that he would be out, of that Simon had no doubt. Out like an old pile of garbage, he thought bitterly, but one of those rare types that never again would be converted to something half as useful as this oil.

Suddenly, Simon felt dizzy, unreal, as if his body were weightless. He couldn't feel the chair beneath him. Perhaps he was having some sort of heart attack, he thought. But he felt neither pain nor fear. The faces of the three men around him seemed to expand. They hung like balloons in black space and then, as Simon examined them, each face seemed to simplify and become the essence of the owner. Thus, Dave Fellows's face became a concentrate of tousled hair, merry eyes, boyish grin—and high-tension intelligence; Jim Lester's was utter boy-scout integrity, a face without a wrinkle of dishonesty or a shadow of prevarication; and Turner's face became the Iago of science, the epitome of deviousness, of sour, jealous skepticism. And he himself? Simon wondered what was his essence as he floated among the balloon faces at Hanratty's. What was he?

"Are you okay?" Jim Lester's voice broke through his reverie. "You look white."

"I'm fine." Simon returned to reality. "Fine," he repeated, trying to shake his mind clear. "But I think we're finished," he said, realizing how appropriate the word was, at least for him. "Perhaps we should leave."

The feeling of unreality stayed with Simon as the four men made their way out of the restaurant. It was heightened outside as Dave Fellows bid them a cheerful farewell and started to run up the street, coattails flapping, toward the hospital.

"Thanks for the hamburger," he called over his shoulder.

Dr. Turner hailed a cab. "Hope I could shed some light of probability onto this," he said as he entered it. "Difficult decisions are our bread and butter in science."

That left only Simon himself and Jim Lester standing on the sidewalk of upper Madison Avenue. Opposite them, the Korean greengrocer in his thriving little shop was busily weighing tomatoes. In the road, gypsy cabs were jostling for the best starting positions for when the light turned green. Two nurses were hurrying toward the hospital and one drunk was going nowhere. Incongruously double-parked in front of Hanratty's, the two Turner-LaMott executive limousines and their drivers waited patiently to return the president and executive vice-president of that great concern back from their hamburger luncheon to their natural midtown habitat. How absurd we are, Simon was thinking, seeing himself as if from a distance. But he found pathos, not humor, in the absurdity.

"Good meeting," Jim Lester interrupted Simon's thoughts. "Funny location; but then Dave Fellows is a genius of sorts, so I guess we have to put up with his idiosyncrasies."

By the time Simon returned, Agatha was as agitated as she ever allowed herself to become. "I have been trying to get you for the past hour at that *place*," she complained. She used the word as if it referred to a men's urinal or worse. "But the person said you'd left."

"Yes, I ran an errand on the way back," Simon said. Immediately he wished he hadn't explained; it was none of her business. He still felt a little shaky, although less alienated from himself than he had been as they were leaving Hanratty's. "What's the problem?" he asked coldly.

"I believe we should discuss it in your office."

Simon raised his eyebrows. "Very well," he said, annoyed at her self-righteousness, but without the strength to object. He turned, entered his office and sat down behind the giant desk. "Well?" he demanded.

Agatha made a considerable production of closing the door and then tugging at the handle to make sure it was fully shut. Then she approached his desk conspiratorially.

"Yes, what is it, then?" Simon was becoming thoroughly impatient.

"Mr. Spinosa's office called for you twice. I explained that you were out and that I would have you call back the minute you returned. But his secretary was very displeased about it. In fact she was quite rude. Told me her boss didn't like to be kept waiting. And I said, well what can I do—"

"Yes, quite right," Simon interrupted. "If that's all, we should call him." He tried to keep his tone normal, as if his stomach had not instantly knotted at hearing Spinosa's name.

"Oh, but you can't. The third call was from Mr. Spinosa himself. He said he was leaving and to give you a message."

"How long ago?"

"About half an hour. And he was just going out then."

"Very well. What is the message?"

"He said to tell you exactly his words." Agatha's voice dropped to an awed whisper.

"What words, for goodness' sake? What did the man say?"

"He said," Agatha replied, her eyes round with more excitement than she had experienced in twenty years at this job, "'Tell Bagnew I said stop hyping our stock—or get out!'"

Simon Bagnew could imagine nothing he would have wanted to do less than to have a meeting with Carlos Spinosa. Yet, here he sat, waiting in Spinosa's reception area, summoned haughtily just the day after his meeting at Hanratty's. Since it was Spinosa himself he was to see, he had not dared say he would not be available until the following day. Indeed, such was his fear of the man that the idea had not even occurred to him.

The reception area of the office Spinosa had chosen for the meeting—one of many he owned around the city—was as ugly and depressing as Simon's already black mood. Its carpet, worn and dirty, seemed to have shrunk, leaving a yard of scuffed linoleum border. The oak desk, poorly crafted and then chipped by rough wear, was work-worn and stained. The two visitor's chairs were threadbare, and one sported a frayed edge. The sole window, grimy and with its paint peeling, faced a dirty brick wall. Behind the desk, which sported only an old-fashioned black telephone, sat a fat and unutterably bored receptionist whose unappealing platinum dye-job was further vulgarized by inch-long black roots.

Why did Spinosa, undoubtedly one of the richer men in New York, choose such an unprepossessing office, Simon wondered. He could, after all, afford any opulence. Hell, the diamond stud he habitually wore to hold his thirty-dollar silk tie immaculately in place was worth enough to refurnish this entire waiting room in Chippendale originals.

Perhaps, thought Simon, who had been waiting over half an hour already, the atmosphere of the place was intended to be gloomy and nerve-wracking. If so, it succeeded. His palms were sweating again. It was a phenomenon he had experienced frequently of late and one he especially hated. It made him feel even more disgustingly insipid than usual, like some sort of concave-chested Jehovah's Witness. "Damn him," Simon muttered, his anger mounting.

The telephone rang shrilly, making Simon start. But the receptionist barely blinked. With snaillike deliberation, one of her pudgy arms crept towards the telephone and, ultimately, transported the receiver back to her ear. She listened wordlessly for a full minute before painstakingly replacing the receiver. "You're to go in," she said without turning to Simon. "Through there." She indicated the correct direction only with the greatest effort.

"Thanks."

"Uh-huh."

Simon walked to the end of the corridor where a middle-aged woman awaited him patiently.

"Please wait in here," she said, ushering him into a conference room only slightly less seedy than the reception area. Simon noticed one of the plastic-covered chairs had a rent in it at least three inches long. "Mr. Spinosa will be with you." She pointedly avoided suggesting that Simon be seated.

Ten minutes longer Simon was forced to wait, pacing nervously around the empty room. Then, just as his nervousness was again starting to be displaced by mounting annoyance, the door flew open and Carlos Spinosa strode in. He seated himself without a word at the head of the conference table and gestured to Simon to sit at one side.

"Now," he said, his voice even flatter and rougher than Simon was expecting. "Why have you not made the retraction I ordered?"

"I, well, I didn't know you had made up your mind."

"I told you I was dissatisfied with your performance."

"But you said I should do nothing until you got back to me." Simon was appalled at the turn of the conversation. How could he be explaining why he hadn't done something in the past when he already knew he couldn't do it in the future.

"Very well. You now understand." Spinosa started to rise.

"No," Simon blurted out. "No, I can't. You see Mr. Spinosa, er, Carlos, it's impossible. Your request . . ."

"My order, not request."

"Yes, well, your order. The point is, it's not advisable. I must explain."

"Yes."

"You see, I have investigated the whole research project in detail. And to make doubly sure that I was in no way biased, I had Jim Lester look into it as well, independently. He would have done so on his own in any case. He's a sound man and, as executive vice-president, he would be responsible—"

"Get on."

"Yes, well, as a result of our investigations, it's quite clear that we really have something in this new technology. It's entirely practical. We've actually seen a sample of the oil made from garbage. Naturally, both Jim Lester and I are absolutely convinced that the technology is sound."

"I'm not." Spinosa's face showed no emotion. His voice sounded even more computer-created than usual. "I insist you announce it has no value to Turner-LaMott."

"But that's not true. There's evidence it will work."

"And I say either it won't or it will be too expensive to be of value to the company."

"But . . ."

"Little man, I am not going to argue with you. Do as I say or get out."

"But Mr. Spinosa," Simon was desperate, "I'm not trying to argue with you. Obviously, I don't want to get out. As you know perfectly well, I need the job. It's just that what you ask is impossible."

"Why?"

"Because I'll be breaking the law."

"So?"

"And we'd be caught almost at once. Look, how can I possibly deny the validity of technology that I announced only weeks ago? If I do that the company will immediately be investigated by the Securities and Exchange Commission."

"You'll say you made a mistake."

"How can I say that when the company's executive vice-president will swear that I flatly refused to listen to his advice? Hell, he may quit over it."

"Look," said Spinosa, "I'm telling you that technology is no fucking good."

"And I'm telling you, Mr. Spinosa," said Bagnew, pushed finally to the point of having nothing more to lose, "that unless you have technical support to back up that statement, my making it against Jim Lester's public disagreement will result in this company being investigated by half the agencies in the federal government." He gulped a deep breath. "Investigated," he added, "up to its ass."

For the first time since he had entered the room, Spinosa was listening. Evidently the toad was not being merely obstreperous, as he had first supposed. He had a point. The very fact that the poor little man would use a swear word showed how strongly he must feel about what he had said. Spinosa allowed himself the most wintery of smiles. "You're right," he admitted. "We got a problem." He rose abruptly and turned toward the door. "I'll take care of it. Don't do anything until you hear from me."

"No sir." Once again, Simon felt like a man reprieved from the gallows.

Carlos Spinosa swept across the room toward the door. "And remember," he rasped, "I won't put up with any more shit. Next time you do what you're told, with no argument." He slammed the door behind him.

19

Jim Lester's classic MG sports car, traditional fire-engine red and still equipped with its original leather strap over the hood, was his third-dearest love. His children and his wife, Mary, were tied for first place, and then came the car. "And it's close," Mary would tease.

He had named the car, which he viewed as a tough

little soldier, Crispian, claiming that, like soldiers who fought at the battle of Agincourt, it did "rouse him at the name of Crispian."

"What does that mean?" ten-year-old Jim Junior had wanted to know. He was lying on the floor in their family room, wriggling.

"It's Shakespeare, son." His father, comfortable in his arm-chair, smiled down at him. "In one of his plays he describes a large battle that took place a long time ago on Crispian's Day. King Harry of England beat a large French army with five times as many men as he had."

"How did he do that?" The boy sat up all attention. Mary Lester laid aside the Sunday paper. She loved watching Jim teaching their son.

"With great swords and enormous courage. Shakespeare describes one of King Harry's allies, the Duke of York, who went down three times but managed to keep on fighting, as 'From helmet to spur all blood he was'."

"Wow!"

"It was a bloody battle, all right. York was finally killed. But in the end, Shakespeare says, ten thousand Frenchmen were killed but only twenty-five Englishmen died."

The little boy's eyes were round with wonder. "Ten thousand to twenty-five? Do you believe that? How did they do it?"

"Well, Shakespeare says that King Harry said it was God who was on his side. 'O God, thy arm was here; And not to us, but to thy arm alone, ascribe we all.'"

"Do you believe in God, Daddy?"

"Well, yes, I think so. But I'm not sure I believe that God wants us to kill people, not even in battle."

"But then why did he let King, uh . . . ."

"King Henry IV."

"You said his name was Harry."

"That was his nickname. Like we call you Jim instead of James."

"Okay, so why did God let King Harry win by that much if he doesn't believe in killing?"

"Maybe Shakespeare didn't get it quite right."

"And anyway, if God doesn't believe in killing, why does he let anyone get killed?" the boy asked angrily. "That doesn't make sense."

"That's one of the biggest questions in life . . . why does anyone ever have to die? Often it doesn't seem fair. But if you believe in God, you believe in heaven too. So that means when someone dies, he goes to heaven and lives forever."

"With wings and things? That's what they say at Sunday school. Well I know I don't want no dumb wings," Jim Junior said with disgust. "I'd look like a girl. So I'm never going to die." He jumped up and ran out of the room leaving his parents chuckling.

"I'm taking Crispian out for a spin. I think he needs tuning."

"Oh sure, he does," his wife smiled at him. "How come that silly car only needs tuning in fine weather?"

"Smart car, I guess." He smiled back at her. "See you, love."

"Take it easy."

"I will."

It was a bright Sunday afternoon. The leaves were starting to turn red and gold. The sky was a perfect fall blue, crystalline and infinite. For contrast, someone had painted a tiny white cloud into the corner of this picture-postcard day. But there was no cloud on Jim Lester's mind as he drove his little car fast but safely down the cliff road. He pretended to listen to the motor, but only as an excuse. In fact, he simply relaxed, enjoying his car, the afternoon, his life.

He saw the black limousine in his rearview mirror when it was still hundreds of yards behind him and observed that it was driving at an excessive speed. Sometimes, he lost sight of it around the bend, but then it would spring back into view, keeping dangerously to one side as it sped around a curve. Cautiously, Jim pulled over to the right of the road, nearer to the edge of the cliff, to make sure the speeding limo had plenty of room to pass. He slowed down conservatively. What was the point of racing, he thought, particularly on a perfect day like this?

The heavy black car tore up behind him and pulled level. Looking to his left, Jim noticed that the driver was wearing dark glasses and looked as grim as death. Jim started to slow further, uncomfortable that the driver was not pulling ahead as he should. What was the matter with the man? Jim held his steering wheel tighter and started to be afraid.

Suddenly the limousine driver wrenched the wheel hard to the right. There was a shuddering jar as the cars collided. The little red MG first buckled and then lifted under the impact. Before he even had time to be really horrified, Jim Lester felt himself flying through the air. The last thing he ever knew was the sound of an awful splintering crash of metal, followed instantly by one terrible searing pain and then oblivion.

Simon Bagnew was watching a football game when he received the first of that afternoon's three terrible phone calls. Janet was out at a church group meeting. The call came directly from Spinosa. "I am calling a press conference for you for three weeks from today," he said. "You are going to announce that the new technology is no good, you were mistaken."

"But . . ."

"The problem you were concerned about has been taken care of."

"I don't understand."

"You don't have to understand. I told you before, you

simply have to do as you're told." The phone went dead.

Simon returned to his football game and pretended to concentrate on it, but had someone asked him the score or even who was playing, he would no longer have known. The sound, which he had turned down when the telephone rang, remained too low to hear. He had only to wait half an hour, lost in his private daze, before the second telephone call, the one he had refused to think about, or acknowledge he was expecting, came through.

"Mr. Bagnew?"

"Yes?"

"This is Police Sergeant O'Malley. You are Simon Bagnew, president of Turner-LaMott?"

"I am."

"I am sorry to have to inform you that, about an hour ago, Mr. James Lester, who was, I understand, your executive vice-president, ran off the edge while driving down the cliff road. He was killed instantly when his car exploded. His wife requested that we call and . . ."

But Simon Bagnew was no longer listening. His face had become ashen and the telephone, as if too heavy for him to hold unsupported, had sunk from his ear onto his shoulder. His body drooped with the sadness of great age and death and despair. "Thank you, officer," he said at last, his tone as empty as if he had been responding to someone holding open a door. "I appreciate your informing me." Deliberately he hung up the phone. "Oh God," he muttered just once. Then, outwardly unmoved by the calamity, he arose and turned up the television set until Howard Cosell, the crowd, and the other announcers were inundating the room with noise.

Slowly he walked over to the liquor cabinet and took out a bottle of his best Scotch, the one he reserved for special occasions. The Glenlivet, it was called, and it cost over fifty dollars a bottle. From the cabinet in the dining room, he chose his most beautiful cut crystal glass—one of the few valuables that had survived the penniless years. He didn't bother with ice but, glass and bottle in hand, returned to the television set and pulled a chair close in front of it. Still moving with trancelike care, he poured out half a tumbler of Scotch. Holding it up to the light, he admired its deep warm brown color, reflecting through the prisms of the cut glass so that it looked like an oily pool of polished amber gems. In slow motion he brought the glass to his lips and started to drink. He continued until the glass was empty. With the same studied care he refilled it. His eyes were full of tears as he stared at the television set, letting it bombard him with its meaningless noise.

Stubbornly, Simon Bagnew continued to drink. He observed the level of the Glenlivet gradually sinking in the bottle as if its decline were his only aim in life. He turned up the sound of the television even more, to its highest level, yet he hardly noticed as the football game ended and an ancient movie, interspersed with strings of local advertisements, replaced it. He saw, heard and felt nothing except the pounding of his heart, the clamp around his throat, the awful sickness in his stomach, the terrible pain of unquenchable remorse.

When finally the telephone rang for the third time, fully expected but totally startling nevertheless, he jumped in terror. At first he refused to pick it up. But it kept ringing, refusing to be drowned by the noise of the television. Eventually, he was forced by the jangling sound to reach over and pick it up. He was physically so drunk by now that he missed the phone altogether the first time and dropped it the second. Finally, he got it to his ear. "Yes," he said, thickly slurring the *s*.

"He's dead," Mary Lester said so softly he could hardly hear her. "You heard he's dead? I told the police to call you."

"Yes."

"And you didn't call me back," she accused. "That means you know too."

"No," he denied, not wanting her to continue.

"It couldn't have been an accident," she said with complete certainty. "Not that way. He was much too careful to just drive off the cliff. He always drives so carefully. So nothing should hurt Crispian. You know he does, Simon. You know what I mean. You *know*. You would have called otherwise."

"No, no, I don't know," Simon's voice was pleading. "No."

"And he knew the road like the back of his hand. The Cliff Road. God, Simon he grew up driving down there. He knew every curve. He couldn't, could he? Simon, he couldn't have . . ."

"Don't know, don't know." Simon's throat burned with an awful fire.

"What happened, Simon?" she screamed. "What the hell's going on?" She burst into hysterical tears.

Bagnew was almost unable to say anything. "Don't know," he managed to mumble into the phone.

"You must know, or you must find out . . ."

"No," he mumbled. "No, I mustn't."

"But—"

"No. No. No!" He couldn't find out. "No!" he shouted again. That was the very last thing he could stand. Get away. Out of himself. Away . . . He hung up the phone before she could continue and staggered back to the liquor cabinet. Taking another bottle of Scotch, he walked drunkenly out of his front door. He half climbed, half fell into his car.

Janet Bagnew, returning from a meeting of the church board, saw him tear out of their driveway and drive erratically away. She had no idea what had happened. But she knew that she was mortally afraid.

20

Simon Bagnew drove into New York automatically, having no goal, nowhere to go, no hope. Once, thinking the road curved when it did not, he almost hit another car. Another time, he lost his sense of balance and drifted so far to his right that he almost smacked against the pillars of a bridge. Each time, when he realized his mistake, he jerked the car away from the danger, overcorrected and swerved crazily down the highway before he finally regained control. In neither case, however, did he lift his foot from the accelerator or feel any of that surge of adrenaline that a near accident would normally have engendered. Partly, it was the alcohol; but mainly, it was that he could relate to nothing but the remorse that overwhelmed him, and the drumbeat pounding of his head.

"Spinosa," the wind seemed to whistle past the car, "Spinosa, Spinosa, Spinosa . . ." And the rush of air bouncing against the telephone poles and fences seemed to answer, "Lester . . . Lester . . . Lester . . ."

Then all the sounds—car tires and air hissing, cars rushing by with sibilant explosions, his own car's engine growling, the blare of horns when he swerved—all this cacophony merged into the pounding of his head and was transformed into an awful rhythmic chant: "Dead and dead and dead and dead and dead . . ." The macabre litany continued endlessly.

When Simon eventually reached New York, he had no memory of the drive, but the knowledge and vision from which he was trying to escape remained as clear and lucid as from the first moment. He drove to his usual garage by habit; there seemed nowhere else in New York to welcome him. He almost missed the turn in the long ramp down to the parking level and scraped the whole left side of his car against the wall. But the impact corrected the car's direction and he made it to the bottom without further mishap. By habit, too, he stopped at the right spot. Then he half-fell out of the car and staggered away without waiting for his parking ticket. He heard not a sound when an irate attendant screamed after him.

"Fucking drunk," the attendant complained as Simon lurched away, and tossed his parking ticket into the garbage can.

The exercise of climbing back up the parking ramp to the street and then the impact of the cold evening air partially sobered Simon. Resolutely he walked from Fifty-third Street, where he had parked, south on Lexington Avenue. To a casual observer, he would have looked like a man, unsteady with drink, hurrying to Grand Central Station or some similar destination from whence he could reasonably find his way home. To a closer observer, like the hookers who offered their soiled wares around Forty-seventh Street, he had a wildness about him that warned them to stay clear. And to someone who knew him, Simon would have presented an extraordinary sight, his eyes unseeing, his face screwed up as if against some nonexistent icy gale, his lips muttering earnestly, but whether curses or prayers was unclear.

Without prior planning, Simon swerved toward a doorway, turning so sharply that he stumbled and almost fell. Recovering, he barged through the door into a bar. It was noisy with an early evening crowd made up partly of locals having a few drinks before going out, partly of businessmen delaying their homeward progress by one—or several—for the road. A few people were obviously looking for pickups and three mildly unappealing but not quite revolting whores were waiting expectantly. Most of the patrons, however, were here to drink—and there was a lot of hard drinking in progress.

Simon shoved his way to the bar, neither noticing nor caring about the complaints of those he pushed. With some difficulty he perched himself on a stool, slipping once and almost crashing to the floor. Finally installed, he managed to swivel the stool until it faced the bar, and hold himself steady against the counter. Methodically, he started to drink, intent only on blotting out his memory.

Simon sat quietly as he drank. He neither talked to his neighbors nor heard them when they commented to him. The babble all around him seemed at a great distance, and he felt insulated from it by an impenetrable cocoon of silence and misery. On the one hand, he could observe himself dispassionately, enveloped in his cocoon, a bloated, sluglike being who aroused in him the same fascinated disgust he remembered experiencing as a boy watching maggots crawl over the carcass of a heifer that had died in a gully one summer and had not been found until it was rotted blue. At the same time, however, he could not distance himself from the depth of the pain, guilt, fear, desperation he felt about Jim Lester. Try as he might to drown out both memory and awareness, the knowledge of Jim dead, the rasp of Spinosa assuring him that the problem was taken care of, the pathetic demand of Mary Lester that he do something, would not leave him for an instant.

But do what? He downed another whisky, hoping to divert his mind. But do what? The question pounded at him. "Do what? Do what?" Words seemed to attack him. "Dead and dead and dead; Do what? Do what? Do what?"

What *could* he do? He had no proof whatsoever that Jim's death was other than accidental. There was no one to accuse, no hope that an accusation would hold. And what of the personal decision he faced? Give in to Spinosa and make the false announcement—or defy the man?

And then what? Over a cliff himself? The ultimate solution, surely. He had embraced its comfort often enough, so why was he shocked now that he might have it inflicted on him? Killed so that some other double-breasted slave could do Spinosa's bidding, vilifying the memory both of Jim Lester and of what minuscule competence and integrity Simon Bagnew stood for?

Simon, ordering another drink and another, observed himself, a stranger. He noted with distaste how his body sagged forward and how his potbelly indented itself against the bar. How sad to have no control over his arms as he drunkenly beckoned the bartender to bring him yet another Scotch. Disgraceful, really, how his tongue slurred his order. How sad!

A tear trickled down Simon's cheek, surprising him. He tried to brush it away and was embarrassed when his hand, as uncontrolled as a newborn's, missed his cheek entirely. Why was that old fart, himself, draped over the bar weeping? If only that poor sot knew what real pain was, Simon thought, or knew the feeling of real guilt. Then how he would weep! Slumped on his bar stool, Simon let his head droop and collapsed half across the bar. I am drunk, he thought. But it's no good. Jim Lester is dead and it's my fault. . . .

"Time to leave." The rough but not unkind voice of the barman invaded Simon's consciousness. "Come on then. Up you get. Go on home. We're closing."

"You're still open," Simon protested with a drunk's excess dignity. "And, anyhow, I've no home."

"'Course you have. Everyone has somewhere," the barman reassured him. "But it ain't here. So out you go." The voice was tougher. "Don't make no big deal."

"I don't want . . ." Simon started to protest.

"Harry," the barman called over the din. "This gentleman wishes to be helped out."

As if by spontaneous incarnation, a huge black man, his

windbreaker jacket filled up with his muscles, appeared at Simon's side. "Time to be movin', man," he said in a deep voice, as gently but firmly as if he were talking to a recalcitrant toddler. "Up we get."

Simon felt his shoulder gripped as by the jaws of a crane. Then an arm of steel encircled his waist and he found himself being conveyed—position vertical, feet barely scuffing the ground—toward the door. "Easy does it, man," the bouncer reassured him. "You've imbibed just a little to excess." Using Simon's body as a buffer, he pushed the door open. "There you go, man," he said, setting Simon onto the sidewalk as carefully as if he were balancing a ballerina on point. He held him a second to steady him and then let him stand alone. "Easy," he repeated as Simon just managed to remain balanced and immobile. Then the bouncer gave Simon the gentlest of pushes, hardly more than a tap, just enough to send him staggering slowly down Lexington Avenue. "Be cool," he called after Simon, his voice full of amusement. "Keep yo' ass upright, my man."

Simon felt as if he had tripped and were running as fast as he could to avoid falling flat on his face. Yet, at the same time, every action was in slow motion. He could move no faster than if he were walking underwater. The air pressed on him as heavily as syrup. Miraculously, he could breathe, but his breath came in gasps, as if he were close to his limit of exertion.

Forever he seemed to stagger forward like this, balanced precariously between standing and falling. Eventually, inevitably, his hopeless attempt at balance failed; without realizing it, he started to tip further and further forward, toppling toward the sidewalk.

It was not the fall itself, or even the pain of its impact, that momentarily sobered Simon. Rather it was his surprise at the reversal of his sensations. First, there was the sudden, sharp pain as his face, which a moment before had been facing upward gasping for air, collided with the paving stone where his feet had been. Then, even as he realized that he was lying spread-eagle across the sidewalk, he felt the rushing sensation of himself falling down and could sense his own arm reaching up, but too slowly to protect his face. At the very end of the sequence, he felt the discomfort of the twist in his ankle on the edge of the pothole that had finally tripped him.

"God," he muttered, reoriented enough by his surprise to be able to clamber back to his feet. "God damn." Futilely he tried to brush his pants clean of the wet mud. "I need a drink," he announced loudly. He ran his hand over his face and felt something wet. With difficulty he managed to extract his handkerchief from his trouser pocket and wipe it over his face. For a moment he gazed at it uncomprehendingly. Why was it red? Then, realizing, he became angry. "Shit," he shouted, "I'm bloody bloody . . ."

Simon's voice trailed off to a cry of mixed amazement and terror as, all of a sudden, out of nowhere, the apparition appeared. It was Jim Lester, all right, clothing tattered, body mangled, covered in blood. He just stood there, as still as Simon himself, but alive although terribly wounded, real although clearly dead.

"Leave me alone," Simon begged.

The figure, ragged and awful, remained still. He was only feet away . . . half in shadow . . . covered in dirt and blood . . . inhumanly dead . . . but alive.

"Oh God," Simon whimpered, excrutiatingly frightened but also full of both remorse and care. He took a step toward the apparition, which seemed to move toward him an equal distance, emerging more into the light and thereby looking less misshapen, more human. Perhaps, after all, he could be saved. Simon stretched out his hand and the creation responded by doing the same. "Let me help you," Simon called to him. "I want to help." He took two rapid steps forward, watching the creature lurch spontaneously the same distance toward him. They were very close together now. Simon took one more step . . . and crashed painfully into the polished marble wall of the building in which he had been seeing himself distortedly reflected. "Oh Christ," Simon prayed and swore. "Oh Christ!"

Staggering now from the impact as much as from the alcohol, Simon turned further south on Lexington Avenue. "Gotta walk," he admonished himself. "Clear the old head."

Past the Graybar Building with its ugly granite facade. On around a corner and past the dirty entrance doors of Grand Central Station where a filthy bag woman cowered in a corner methodically counting her treasures, tiny pieces of trash meticulously gleaned from city gutters and arranged around her in a pattern of infinite importance. On again, crossing Forty-second Street without regard to the light which, fortunately, was green. On down to Forty-first Street where, deciding to cross Madison, he was almost run down by a newspaper truck driven at breakneck speed by a driver expecting no pedestrians at two A.M.

Gradually, Simon lost all sense of place or time. Somewhere near Twentieth Street he found an all-night bar and drank some more. Somehow he staggered on, falling several times until his clothes were covered with dirt and his face looked as if it had been unwashed for days.

Eventually, as the road widened, he realized that there were other men around, as dissolute as he, leaning in corners, fallen and unconscious in doorways. Those still awake were swigging from bottles without labels. Lowering himself, half-falling, next to such a one, Simon proferred him a five-dollar note, it seemed, or perhaps a ten; and the Bowery drunk, wise in the values on this strip, sold him his bottle gleefully. Simon drank great gulps.

Then, at last, he felt his thoughts start to blur with the onset of oblivion. If he could only drink enough to be gone, absent from every thought. With a groan he realized that the bottle was empty. But it was enough. His head fell backward against the wall and he passed out.

Oh, but the dreams. Crawling, slimy beasts beset him, creatures with the face of Spinosa and the broken body of Jim Lester. They insinuated themselves, hugging and loving him. When he tried to beat them away they embraced him until, to his horror, he found himself first accepting, then welcoming and finally lusting for them. In his self-disgust he tried to run away, but he was frozen; he tried to turn away, but his head would not move; endeavored to close his eyes, but his eyelids became transparent. Thus, he was forced to watch with mounting fascination as the creatures he abhorred and yet lusted for started slowly and methodically, with sharp knives, sledge hammers they swung as easily as softball bats, blue-steeled machetes, to mutilate each other, to carve up, to do to death ...

When the police found Simon forty-eight hours later, he was whimpering with terror, half-lying on his back like a dying cat feebly trying to protect itself from some demon attacker.

"This one needs to go," the younger cop said to his partner. "He's in a bad way."

"Yeah." His partner's face wrinkled in disgust but he didn't move.

"Come on then, Fred. I can't handle him alone."

"Stinks."

"Yeah. But he's still gotta go."

"Smells like he went, is all. God, how I hate this job! Drunken bums. Oughta shoot the fuckin' lot."

"So you coming or not?"

"Okay, okay." Fred grumbled. "Let's do it." He moved

toward Simon, who cried out in terror and wriggled and squeezed himself as far back into the corner of the wall as he could. "Up you get then." Old Fred grasped one arm and his partner the other. "Let's go, then." His voice was surprisingly kind.

Together the two cops pulled Simon to his feet. He muttered incoherently.

"It's okay," Fred reassured Simon. "Goin' to get you cleaned up, is all."

Simon whimpered louder.

"Okay, okay. Just take it easy. You'll be fine." Fred's voice was as gentle as if he were talking to a hurt puppy.

The younger cop looked at his new partner in surprise. Back at the station they had warned him that the old man chewed up rookies together with the nails he ate for breakfast. Holding Simon's other arm he smiled at his partner. "You're not so tough," he grinned. "How long you been doin' this?"

"Ten partners like you, kid. Two dead. I only got a year to go. Tough enough."

Simon's body started to sag between them.

"Up!" Fred ordered sharply but still not unkindly. The word cut through Simon's consciousness and he pulled himself more upright.

"What you doin' here anyhow? I never seen you before," Fred asked. "He's no regular," he added to his partner. "Look at his clothes."

"So what do we do?"

"Shove him in the van, deposit him at the hospital, and hope he don't throw up or shit before we get there. Just like with all the others. Inside, you poor sot," he added to Simon and lowered him onto the bench in the back of the van. "Hang on so you don't fall off the seat."

"I'm okay," Simon said thickly. "I'll leave now."

"Sure you will." The two cops shut the door and drove him away.

* * *

Janet reached Simon some five hours after he had been admitted. The hospital routine was ponderous and it was midafternoon before they finally reached her. She was out of breath when she arrived, but otherwise, on the surface, as prosaically efficient as ever.

"You've had a difficult time, I'm afraid," she said, looking him over. He was clean but scratched, bruised and terribly haggard. The flesh of his face was so gray and loose that it seemed virtually dead, as if, at any moment, it might dislodge itself and slip off his skull like the frosting on a cake left out in the sun.

"Yes." His eyes filled with tears.

"We'd better get you out of here, then," she said briskly. Her no-nonsense manner brooked no weakness in either of them. Oh, my God, she was thinking, what has he done, and why, oh why? But she had promised herself not to ask the questions that bombarded her. "Then, if you like, we can talk later," she bit her lip to avoid saying more.

"Yes," he repeated weakly, knowing that he must tell her the whole story eventually—and knowing too that such was his shame that he probably never could.

Janet helped her suddenly aged husband out of bed with the partial sympathy of a good professional nurse. Don't baby him, she warned herself. He must neither be criticized for his drinking bout nor have it endorsed by excessive sympathy. Moreover, try as she would, Janet could not quite eradicate some of the waspish disgust for all weakness that her upbringing had imbued into her austere New England soul. Why would her husband let himself go like this? Could anything be an adequate excuse? On the Bowery they had found him, so the police had informed her. The Bowery! How could he? People just didn't do such things.

"Come then," she said, holding his arm to steady him

as he swung his legs out of bed and struggled to stand. "I've brought you clean clothes."

His coarse hospital gown was creased up behind so that his sagging buttocks hung below it.

"Go change in the bathroom," she said, brushing his nightshirt down almost crossly. She steadied him as far as the door. "In you go." She handed him his clothes and then closed the door firmly behind him. He was quite capable of dressing himself, she decided. After all, there was nothing wrong with him except the hangover of his binge.

The old man in the next bed had been watching silently ever since Janet arrived. "What's the problem, then?" he asked, his voice creaky. "Got a drinking problem, does he?"

"No, he does not," Janet flared. How dare the old indigent say such a thing? "He's perfectly fine. Just needs a rest."

"He had a drinking problem when they brought him in," the old man cackled with finality. "Whether you wanna know or not." He rolled over away from Janet. "Drunk as a fucking Injun," he muttered. "Drunk out of his fuckin' mind."

Janet tried not to hear, and hearing, to pay no attention. But the words struck at her like lashes. Oh, what was wrong with him? All these years he had been such a good man. But now he had become different, staying away at nights—and when he was home he was either arrogant or secretive and secluded . . . and drunk, just as the old man said. She took a deep breath to steady herself. But he *would* recover; just as he *had* got a new job. She'd see to it. That there might be any other outcome she was far too determined—but, yes, at this moment also far too desperate—even to consider. After all, she concluded, he *is* my husband.

Simon emerged, still pale and drawn, but adequately dressed now and more composed. Her heart was wrenched looking at him. "Feeling better?" she asked. Oh yes, she was thinking, I really do love the man.

21

The Greenwich Hospital was outstandingly tasteful, a gem even in this wealthy community abounding in good taste—more like an understated luxury hotel than a hospital. It was surrounded by the sort of lawns always called 'spacious,' and it was comfortably shaded by a veritable arboretum of imported trees. In front of the building ran a two-lane residential boulevard also lined with trees. It was a cul-de-sac, naturally, and therefore devoid of all traffic but for the occasional car seeking a parking spot. Everything around the hospital—most certainly including the people entering and leaving—was immaculate: lawns, shrubs, circular driveway, windows glistening in the sun, all were a cliché of affluent neatness.

The strollers, this dappled Saturday morning, fit their setting. The men, resplendent in lime-green blazers and plaid pants, the women in pleated skirts or designer jeans topped by very expensive shirts or sweaters, denoted wealthy Wall Street or, at least, well-to-do Madison Avenue, as obviously as khakis announce the military. They went beyond affluence, however, to the point of arrogance. Even in front of their hospital—where surely their peers occasionally died—they exuded a degree of security that bordered on the insufferable. Certainly the rich have medical setbacks, their manner implied. Indeed, heart attacks, ulcers, even cancer are the burdens we leaders have to bear even more than does the pack. But that is just life, to be recognized, accepted, endured, but always quietly and with style. The fact that we suffer dread diseases just like the hoi polloi, need not imply that we, the elite, are not superior in every other respect . . . or that we are not to the manor born and destined to be still firmly in it when we die!

Janet parked the car under a tree. Their old family station wagon was quite appropriate here: Greenwich people did not show off their wealth by owning Cadillacs. An occasional Mercedes—preferably ten years old but perfectly kept—was acceptable. Otherwise, a middle-aged Chevy for her, and an even older one for him to take to the golf course, plus an MG for the kids, was about right. Oh, and of course during the week there was Willie or Sam or whatever the driver was called to drive Dad around in the limo. Janet fished in the back seat for a carrier bag, hopped out of the car and hurried into the hospital.

Here, too, the aura of confident, conservative wealth was as pervasive as the Muzak that played unceasingly. One might be sick, might even die, but there was no need to be showy, hysterical or in any other way obvious about it. Doctors at the Greenwich Hospital tended to wear elderly sports jackets and donned white coats only when absolutely necessary. Candy-stripers abounded, mostly preppy girls with easy manners, or ladies of a certain age, eyes sun-wrinkled from sailing and tennis.

Janet, for all the impoverishment of the last few years, fit into this environment. Her heavy walking shoes imitated those of the kind lady behind the reception desk precisely. Their voices were as the voices of sisters.

"Janet, how nice to see you," the receptionist beamed,

quite ignoring the fact that Janet had been in to see Simon twice a day each of the four days he had been "resting" here. "Did you get everything you wanted?"

"Well, almost. I got a new skirt and shoes. But they didn't have any blouses. Nothing suitable."

"Oh, I know." The receptionist was all sympathy.

"Mostly day-glo or see-through." The two women chuckled together. What was the world coming to? "It's such a nuisance."

"Of course."

"Well, I'd better be getting up to him." Janet's tone implied that duty called. "Nice seeing you."

"Really," the receptionist replied. How could such a sensible person have a drunk as a husband? Thank God her Todd never took too much. Never had, even when they were kids. Didn't do too much of anything, in fact, except make money and complain about politicians.

Janet hurried back to the elevators. How she hated that look of mixed sympathy and scorn. How well she recognized it! Everyone was so kind to her, but they knew, didn't they? Her husband wasn't in the hospital because of cancer or kidney stones or a heart attack. Those afflictions you couldn't help. But he didn't *have* to drink. She had to recognize that, even as she tried to understand and forgive. He'd never been weak before, but this time he'd caved in.

In a sense, the problem was continuing, she worried. He hadn't had a drink since she'd found him in New York, at least not as far as she could tell. But his health had become steadily more precarious. He was on the edge of pneumonia, the doctor said, and he had a kidney inflammation that kept him bedridden and in pain. For some reason, it wouldn't respond to the medication the way the doctor thought it should. Was Simon bringing that on himself in some way? Moreover, he was both depressed and agitated, unable or unwilling to get himself out of bed or to telephone his office for hours on end; and then, in a complete switch, he would demand petulantly and sometimes aggressively to be given a business suit so that he could go to the office where he belonged.

Yesterday, Janet had called his bluff and offered to drive him home. But he had instantly found himself too weak. Was he just giving in to his disease as he had to the alcohol? Couldn't he shake off his ill health, or at least help to overcome it? She would! Janet was ashamed of the thought the moment she formulated it, but it nagged at her in spite of herself.

Janet Bagnew alighted from the elevator and walked rather slowly, almost unwillingly, toward her husband's room. Outside, she hesitated a moment. Then, pulling her shoulders back with a conscious effort, she took a deep breath and pushed open the door. "Hello, darling," she said cheerfully. "I've had a fine time shopping. Lots of skirts and shoes, but not a suitable blouse in the length and breadth of Greenwich. All day-glo or see-through."

"Really?" Simon couldn't help smiling both at her bubbling cheerfulness and at the thought of his Janet in a see-through anything. "Perhaps not wholly appropriate," he agreed drily.

"So I brought you some cookies instead. Peak Frean's."

"If I'm a grownup or plan to be one?" Simon asked, quoting the sophisticated commercial. "I'm working on it." His tone was bitter.

"Oh, come on. We've been through that."

There was a pause.

"I really appreciate you're not asking me anything," Simon started hesitantly. "You must want to know what happened."

"You'll tell me when you're ready." How touching that he had realized.

"Yes," he said pensively, wondering when the hell that would be.

Simon had a friend who had described his body as being on a programmed shutdown. That was just how his own felt now. He could observe quite clearly how it was being battered by his guilt and fears. Thank God, he thought for the thousandth time, for the drugs they gave him, drugs to decongest his lungs, lower his blood pressure, cure his kidney, kill the pain, let him sleep—they all helped his mind. The doctors had not helped his body much, but inadvertently, they had kept him sane. In the last forty-eight hours, he found he could again sleep without nightmares. He remained desperate with remorse and worry when he let himself think about Jim Lester or Spinosa. But he could tune them out now. The hours of sleep were oblivion, and he had never been as grateful for anything in his whole life. "Yes," he repeated softly, "I'll tell you when I can."

Tell me what? Janet wanted to scream. He'd told her of Spinosa and Galsworthy, warned her that he might be fired yet again. All that was bad, but what problem could be so awful that he had to be so defeated and so maudlin? She wanted to shake him, forcibly imbue him with the determination he seemed unable to generate for himself. One just doesn't give in, Janet felt. It was *wrong*.

Pursing her lips, she held her peace. Surely he would confide in her eventually. And regain his courage, and his dignity. "Yes, dear," she said with as much tenderness as she could muster. "I know; I do understand." But, in fact, she realized, she understood nothing about what made him behave this way.

"I think I feel a lot better," Simon said, suddenly manically cheerful. "I went for a walk down the corridor earlier."

"Oh, that's good." Perhaps she had been too harsh in her judgment.

"The kidney pills seem to be starting to work. Pain's less." He paused to smile at her. "How are you?"

Janet was surprised. Simon had shown not the least interest in any but his own problems for days now. Even before his—she hesitated even before phrasing it to herself—his attack (no, that was too dramatic), his *bout* (that was better)—even before his bout he had seemed entirely preoccupied and self-centered. She'd known that something was wrong. "Why, I'm fine," she answered, her surprise flustering her slightly.

"You've had a lot to put up with," he continued sadly.

"Oh come. It's not that bad."

"But you have." His eyes filled with tears. "I've let you down. You and Susie." He was close to weeping.

"Simon, you haven't." She said it sternly, fighting her growing embarrassment at his weakness. It was all right for men to cry, she had read in some magazine. Well not to her. "I'm fine," she insisted. "And so are you. We've just had a little bad luck. It will pass."

"If only I had your strength." His face sagged lugubriously and a tear rolled down one cheek.

"Stop it," she snapped at him. "I won't stand that sort of talk."

"But it's true."

"Rubbish."

"Please don't be cross." The tears overflowed, making his cheeks, the sides of his nose, his chin, glisten. "I just don't have it anymore," he wept. "It's all too much."

"Stop it, Simon." She practically stamped her foot, now at the very end of her patience. "I won't allow this sort of self-pity. Just stop it!"

"First I'm out of work for years," he continued in a singsong voice, as if he had not heard her. "Then, as soon as I find a job, I swell up with the pride of it and ignore you. You, who have stood by me, scrimping and saving, through all the bad times. Now this binge over which I had no control . . ."

Finally, Janet's patience snapped. "Be quiet this instant," she stormed at him. "You have no right to feel so damned sorry for yourself. Pull yourself together." She paused to look coldly at him.

His chin quivered, his eyes and jowls drooped like a Saint Bernard, his belly formed a vulnerable mound under the rumpled sheet.

Her examination of him was full of anger and contempt. "Be a man," she said witheringly, "or I want none of you."

"But, Janet . . ."

"I never complained when you were out of work. Those things happen. They prove nothing. Neither did your daughter. There is nothing to be ashamed of in trying, not even if you fail."

"But . . ."

"But nothing. The only shame is in quitting. Shame is in giving in." She paused and then, not fully aware of how awful were the words she was about to utter, decided that she had gone so far that she might as well say the whole thing. "I have never doubted that you were the right man for me, Simon. Not when we argued occasionally. Not when you lost your job and were despondent. Not even recently when you started having an affair with someone else. . . . No, don't stop me. I know those things happen and I was confident you would come back to me. You were always courageous, you see, tough and resilient, even in adversity. And because you were strong, you gave me strength. I could keep our lives in perspective. Of course we would be all right. People like us always make it. We are well-bred, intelligent, healthy. My God, what can go wrong if we keep trying? Who or what is powerful enough—except disease, accident, death—to stop us?"

Simon cringed back into his bed.

"But now, for the first time in my life, I wonder whether I am misled," she continued, her voice as unforgiving as crystal. "I wonder where your courage went. Or has it been an illusion—my fantasy, perhaps—all along? What are you, Simon, the man I married and love, or a soft-underbellied crybaby? I don't know what has caused this breakdown, and I don't care." Her anger raised her voice and for once she was passionate. "But I do know that nothing gives you the right to lie down in defeat like this. There's no excuse. It's as bad as suicide. And that I consider the ultimate degradation."

A vision of the final solution that had sustained him for so long flashed across Simon's mind. Thank God he had never talked about that, he thought. Not that he would have done so as long as there was the slightest chance that he might be forced to resort to it.

"I wouldn't expect you, even now, to sink that low. But what you are doing is akin to it: a sort of emotional or psychic suicide, a giving in that is almost as bad." She paused for breath, her chest heaving with anger. "How can you, Simon?" she demanded. "What sort of a man have you become?" She paused and then, with all the bitterness and disappointment of the last days welling up inside her, all the years of trying to hold up her head now negated by his drunkenness, all she had labored so hard to maintain torn down by his irresponsibility, she added her final, scathing question: "Or are you still a man at all?"

Slowly Janet arose from her chair. "That's all I have to say, Simon," she announced in her normal voice. "I'm sorry that I have offended you. But it had to be said." She started to bend over to kiss him, thought better of it, touched him on the shoulder with a gesture both disdainfully distant and unbearably intimate. "Call me this evening," she said. "I'll be home. Tell me whatever you like." She started toward the door. As she left, she half-turned back to him. "Take care of yourself," she admonished. Then she left.

"How is he then, your husband?" the receptionist asked as Janet walked past her desk.

"Oh, fine." Janet was startled out of her reverie by the question. "He'll be just fine," she repeated. She started to walk away, but she was almost too distraught to move. Desperately she wished for some outlet for her swirling emotions. If only she could scream or cry. If only she could tell someone. "It's only that . . ." she started to say to the receptionist.

"Yes, only what?" The woman sensed a wonderful piece of scandal about to be revealed. It wouldn't be the first time. Even the toughest ladies sometimes went to pieces at a bedside. Then they had to tell someone about it, and she was usually the first sympathetic ear they found.

"It's only that . . ." Janet realized what she was about to say and bit her tongue. It was no one's business but her own. "It's only that I wish they knew just how fast he'll respond to the drugs. Some take longer than others to work." Resolutely, she turned and started toward the door.

"Oh, I quite understand, dear," the receptionist called after her, acutely disappointed. Instead of a confession, all she'd got was Janet's traditional New England reserve. Such hoity-toity airs she puts on, the receptionist was thinking. With what right? Her man picked up as a common drunk—and everyone knows that he'd been out of work for years. "See you tomorrow, then. Have a nice evening."

"Thank you," Janet called back without breaking stride. She spun the circular door so hard that it clipped her heel as she went through it. "Damn," she muttered, surprising herself with the sound of her own voice.

Briskly, Janet walked down the circular driveway and crossed the boulevard to her car. As she pulled away from the curb, another car, very similar to her own, slid into the space. Nothing had changed as a result of her visit . . . except that, for the first time in her life, she was deeply, violently angry at her husband.

Simon lay very still in his bed after Janet left. He held onto the edges of the mattress as if even the slightest motion might tip up this tiny raft of safety and leave him drowning in some great ocean of reality. At first his tears flowed unabated and he made no attempt to dry his cheeks. Eventually they stopped. And a long time later, as they dried astringently and started to itch, he wiped at his cheeks with the back of one hand. His face seemed numb; and the sensation on his hand was cold, as if he were rubbing foam-filled plastic. Quickly he stopped and grabbed the mattress again as a child, daring to ride his bicycle one-handed for the first time, will grab for the handlebar again, scared by his own daring.

A nurse bustled into the room. "How are we, then?" she demanded in tones reserved for children, senile ancients and hospital patients. "We okay?"

Simon grunted.

"Good, good." She straightened a sheet and hurried out.

Simon continued to lie quietly, gripping the sides of the bed. But his mind, as numbed as his body up to now, was starting to function.

"Jim Lester," Simon muttered, able to say the name for the first time in days without being immediately destroyed by the horror of his death. I've got to face him, Simon was thinking. Dead. And it's my fault.

But for the first time he corrected this thought. It was his action that had caused Jim's death, no doubt. But hardly his fault beyond that. He would never have urged Jim to inform himself, and then used him as an excuse with Spinosa, if he'd had the remotest idea of what would happen. How could he know, or even suspect? People didn't do such things. Unconsciously, he was repeating Janet's earlier thought verbatim. Their actions might be at odds, but their values meshed. Did his ignorance exonerate him? Oh, no, by no means! He was the cause of Jim's death all right, as surely as if he had forced the car off the cliff himself. There was no getting away from the fact that the result of his talk with Spinosa was that a good man was dead, his wife heartbroken and his kids fatherless. But the fact that Simon had no way of knowing the results of his action did perhaps somewhat mitigate his culpability. Simon eased his grasp on his mattress.

Very slowly, like an old electric fan stiff from a winter's disuse, Simon's mind was starting to operate. The reflex emotions of panic, terror and remorse were slowly being marshaled into some kind of order. For the first time in days he could go beyond the fact of Jim Lester's death and realize that, while he was its cause, Spinosa was its vehicle. And with that thought came the certainty that he had to do something. Things could not be left just like this. It was too . . . he could not yet find the right word. Unfair? Untidy? Those words could not nearly explain the strength of his feeling that something had to be done.

But what could be done? He could not prove Spinosa was in any way involved. There was not even a hint, as far as he could tell, that Jim's death was other than an accident, another driver fallen asleep at the wheel. Even if he could somehow prove that Jim Lester had been murdered, even show that Spinosa was implicated—prove, for example, that Spinosa told him about the "accident" before it happened—what good would that do? Another accident, this one to him, would be the only result. He wondered how they would go after him. Another automobile wreck? Or a "suicide" out of some high-storied building? Simon Bagnew, the man who for years had accepted suicide as his personal final solution, and had found great comfort in it, shuddered with horror at the thought of being killed.

Creakily, Simon rolled over onto his side, pushed his legs over the edge of the bed, and used the leverage of their weight to help himself sit upright. After a few moments' rest he rose unsteadily to his feet. Slowly he walked toward the closet and swung open the door so that he could gaze at the full-length mirror inside.

What he saw, he decided, was pitiful. Staring back at him was an aging man with a weak chin, wearily rounded shoulders, and a potbelly. His receding hair gave him a flat-foreheaded look, a little like a toad, he thought. And how his slightly bulging eyes, puffed lids and jowls accentuated that appearance! His chin was stubbly and his eyes damp and bloodshot.

"I must stand up to him." He said it simply. His voice quavered like an old man's, but the words reverberated with his conviction. "Perhaps I can't; but I must try. He wondered whether, in the end, he would be able to stand up to Carlos Spinosa or not. Somehow, he doubted it. But he did feel, at least at this second, that he would make the attempt. How he would fight, he had no idea . . . so far, there seemed not a single reasonable option, absolutely no hope. Worse, even if he found some workable plan, would he have the strength, the courage, to make it stick? He doubted it.

Simon Bagnew turned away from the mirror and, moving a little faster, went into the bathroom. He started to shave. The water felt good on his face and, when he had finished, the sting of his after-shave felt wonderful.

Did he hold any cards at all? Simon wondered for the hundredth time. All he could decide to do for now was to promise to do everything Spinosa asked.

22

Although he looked haggard and his liver condition added a sickly olive tone to his already gray pallor, Simon Bagnew had put in long, hard days at work since he released himself from the Greenwich hospital two weeks ago. He seemed both driven and efficient. The employees of Turner-LaMott buzzed at the change.

"What's happened to him?" asked the attractive but sharp-nosed woman whose title was group product manager, sleeping products and tranquilizers, but who was usually referred to as the sleep grouper. "He looks like he died and they forgot to bury him."

"Yeah, but he's in there pitching, you have to give him that." Her colleague, another group product manager, replied. "I don't know what happened. But he's working his tail off, even though he does look half-dead. You have to admit it, the man's got guts."

"I suppose . . ."

"And have you noticed how decisive he's become?"

Sam Peters, the deceptively mild-looking, but highly political sales manager, overhearing what they were discussing, paused in his methodical progress down the corridor. "And he's talking so lucidly, too," he agreed. "Not one mixed metaphor or 'in my experience' in over a week!" He started to move on.

"They say he was attacked by a bottle," the sleep grouper stopped him, pleased to gossip. "He sure looks ready to throw up any second."

"Doubt it. No one's ever seen him with too much."

"Maybe he's gone on the wagon."

"Don't think so. He'll take a drink now and then. Maybe a glass of wine at lunch." Peters sought to impress with his inside knowledge. "That's not the sign of an alcoholic. They're all feast or famine. One's too much and never enough."

"Guess you're right. But what's it all about?"

"Ahh . . ." Peters loved to appear mysterious.

"I heard one of the directors, that Spinosa guy, he's called some sort of news conference."

"So?"

"Don't ask me." She paused.

"I figure you'd know if anyone does."

He fell for the challenge inevitably. "No idea," he said importantly, doing his best to pretend he knew more than he did but couldn't repeat it. "Of course Spinosa's behind it. But I'd better not discuss it."

"Oh, I thought you were informed," the grouper goaded. "But . . ."

"Well, I can tell you this. It's going to be a hell of an announcement. Every member of the press I ever heard of is being invited." Sam Peters paused impressively. "And judging by the wording of the announcement, they'll all come." Responsibility for the mail room fell under sales, so Sam saw every important mailing—even if he didn't necessarily know what it meant.

"Since when do more than a handful of reporters turn up for a Turner-LaMott news conference?" the sleep grouper asked innocently.

"Since the last time—when they got a lot more than they bargained for."

"That's true. But they can't expect a bombshell every time," she tried to probe.

"Sorry," Sam said, "but I can't say more." He moved off, stately as a barge and well pleased with himself. In spite of his ignorance, he had managed to maintain his reputation for being in the know. No doubt, future events would suggest that, all along, he'd been privy to more than he'd been willing to tell. For one thing was certain: whatever was to be announced, it was to be big news.

If Simon seemed more decisive, it was because all other decisions became so minor and easy compared to the critical one of what to do about Carlos Spinosa. He thought about nothing else, day and night. With little hope of success, he had tried to delay the press conference. "But Carlos, I'm indisposed." he had complained. "And there's such a lot of groundwork."

"No delays," Carlos had rasped. "See to it."

"Very well." He had to pretend to go along with everything Carlos wanted. That way, his enemy would not be prealerted when he struck. Simon laughed bitterly at the thought. Struck with what? Stones against tanks? God, but how absurd he had become. . . .

So the preparations for the press conference continued. As Sam Peters had indicated, all the key reporters would attend. The announcement each had received was terse but compelling:

> I shall be making an important announcement, affecting the future of the Turner-LaMott Corporation, on Wednesday, September 1st at 11:00 AM in the Cotillion Room of the Pierre Hotel, Fifth Avenue and 61st Street, New York. We would, therefore, appreciate your attendance or that of your deputy.
> We have no doubt that the announcement will have a significant impact on the value placed upon the company by the investing public.

That meant that Turner-LaMott's stock would gyrate; and that meant every reporter had to be present.

The days passed for Simon as slowly as if he were counting the seconds as they piled up into minutes, and the minutes into hours. He felt alternately terrified at what was bound to happen, frustrated because he had no counterplan, frantic that the time was drawing ever closer and, paradoxically, equally frantic that time was moving so slowly that it seemed to hold for long periods virtually without moving at all.

A thousand alternatives skittered through his brain. He could defy Spinosa and take the consequences. That would foil the bastard. And he could protect his life, perhaps, by telling Spinosa that he had left a letter describing that he was to be killed and why. But that would not help. Even if he were not killed, he would be fired and his successor would make the announcement anyhow, certainly contradicting what Simon had said previously and probably publicly ridiculing him as well. After that there would not even be the slimmest chance in the world that Simon could find another job. If that were to be the path he chose, it would be better not to write the letter at all. That way Carlos would institute the final solution Janet abhorred—which he himself would probably be too weak to carry out.

But what if Carlos didn't bother to have him killed? Firing him would be enough. Carlos would have his way . . . and he, Simon, would be hopeless, utterly ruined for the rest of his life. Even his family would be out of work.

The easiest path, of course, would be to do precisely what Spinosa asked. Oh, how tempting that was. Instead of misery, penury and disgrace, he would remain a senior, successful—

The telephone rang, interrupting him at the very moment of this daydream. Spinosa indulged in no greetings. "Ten days left," he said. "You are proceeding?"

"Well, yes, Carlos. I am. The invitations go out tomorrow and—"

"And you are thinking of alternatives."

"Well, I . . . Of course not. I don't know what you mean."

Carlos ignored the denial. "I have them all covered. You *must* make the announcement I ordered."

"Yes." Suddenly Simon was angry, perhaps more coldly angry than he had ever been before in his life. And, with the anger came a new insight, a realization that whatever he did there was no way out. Even if he agreed with Spinosa, sold his integrity to this evil man, it wouldn't help. He'd still be made a scapegoat in the end. "And once I make the announcement," Simon said glacially, quite certain now that he was right, "then what?" It was a rhetorical question. "I'll tell you what. Then you'll fire me anyhow. If that's what you mean, yes, I have thought of that, Carlos. Perhaps I am not as clever as you, but one would have to be even stupider than me not to think as far as that. So why should I make the announcement? Why should I? How can you force me?" A great burden fell from Simon's shoulders. He was free. . . .

Spinosa emitted a strange grating sound, more like the clicking of a geiger counter than anything human. With horror, Simon realized it was the voice of the gray man chuckling. "I wondered how long you would take to realize." For a moment Spinosa's voice sounded almost friendly. "Of course you are right. But there is a carrot."

"What?" Simon was thoroughly confused.

"I have anticipated your rebellion. An employment contract is drawn up. I will send it over in an hour. It says that if we fire you we must indemnify you. One million dollars."

Simon almost groaned. Instead of the heady freedom of a few moments ago, a vice gripped again at his heart. How could he possibly refuse now?

"Also," Carlos was continuing, "there is a key man life insurance policy that pays the same amount to your family if you die. Double if death is by accident, unknown causes . . . even murder." He hung up.

For minutes Simon's head whirled. "The bastard," he muttered. "Oh, the unmitigated, unforgiveable bastard." There were no words in Simon's vocabulary to express adequately his loathing.

The contract Spinosa had promised arrived promptly. It sat now, as dangerous as a letter bomb, isolated in the locked drawer of Simon's desk at home. He dared neither look at it, for fear of being seduced, nor show it to anyone, his lawyer, wife, even Sandra, for fear of its being repudiated by them on his behalf. Give up a million dollars? Not bloody likely. Sell his soul? He wasn't sure he could do that either. "The bastard," Simon would mutter venomously. "Oh, that filthy bastard."

Sometimes, instead of trying to think coherently, Simon fantasized. What would happen, he dreamed, if he walked onto the platform a week from Wednesday, after having pretended until the last minute that he intended to repudiate the patents publicly, and then, in ringing tones, he endorsed them even more strongly. . . ? He played with that idea for a day. What could go wrong? They could assassinate him where he stood. But once he had said the words, it would be too late from them to issue a denial.

Simon stopped dreaming and began to think in earnest that he may have found the path. And his family? Well, if he lived and stayed employed, they would be fine. But that was impossible. If Spinosa didn't kill him, which was unlikely, he would surely have to fire him. He would have no other option. For if Simon could defy Spinosa with impunity on this, he would be completely free. Nothing could bind him then. But if he were fired, a million dollars would accrue to him. How wonderful life would be with no money problems ever again. But no, that would never happen either. It would be tantamount to a clear victory for Simon. And that, Spinosa would never tolerate. He would certainly kill again before he let Simon get away with a coup like that. There was no doubt of it, he would be as good as dead if he so blatantly defied Carlos. But what of it? On his death, Janet and his children would be even richer . . . two million dollars if he died by accident. And not only that—Simon's spirits soared—but if he were clever enough he might even avenge some part of Jim Lester's death by throwing suspicion for his own onto Spinosa's head.

He started thinking through how Spinosa's attack might come. If he only knew that, he could warn the police that he was in danger—and, in warning them, implicate Spinosa. But he didn't have any idea how it was going to be done.

Of course! The revelation hit Simon like an explosion on a peaceful night. He musn't wait to be killed. To fix the blame, he had to plan how to kill himself, and where, and in what way. By planning the whole thing, he could make his death more than the weak suicide Janet despised: he could make his own death an act of sweet and violent revenge on Carlos Spinosa. If he were really clever, he might even frame Spinosa so well that the gray man took the full punishment he deserved—but for a crime he didn't commit.

Simon started planning his revenge on Spinosa in earnest. A nice touch, he decided, would be if he did it in a sports car as much like Jim's as possible. That would make sure everyone remembered the coincidence. Beforehand he would send registered letters to the appropriate authorities to be opened only in the event of his death. One would go to his own lawyer; one to the company's lawyer; one to Harrison; one, most carefully phrased, to his family; and maybe a final one to the *Wall Street Journal* where he trusted one of the senior editors.

Each letter would explain that the announcement he was making would place his life in jeopardy. It would point to his suspicion that Jim Lester had been forced off the cliff. It would explain how he was defying Spinosa's repeated requests and explain the whole matter of the technology and the supporting patents. It would affirm yet again that the technology was sound and valuable.

Excited now, Simon had reached a decision. "I don't want to be disturbed," he ordered his secretary. "Not for anyone. No exceptions. I'm not here."

"Yes, sir." She had never seen him as tough.

He closed his door firmly and started to write the letters. The first draft took him an hour. It was clear, persuasive. What flaw could there be? He started to polish it. Another hour later, he was well satisfied. The problem seemed resolved. He patted the outside of his jacket where the finished letter nestled inside, and smiled to himself. What a relief!

"I'm available again," he told his secretary cheerfully. "But not for long. I'm quitting early today. Please get my wife on the phone. Oh, and would you make a reservation at the Stonehenge Restaurant for, say, seven-thirty. It's out in Wilton. The nicest place I know within an hour's drive of my home." He turned back into his office. Nothing could go wrong. Janet would never have any idea that he had not been killed. Quite the contrary, she would think the path he had chosen was wonderfully brave. The only minor problem that remained was finding a typewriter on which to prepare the letters. No, better still, he would write out all five versions in longhand. That way there could be no claims that the letters weren't authentic.

The intercom buzzed and Simon picked up the phone. He felt unshakably content. "Mr. Spinosa on one, sir."

"Thank you." He punched the button. "Yes, Carlos,"

he said, his confidence not reduced even by the hated sound of that voice. "What can I do for you?"

"I imagine that about now you have, or you will, decide that it is in your power to double-cross me." The certainty of the man was the ultimate arrogance. "I would be surprised were you not to reach that decision. If you have not, I am disappointed that it has taken you so long."

For a few more seconds Simon's world remained poised only on the brink of ruin—as a snowball tossed high in the air will stand still at the apex of its parabola before plunging downwards to crash inevitably to powder.

"You believe you can mount that platform and say the opposite of my command." Again the depth of Carlos's certainty extended his assertion beyond accusation into accepted fact.

Unable to remonstrate or deny, Simon merely grunted like a man hit in the solar plexus. The snowball started to accelerate downward.

"Don't." The word was the hardest, most vicious Simon had ever heard. But it released that anger in Simon that, more and more frequently now, was close to the surface. "Why the hell not?" he yelled, suddenly out of control, knowing already what the answer would be. Knowing . . .

"Suicide is not covered by the insurance."

"It would not be suicide." Such had been Spinosa's certainty, that Simon was ready to argue the point as if the two of them were equally well-informed about the letter in Simon's pocket. "You could not make it appear to be."

"Of course we could."

"Why would I want to kill myself? No one would believe that."

"Because you have been embezzling."

The snowball crashed to the ground. "But . . ."

"I have the proof in front of me. A clever, complicated piece of computer fraud. That would explain any crazy accusations you may have written before you killed yourself." He paused. "Any stupid letters." He filled the words with utter contempt.

Simon hung his head in exhaustion. How could he fight? He felt ashamed at his childishness for having thought he had found a solution.

"Or perhaps," Carlos Spinosa was continuing, "you committed suicide because you heard that your girl friend, Sandra McGuire, I believe that's her name, just died in a car crash. She had been snorting some of Turner-LaMott's more potent drugs. Seems you stopped seeing her. She was blown out of her mind. One wonders where she got them. There was a note with your name on it."

With the gentlest of clicks, a tiny sibilance like that of a sad mother clicking her tongue at her naughty child, the phone went dead.

Agatha entered. "I made the restaurant reservation," she said. "And your wife called while you were on the phone, so I told her. She said she had a meeting near there anyhow, so she'll meet you at the restaurant. Seven-thirty. She said to tell you she's absolutely delighted."

"It is going according to plan." Spinosa was supremely confident. "That is the third time you have asked me to repeat myself. It is enough."

"Of course I worry, old chap. Who wouldn't with that much money involved?" But Oliver Chapin did not, in fact, sound particularly concerned. Spinosa was rarely wrong—and almost never willing to be this definite if he had any doubts at all. "A great deal of money, you must admit."

"Certainly. You would not be interested in a small deal."

"Indeed," Chapin sounded even more avuncular than usual. "So you feel we should proceed?"

"Just make sure you have the funds ready by Wednesday." Spinosa hung up, carefully removing his speaker from the scrambling mechanism that would have made it impossible for Chapin to record the conversation had he wanted to.

Thoughtfully, Oliver Chapin replaced his receiver too.

"Remember to take it off that scrambler," Sidney Rosenberg, who had been listening on the extension, reminded him.

The Pierre Hotel reeks of money. Old money, new money, it doesn't much matter as long as there is a great deal of it. And the hotel's Cotillion Room is the epitome of that feeling of richness. Not very large, it is chandeliered, mirrored, carpeted—New York's closest approach to Louis XIV grandeur, a modern-day American version of Versaille's Hall of Mirrors. Foot for foot, it is probably the most expensive banquet room in the city. Thus, it is normally used for business functions only by cosmetic companies and others who wish to borrow elegance and prestige from its surroundings. Staid and solid companies like Turner-LaMott generally prefer more mundane settings like, say, the Sheraton-Statler some thirty blocks south opposite Penn Station. Indeed, it was Spinosa who had chosen the site and Morgan Galsworthy who had passed on the information to Simon.

"Why do we need to be that opulent?" Simon had asked. "Surely a less expensive place will do?"

"Indeed?" Galsworthy had enjoyed himself. He was at his best when giving Simon commands he had no doubt would be carried out. "I think not. My associates and I feel that bad news is best told in the most prestigious setting." He paused to chuckle as throatily as a brook. "The contrast adds to the surprise," he explained, "and hence the news value."

Watching from behind a screen at the far end of the

room as the crowds of reporters pushed their way into the Cotillion Room, Simon realized that Spinosa had been right. The unusual setting for the press conference added to the air of expectancy. He could hear the buzzing of the audience, quite different in tone than at the normal run of such events. Senior business correspondents for the *Wall Street Journal*, *The New York Times* and the news services had come in person and were busy interviewing any Turner-LaMott staff they could find—and pumping each other—to see if anyone could give them a lead on what was to be announced. No one could. Junior reporters were jostling for position, not sure in this unaccustomed room where was the best place to station themselves. In the entrance foyer, Turner-LaMott's staff had set up a battery of ten telephones. But, just to be safe, several of the public telephones were occupied, apparently in perpetuity, by cub reporters working for the major newspapers so ably represented by the senior reporters inside the Cotillion room. It was only ten minutes to eleven and already all seats were filled and several reporters were standing around the edge of the room.

Simon Bagnew heaved a weary sigh. With an obvious effort he pulled back his shoulders and started walking toward the gap in the screen from whence he would emerge to make the announcement. From there he would proceed some twenty paces to the speaker's rostrum situated off-center on a slightly raised platform. There were to be no introductions, no pomp, no ceremony. The importance of the announcement would carry its own impact.

"I'll introduce myself," Simon had told his vice president of corporate relations.

"But you can't." The man was shocked. "You have to be introduced by someone else."

"Why do I? I'm quite capable of telling them who I am."

"But, Simon . . ."

"I'd prefer it." Simon had been firm.

Looking small and terribly haggard, Simon emerged from the screen and started on his short—but infinite—journey to the podium. His hand shook and he looked gravely ill. He walked with the unsteadiness of a man at least twenty years older.

Janet was sitting near the front of the audience, but far to one side, amidst all the Turner-LaMott executives, insulated from the reporters who were, for the most part, on the other side of the hall, near the telephones and the exit. Janet's heart went out to her husband. How frail he looked, how terribly sick. Thank God he had finally talked to her. Now if only he made the right decision.

Out of the corner of her eye, she noticed that Carlos Spinosa was rising. He had been sitting in the front row next to Dr. Turner and just to the left of the rostrum. Simon would have to pass almost in front of him to reach it. As Simon approached, Spinosa moved forward a couple of steps to intercept him. What was he after? Could he say anything now to make Simon change his mind? Oh God, Janet prayed, give my husband the strength to do what is right, and the wisdom to know what that is. It was such a tough decision Simon had to make, so full of risks. But then, if he didn't fight, but simply caved in, he'd hate himself for the rest of his days. What sort of a life would that be—what sort of a marriage?

Simon, also observing Spinosa moving toward him, tried to accelerate. But his limbs seemed unwilling to respond to his mind. He could barely move at all. How he wished he could reach the rostrum without the bastard catching him. He sweated with the exertion of trying to speed up. But, no, Spinosa was at his elbow. "You better make it good," he whispered in his grating voice. "Remember, the technology is no good." He paused. "No fucking good at all," he repeated, pounding his message home.

"I remember what you told me," Bagnew agreed. He

couldn't understand why he was trembling so hard. There was nothing so terribly difficult about what he was going to do. His decision was made. All he had to do was to say a few words. It was just the awful impact they would have on the rest of his life that made him tremble so.

"I trust Sandra remains well," Spinosa said. Then, to Simon's horror, he added, "And of course your wife and your daughter Susie too." He turned, as gracefully as a dancer, and returned to his chair.

Simon seemed to choke for a moment, then his foot caught on a tuft of carpet and he stumbled enough to make his wife gasp. What had Spinosa said to him? she wondered. If possible, Simon had paled even more. Oh, don't lose courage now, my love, she prayed.

Somehow Simon managed to recover enough to mount the podium. The microphone picked up his labored breathing and his grunt of effort as he pulled himself up onto it. For a moment he was silent. Then, with an obvious effort, he pulled himself taller. "Ladies and gentlemen," he started, his voice sounding as hoarse as if he were barely recovered from a major bout with the flu. "I am Simon Bagnew, president and chief executive officer of Turner-LaMott. First, may I welcome you all here. We shall not keep you very long." For a moment Simon wavered.

Janet held her breath. Had Spinosa said something new to him that had changed the plan?

Then Simon started again with more conviction, in a stronger voice. "I'm afraid that I have some news that may not be pleasing to everyone in the room." He looked meaningfully at Spinosa, whose face remained entirely impassive. "It is about the technology covering the new, genetically engineered, waste-consuming, oil-producing microorganisms about which I made an announcement some weeks ago."

There was a painful silence in the audience as Simon

paused to take a drink of water. A single hurriedly suppressed cough sounded so loud that its perpetrator, an experienced veteran of countless news conferences, blushed with embarrassment.

"It appears," Simon continued at length, "that Turner-LaMott will, after all, gain no benefit from those patents."

There was an instantaneous eruption of noise in the audience. "Why?" "Explain!" "What happened?" The roar of questions drowned Simon Bagnew's next words.

"The technology I described to you, and the patents attached to it, will be of no value to this company," Simon tried to shout over the din. "I'm afraid we cannot proceed with the project."

Carlos Spinosa, to the astonishment of those observing him, was smiling broadly. He looked, Janet Bagnew decided, like a barracuda baring its teeth more than like a man pleased. But there was no doubt that this was his look of victory. Drained entirely, Janet slumped into her seat, her face totally expressionless.

Vainly, Simon tried to make himself heard above the uproar in the room to provide an explanation of what had happened. But the explanation was of little importance. Few of the reporters remained in the room to listen.

The ten phones in the foyer were already proving completely inadequate to the demand, and both the *Times* and the New York *Post* reporters were busy dictating their stories into the lobby's public telephones. The *Wall Street Journal* reporter was hurrying across the street to the Turner-LaMott offices, dictating the first part of his story into a tape recorder as he went. The AP and UPI men had finished their first reports and the ticker tapes were even now carrying their messages that the patents were valueless.

The stock of Turner-LaMott was already beginning to plummet.

23

Oliver Chapin, the Deacon, was at his most ecclesiastic, more monkish by far than the real monk who was accompanying him on the tour of one of New York's finest Catholic hospitals. They had reached the maternity ward and Oliver was ushered into the corridor from which, through a glass wall, he could see the crèche where a dozen newborns lay swaddled tightly in tiny cribs. "How totally adorable they are." He beamed at his guide. "I find it thoroughly . . ." He searched for the precise word. ". . . miraculous to see such tiny babies. How does the song go. . . ? 'Every time I hear a newborn baby cry, da da te da, or see the sky . . .'" He hummed the tune, his voice cracking slightly as it picked its way up the register, 'then I know why I believe.'" Oliver chortled with unalloyed pleasure.

"God's work," the monk said sourly, for his part less than approving both of the babies and, if truth be told, of Oliver Chapin. As for the babies, well—the monk pursed his lips—why had the Lord chosen to develop such a questionable method of implementing his miracles?

"God's work, indeed." Chapin's agreement was as ecclesiastic as everything else about the man. "And I am so pleased that, in at least some minor way, the Chapin interests can help to make the world a little safer for these babies."

"And we are most grateful for your gift. The new equipment is invaluable." One should not look a gift horse in the mouth, the monk decided, however bad its teeth were likely to be. What was it Father McCollough had said when they told him of the Chapin donation? "Thank you Lord, it seems thou hast started to endow Oliver Chapin with a conscience. Were it to grow to average size, our hospital would be the richest in the land." Perhaps, the monk thought, even a good priest like Jack McCollough had to become cynical running a big institution like this. "Father McCollough," he continued aloud to Chapin, "tells me that, as a result of your gift, we have saved eight babies this month alone."

"I hope that there will be more, much more." Chapin was greatly moved. "Eight babies," he muttered to himself. "What a wonderful thing." As soon as he had his problems with Caro Pollo cleared up—and the Spinosa thing, which was drawing all his cash just now, had been completed—he would see to it. A large donation certainly. Perhaps a very large one indeed. But first Caro.

"Of course there is always so much left to be done. . . ." The monk interrupted Oliver's reverie only after the statistic had hung in the air long enough to speak for itself.

"Indeed." Chapin decided he did not wish to hear more about the hospital's needs just now; Pollo was too heavy on his mind.

Smoothly his guide moved him into another corridor, this one with drapes over its visiting wall. Briefly, the monk spoke into an intercom telephone attached to the wall and the curtain parted slightly. "This is a sadder crèche, I'm afraid," he explained. "It's the babies' intensive care unit."

Chapin could see tiny oxygen tents over some of the cribs and feeding tubes over others. Several nurses, in surgical gowns and masks, bustled between them. "Many babies survive here, but sadly many do not," Chapin's guide explained. "That too is God's will."

"Are you sure?" Chapin demanded sharply. "I'd not argue theology with you, but dying babies. . . ? Can nothing be done?"

"Not always. Although we are making progress." The

monk hesitated fractionally. "Of course, research is frightfully expensive. Money is always a problem. The more we have, the faster we find cures. And with the government cutting back . . ." He let the sentence hang yet again.

It was becoming a habit, this monk's abandonment of pregnant sentences, Oliver reflected cynically. "Very difficult," he agreed, still fighting his instinct toward generosity.

"There are so many reasons the babies are ill. Congenital defects, chicken pox in the mothers, damage during birth, herpes infections, mothers addicted—"

"How disgraceful," Oliver Chapin interrupted, genuinely shocked. "That a woman would addict herself and then allow herself to become pregnant." He shook his head in sincere dismay.

Suddenly there was a commotion around one of the beds. Oliver could see a young nurse, her forehead creased with concern, issue a series of quick, efficient orders. Seconds later another young woman, evidently a doctor, rushed in. She examined the electronic dials on the machine connected to the minute being in the crib. Hurriedly, she filled a syringe from one of the bottles in a medication tray, leaned over the crib and plunged the needle into the mite lying there. For a few seconds she remained tense and watchful; then her shoulders slumped. One of the nurses lifted a corner of the oxygen tent covering the baby and the doctor placed a stethoscope on the baby's chest. She listened, then turned away, a picture of dejection.

Oliver, looking at the tray, noticed that several of the bottles had the very recognizable logotype of Turner-LaMott on the corner of their labels. He was profoundly relieved that the bottle the doctor had used was from a different manufacturer.

The monk crossed himself piously and muttered a prayer under his breath. Then, "God's will be done," he intoned.

"If it is God's will to kill babies," Chapin said angrily, his face puffed pink with emotion, "then death is no evil to God."

"You are right," the monk said, suddenly speaking from the heart. "But at least babies really go to heaven."

"And bad men to hell?"

"Indeed. I know it's old-fashioned, but that's what I believe."

"So the faster it happens, the better?"

"God's will is to give men time to repent. It is tragic if that time is somehow not allowed to them. But babies are not given time to sin—and therefore there is no tragedy in their death."

"And he who has time to repent and won't?"

"He is worse than he who has no time—for he has not merely forgotten, he has rejected God."

"Indeed, indeed." Oliver Chapin, still feeling shaky from seeing the baby die, had firmly made up his mind. "I shall certainly give more money to help here," he promised. "But I must finish certain transactions first. It won't be long." He started to walk back down the corridor. "Oh, and your words have been most helpful," he assured the monk.

"I'm glad . . . but how?"

"I must go now." He shook hands with the monk and started to leave. Turning, he said, "It's just that from what you said it's clear that some men shouldn't be given the time to repent."

"The saints who don't need to?"

"Indeed, indeed," Chapin called over his shoulder as he left. "And those whose sin is so deep they'd never even try."

Caro Pollo, again holding court in the dirty bar he often used as his headquarters, was enjoying the sound of his own voice even more than usual. His voice, for such a little man, was surprisingly loud and, into the bargain, angry and piercing enough to cut through virtually any argument or fight.

"We ain't made no fuckin' progress at all," he was declaiming. "We ain't got no more of you-know-what to sell. Shit, we got less. Right, Harry? Am I right?"

The ex-prize fighter next to Pollo nodded his small head vigorously. "You got it, boss," he grunted. "You got it." He buried his face in the foam of his beer, gulped half the glass and belched loudly.

Pollo leaned his chair back precariously. "There," he said, his point proven. "An' what we done about it?" He glared at his listeners, hostile ugly men around the bar table. "Fuck *all!*" he said and crossed his arms. "Well, I tell you this boys, I've had it. I ain't standing for it another day. Not one more fuckin' day. Shit, we're losing money so fast it'd make your head spin."

Caro Pollo kicked at a loose piece of filthy carpet and glowered at his listeners who nodded in agreement but remained silent. It was one thing, each of them realized, to have uncharitable thoughts about the Chapin empire . . . even to complain about the lack of supplies. That was, after all, a fact of life and a most unfortunate one if you happened to be in the business of supplying the stuff or of running a business machine, like prostitution. It was the oil that kept the human components nicely dehumanized and running smoothly. But it was quite another thing, each of them felt strongly, to challenge Chapin head on and state in public forum that you planned to do something about it. Gutsy little bugger, you had to give him that. But how. . . ?

"Too fuckin' right," Pollo tried again to elicit a response. "I'm goin' to do something."

"Yeah?" Ricardo, a swarthy Italian, a little older than the others asked. He tried to keep the suspicion out of his voice. There was no point in antagonizing Pollo unnecessarily. God knew he was angry enough all the time anyway. Nasty little shit. "What you planning?" The suspicion crept in anyhow.

"Tell him. That's what. I'm going to meet the Deacon personally an' tell him that I, Caro Pollo, have had it." He smiled nastily. "Then we'll work out a deal together."

Ricardo looked even more skeptical. In twenty years he'd never heard of the Deacon bargaining with anyone. "The old man don't do much business personally," he suggested tentatively. "What you got that he wants?"

"Don' worry. He'll deal with me okay." Pollo tilted his chair so far back that it hung in midair, kept in perfect balance by a series of tiny precise movements of Caro's legs. Caro felt as if he were flying, gliding, such was his confidence. Today, his senses told him, he could do anything. "He ain't got no option but to see me, does he? I'm the biggest customer he's got."

"That hasn't cut ice before."

"Well it better this time."

"Yeah?" Ricardo remained unconvinced.

"Listen, fuckers. You don' believe?" Suddenly Caro cracked his chair forward, back onto its four legs, making the table shake and spilling beer from several glasses. He leaned toward them, chin out, teeth bared, a hyena suddenly vicious and ready to attack. "What do the rest of youse boys think? You think the Deacon won't discuss with me?"

There were noncommittal grunts around the table, but the body language was noisy. Two men stretched their arms above their heads; one crossed his legs, pushing himself farther back into his chair; yet another hugged a hand under his opposite arm.

"Well?"

"Dunno," someone mumbled.

"Youse as much good as warts on the tits on a fuckin' bull," Caro stormed. In fact, though, he was delighted by their disbelief. It would make his punch line that much more powerful. He was reveling in his secret!

The bar was as deserted as it usually was when Caro's group convened. Except that today, too drunk to understand the risk, a misshapen old man snored softly across a plastic tabletop in the corner. With a grunt, he shifted position and, unstable to begin with, tipped himself off his chair. There was a crash as he fell.

"What the fuck. . . " To a man, Caro's group reacted like startled deer either jumping up or grabbing for a gun or, in one case, diving for the floor. Caro Pollo himself, however, who would normally have reacted at least as nervously as the group, remained unmoved. He had been idly staring at the drunk so that, of all his cronies, Caro was the only one to realize immediately that there was no cause for alarm. "Relax, boys. Calm your nerves," he crowed. "Siddown, for Chrissake. You gonna shoot the old fuck for falling off his chair?"

Gradually the men resumed their seats, some shamefaced, others plainly relieved. "Better to be careful," Ricardo summarized.

"Better get it right," Caro interrupted. "No one said nothing about bein' careless."

"So?"

There was an expectant hush. Caro Pollo, always the runt of the litter, was a big man now. All of them, every one of these men who between them controlled hundreds, maybe thousands of workers—hookers, pushers, pimps, garbagemen, enforcers—was hanging on his, little Luigi Pollo's, words. "There's gotta be two sources. Otherwise, we'll always have these shortages. We need the merchandise, an' if he can't supply, then there's gotta be an understanding that others can. . . ."

"You?" The word carried a mixture of awe and disbelief.

"Sure, why not?"

"The Deacon would never—"

"Fuck the Deacon. He ain't supplying enough. An' I say I can."

"He'll never agree." Ricardo was as certain as he was of the scar he still carried on his thigh from the last war that erupted when someone tried to fight the Chapin empire. It still throbbed at night sometimes.

Several heads nodded in agreement.

"He fuckin' will," Caro savored every moment of his announcement. "I already talked to him about it on the phone." He paused to survey his audience, relishing their looks of astonishment. "An' you know what he said?" He waited as if expecting an answer. "He said 'Caro, my boy'—you know how he speaks in that fuckin' superior tone—'Caro my boy, you got a point.'" Pollo's imitation of Oliver Chapin's tone was dreadful.

"That don' mean—"

"Wait. There's more: 'Caro, my boy,'" he says, "'what you and I should do is to work out a compromise.' That's what." As Caro's elation grew, his voice became high pitched. "'A compromise, my boy'" Caro repeated, still mimicking Chapin. "'So that you and I can share in the supply,'" Caro finished. He surveyed his audience in triumph. "Share the supply," he crowed. "The fucker's given in! Hey waiter," Caro yelled to the barman in the gloom at the end of the room. "We wan' another round over here."

"Yes, sir."

"And hurry it up."

"He's gonna let you share?" Ricardo's disbelief made him careless.

"You doubt what I'm saying to you?" Caro Pollo turned on the older man, instantly belligerent.

"Just surprised."

"Don't be. It's obvious. He don' have no other choice."

"When are you meeting?"

"Tonight!"

The waiter-owner brought the drinks and all the men remained silent until he quickly retreated to his kitchen.

"How do you know it's not gonna be a trap?" Ricardo asked as soon as the waiter was out of earshot.

"Because he's got no reason," said Caro, playing his listeners along. "And," he added as their looks of disbelief at that naïvete mounted, "because I got it figured so he can't."

"How?"

"We're meeting alone, just him and me. At low tide. Way out on the edge of the water on Coney Island Beach."

"Alone—on Coney Island?"

"Yeah, smart-ass. It's empty this time of year. And there's rain forecast. A storm." He smirked at his cleverness. "Old Ollie will have to walk about a hundred yards across the sand to get to me. Alone."

"They could sharpshoot you."

"Sure. And Mister Bo would hit Old Ollie right back," Caro said, referring to the finest marksman in the Pollo organization—and probably in the whole of New Jersey.

"Or he could bring a gun."

"Yeah," said Caro Pollo slowly, unconsciously imitating a thousand TV shows. "He could." From nowhere, a small but potent pistol appeared in his hand. Caro pointed at his questioner. "I wish he'd try," he said softly as the other man instinctively started to raise his hands. "I just wish he'd try."

Both the weather forecast and Caro Pollo were right. At dusk, in the pouring rain, Coney Island Beach was entirely deserted. It was also depressingly drab and dirty. Litter abounded. The sand, smoothed by the rain, was hard and gray, and gray too was the water, so that the edge between the sodden sand and the wavelets—also beaten down by the torrent—was more a matter of degree than a clear delineation. Other than the hum of the rain hitting the ground, there was no sound.

Caro Pollo, purposely early, waited in his car with three henchmen at the road edge of the beach. He had already reconnoitered thoroughly to make certain the beach was deserted. The rain reduced visibility enough to leave figures visible but unrecognizable. Pollo was damp from his explorations, and the car windows steamed up annoyingly. But, apart from these minor inconveniences, goddam but he'd worked it out smart! The excitement—and, in spite of himself, the apprehension—built.

At ten to eight, Caro Pollo couldn't restrain his impatience. "Time to go," he announced. "Where's that umbrella?"

"Thought you said you'd wait till the Deacon showed. It ain't time yet."

"Never mind what I said. How can a man see what's going on with the windows all steamed up. How was I supposed to know you didn't have no blower system?" He grabbed angrily at the umbrella, a brown-and-tan striped golfing version chosen to blend into the surroundings as well as to give maximum protection. "Fuck, I can't see a thing," he complained, angry merely to cover his nervousness. "You guys stay here, I'm gonna start moving out onto the sand. Don' move when old Ollie gets there as long as his car stays on the edge like us. But if he starts to drive in, or if there's more than one guy walking, you go for it. Got it? Go like hell!"

"Sure, boss." They'd heard the instructions fifty times."

"The sand's hard as a road, so you won't have no problem."

"Shouldn't you better wait till the Deacon starts in?"

"I ain't going anywhere. Just outside so I can see," Pollo assured him, realizing he dared not move far onto the sand until he could see his adversary doing the same. He got out of the car, hoisting the umbrella and pulling his plastic rain cape around him. For a moment the car door stayed open and the rain splashed inside. The passengers flinched from the drops. So heavy was the rain that it fell off Caro's umbrella in a circular curtain, until he seemed to be enclosed in a semitransparent veil.

"Fuck." The cloudburst weighed on the umbrella as heavily as if Pollo had been under a shower, spraying everywhere. "Fuck," he muttered again as some of it trickled down the inside of his shirt. Even though the night was warm, he shivered.

Slowly, Caro Pollo started to move away from the car, peering through the sheets of rain. Dimly, on his right he could make out the boarded-up huts behind the Coney Island boardwalk, two or three lights barely visible in the distance. To his left, the apparently endless expanse of beach and rain. . . .

Two disembodied headlights pierced the grayness about fifty yards ahead of him as a car eased down one of the access roads toward the beach. Pollo felt his stomach tighten. A second later, the limousine eased its long snout out from behind a hut. It crept forward another few feet until the whole car was clear of the hut and in full view. Then Caro saw it jerk to a halt. For a moment nothing happened. Then a door opened and a large umbrella, even wider than Caro's own and from this distance apparently quite black, emerged. It was followed immediately by a tall, obviously athletic man who jumped out of the car quickly, adjusted the umbrella and bent to open the car's rear door. Very slowly, a much shorter man, evidently Oliver Chapin himself, emerged. He was protected from the rain by his escort who held the umbrella most carefully over Chapin with no thought for the water pelting onto his own back. Chapin took the umbrella and started walking slowly toward the sea. The man, now completely unprotected against the rain, watched a few moments and then jumped back into the car. Its headlights jerked off and on twice in the prearranged signal. The figure of Oliver Chapin, a dark gray silhouette against the lighter gray rain, continued to walk toward the water's edge, angling slightly toward his left.

"That's it," Pollo muttered and gave his own driver the thumbs up signal so that he flicked his headlights off and on twice in response. Then he too started toward the sea, angling to his right so that his course would intersect with Oliver's at the water's edge. By prior agreement both cars switched off their headlights. All that was left in the gray, drenched light were two small figures, one more rotund than the other, making their way at a measured pace toward a rendezvous at the water's edge.

To Pollo the walk seemed interminable. He was as jumpy as a hare. His knuckles cracked as he pressed his fingers into his palms, clenching and unclenching his fists. By Christ, he thought, he'd won! The Deacon himself, on a foul day like this, come to talk turkey and make a bargain. What could go wrong. . . ? He kept his eyes glued on his adversary. Couldn't he walk faster? Getting old? He thought he detected a slight limp in Chapin's walk. At least this was going to be a better meeting than the last one in old Ollie's Brooklyn building. You couldn't argue with a man on his own ground.

But this, Caro gloated, this was perfect. The Deacon's car was no closer than Caro's. They'd never shoot, not with their man just as vulnerable and with Mister Bo's telescopic sights perfectly trained on the Deacon's bald head. They were evenly matched at last. Except that, man to man, Caro Pollo knew he was by far the younger and faster. "I got him now," Caro Pollo gloated. "I got the fuck now."

The two men were now only twenty yards apart, easily close enough to recognize each other. The rain, still heavy, had abated somewhat.

"Hello, hello," Oliver Chapin waved his hand as he approached. "How are you, my dear fellow."

Pollo, nonplused, muttered an inaudible reply.

"What a strange place to meet," Chapin continued. He stretched out his hand toward Pollo who, startled, hesitated before doing the same. "It's been a while. How are you?" Chapin sounded as convivial as if he were at a cocktail party.

"Fine, thank you."

"Terrible night you picked."

"Yeah."

"But suitable. I'd say this was a clever idea of yours. Not that I'd double-cross you even if we met in my apartment. And of course, I'd trust you if we met in yours. But I agree that it's always better to be safe than sorry." Oliver Chapin prattled on, his hand on Caro Pollo's own. The two umbrellas touched and overlapped forming a canopy over both their heads. The two men strolled slowly along the water's edge. "Well, well, well, I never thought I'd be perambulating here," Oliver said. "We should really have a Nathan's hot dog, shouldn't we? De rigueur, I should have thought."

"Yeah." Pollo was becoming uneasy. He didn't understand what was happening. "Listen," he started abruptly, "I don't give a shit about no hot dogs." He shook Chapin's hand off his arm and pulled apart from him so that they continued to walk side by side but apart, like lovers who have tiffed. "What I wanna know is what you plan to do about the short supplies."

"Of course, of course. It's all under perfect control. You worry too much."

"Yeah. That's what you said months ago. An' nothing's happened."

"You're right. Quite right. These things take time." Oliver Chapin stooped to bend down and pick up a flat stone from the beach. He skimmed it expertly over the water so that it skipped half a dozen times over the oily wavelets, like a live thing, before dying and sinking. "This is just the right place to discuss it," he said, suddenly businesslike. He turned toward Caro Pollo who, likewise, had stopped.

The two men faced each other, each with his legs apart, his umbrella handle resting on his shoulder so that the umbrella fitted behind his head like a huge halo, each with his free hand straight down beside him. The only difference was in their dress: Caro wore a slicker, Oliver Chapin a tan Aquascutum raincoat.

"So what would you like?" Chapin asked, reasonable.

"We're gonna split, that's what." Caro Pollo's tone was determined, but he was talking too fast. "Since supply's the problem it's become, two organizations—mine and yours—bringing in the stuff will do better than you alone."

"And why would I agree to that?" The Deacon's voice could not have been more plummy if he had been asking about his hostess's gown at a garden party.

"You got nothing to lose . . ."

"Perhaps not," Chapin agreed. "You may be right." Suddenly he stopped, alert. "What's that noise?" he demanded, taking a step back.

"I don' hear nothing."

"Damn right." The elder man jumped backwards again, evidently terrified. "What the sweet Jesus are you trying to pull?"

At that moment Caro heard it too, a ground-vibrating roar, virtually beneath his feet. Instantly his gun jumped to his hand. "What the fuck?" He spun around searching vainly for the roaring, unseen enemy, backing away from the sound, first one way then the other, oblivious now to Chapin who, crouching low, was just as frightened as he.

But Caro Pollo's terror was nowhere near its height. For suddenly the beach seemed to shake as with a massive earthquake, and with an even mightier roar, the ground only feet away from Pollo heaved and cracked. Caro, too, crouched down, terrified and snarling, but still completely uncomprehending. In slow motion, but very quickly, a large metal snout, for all the world like a mechanical hippopotamus, emerged from the sand. Instinctively Caro fired at it, still uncomprehending. But the bullets bounced harmlessly off the vehicle's side as, with engine steaming, it drove up its underground ramp, pushing through the sand and the planks holding it. Comprehension dawning, Caro loosed another fusillade.

But Caro had recovered far too slowly. Just as he was about to wheel back toward Chapin, squatting behind his umbrella, three gun muzzles seemed to grow like sprouting plants out of the side of the vehicle. Sand-encrusted hands raised themselves behind the muzzles. Six eyes squinted at their target. Caro Pollo screamed once pathetically and his sphincter muscle lost control. Simultaneously, the three gun muzzles pointing at Pollo barked out short accurate bursts of machine-gun fire. And Luigi Pollo, sarcastically called Caro because he was such an undear child, youth and man, seemed to disintegrate into a great arc of spattering blood and semi-solid fragments of flesh and bone and clothes. One moment there was a man; the next an explosion of juicy gore.

"Jesus Christ, what the fuck happened?" The marksman in Pollo's car yelled at his companion. "There's a fucking car coming out of the sand."

"Shoot the bastard, Bo. Shoot him," one of the other men in the car screamed.

"Shoot him? Fuck, I can't even see him."

"Shoot, goddammit. They've got Caro."

"There's a goddam jeep out there . . . the Deacon's completely hidden."

The driver started the limo. "Let's go," he yelled. "They've fucked us." He put the car in gear.

"There's a whole army of them out there," said the marksman, quietly.

"And there's the Deacon's crew back over there," said

the third man, pointing to the limousine that had switched its lights on. "They're coming this way, looks like."

"Yeah," said the driver. "Shit." He put the car into reverse. "Better get out of here."

"Fucking right," the marksman agreed. "Let's go." The limousine accelerated backwards, turned with a screech of tires, and tore away.

On the beach, with a final roar of its engines the mechanical monster drove completely clear of its underground garage, vibrated itself clean of most of the residual sand and stood at the surface, as ordinary an armored jeep as one could hope to see. Unhurriedly, Oliver Chapin walked toward it. The door was opened from the inside and he climbed in. Then, without further delay, while the remains of Caro Pollo, steadily washed by the drenching rain, continued to spread into a giant, oozing stain on the sand, the jeep carrying the Deacon drove away.

"Lovely, lovely," said Oliver Chapin to the driver. "You did very well. Very well. Now all I've got to do is to complete one more little deal—and then we can have some peace and quiet again." In high spirits, he beamed at the other men crowded into the jeep.

24

The drama of multimillion dollar decisions made with barely a moment's thought, the palpable tension of the twenty young men and women concentrating every ounce of their mental energy on the video screens in front of them, the lizardlike speed of their fingers playing over the computer keyboards, their insistent barely audible mutter into telephone receivers nestled like permanent deformities between chins and shoulders . . . all this frenetic effort was rendered otherworldly by its near silence.

Only a few years earlier, Spinosa recalled, the trading room of a typical investment house was full of mayhem. People would shout orders, ticker-tape machines would clatter, messenger boys would run. But the highly sophisticated trading rooms of the most advanced of the investment bankers today were no longer like that. Gone was the debris and the bustle, instead there were silent rows of aseptic computer screens, satellite hookups, word processors, memory banks . . .

Only the young could stand it, Carlos Spinosa thought a shade bitterly. Eventually their electronics would overtake him, but by then he would be too old and out of it anyway. In the meantime, he reassured himself, a few words at the right moment plus a rapid command of mental arithmetic was enough to keep him on top. And that—plus the wonderful relaxation of an occasional Puccini opera remembered in its entirety—was enough challenge to feed his brain. He had felt that sense of power running those women eons ago in Brazil before he died; he'd felt it in the early days of his resurrection as he bargained for the poppies in Turkey or sold them to the old men from Chicago; he'd felt it even more strongly in the vibrating dramas of big business and high finance when he'd first invaded Wall Street as a lowly speculator and seen his thousands become millions.

But now! Now that drama of money had reached its peak. The concept was not so much beyond imagination as beyond *daring* to imagine. A million dollars would, correctly invested and supported by adequate mortgages, make you the owner, that is give you the *power* of ownership, of, say, a hundred houses: a whole village including possibly the church, tiny town hall and fire station. But a hundred million! That would let you be the owner, landlord, baron, *boss* of ten *thousand* houses, with office buildings and supermarkets, drug stores and a school, a library and movie house and motel . . . the whole town, from McDonald's franchise to funeral parlor! That sort of wealth, even to imagine it, was awe-inspiring. Oh, and it was going well, this ultimate *colossal* play; Oliver Chapin could be well pleased that he had entrusted him, Carlos Spinosa, with this deal.

For a moment, Carlos allowed his face to lose its frozen immobility. The effect was as improbable as watching the faces on Mount Rushmore smile. He caught himself and purposely reset his face in its habitual, grim, unyielding mask. No one would have dreamed that an elated aria from *Madama Butterfly* was trilling through his head as he watched the computer terminals respond to the complicated orders he had placed all over the world in the last few days.

Carlos Spinosa turned abruptly away from the trading room and marched toward a private office kept permanently available to him. "Keep me informed," he said to the woman guarding his door.

"Yes, sir."

He entered and slammed shut the door. Restlessly he paced across the deep carpet. The room was as silent as a sensory deprivation chamber—and almost as impersonal. Extraordinary, Carlos thought, how much power can be wielded across the globe from a place like this, that has no feeling of power, no feeling of anything at all. He walked to the window and stood before it, legs braced apart, arms akimbo, and let his imagination roam.

The stock of Turner-LaMott fell precipitously. It had been hovering around thirty-two dollars a share for weeks, "taking higher ground" but never "breaking through the low thirties barrier," as the Wall Street jargonists described it. But by noon of the day after Simon's announcement it had lost some fifteen points and was down to about seventeen dollars. But then, suddenly and surprisingly, it stuck. Although "sell" was on the order sheet of every pension trust and money fund on the street, the price held up, even climbing back a bit, on the afternoon of that first day, to almost nineteen dollars. Turner-LaMott was the most active stock on the big board on the first day, and on four of the next seven trading days following the announcement.

"Managed to get you out at nineteen and a quarter, a point above what you paid," a customer's man, professionally at ease in the role of perennial optimist, assured his client.

"And only fourteen points below its peak."

"Indeed, indeed. We should have sold then. As the comedian said, 'It's easy to make money. Buy cheap then wait 'til you can sell dear . . . and if the price doesn't go up, why, don't buy.'"

"That seems irrelevant. The point is, shouldn't you have known?"

"Wish I had. But it was a total surprise. No one could have expected it. One of the biggest high-tech breakthroughs of the decade one minute—and screams of false alarm the next. No one could have guessed. Hell, if they had, the stock would have never gyrated like that."

"And the insiders. . . ?"

"Hell, the rumor is they're the ones lost the most. For a fact, Carlos Spinosa—"

"Is he involved?"

"On the board."

"So how could you recommend . . ." The customer, finally, had a complaint worth bitching about. "The man's a crook."

"But a clever one."

"That makes it worse."

"He bought a big block at thirty. Three thousand shares. About a hundred grand. If there's one piece of proof they didn't know on the inside, it's that. Spinosa's not in the habit of buying at thirty and selling at seventeen."

"That's what he did?"

"It's on the books. He has to declare, you know, since he's a director."

"Then he must think it's going farther down?"

"I'm damn glad I was able to unload you where I did." The customer's man came the full circle.

"I suppose."

"Now, I've got this new opportunity . . ."

There was a tentative buzz on Spinosa's intercom. He turned slowly and pushed down the speak button. "Yes?"

"Mr. Jack Raymond would like to talk to you," said the voice of the guardian. She sounded as empty of emotional content as the office itself. "May I send him in?"

"Yes."

There was a click as the door unlatched and a young man, hardly fully adult, hurried in. His cheeks, Spinosa noticed, were still round with remaining puppy fat, but already his brow showed the trader's tension. "Yes?" Carlos demanded.

"We've reached nine point eight percent for Gencom."

Spinosa didn't need the picture painted. Under SEC rules, ten percent ownership of a company was the maximum any one investor or investment group could own without publicly declaring their position. What the worried young man was saying was that, having reached that level on behalf of Gencom, a company evidently advised by Spinosa, he needed new instructions.

"Then stop."

"But sell pressure's strong. I doubt if the price can hold."

"What are we in at?"

"Averages about eighteen. You could see a spiral down when we stop taking up the slack. Down to twelve or thirteen I'd guess. But it's hard to know how deep the selling is."

"And if we continue?"

"Well, we'll have to issue a statement at once. Even then, I'd guess we'd have to hold off for a few hours. But that wouldn't hurt, because the announcement itself would hold up the price. Might build it quite a bit."

"Okay." Spinosa had apparently lost interest.

There were a few moments of hesitation as Jack Raymond waited for clearer orders. Eventually it became obvious that Carlos Spinosa would say nothing more.

"What should I do then?" Raymond asked at last.

"Nothing."

"But . . ."

"Just stop buying."

"Very well, sir." The young man left the room shaking his head. What the hell was Spinosa up to, he wondered? And how could he expect to keep up with what was going on? There hadn't been a computer terminal in the whole damn room.

In Miami, the old man sat in a corner of the almost empty coffee shop. He barely glanced up as the waiter approached him deferentially.

"Message for you sir."

"Yup."

"From New York. Says 'We have stopped.'"

"Right." The old man nodded his head decisively. Then, with clumsy fingers he extracted a small message pad from the pocket of his rather frayed jacket. The notes on the pad sported the name of a distinctly second-class hotel. He scribbled a short message with shaking hand and handed it to the waiter, who hurried away without another word to give it to a boy waiting outside on a bright red motorbike. "Forty thousand TLM" the note said. "And get me a hundred too," the waiter added. "The old man's never wrong."

"Okay, man. Guess I'll do the same." The motorbike roared away to deliver the note personally to the Miami office of Merrill Lynch.

In Palermo, the setting sun still beat onto the ripples of the swimming pool and the girl stretched, showing both a teenager's languor and a woman's self-awareness. It was time to change, from bikini to minidress, from Margarita's to Campari . . . She hadn't seen Gino all day. Perhaps he'd have time before they had to go down and meet the others. Unconsciously, she ran a hand up the inside of her thighs as all her muscles tightened and she yawned.

The telephone startled her, inexplicably making her feel guilty. "Yes," she said, her voice modulated even in its impatience.

"Christina, my darling."

"Oh hello, Joe," she said, disappointed.

"Sorry it's only me?"

"Oh, no Joe. Of course not." She was at pains not to antagonize Gino's manager. "Never make enemies," her mother had warned her. "And make all the friends you can," her ex-college roommate had added. "Especially if they're rich." Christina giggled at the thought. "I love talking to you, Joe," she went on. "It's only you usually have to give me bad news."

"Yeah. But I got nothing bad this time. Only a message."

"For Gino?"

"Yeah."

"But I don't know when I'll see him. Shouldn't you call direct?"

"No. He said to give it to you to pass on."
"Okay. If that's what he said."
"I don't know what it means."
"You don't have to," she said drily. "No one ever does. Just tell me the message."
"It's only two words: 'We've stopped.'"
"Oh, I just remembered. Gino said you might be calling with some message. He said no matter what you said to tell you to take a message back." She giggled again. "You won't know what this means either."
"What is it?"
"Just two words: 'Twenty thousand.'"
"Okay. Wilco, as they say in America." Joe hung up.
"Shit," she said, wishing for a moment that she was back in America herself. She leaned over to pour herself a last Margarita from the pitcher. There was no need to hurry in to change. If Gino was using her to relay messages, whatever they meant, one thing was sure, she wouldn't be seeing him tonight. She could feel the disappointment in her loins.

The Herr Generaldirektor of the Schweizer Vereinigte Exportbank, Dr. Willie Ruhrmann, was resting his ample-bellied body in his favorite armchair and reading the *Züricher Zeitung*'s cultural section. In the mornings he always read the business section; at night, before supper, he read culture; he never varied. The Frau Direktor sat in the chair opposite him smiling, regarding the ample figure of her husband with placid approval. She was busy crocheting her ninth placemat of the week. When the telephone rang, they both looked at it with a mixture of surprise and mild annoyance. It was not unheard of to have their evening hour interrupted like this, but it was rare and not to be encouraged. Anna would get it in the kitchen, of course, but even so . . . The Herr Direktor went back to the contemplation of his newspaper and his wife to the contemplation of him. The telephone stopped ringing.

Anna knocked tentatively on the door. "Excuse me, sir," she said, pushing the door hesitantly and putting only her head through the narrow gap. "There was a gentleman on the phone."

Yes, Anna." Why could she not wait until after supper as she had been told. Oh, but servants these days!

"I know I shouldn't disturb you; but he said it was urgent that I pass on the message to you." She paused and then added with considerable awe, "He had a very loud voice, sir."

"And what was the message, my dear?" The Frau Direktor interrupted her maid's breathless recital before her husband could puff himself up into a froth the way he surely would in just a moment. So bad for his blood pressure. "Just tell us and then you can go back to your work."

"Yes, madam," Anna said gratefully. "It was a simple enough message, madam, although I don't understand it. But he made me repeat it, so I know it was right. I'm quite sure, madam."

"What was the message." The Herr Direktor's patience was already at its limit.

"Oh," said Anna, with pleasure, "that was only two words. The man with the loud voice said to tell you, 'We've stopped.'"

"Thank you, Anna," the Herr Direktor said, a surprising amount of kindness in his voice. "You were quite right to tell me." He smiled at her, quite oozing charm. "That will be all, thank you." As the girl left, the Herr Direktor's behavior became even more surprising. For the first time since his wife could remember, he put down the newspaper, arose and went to the telephone. Quickly he dialed. There was a moment's pause. Then, "Fifty thousand," the Herr Generaldirektor ordered abruptly.

"Immediately, tomorrow morning. Is that clear?" He paused another moment and then, without another word, hung up the telephone and returned to his seat. "My goodness," he said to his wife with a happy sigh, "what a terribly disrupted evening!"

"Yes, dear," his wife replied, sighing too, but rather less happily.

And still the price of the Turner-LaMott shares held up. Large blocks traded . . . but for every buyer disenchanted with the company and afraid of a further precipitous drop, there seemed to be at least another—usually from overseas, it was noted by more than one astute Wall Street trader—who was willing to buy almost any quantity. Nineteen, nineteen and a half, twenty—the price of the stock edged upwards. Gradually the volume dropped. Few buyers wanted to pay more than twenty; but the sellers had new courage: many decided they might hold out for more.

Carlos Spinosa had returned to his favorite office, this one in a brownstone on East Sixty-second Street—an elegant environment, beautifully furnished in Louis XIV antiques and superb Persian rugs. Only one assistant and a secretary of very long standing worked here. The assistant, young, brilliant, Harvard-trained, a genius with computers, was well paid. Some quarter of a million a year, including his bonus . . . just enough to pay for his habit, which was getting worse. He wouldn't last much longer, Carlos reflected sadly. In the meantime, he was invaluable.

"We need thirty percent to get complete control," Carlos was saying to him now. "That's the way it's set up."

"I don't understand, sir."

"You're not supposed to," said Spinosa, showing rare pride, "nor do the Feds. But it won't work if we can't buy enough. Can't we buy faster?"

"But already we're pushing the price up. It's back to twenty-two."

"Fuck it, it'll go up to fifty when we let the news out. Buy more."

"Very well, sir."

Gradually the Turner-LaMott stock price rose—and the calculations from the minicomputer on the desk in front of Spinosa's assistant showed how his group's total spending was rising too.

By the time the stock reached 25, Spinosa had bought 400 million dollars' worth. He managed to acquire another 50 million dollars' worth of stock as the price inched up to 27½. By the time it reached 28½, he had spent a total of 605 million dollars.

"Well, my dear chap, and how are things progressing?" It was Oliver Chapin sounding as jocular and relaxed as ever. But there was an edge to his voice that Spinosa detected immediately. Not even Chapin could play with sums like this without the tension mounting almost unbearably.

"Fine. We've got twenty-five percent of the stock, average purchase price about twenty-four dollars. You've spent five hundred million dollars plus the one hundred million I earned for you. Only about two hundred million to go, I guess."

There was an ominous pause on Oliver Chapin's end of the line. "That's rather more than you anticipated," he said at last. The edge in his voice had switched from mere tension to something far more dangerous . . . a nascent anger, not yet formed enough to cause action, but highly threatening nevertheless, like a bull pawing the ground but not yet sure exactly where or when to charge.

"These things cannot always be predicted with complete accuracy," Spinosa said quickly. "But you said control. And that's exactly what you're getting."

"For seven hundred million dollars? That's quite a bit for control, I should have thought."

"It's six hundred million dollars. A hundred I earned for you. But you're right, it is a lot." There was no point in arguing with Chapin in this mood. "But, of course, you'll get it all back. It's no more than a loan."

"Right you are," said Oliver Chapin, flattening out his vowels a little. "So long as it's only a loan, and we end up with control, I'll go along."

"Thirty percent of the company. With that, as we discussed, you can do what you want and—"

Oliver was brisk. "I'll know what to do once I have it." Then, his voice dropping to barely a whisper, his accent changing to reveal his raw heritage, he added, "I know you'll make *sure* we get it." Even Carlos Spinosa, who thought himself inured to every form of threat, shuddered.

25

Carlos Spinosa, normally as impeccable as a Brooks Brothers mannequin, astonishingly sported a five-o'clock shadow. His eyes were sunken and shadowed and the normally razor-sharp creases in his pants were bagged out at the knees. He looked as unkempt as any ordinary man after a long night. In fact, apart from cat naps of an hour or so out of every four or five, Carlos and his assistant had remained in his office now for seventy-two hours, glued to the telephone and the computer screen, poring over printouts. Occasionally, he would listen to an incoming call—or place an outgoing one—and then, his rasping voice never varying its intonation, issue a brief order or two before hanging up abruptly.

Gradually, his percentage of TLM ownership grew. From

Sicily and Liechtenstein, from Venezuela and Hong Kong, from Miami and Costa Rica the news kept coming in. Gruff voices or impenetrably succinct telexes announced "ten, total forty-three" or "four, total twelve" or, occasionally, only "half, total eight point three and blocked"—describing on each occasion the amount purchased since the last report and the total purchased to date. Sometimes, especially from the tinier outposts of Spinosa's network of apparently unrelated co-operators, someone would block out at a low level, knowing how quickly rumors can build in a small town and mindful of Spinosa's twice-repeated warning—and for such a taciturn man, twice had the impact of a harangue—that on this one there should be no risks taken.

"How far?" Spinosa was exhausted but not an ounce of concentration seemed to have been lost, nor had his remarkable aptitude for mental arithmetic slowed.

"Twenty-eight point three," his assistant summarized. "At an average of twenty-four and a quarter. Price is almost twenty-nine now so the remaining one point seven percent should end us with the thirty percent you want at an average of . . ." He turned to his calculator to compute the final average they could expect.

"Twenty-four and a half," Carlos interrupted.

"You're right, of course," the younger man agreed, finishing his calculation.

"Of course." Spinosa was merely admitting to the irrefutable fact that he was a genius at calculation. "I think it's time to report to our friend."

"I think so. I'll get him on the phone."

"No, we should meet. Call Rosenberg. He'll want to make the arrangements."

By the time the meeting between Oliver Chapin and Carlos Spinosa took place—this time in a nondescript but comfortable safe house that Sidney Rosenberg had decided was a justifiable sacrifice considering how far along the deal had progressed—Spinosa's total ownership had indeed reached the thirty percent aim. It had cost almost exactly the seven hundred million dollars of Spinosa's most recent prediction.

"So we got the thirty percent," said Oliver Chapin, leaning back in his armchair and rubbing his stomach as if he were talking of some superlative meal he had just enjoyed. He peered at Spinosa beatifically. "But then again, I'd have to say that seven hundred million dollars is a fair sum."

Spinosa inclined his head fractionally in concurrence. "Indeed."

"So perhaps you wouldn't mind explaining how we intend to obtain the rest. Just to reassure me again, just so I feel, how should I put it, tranquil, on 'Golden Pond,' as it were, if you recall the film. Why is it, for instance, that we don't need fifty-one percent . . . take me through that again."

Spinosa, as always, was aggravated. It was sheer perversity that made Oliver play the innocent like this—probably so he could boast later how he, a naïve lad from a poor but honest family, had made it all alone in the big time. Oliver always hated to be reminded that he'd studied accounting at night school for five years.

"The point is," Spinosa said with a sigh, accepting that Chapin had surely bought himself the right to be humored, "that you don't actually want to buy Turner-LaMott."

"What's that you're telling me?"

"What we're going to do is buy just the pharmaceutical part of the company. You don't want their shampoo business, nor their diet aids, nor any of the rest of it."

"Okay. If you say so. But how?"

"We've been over this before, Oliver."

"No doubt, no doubt at all," Oliver agreed jovially. "But a little repetition is a thoroughly good thing." He beamed at Spinosa, but it was clear that he was adamant.

"For an investment of seven hundred million dollars, you will concede, I've acquired the right to be just a little redundant."

"Very well."

"Lovely." Chapin reclined further.

"In summary, it works in three stages. First, in about three weeks' time, we'll announce that the technology is good after all. That'll drive the price of the stock up from the average price you paid, which is about twenty-four dollars, to the mid forties, quite possibly even fifty."

"We paid an average of twenty-four and a half. At forty-nine we'd double our money," Chapin agreed shrewdly. "But that's theory. Because if we ever tried to sell out, the market would be flooded and the price would fall dramatically. We'd probably still make a profit, but we'd miss the control we want."

"Right. We won't try to sell, though. We'll consolidate all our stock in your hands. You'll declare that you're buying at the market price . . . and you'll keep buying until you've bought out all your agents. You'll probably get a few other offers, and you can buy them too, but not many because everyone who's arm's-length will be holding out for a higher price."

It was an extraordinarily long speech for Carlos Spinosa, and Oliver beamed his appreciation. Instead of commenting on it, he continued, "But that still doesn't do anything—just formalizes where we are now."

"Correct. So the third step becomes the key. You make a very simple exchange offer. You offer half your stock in exchange for the pharmaceutical part of the Turner-LaMott Company. It's worth about three hundred million at book so that your offer of half your stock will be about twice its value . . . that will be considered generous. As for the other half of your stock, well, you sell that. You should get about six hundred million dollars for it at the price to which I'm anticipating the stock will rise."

"Why won't that push the price down?"

"Oh, that's very simple. For one thing, we're selling only half your stock—fifteen percent of the whole rather than thirty percent. That makes a very big difference. The other reason the price will hold up, even while you're selling, is because the exchange offer will be at fifty dollars per share. That will have a huge psychological impact." Carlos Spinosa allowed his face to exhibit the vestige of a sour smile. "In other words," he said with satisfaction, "you get all your money back—and you end up with full ownership of that part of the business you really want."

"The part that makes those rather interesting white powders," said Oliver Chapin with equal satisfaction. "Yes, that's what we want. Both their manufacturing and their distribution."

"I have no opinion about that," Spinosa said coldly. "I'm interested merely in engineering the deal you want."

"Absolutely, old chap," Chapin agreed, without suggesting that he accepted any rebuke. "But tell me, why do we have to go through this whole scheme in the first place? Why not just make the money on the stock and use the profits to buy the pharmaceutical company?"

"Because they'd never sell. The only reason you can force the exchange is because you own that much stock in the first place. You don't have a voting majority, of course, but your minority is so large that you could probably launch a successful take-over bid for the whole company any time you wanted."

"If I had the money."

"They have no way of knowing that you don't."

"Indeed, indeed. And perhaps I do!"

"Perhaps," Spinosa agreed, but he doubted it. "In any case, the Turner-LaMott people will be delighted to be rid of you and the threat you pose by swapping their pharmaceutical division for all the TLM shares you'll own. They end up with a smaller company—by three hundred million dollars' worth—but they have six hundred million dollars less stock outstanding. In other words, any remaining stockholders—which undoubtedly includes the management—will be a fair bit richer personally."

"So they'll agree," Oliver summarized.

"From your point of view there's another huge advantage," Spinosa continued. "Under this approach, you no longer own any public stock. You'll have 'gone private' with the Turner-LaMott pharmaceutical division. You'll control a private company with no need to explain anything to shareholders, the stock exchange, the Securities and Exchange Commission or any stockholder or reporter who wants to ask what's going on. In other words, you'll have what you want: control of—"

"Of a company with eight factories and over a thousand sales people," interrupted Oliver Chapin with a chuckle of enormous pleasure, "specializing in the international manufacture and distribution of a wide variety of drugs." He beamed at Spinosa briefly. Then, switching the subject right back to the beginning, he asked again, "But repeat why you're so certain the stock will rise."

"Because the technology's hot," Carlos Spinosa said tersely, tiring of this game of explanations.

"Yes?"

"You've got the best of all worlds," Carlos gave in with a sigh. "High tech, pollution control and energy are the three hottest buttons on the street. Look at the multiples high-tech stocks are getting." Spinosa paused while Chapin nodded so vigorously in agreement that he looked likely to damage his neck or shake loose his head. "You've got all three," Spinosa continued. "And in a form that's easy to understand, perfect for the media to report. There's no doubt that when we declare the technology's good after all, the stock will soar. Everyone will know that we're for real. Having once announced it wasn't working, we'd obviously not reverse ourselves unless we were damned certain."

"Wonderful," said Oliver. And then, more sincerely flattering than he had been in many years, he declared, "truly a simple and wonderful scheme."

26

Simon Bagnew stiffly emerged from his limousine. "I should be about an hour," he said to his driver. "Goodness knows why I'm wasting even that much time." The grumble was really to cover his apprehension. Although, according to his doctor, the occasional flutter of his heart—he had recently become aware of a sort of double beat in his chest—was not serious, it was still "worth looking into."

"What does that mean?" Simon had asked. "If it's not serious, why worry?"

"We ought to know what's causing it."

"Why? Can it lead to anything?"

"Nothing to worry about." The bland assurance had, of course, added to Simon's concern, and his heart had immediately jumped arhythmically as if in sympathy. "We'll just give you a stress test to check you out. No problem."

If the doctor could afford this Fifth Avenue rent he must have a good practice, thought Simon. However the waiting room he now entered immediately eroded his confidence. Nothing here suggested that his doctor had any particular medical talent: these elderly, overweight women looked as if they had nothing better to do than eat and visit that nice doctor on Fifth Avenue. That and take a few of his tranquilizers and barbiturates whenever sheer boredom wasn't enough to put them to sleep.

He gave the secretary, a sweet girl with a lovely smile marred only by the thin line of hair on her upper lip, his name and insurance number. She seemed more interested in the latter. "There'll be just a few minutes' wait. Please take a seat." She had evidently said it many times before.

Simon entered the waiting room and sat down heavily. He looked with mild distaste at the dog-eared *New Yorker* and *National Geographic* magazines. God, he thought, could I really have brought a heart condition on myself with that idiotic drinking? How could I have allowed myself to sink so low? A heart attack, he thought, and it would all be over. How unfair that would be.

Not so much unfair as ironic, he had to admit. Just as he had made the decision . . . Ah, the decision. How long would he have to wait before he would know whether he had chosen rightly? He felt his heart flutter again.

"Mr. Bagnew? You can go in now. Please disrobe completely and put on the gown. We're going to do some tests, X rays and so forth, before the stress test itself."

"Very well." Simon entered the cubicle and started to undress. What a dehumanizing experience. Damn gowns had to be put on backward for some reason. Impossible to do up the ties, and your ass was forever trying to moon out of the slit. He brushed his hand through his thinning hair and completed changing. "I'm ready," he said, poking his head out of the cubicle and feeling foolish.

"Be with you shortly," a nurse called.

The wait, standing upright in the changing cubicle, seemed interminable. Why were all doctor's offices devoid of anything to read but ancient magazines in the waiting rooms?

"If you'll follow me, please," another nurse interrupted his reverie, "we'll proceed with your tests." She was young but angular and unappealing.

"What tests are they?"

"Just routine." The nurse evidently assumed senility in all her patients. "We'll not have to worry about anything."

"We are not worried," Simon said tersely. "We are merely interested."

But the nurse pretended not to hear. "Now," she said, pushing him gently toward an x-ray machine against the wall of the sparse room they had entered. "Let's push our chest against the flat part there, round our shoulders . . ."

Simon, who had been x-rayed before, placed himself in the correct position."

"Very good," the nurse enthused at his unexpected competence.

The tests took almost an hour. Annoying though the nurse was, Simon had to admit that she was competent. Able staff in business usually suggested an able boss. Perhaps the same applied to medicine.

"There. Now. We're all done. Just the stress test to go. Of course, only the Doctor"—she pronounced the word in awe, her voice dropping several notes—"only the Doctor supervises those."

"Of course!" Simon agreed. But the sarcasm was entirely lost on her.

"So we'd better change into our running clothes," the nurse suggested. "The Doctor will be along shortly." She started to leave. "It was nice talking to you," she said shyly, surprising Simon.

"And you," he agreed lamely, but she had already left.

"Well, well. I see you're all set." The doctor's manner was breezy and familiar. "Nothing to this stress test, of course, but they help us evaluate what's going on."

"How?" Simon asked.

"Let me explain," the doctor said. "You step on that

machine and first walk and then run . . . and you keep at it until you feel too tired to continue. All the time you're wired up to our instruments so we can measure your pulse, heartbeat and so on. And that tells us a great deal."

"What does it tell?" Simon asked stubbornly.

"What's going on." The doctor remained vague but cheerful. "Now, if you'd just sign this form, we can be getting on." He saw Simon's questioning look. "Oh, there's nothing to worry about," he reassured. "The form just holds us harmless in the very improbable event that the exercise is somehow too much for you."

The stress machine, its continuous belt tilted uphill, faced a wall on which there was a picture of a scrawny woman, her face drawn with strain, winning a marathon. Was it offering encouragement, Simon wondered, or a stern warning? The belt was moving slowly so that Simon merely had to stroll up its gentle gradient.

"Hold onto the rail in front of you to keep steady," the doctor advised. "How do you feel?"

"Jaunty," said Simon, hoping it was a description others had not used before him.

"Good, then we can speed you up a bit."

Three minutes had passed on the clock on the side wall by the time Simon had to start trotting to keep up with the machine. It was some time since he had taken any exercise at all, and after less than a minute the jogging made him pant. Worse, he could feel the excess flesh on his body jiggle. It was a most unpleasant sensation, he decided. He'd simply have to get back into shape. It was absurd to be this affected by jogging barely a minute. He clenched his fists around the railing and determined to continue.

"You still okay?" the doctor asked. "Keep it up until you've had enough. Remember, we'll stop at once at your signal."

"I'm fine." Simon kept his answer short, needing all his

breath. He pulled on the rail to help him keep up with the belt.

"Excellent, excellent. Then we'll speed up just a little."

Two minutes. Simon realized he was close to exhaustion already. Even looking like that damned marathoner would be better than being this untrained.

Three minutes. He felt awful.

"You still okay?"

"Fine."

"Then up she goes."

Three and a half. He was panting like a steam locomotive and he could feel his pulse pounding in his ears.

Four. He just couldn't keep going much longer.

"Enough!" It was the doctor's decision to pull him off the machine, not his own. Simon was perversely proud of that. "Over here, lie down." The doctor spoke with urgency, guiding him backwards so that he should not trip over the wires affixed to his body. "Excellent. You did very well. Very well."

Simon felt the room reeling. He barely managed to reach the table and lie back on it gratefully. He would have fainted, he realized, had he remained on that damned machine another few seconds.

"Now we'll see how fast you return to normal," the doctor explained. He looked at Simon's heaving chest. "You're a shade out of condition, you know."

"I know."

"But pretty competitive."

"Yes," Simon agreed between gasps. "I know that too."

Simon arrived in his office by noon. Even after a shower at the doctor's office, he felt hot from his exertions. He wondered what the findings from the stress test would be. It would be a week, the doctor had told him, before the results were analyzed. He would just have to try not to worry about it before then.

"Any messages?" he asked his secretary, resolutely putting his fears aside.

"Only Mr. Spinosa's office."

"Yes?" He tried to keep his voice neutral.

"They said . . ." His secretary tried to appear nonchalant, reveling all the while in the sensations she knew her message was causing in her boss. "They said," she repeated, "that Mr. Spinosa intends to visit you today."

"When?" Simon asked too loudly.

"They weren't certain. I said you'd be in by noon. They said to stay here. He'd be by."

"Thank you." Simon walked into his office thinking furiously that it was typical of Spinosa to keep Simon off balance, unsure whether to go out to eat or not. But what was he to do about it? For a second, he considered going out to eat anyhow. But no, he had no alternative; his only choice was to swallow his pride and put up with the man . . . that is, if he wanted to keep his job. And that he wanted desperately.

Simon sat down behind his desk and reached for the pile of papers in his In basket. Normally the routine of going through his mail had a pleasantly calming effect. But he was too agitated now to concentrate on the papers before him. He'd done what Spinosa wanted, but the damned man was so unpredictable, God knew what he might do next. Bagnew slumped behind his desk, looking more like a half-empty sack of grain than the captain of industry his title made him. His body was bloated and unshapely, his face puffy and too red; his hair thin and untidy.

The intercom made Simon start. He had never got used to the damn thing and his occasional complaints to Agatha had resulted in no change. "Yes," he snapped into the phone, suddenly angry. "What do you want?"

"Mr. Spinosa is here to see you."

The energizing annoyance that had made him sit upright a moment before now evaporated instantly. "Please send him in." Simon arose and tried to smooth out his rumpled suit. "Come in, come in," he said as the door opened slowly. "Come in." There was a moment of emptiness. Then Spinosa, immaculate as always in a gray silk suit, a slightly lighter silk shirt, and a tie which combined thin diagonal stripes of grey and maroon, entered. He moved as precisely as if he were on stepping stones, a way of walking that gave him the appearance of great fastidiousness, a sort of exaggerated self-awareness and care. It also made him seem taller, more erect, and thus, more elegant and somehow crueler than ever.

How austere the man was, as gaunt as an ascetic. With a beard, he would be an Italian saint, Simon thought irrelevantly; without, he is a Spanish inquisitor. "It's good to see you," Simon said formally and stretched his hand toward Spinosa. Wordlessly, Spinosa shook hands. The skin that touched Simon's moist palm seemed cool and parchment dry.

"Please have a seat." Simon gestured and turned toward the sofa, but Spinosa did not move and Simon was forced to stop and turn back. "To what do I owe..." Simon started and realized how silly the phrase would sound—"this pleasure," indeed! "What can I do for you?" he asked instead. And then, again correcting himself and now sounding brusque to the point of rudeness, "What do you want?"

"You did well at the press conference." Spinosa's voice was cold.

"Thank you." Simon had no idea what to think. He felt his stomach contract into a knot as hard and heavy as a bowling ball.

"It's too bad that you have so misled our investors."

"But," Simon started to remonstrate, "I only did what you—"

"Two entirely contradictory statements almost back to

back," Spinosa interrupted. For the first time since Simon had known him, he smiled broadly, a chilling sight. "I have, therefore, been asked by the board of directors to demand your resignation, effective immediately." Spinosa's smile did not falter in the least, but now it looked as sour as that of a monarch forced to bestow a knighthood on a subject unworthy of the honor. "I shall take over your position."

"But . . . good God . . . but I did only what you told me."

"You have now repeated that foolish remark twice. Be assured, it will not help you. Just a few weeks ago you announced a major breakthrough in new technology; then, last week, you suddenly announced it was of no value to Turner-LaMott. That is clearly irresponsible. How could I—or anyone—possibly have told you to do anything so absurd? You are incompetent. You are therefore fired." Spinosa turned on his heel and, picking his way as carefully as before, moved toward the door. "Kindly make sure you vacate your office by the end of this week."

Simon Bagnew felt the room start to spin. This couldn't be happening to him, not again. It was even more unfair than the last time. Had he not followed Spinosa's orders completely, even where most people would have felt they were entirely wrong, immoral even? "You can't," Simon protested, "you can't fire me. I have a contract." For a moment the thought gave him courage. "You'll owe me indemnity." But his brave front was short-lived.

Spinosa turned back toward Simon. "A contract," he asked sarcastically, "that allows you to defraud the investors?"

"I never . . ." Simon started. But already he knew what was coming.

"We have run across buy orders for stock placed by you immediately before the first announcement . . . and sell orders immediately before the second announcement. Just from the ones we've managed to trace so far, you have gained about a hundred thousand dollars. Probably there were many other orders, and many accomplices. No doubt we'll find at least a few of them too. Already we have a sworn, notarized affidavit from one broker you retained to handle secret transactions. He not only says under oath that you asked him to place the orders, but that he warned you it was illegal and, swearing him to secrecy, you told him to go ahead anyway."

"God damn you, Spinosa. You know that's a frame."

"If it is, which I deny, it's one that is water tight," said Spinosa slowly. "You are fired, effective immediately. If you make any fuss, you will also be criminally prosecuted."

"But you promised me a million dollars if ever you forced me out of the company."

"That is what your contract says." Spinosa seemed almost friendly. "But how much can you collect from prison?" He turned elegantly on his heel, leaving an indentation of crushed pile in the carpet.

Bagnew, utterly shocked, heard him singing the final aria from *La Bohème* under his breath: "Your tiny hand is frozen." The words were cut off abruptly as the door closed behind him.

As if in a trance, Simon moved back to his desk. As laboriously as an old, old man he sat down in his huge leather chair. "Oh God," he said aloud just once.

He felt his heart suddenly speed up, as panicked as an entrapped bird fluttering to escape. "No," Simon said loudly. "Not that." Later, once everything was clear, a heart attack would be acceptable.

But his heart continued to beat very fast, and when he tried to arise he felt too faint. Leaning forward, until his head rested wearily on his arms crossed on the shining desk, Simon fell asleep as suddenly and as completely as if he were in a coma, or already the victim of the heart attack he so feared.

27

Janet Bagnew, wearing a well-cut, sensible suit—ready for anything—left the house, carefully locking the door behind her, a look of infinite determination on her face. She drove down the driveway in the family station wagon, briefly stopping at the mail box. Bills, nothing but bills. Looking at them with distaste, she tossed them onto the back seat. Then she turned carefully left toward Greenwich and, beyond the town itself, the New England Thruway toward Manhattan.

Of course she would be back here. Even though the house was now sold to that nice young couple, there were *loads* of tasks left to complete before the Bagnew family found its way clear of the place permanently. Closing on the contract wasn't even for another ten days.

But this departure nevertheless felt like the final one. She glanced back at the house, just visible as she reached the rise in the road, and felt as if she were saying a permanent good-bye. It had been a good life, by and large, she reflected. Susan had become strong there. There was a lump in Janet Bagnew's throat as she drove away. It's past and done, she chided herself. Remember it for the good things, but concentrate on the problems at hand. She pressed her foot more vigorously onto the accelerator and sped toward New York and everything that awaited her there.

Janet Bagnew knew New York only as a suburban matron visiting for an afternoon's shopping or an occasional evening theater or concert. Now, for the first time, she was to become one of the huge pool of urbanites—over nine million they said—who jostled together to make up the five boroughs of the city. If you read the paper, you might think mugging, pillage and rape were the standard means of livelihood. But Janet was far less concerned about that than about what her life and Simon's would be like under these new circumstances. At least, she thought with sudden amusement, if you could take everything that had happened in the right spirit, it certainly added up to an exciting time.

Janet drove the old station wagon steadily down the East Side Highway, ignoring both the occasional joyriders cutting in front of her and the anguished rattle of her car protesting the bumps and potholes. At Thirty-fifth Street, she exited right and then moved slowly west across town through heavy traffic. On Lexington, she turned left and edged the wagon slowly southward.

Lexington Avenue's cachet falls gradually but inexorably as one moves south from Fifty-ninth Street, the location of the main store of Bloomingdale's, the trendiest department store chain in the world. As far as Forty-sixth Street, Lexington remains acceptable, held together by a number of more or less luxurious hotels and the rear entrances of several prestigious Park Avenue office buildings. But then it is pulled down by the sleaze attracted by the rear entrance of Grand Central Station and the front entrance of the Post Office. Bag women and crazy old men, both of indescribable filthiness, live out their miserable lives here; and prostitutes parade. The avenue improves again slightly in the thirties, by pretending to be luxuriously residential. But by the twenties it has become a lower-middle-class working area, although still decent. Beyond that, however, where Lexington becomes Irving Place and then terminates at Fourteenth Street, the rot sets in. Poverty, drunkenness—all the sleazy aspects of the battle of survival in a big city—come into the open.

At the very edge, between the poor-but-honest and the

depraved, sat the Ace Hotel. Its doorman was dirty and seemed more preoccupied with a variety of street transactions than with his task of keeping guard over the hotel's entrance. He looked up in surprise when Janet Bagnew pulled up. Clearly, she had come to the wrong place. "You can't stop there lady," he said, not unkindly, but prepared to be belligerent if necessary. "That's my unloading area."

"Oh, that's okay," she said, smiling warmly, alighting from the wagon and handing him her keys and a dollar. "I won't be needing the car for a while so you can move it if you like."

"Okay," he said, "I'll take care of it." He didn't bother to hide his astonishment.

Janet Bagnew entered the hotel lobby with a firm step. Once inside, however, she stopped and looked around to make sure no one in there knew her and that no one was following her in. Then, quickly, she walked across the lobby and out of the rear exit. She jumped into a taxi. "The Carlyle," she ordered.

"Huh?"

"Madison and Seventy-sixth."

"Yes, ma'am." The cabbie looked at her with even more surprise than had the doorman.

"You don't know it?"

"Oh, sure lady." He took off with a squeal of tires. Not many people left the Ace to go to the Carlyle, perhaps the most elegant hotel in New York. A cleaning lady, perhaps? But no, her suit looked better than that. Ah, well, people had strange habits. He shrugged his shoulders, worrying for a moment that she might not have the money to pay, and he glanced at her appraisingly in his rearview mirror. She seemed well-heeled enough. Perhaps, he thought suddenly, she owned the Ace hotel. One of those freakin' slum landlords he'd read about in the *Post*. The thought gave him considerable relief.

Janet sat back and tried to relax as the cab rushed uptown, wedging herself into her seat to avoid being excessively jostled. Once she was reasonably comfortable, she started to amuse herself by watching the people. What an endless and marvelous array New York offered . . . the elegant and impoverished; the sensible (like herself) and the bizarre; the relaxed and happy, judging by their untroubled faces, and the terribly pressured, their faces deeply creased. Every race, color, creed, profession, type, status of person, mixed into one great urban stewpot. . . . It seemed only moments before they arrived.

"Three-sixty, lady." The cabbie felt an immediate twinge of anxiety. What if she . . .

"Keep the change," Janet said recklessly, handing him a five-dollar bill, noticing that this left her only with one ten-dollar bill in her purse.

"Thank you, ma'am. Thank you very much."

The friendly doorman, in pressed uniform and crisp, spotless shirt, was a perfect contrast to the man at the Ace. He held open the cab door and smiled her into the hotel lobby, small, marbled and exclusive.

With only the barest hesitation, Janet turned toward the elevators to the left. The elevator operator stood aside to let her enter.

"The top floor," she said quietly.

"Certainly, madam." He slammed the door and the elevator rushed her upward. It arrived in seconds, lurching her stomach.

"Thank you," she said anyway.

Stepping out, Janet Bagnew hesitated only briefly before walking over to the apartment on the left. The door was ajar. She knocked, entered and found herself in an elegantly appointed vestibule. On the left was a large gilt-framed mirror, on the right a doorway which evidently led into the suite itself. Glancing into the mirror, she inspected herself quickly, picked a piece of lint off her skirt and straightened her hair. She was just about to open the second door when it was pulled open from the inside.

"Well, my dear, how nice to see you." Foster Harrison smiled at her warmly. "How very nice," he repeated, taking both her hands in his and bending down to kiss her cheek. "Come in, do come in. We're waiting for you." He pulled her into the room behind him as if he were the tug and she the tender.

"Hello darling." Simon Bagnew put down his champagne glass as soon as he saw her and hurried over to embrace his wife. "We were just starting to celebrate," he said.

"You look wonderful," she said. "Just wonderful."

"Never felt better."

"Quite a victory, quite a victory," said Harrison. "It was a brilliant scheme you thought up, Simon."

"Janet had as much to do with it as I did."

"Anyhow, damned good! Here's to all of us."

The three of them toasted each other with champagne, all looking very serious but thoroughly satisfied. "I've ordered dinner to be sent up," Harrison continued. "Caviar, giant filet mignons, Mouton Rothschild, the whole works."

"I'm glad," said Janet Bagnew. "It hasn't been every day we've known we can afford it."

"And now we can," her husband said. "Even though there's still a hell of a lot of work ahead of us."

"Yes, even I believe it now," she said. "I even left our station wagon where I'm sure it will be stolen before I get back!"

The two men laughed. "But you weren't followed?" Simon asked suddenly concerned. "I don't think they'd realize yet, but . . ."

"Of course not. I did just as you told me, in one door and out the other. Very James Bondish I felt, too." She paused, looking a little worried in spite of her light tone. "It won't go on too long, will it?"

"No. As soon as the whole thing's in the open, it will be over," Foster Harrison said reassuringly.

"I'm sure of it," Simon agreed.

"Okay," she said, taking a tentative sip of champagne. "If you say so, I choose to be convinced!"

"You're a very brave lady," Harrison said. "And you have a very courageous husband. It took a lot of guts for him to come and tell me the whole story. He had no idea what my reaction would be."

"We talked about it a lot before he came," Janet admitted. "We decided we had no choice."

"I'm glad you made the decision."

"So am I," said Simon with heartfelt certainty. "I just wish I could be there when Spinosa finds out."

28

The limousine in which Carlos Spinosa habitually traveled was a stretched Mercedes 500. It sported not only a television set but an entire video console capable of everything from picking up private satellite transmissions to playing electronic games. It had two telephones and a complicated mobile unit that could provide passengers with the very latest stock market quotes from New York, Munich, Tokyo, wherever, at any moment—provided, of course, the car did not happen to be in a tunnel.

On the outside, the car was as gray as a bullet. It gleamed with polish, but since there was virtually no chrome to add contrast, the overall impression was flat. Even the car's windows were covered with one-way mirroring that looked gray from the outside. Every inch, body and windows, was bulletproof.

In the front seat, insulated from the grand and spacious interior where Carlos Spinosa lounged elegantly, the uniformed chauffeur, in jaunty cap and sunglasses, looked affluent and tough. His upright position, constantly moving head, darting eyes and slightly worried expression made him seem as wide awake and ready for trouble as a fighter pilot in a combat zone. The close observer would have been right had he guessed that the man was indeed a fine athlete, a fighter of near-Olympic standards, but thoroughly experienced too, at torture and murder.

Not a man given to excessive self-indulgences, Carlos Spinosa nevertheless reveled in the chamois softness of the mouse gray leather lining the car. He enjoyed nothing more than being sped along at a hundred miles an hour while pouring himself and Bella a glass of perfectly chilled Dom Perignon from the car's refrigerator, as the superbly balanced and modulated stereo unit enveloped him in his beloved Puccini arias. Occasionally, a young traffic cop, not sufficiently seasoned to be intimidated by the size and grayness of the car, stopped them for speeding. But there were damned few cops who couldn't be persuaded they had made a mistake by the mention of a few well-chosen names—and a hundred bucks. The driver handled these transactions, of course, but Carlos was the one who enjoyed the sense of security his ability to buy off the police brought. If he had only been able to manage that back in Brazil. . . .

Now Carlos's limousine raced north on the Merritt Parkway through "back country" Greenwich and Stamford, toward Wilton. He was looking forward to the meeting with the innovative technical staff at TULIPS, and with Dr. Winthrop Turner, far less innovative but more reliable. Neither Carlos nor the driver gave a damn that the sky was azure and the fall foliage—the blazing yellows and reds of the maples, the everlasting deep green of the pines—was so splendid that tourists thronged to see it. Carlos, his pleasure incorporating both elation and the tense anticipation of victory, thought only of the giant coup he would soon have completed.

Only one more major play to go: an exciting, persuasive and thoroughly professional press conference replete with facts, figures and graphs reestablishing the validity of the technological breakthrough. Ideally there would be an actual live demonstration of what those little bugs could do. Even a press made thoroughly skeptical by Turner-LaMott's previous contradictory claims could not fail to believe what they saw for themselves. Yes, this was one event he intended to handle all the way. Just for once, he wanted to emerge as the hero, to take the credit for launching technology that would not only be profitable, but would also be a great boon to humanity.

Ah, but the impact on the stock! If he could make the press conference dramatic enough—and he damn well intended to—he could push the shares to fifty dollars, even sixty, perhaps more. Rapidly he calculated his share of the total profits, his commission on the Chapin profits, plus his full profit from his own investments. Even the most conservative forecasts resulted in astronomic profits, sums that went beyond wealth. With his knowledge, experience and ambitions—and that kind of money—he would be among the world's most powerful men.

And all without risk! He almost chortled. Not since his first successes in São Paulo—before the disaster—had he been as sure of what he was doing, as confident that he had his destiny by the balls. Then, of course, he had become overconfident and therefore careless. That lesson had been unforgettable! No, nothing could go wrong now. The technology was sound—his internal spies as well as everything the poor toad had told him proved that beyond any doubt. And it was enormously valuable. Best of all, no one could blame Spinosa for the earlier confusion. He had been only a director when the toad had made his announcements; no one could suggest that, as such, he should, or even could have stopped them. And the moment he took over the reins of power himself, why he immediately fired the incompetent little man, corrected the misinformation and proceeded to run the company properly.

The one problem that had worried him had been stockholder suits, and on that he had received very careful advice from old Amos.

"What about a class-action suit from investors who lost money as a result of the first announcement, which proved to be false?" Carlos had asked, leaning forward in intense concentration.

Amos McCarthy looked more like a retired sailor than the million-dollar-a-year senior partner in one of New York's oldest and most prestigious law firms. His face seemed to be made of badly tanned, hopelessly crinkled leather; his white hair was wiry and unruly; he seemed as uncomfortable in his suit as a dock worker at a wedding. But his simple, down-to-earth advice was potent with a mixture of his own experience and the painstaking research of a dozen juniors, each a brilliant academic lawyer. "Well, Carlos, I'll tell you. You'll get suits, all right. Plenty. Every loser that's got a cousin that's a lawyer will sue."

"Of course."

"But I'm not so sure they'll win. Make a lot of fuss for you. Keep me and my boys pretty busy. Cost you a pretty penny. Mebbe even a million or two."

Carlos remained silent, knowing he would be glad to pay, but by reflex unwilling to concede the point before it was necessary.

"But in the end I'd guess you'll win."

"Why?"

"For one thing, any investor who bought TLM stock

before the first announcement hasn't lost much. . . . Even after the second announcement, the stock didn't fall that far below its original price. Sure, they could have sold higher . . . but that's lost opportunity not real damages. They don't have much of an argument where they didn't actually lose."

"And for those who bought high after the first announcement—and sold low after the second?"

"Well, hell, they bought and sold in a few weeks . . . that's speculatin'."

"Obviously."

"They were gamblin'. The courts don't hold much sympathy for that sort of thing. After all, if they'd won their bet, they wouldn't have been willing to give the money back." Amos paused and the creases in his forehead deepened so drastically it seemed his skin might crack. "The only thing is . . ." he started.

"Yes?"

"That we got to be darned sure no one inside the company planned this thing."

"Of course."

"If the court ever felt that the management of Turner-LaMott knew that the technology was good when they said it wasn't, why then this would be a big problem."

"There can be no such proof."

"Well, mebbe." Old Amos was not easily convinced. "No disgruntled employee? Not that president of yours that you told me was to blame? Nothin' in the files?"

"The only thing I have found in the files," Carlos Spinosa had assured the elderly lawyer, "is a detailed confidential memorandum from Jim Lester who was executive vice-president of the firm at the time—and far more experienced than Bagnew—to the effect that in his view the technology was impractical."

"Could be a forgery."

"His secretary will swear it was written by him. He never signed copies of internal memoranda so that's why his signature is not on it."

"And the original?"

"That was sent to Simon Bagnew. That is why he was forced to make the new announcement," Spinosa said emphatically. "He certainly should recall it, even though he is not likely to be friendly to us. Why, otherwise, would he have made his announcement?"

"Indeed."

"But even if he were to become irrationally uncooperative, it wouldn't matter. His very experienced secretary, Agatha Caruthers, will recall giving him the document. She will also swear that he asked her to destroy any copies of it she might have made immediately, which she did."

"Evidently, he was thinking of suppressing the bad news," Amos said dryly.

"Probably. But he was forced to announce it because Jim Lester knew and would have sent copies to all sorts of people if Bagnew hadn't announced it. Jim Lester turns out to have been wrong in this case, but for some reason he was convinced. And he was a truly honest man. We know that, at a meeting between Bagnew, Turner, Dave Fellows of TULIPS and him, not long before his letter, Lester felt the technology was valuable. But he must have found something in the meantime because his letter states clearly that he'd changed his mind."

"And Jim Lester is dead."

"Yes," agreed Carlos. "I'm afraid he died in an automobile accident."

Carlos Spinosa lay back even further into the soft padding of the limousine's seats. He stretched his legs and crinkled his toes, watching his knitted cotton socks crease and smooth themselves with each movement. His brightly polished church shoes—two hundred dollars a pair—lay next to him on the car's deep pile rug, like a footwear shot for some men's fashion magazine. "Foolproof," Carlos muttered to himself. "Absolutely foolproof."

Dr. Turner—no relation—was waiting nervously at the entrance to TULIPS as the gray limousine drove up. It stopped so suddenly that it threw up gravel like a skier throwing up a shower of snow as he slides to his halt. Instinctively, and to his considerable annoyance, Dr. Turner jumped backwards. He had hardly regained his dignity before Carlos Spinosa was out of the car and standing before him, entirely self-possessed.

"Good morning." The greeting was a major concession for Spinosa who normally dispensed with all forms of protocol as unnecessary and time wasting.

"Good morning, sir." Dr. Turner hesitated, wondering whether "Carlos" would have been better. "Welcome to TULIPS."

"Is everyone ready?"

"Indeed. All the players are waiting inside."

"It's no game."

"No, no. Of course not. I didn't mean . . ."

But Carlos Spinosa was already moving rapidly into the building. Dr. Turner, too rotund to do so with dignity, had to scamper to catch up. In the courtyard, the driver remained next to his limousine, his body alert, a sentry and protector. He made it clear that no one would touch his car.

"Carlos, old fellow, how nice to see you. It's been only—what?—three weeks, since you were here before." Dave Fellows slapped the startled Spinosa on the shoulder. What have you been up to?"

Dr. Turner hurried up, appalled at the familiarity. What did these fellows up here think, behaving like this. "Dr. Fellows," he said acerbically. "Last week the board elected Mr. Spinosa chief executive officer of Turner-LaMott."

"So that's what you've been up to!" Dave grinned boyishly. "Come to think of it, I thought someone had mentioned to me that you'd replaced dear old Simon." He paused looking perplexed. "Oh I know who it was," he brightened at the recollection. "Of course it was Susie." His look at Spinosa was, for just a second, shrewd enough to belie his ingenuous manner. "She's Simon Bagnew's daughter," he said, again playing the innocent. "And my lover."

Dr. Turner choked into a fit of coughing.

"I know," Spinosa said, unperturbed.

"I had assumed you would."

Dr. Turner watched the exchange with astonishment. "Now look here," he tried to interrupt.

"She is an unusually attractive girl," said Spinosa, ignoring the research director. "You are to be congratulated."

"Thank you."

"And you are evidently an unusually talented scientist," Spinosa continued. "As long as we retain your loyalty, I shall remain very pleased to have Turner-LaMott support your research."

"Loyalty? Oh, I say, I don't think it applies," David said with a laugh. "I do my research work with all the other chaps here, usually with that cantankerous old fellow over there who's my closest partner in crime." He pointed to Lee Carello who sat in the corner of the room immersed in a book and quite oblivious to the visitors. "Also with Harriet, who's usually so depressed she can't work at all. Just occasionally, we do some super work." He smiled warmly at Spinosa. "Usually not, though, I'm afraid." His smile turned to a look of rueful chagrin. "If we do, and something worthwhile for Turner-LaMott comes of it, well, that's fine. But if good old TLM can't use what we discover, why that's hardly my concern." Suddenly David was totally serious, any semblance of boyishness forgotten. "You pay me and provide me with support systems to search for new truths. As long as you continue to offer me an opportunity to do my research unsupervised, as you have up to now, I shall continue to work here. If you wish to change the deal, I shall be forced to work elsewhere. It's terribly simple isn't it?" Dave Fellows, Ph.D. (Cantab), M.D. (Yale), looked Carlos Spinosa straight in the eye. "Loyalty doesn't come into it," he concluded.

Dr. Turner, speechless, looked on in horror, but Spinosa seemed both unsurprised and unoffended. "But you will help us turn your discoveries into commercial propositions by teaching us all you know on a given subject."

"Of course." The agreement was friendly. "As long as it doesn't take too much of my time away from my work."

For the first time, Spinosa frowned. This young man could conceivably hurt his scheme by being uncooperative and not providing the practical research staff, headed by poor Turner, with all the theoretical information they needed. Not that it would be a big problem, since, as far as Spinosa's informants knew, all the theory TULIPS had developed had already been conveyed to Dr. Turner. But if not, Spinosa reasoned—shrugging almost imperceptibly—there would be ways of convincing this independent genius here . . . especially now that he was so in love with the long-legged Susan Bagnew. "Helping us shouldn't take much time." Spinosa remained conciliatory, although the rasp in his voice did seem a little harsher.

"Absolutely," said David Fellows, once again the very picture of the boyish, naïve Englishman. "For one thing, I don't actually know enough to take up much of anyone's time in the telling, do I?" He laughed happily. "It was good to see you again, Carlos. I've got to be going now." He started to turn away.

"Wait." Spinosa barked out the order. His patience was at its end. "First tell me about the garbage-to-oil technology."

"Oh that," David said, "we did that months ago. I've almost forgotten it."

"But you could recreate your techniques."

"Suppose so, if I wanted to. But what's the point? Dr. Turner knows all about it, don't you Doc?"

"Is there nothing more you need to know then, Dr. Turner?" Spinosa asked.

To Spinosa's surprise, Turner looked acutely embarrassed. "I'm afraid I don't understand what you mean," he said.

"I'll be going, then," David said.

"I said wait," said Spinosa angrily. "What don't you understand?"

"Well, why would Dr. Fellows be required to clarify that technology? Our contract doesn't call for any form of technical assistance. If it did, I suppose he'd be willing to help. But I can't see that we'd ever waste TULIPS time on it. In any case, the technology is crystal clear. There's no mystery at all; once the basic genetic work is done, it's done. That's all—"

"Absolutely," David interrupted. "Look here, I really must be going—"

Spinosa's growl, coldly violent, interrupted him. "I have no idea what you're talking about, Turner. And I don't think you do either." He stared imperiously at the now reddening research director. "And as for this genius over here, I think whatever he's up to can wait until we get this cleared up." Neither of his listeners moved, but whereas Turner was evidently frozen by the power of his new boss, afraid for himself, David Fellows seemed held only by curiosity about what would happen next.

"I say," he remarked to no one in particular, "how interesting this is!"

Spinosa ignored him. "What I am here to learn about," he continued, "is exactly where we stand in the development of our oil-producing microorganisms, and in the processing of the many subsidiary patents that I know have been applied for. Is that clear?"

"Yes, sir. It's clear," Dr. Turner said hesitantly. "I realized before that's what you wanted to discuss. That's why I don't understand. As you know, we obviously have no further interest in that technology or in those patents."

"What the hell do you mean?" For the first time Spinosa's anger started to slip out of control. "I suggest you get interested damn fast if you want to work here for more than another five minutes."

"But, we don't own any of those patents anymore."

"Come now, don't be particularly stupid," said Spinosa, now holding his temper in check only with the greatest difficulty. "Of course we own them. Stop wasting my time."

"But we sold them. Mr. Bagnew sold them before he left."

"What?" said Spinosa. "Say that again. He sold what?"

"The technology rights, and all the patents connected with the oil-producing organisms."

"But that's impossible. How could he sell them? It took years to develop them." Spinosa simply couldn't believe his ears. Clearly, there was a mistake. "Now, goddammit," he said furiously, "stop playing idiot games with me." Spinosa's elegance had slipped and his accent seemed more foreign.

"Yes, I explained to Mr. Bagnew that I thought those patents were worth millions," said the research director. "Of course. But he pointed out that you felt strongly that the technology was, in fact, of no value to the company."

"No value?" Spinosa exploded. "But . . ."

"I must admit, I didn't understand either," Dr. Turner continued. His dignity had returned now that he felt himself to be on safe ground. And with it had come a sense of outrage that Spinosa had so insulted him just moments ago. It was good to see the man so agitated, Dr. Turner decided. Very good indeed. "It was only when Simon Bagnew explained that you personally had specifically and forcibly required him to make a public announcement that the patents were of no value to us that I realized you must know something the rest of us didn't."

Carlos Spinosa stood, aghast. He seemed gray, gaunt, blasted; but above all, he looked utterly lonely. "Go on," he said, his voice low, flat, with its disbelief starting to be overlaid with understanding. "Proceed."

"Well, even then I wasn't quite sure," Dr. Turner said, as if he were relating some juicy piece of gossip. "I would normally have asked Jim Lester about it, of course. But that awful accident . . ." He paused, looking lost. "Oh yes, I was saying that I still wasn't convinced. But . . ."

"But what?"

"But then, when I saw you at the press conference I knew what Simon had told me was correct."

Dave Fellows was watching the interchange before him with intent interest, a slight smile on his face.

"Go *on*," Spinosa insisted. "What convinced you?"

"Why you did, sir." Dr. Turner sounded quite triumphant.

"Me?"

"Indeed, Carlos," Dr. Turner continued easily, quite enjoying himself now. "I was sitting next to you when Simon came in to make the announcement. You don't remember? Simon had worked with me on selling the technology. We'd found a buyer and the contract was finalized. But I was still not convinced that the board would want us to sell. And I didn't know what Simon was going to announce to the press. The buyers had signed the contract and so had Simon, but I hadn't. And Simon felt it should have my signature on it too so that there could be no doubt at all the key people of Turner-LaMott were in agreement. I was having real trouble making up my mind and thought, maybe, we should check it out with the board. At one point I suggested talking to you personally. Simon thought the technology valueless, as I said. But . . ."

"Get on with it man, for God's sake get on with it." Spinosa's fists were clenched, his cheeks cavernous.

"Well, you walked straight up to him," Dr. Turner continued huffily, "and I heard you tell him quite clearly that the technology was no good. You warned him that he'd better not pull any punches in making that announcement. Actually, Carlos, you repeated it twice. And you put it in very strong terms."

Spinosa made a brief choking sound but said nothing. He seemed to be out of breath so that, even though he was still immobile, his chest heaved. His face had become as gray-white as his fine silk shirt. Except for his eyes, which darted here and there in panic, his entire head seemed to have become as still as a block of rough granite.

"It was at that point that I realized that you must know something that I was missing. Clearly you felt very strongly that the company should not proceed. At that point, selling the process obviously made very good business sense."

"Clearly," David Fellows agreed.

"So when Mr. Bagnew came to me right after the press conference and asked me again to countersign the contract, of course I complied."

"Who bought them?" Spinosa asked, his voice now barely audible. If possible his face had become even grayer. He swayed slightly. A mental image of that awful prison in Brazil flashed through his mind. "Who?" he repeated, and the word was barely a croak.

"A group of businessmen," Dr. Turner said reassuringly. "They were warned that TLM felt the patents were no good. We quoted our concern specifically so that there would be no misunderstanding. But they assured us they wanted them anyway. We got over a million dollars for them."

"Is the contract binding?" Spinosa asked weakly.

"Indeed it is," Dr. Turner reassured him proudly. "Because of the controversy about the value of the patents, both our lawyers and theirs made doubly sure that the contracts are absolutely watertight. Don't worry," Dr. Turner said emphatically, "there's no way that contract can be broken if anyone changes his mind."

"Who?" Spinosa's demand was more urgent, his face contorted.

"Oh, that. Well, I'm not sure who was behind it. We just talked with their lawyers. But it was an investor group. And I believe it may have been headed by our ex-chairman, Mr. Harrison."

"Oh God," Carlos Spinosa groaned. "Oh God." He clutched his stomach in pain. Slowly, as stately as a giant pine falling, he collapsed onto the carpeted floor.

29

Oliver Chapin had gained stature in adversity. As he stood at the far end of the long room, he no longer resembled a lowly, jovial monk. To call him Deacon now would have been disrespectful. For there could be no doubt that today he was the highest of churchmen, the bishop perhaps, or the monastery's mighty abbot—and a stern and unyielding zealot able to strike fear into the heart of even the most unrepentant sinner. The room was sparsely furnished with a long refectory table, a dozen beautifully proportioned but unremittingly severe Shaker chairs and two winged arm chairs of hard cowhide. The floor of rough-hewn stone slabs reinforced the feeling of monkish asceticism. Behind Oliver was a giant fireplace, smoky with a century and a half of roasting fires. Its pillared sides and tall mantel framed the old man as if he were the subject of some early Dutch painting. On either side of the fireplace, tall windows, their panes darkened by the rain streaming down them, cast a dirty light into the room accentuating its cold ecclesiasticism.

The room itself was the main dining hall of a giant stone farmhouse located in rural Pennsylvania not far from Bethlehem. It was the safest of the safe houses set up by Sidney Rosenberg. In good times, neither Oliver Chapin himself nor anyone known to be even distantly connected with him ever visited the farmhouse. Rather, it was kept strictly in reserve, unguessed-at by police, FBI or any of the friends, acquaintances or enemies of the late Caro Pollo or his feuding successors.

But these were not good times, and Oliver had decided the house was needed for this one night at least.

Sidney Rosenberg and Oliver had arrived separately from different directions. Sid had taken the longer route. Walking nonchalantly from his apartment on Manhattan's Upper East Side, casually dressed, he had sauntered into a small, chic restaurant specializing in health food salads. He ate there often and the proprietor, an ex-schoolteacher who preferred feeding willing patrons well to forcing stale knowledge into unwilling students, greeted him warmly. It was still a little early so Sidney had his pick of tables. He sat near the rear, his back to the wall, able to survey the whole restaurant.

Only two couples and a threesome entered in the next twenty minutes and Sidney memorized minutely the appearance of each person. He ate a light salad quickly, excused himself to the proprietor for having to rush out so fast, and slid out of the restaurant's back door into the alley. It was a long, empty passageway with a high fence on one side and windowless walls on the other. No one could observe Sidney as he walked rapidly to the end of the alley, and no one followed.

Emerging, Rosenberg ducked quickly into the subway not fifty feet away. The platform had only two people on it, and when the train arrived, both got on while Sidney waited patiently for the next train. He emerged two stations further on and hailed a taxi. The cab crossed over the Fifty-ninth Street Bridge and dropped him at an anonymous corner of Queens Boulevard, where he stopped briefly to buy a slice of pizza.

Still alert to the slender possibility of pursuit or recognition, he walked the two blocks to an undistinguished Chevy with a pock-marked bumper and rust marks on its door, which he kept garaged there in the name of William Crane. He drove up Queens Boulevard, that thriving proof of the effectiveness of franchising and the free-enterprise system. Just beyond the giant cemetery, which never failed to depress him, Sidney turned right onto the Van Wyck expressway . . . a terrible misnomer for one of the slowest arteries in the city. Thence, onto the Belt Parkway, so old by highway standards that it still boasted wooden telephone poles, on over the Verrazzano bridge and through Staten Island, and on to the ugly marshlands and suburbs of New Jersey. Always keeping well within the speed limit, Sidney continued westward. Eventually, bored and drowsy, he exited onto a road that wound through well-kept fields, past painted barns and myriad antique shops until it reached a narrow unpaved road. Half an hour later, he arrived at the old farmhouse itself. He parked in the shed at the back and entered the house through its servant's entrance.

Oliver Chapin had left New York driving himself in an ordinary-looking Buick registered in his own name. He had made no attempt to avoid being followed and had noted that at least one car, a powerful and overblown Corvette, did seem to be tailing him. Perhaps there were others. It was about eleven-thirty at night as he pointed his car toward the East River Highway. There was a slight smile on his face.

Up the East Side Highway, its traffic becoming thinner the further north he went, Oliver drove conservatively, accelerating very slowly, never switching lanes nor exceeding forty. The tail kept pace about fifty yards behind him. And Oliver noted that there was another car too, a fat and ugly Thunderbird, a few yards behind the Corvette. No doubt he had a double escort—and both pretty typical of the taste of the remaining Pollo family. Oliver's smile broadened. How stupid they were. He'd pulled the same trick back in '56, and they didn't even remember.

Signaling well in advance, Oliver pulled his Buick left onto the Triborough Bridge. The two cars behind speeded up to be able to see which way he would go after he'd cleared the toll. Right led to the Bruckner Expressway, an overhead road leading directly to the New England Thruway and continuing north—through the wealthiest of New York's exurban communities—Larchmont, Rye, Greenwich, Stamford, Darien, all the way to Boston. Left hurried out to New York's airports, LaGuardia and Kennedy.

It was at exactly the moment that the two following cars had committed themselves to wait behind two other cars at the toll gate—apparently anxious not to approach too close—that Oliver himself cleared the tolls. And it was at that precise instant, too, that his elderly Buick shook itself out of its lethargy and changed into a finely-tuned racing machine. The sudden roar of its engine—by Ferrari, not Buick—coupled with the whiff of high-octane racing fuel exhaust, startled the toll collector. But it surprised the two stalled hounds far more as they saw their rabbit turn to a hare and accelerate away from them at a truly astonishing rate. Zero to sixty in five seconds was the actual timing, and up to a hundred in a few seconds more. The Buick, taking the right fork up the Bruckner, was a mile ahead and tearing along the expressway before the other two had even cleared the toll. By the time they had fully appreciated how the old man had duped them, he had already parked the car in a public parking lot off Bruckner Boulevard amidst a sea of other cars from which it was superficially indistinguishable. With a touch of a button hidden under the dashboard, he had swivelled the license plates. And, all that accomplished, he was already contentedly munching away at a Big Mac and a large order of French fries. Dressed in jeans, an open shirt and a padded waterproof windbreaker, Oliver Chapin looked as similar to the other lonely men at the late-night McDonald's as did his car to the others in the lot.

The two men had radioed in that they had lost Chapin going toward New England. It was less than twenty minutes after they had started tailing him. But by the time they had given a detailed description of the Buick he had been driving, including its previous license-plate number, Oliver was already behind the wheel of a medium blue two-door Ford that had been parked on the same lot, and was driving out toward the Verrazzano, to follow the same route Sidney had taken a few hours earlier.

Next to Chapin on the front seat slumped Carlos Spinosa. His beautifully tailored gray suit was uncharacteristically wrinkled, and there were two large stains in the pants and an unsightly rent down the shoulder seam of the jacket. His shirt was loose and his tie, also dirty with large encrusted spots of something unrecognizable, was pulled almost off. At first glance Spinosa might have seemed merely asleep, except for the fact that his head was resting directly on the door and banging against it painfully each time the car swerved or bounced. Clearly, he was unconscious.

It was almost midnight when Oliver Chapin reached the farmhouse, by which time Spinosa was starting to groan and twitch. He would gain consciousness soon—and with it, Oliver thought, the awful headache he deserved.

Oliver eased his Ford in beside Sidney's Chevy and closed the shed doors. By that time, Sidney, alerted by an internal alarm, was already hurrying into the shed from the house. He anticipated that it would be Oliver, but he was alert anyway, careful by reflex.

"Evening, my boy." Oliver Chapin exuded cordiality. "No trouble getting here I take it?"

"None." Sidney was taciturn to cover his tension. Not that he felt in any immediate danger. But the Chapin empire's situation was desperate . . . and, for the first time in his career with Oliver, Sid had to admit that what had gone wrong was at least partly his fault. "And you had no problems either?" He made an effort to seem relaxed.

"None at all, my boy. None at all. A little dyspepsia, perhaps, from eating my McDonald's French fries too fast." He beamed at Sidney. "But I loved them," he confided. "Well, give me a hand with the Brazilian here."

"Did you have any trouble with him?"

"Not once we eliminated the chauffeur." Oliver smiled. "Beautiful boy, that one."

"Did he fight?"

"No chance," said Oliver scathingly. "Those college athletes are all the same, you see. They need rules to know how to breathe. If you don't stick with their rules, they can't function."

Sidney didn't understand, but preferred not to say anything. He hated violence and generally chose to ignore its existence.

But Oliver was elated by the victory. "He was protected against guns, bombs, knives . . . all of that. It never occurred to him that we'd poison his hamburger!" He laughed uproariously. "If McDonald's can do it to me every time I eat there," Oliver chuckled, burping to make his point, "I figured we could do just a little more to Pretty Boy."

"And Carlos?"

"Must have scared the shit out of him! He'd no sooner watched his driver die, than he started becoming sick himself, screamed for a doctor . . ." Oliver Chapin laughed happily again. "Fortunately, that limo of his is sound proof so no one heard. In fact, it took the boys twenty minutes to pry it open after he'd quit yelling and vomiting and passed out."

"So you're here." Sidney tried not to sound as if he had mixed feelings about it.

"Certainly am. Now let's get him out before he wakes up."

Together the two men dragged Spinosa out of the shed and into the house. He was semiconscious by then, able to use his legs to some degree, but probably still unaware of his surroundings. Up the stairs they moved him and dumped him unceremoniously onto the low camp bed in a small, windowless room at the top. Originally, it had no doubt been some sort of storage room. The walls were of stone; the door of thick oak, bolted from the outside.

"That should hold him for a while, I should imagine." Oliver rubbed his hands together in satisfaction.

"As long as you want."

"Tomorrow we'll hear what he has to say."

"But we know that, don't we?" Sidney wished he could muster up some hope.

"Probably, probably. But you never can be sure. He's a wily one, our Brazilian. Maybe he still has a trick up his sleeve."

"I doubt it."

"So do I, so do I. But there's no harm in playing the last card in the hand if it doesn't cost you extra."

"I guess," Sidney agreed without conviction.

"We'll worry about it tomorrow. Now I think, a brandy and then, as I tell my grandchildren, everyone scampers off to bed."

Oliver Chapin stood now at the head of the long dining room. The room was kept at seventy-four degrees by central heating—a concession to modernity made by an owner before Chapin's incognito front man, but long after the original builder—but its austerity made it seem colder. Thus, Sidney Rosenberg wore a sweater under his sports coat and heavy pants. Oliver wore a dark suit, white business shirt and conservative tie. Draped over it, like an opera cloak, he had a navy blue raincoat. When it occasionally caught the light, its folds showed a metallic blue sheen. He looked taller, dressed like this, and more imposing and dangerous than even Sidney, who had long recognized the raw power of his boss, had ever seen before.

"I believe the time has come for us to interview our friend." There was no trace of sarcasm in Oliver Chapin's words. "Would you fetch him, please?"

"Of course," Sidney agreed quickly. "But isn't it a bit risky, Oliver? After all, there's no one else here and Spinosa could get violent."

"He won't do anything." Chapin's certainty was absolute. "He's beaten."

There was little point in disagreeing with the old man when he was in one of these moods, but Sidney tried anyway. "I'm sure you're right. But, Oliver, why take the risk?"

"Because we need to hear whether he has a solution."

"How can he?" Sidney was hanging onto his composure only with great difficulty. Millions, hundreds of millions, the Chapin empire had lost by the miscalculations of

Spinosa . . . oh God, and perhaps by his own . . . and now Oliver wanted to interview the man, seek his advice.

"It is right to give the man a last chance."

"And if he were to resist?" Sidney asked, phrasing the question carefully to avoid seeming argumentative, "or if he were to have no solutions?"

"In either case, of course, I would kill him." The statement was made with such finality that Sidney Rosenberg shuddered. He had never seen a dead man, except at a funeral. He was an accountant.

"Go. In fairness, I give him his final chance; and in fairness, he will take it. Only a man of astonishing pessimism will believe his life is over while he is still given the symbols of life to build his hope. And, while hope exists, he will grasp for it. I am our friend's hope. He will come to me. You will see."

"Oliver . . ."

"Enough."

The order, issued in a quiet voice and with enormous dignity, was irresistible. Without another word, Sidney Rosenberg left the room. Methodically he climbed the stairs to the small room in which Carlos Spinosa was imprisoned. With the greatest trepidation he unlocked the door.

Slowly, creakily, Carlos Spinosa arose. Even Sidney was shocked by his appearance. Gone was the arrogant industrialist, confident in every social situation, self-possessed in the back seat of the taxi with Oliver at his feet, wonderfully effective in negotiations. Instead, Sidney saw an aging man, shoulders bowed, face as pinched as an exhausted fox who hears the hounds baying. Spinosa swayed slightly and put out a hand to steady himself against the wall. "Listen, Sid," he said desperately, "I can explain. I really can. I'll get it straightened out. Please . . ."

"Of course," Sidney agreed. So the old man had been right again. "That's why Oliver wants to see you."

"Oh thank God." Spinosa wiped a hand over his face. It

looked like a claw and it shook so hard it seemed to shake the face itself. "I know he'll understand."

As they walked down the stairs, Spinosa kept as close to Sidney as he could, like a child seeking safety behind his mother's skirts. Sidney noted that he stank of sweat—the acrid stench of panic, not the mere musty odor of exertion—and sourly of vomit.

They reached the bottom of the stairs and, a few steps further, the massive door leading to the long dining room where Oliver waited.

"Through there," Sidney indicated.

With an obvious effort, Carlos Spinosa pulled himself straight. He tugged at his suit jacket, pulled tight the knot in his tie and, taking his time, pulled a comb through his hair. The effect was astonishing: where before there had been a beaten, frightened man, the Spinosa who now stood before Rosenberg was once again the successful entrepreneur. His crumpled, dirty clothes had become merely an accident, not a statement; his sunken cheeks and general pallor merely the signs of a hard night and a stomach virus, not of a failure of nerve.

Now, it was Sidney who experienced fear. What if Spinosa stood up to Oliver, perhaps outbluffed him after all? Could he blame him, Sidney Rosenberg, for the whole mess? Could this whole event have been staged, somehow, by Spinosa. . . ?

"I am ready," Spinosa interrupted Sidney's thoughts. His voice had regained most of its former power. Any remaining weakness, like the dirty suit, could be explained by the discomfort of his abduction. He pushed open the door and, with Sidney a few steps behind, he entered.

Whatever Sidney had expected, it was not this elaborately jovial, charming host. "Come in, come in my dear chap," Chapin beamed at Spinosa. "How are you? I do hope your journey here wasn't too uncomfortable. Most unfortunate, the circumstances. And I must apologize about your driver. A shame, that; good ones are so hard to find. But I knew you'd understand. He was being a bit overprotective, and we had to get you here privately, don't you know. Can't be too careful with that awful Pollo tribe still wandering about. Like a chicken without its head, lots of flapping but no future." He chortled with pleasure. "Do have a drink. Bit early in the day for cognac, perhaps. But no, you're probably still on last night's time schedule—perhaps a beer, or coffee?"

Carlos Spinosa stood astonished as Oliver prattled on. He, like Rosenberg, had not known what to expect. But warm chatter and social ebullience was totally unexpected.

"Well, what will it be?" Oliver asked a trace more sharply.

"Coffee. I'd like a cup of coffee, please, black."

"Ah, good, good." Oliver Chapin was all smiles again, but he didn't move. "Unfortunately, we don't actually have any coffee."

"It's all right."

"You love coffee, I know, all Brazilians do. Used to be a song about it. Something about 'An awful lot of coffee in Brazil.' You remember it?"

"No."

"No matter, not important. Now where were we?" He looked at Spinosa inquiringly, pushing his round face expectantly up into his guest's more angular one. "What were you saying?"

"I hadn't—"

"About our investment, wasn't it? Something about Turner-LaMott maybe?"

Rosenberg watched with fascination as Carlos' face started to sweat, the skin dry one moment and beaded with moisture the next.

"Well yes, of course, I'm ready to explain . . ."

"Oh, that's good." Oliver Chapin's voice remained so

friendly. "Because, we do need a bit of an explanation, don't we?"

"Yes, well, what happened was—"

"Actually, old man, I don't much mind what happened," Chapin interrupted. "What's past is past, isn't it?" Once more he beamed at Spinosa, again pushing his face up under the taller man's nose. "What I really want to know is what you're planning to do about it now."

"Well, I'm not sure that—"

"You see, the way I read my newspaper, it seems to me that the price of Turner-LaMott appears to have fallen to about sixteen dollars a share, if you can believe that. Now, I'm sure you are going to resolve that problem in your normal efficient way. That's why I'm so glad we're meeting."

"I—"

"The problem is," Oliver Chapin continued relentlessly, "that it seems to me—although, of course, I may not have it right—that at sixteen, we've lost about one hundred thirty-three million, plus the hundred million you earned us. Two hundred and thirty-three million . . . As some of my rough friends might say, 'that's a lotta bread.'"

"Of course, but—"

"What seems to be even worse is that almost all our assets, seven hundred million or so, before the loss, are tied up in Turner-LaMott. And somehow, we don't seem to have control. If we start to sell our stock at all fast, we'll just push the price down further—and lose more. At least," Oliver continued, "that's how it appears to me." He was almost whispering now, and the warmth had left his face and evaporated from his voice. He looked lethal. "But of course, I'm still sure you're going to explain to me where my thinking is incorrect."

"Yes, but—"

"I know you won't renege now. I'm quite confident, Mr. Spinosa, as I said to Sidney here only this morning—

didn't I, Sidney—that you already have a plan to live up to your promise."

"Of course," Sidney lied his agreement.

"So, stated very simply, Mr. Spinosa, what I want to know is how are you going to get back the full seven hundred million cash you owe us—and gain control of Turner-LaMott's pharmaceutical division into the bargain?"

Carlos Spinosa made an enormous effort at control. Although the sweat on his forehead continued to gather in tiny pearls, now coagulating into droplets and then coursing slowly down his forehead, he managed to stop his hands from shaking and to force his voice to sound confident. "I am certain that the TLM stock will rebound."

"To thirty—or to forty or fifty, as you told us?"

"It will come back far enough to wipe out most of your losses."

"But control . . ."

"Remains a good possibility . . ."

"And our cash?"

"Also a good likelihood that it can be rescued over time." Spinosa seemed to relax a little further. Perhaps, after all, he could buy some time from this old man, convince him that he actually did have some tricks left up his sleeve. "Yes, I do believe that the scheme I am completing now, while it may take a little longer, will greatly improve the chances—"

"I'm not interested in chances or likelihoods or possibilities," Oliver Chapin said in his softest, roundest voice. Then, suddenly, appallingly, his voice rose to a scream, his face contorted with rage. The vein on his neck swelled and pulsed. "I want my fucking money!" As fast as Oliver's rage had started, it seemed to end. Only the reverberations of his screams remained. "And I want it now," he added, the words icy.

"But you can't . . ."

"Indeed I can. You owe me money and I intend to collect it from you just as I would from any other two-bit piker." Oliver Chapin paused. "You see, it was not all my own money. It was mostly our group's money. Personally I put in only about five percent of the whole; they put up the rest. And I'm afraid that they will want it back. Even if I were willing to let you off the hook, I fear my partners would not be so lenient." Calmly Oliver reached behind the armchair next to him. The next moment Spinosa and Sidney Rosenberg realized that the old man now cradled a sawed-off shotgun in his arms. It was a weapon of grotesque force, but he held it with as much tenderness as if it were a fragile thing. "I want it back, Carlos. That money," he said in his softest voice. "Do you have anything planned to get it back?"

"No." The single word encapsulated fully the depth of Spinosa's despair. "Please. Give me time. A few days."

"Then you must give us *your* money. All of it, until you have paid back what you owe."

"I cannot do it. You would force me into bankruptcy. Then what would you have?"

Oliver Chapin cocked the gun and pointed its barrel at Spinosa. "Then I would not have a mutilated man on my mind," he said. With that he started to pull the trigger, as cooly as if he were firing a BB gun during target practice.

"No. God, no!"

But Oliver Chapin's arm did not waver and his finger continued to tighten.

"No!" Spinosa screamed again, his terror absolute.

But the crescendo of the scream was cut off by the shattering blast of the shotgun, which sounded louder in the confined space than anything that Sidney had ever heard.

"Christ!" Sidney whispered, too stunned to move.

At the same moment, there was another scream from Spinosa, this one as much of pain as terror, as he was smacked flat onto the floor by the blast.

Even as Sidney gazed with horror at Spinosa writhing on the floor, he realized that the man was not mortally wounded. Oliver must have moved the gun away at the last moment. Had it hit Carlos full blast there would have been little left of him. The plaster to the left of him had quite caved in, like an eggshell hit hard with the back of a spoon. Even so, enough stray pieces of shot had hit Spinosa's leg to render his pants leg a tattered mess and his leg inside it as bloody as if it had been mauled by a shark.

"Oh God, oh God," Spinosa was whining now. "Oh God. Leave me alone. Oh, please." His legs were pulled up to his stomach so that he lay in the fetal position, nursing his wounded leg. His begging and tears became a litany, mournful and meaningless.

"Shut up." Oliver Chapin ordered matter-of-factly. "You are scratched, not badly hurt." He sounded gruff but, in spite of it, surprisingly kind. "This time, I went easy on you. Next time . . . well, look at the wall!" He chuckled.

"What do you want?" Spinosa struggled to his feet and stood upright with an effort, supporting himself against the back of a chair. "You bastard," he said with sudden venom. "What are you trying to do? What do you want?"

In the instant his anger had changed him again. Where a moment before he had been a pathetically whimpering child, now he had regained much of his dignity and stature.

Sidney was again amazed by the transformation. He was not sure, however, whether Spinosa's new strength was real, or merely the final dignity of failure.

"Let me assure you," Spinosa said in his normal gravel monotone, as if he were negotiating yet another business deal, "that I will do everything I can."

"I'm so pleased," Oliver said, for his part treating Spinosa as if he were an honored business guest.

"Well?"

"I have a little contract here for you to sign. It's quite

simple, really. All it states is that you will turn over all your assets to a new company that I have set up. In return, you will have a thirty-three percent share of that new company for as long as you want. Or at least until I decide to buy you out, which I can do at any time, at a price to be basically determined by an arbitrator of my choice."

"What assets has your company?" Carlos asked.

"Your assets, Carlos, old man. That is all. Just your assets. And, of course, my considerable know-how. That's what makes it such a good deal."

"And if I refuse?"

"Look at the wall!"

"Very well." Carlos held out his hand for the paper. "I will sign."

"No, no." Oliver Chapin shook his head. "We have lots of work to do first. It is not easy to give away fifty or sixty million." He looked at Spinosa speculatively. "That is what you have, is it not?"

"Why nothing like that, I'm afraid." Spinosa said it so naturally that Sidney Rosenberg believed him. Evidently, his boss had been misinformed. But by whom? And why hadn't he involved Sidney in gathering the information? There could be only one answer to that, and it turned Sid's stomach to liquid and let him taste it in his throat.

"I think you do," Oliver Chapin spoke as if to a child, sounding more sad than angry. He moved the gun fractionally and he placed his finger back on the trigger. It was enough.

"Yes," Spinosa cried. "Yes, yes. You are right."

"This is the list we have," said Chapin. "Would you add to or subtract from it, please."

Spinosa looked at it. "It seems correct."

"You lie." Oliver's trigger finger tightened. "You know there is a million or so in the Geneva account..." Chapin's voice grated almost as harshly as Spinosa's own.

"I shall ask you only once more. If you do not fill in what I already know, I will assume you are also hiding other things." He paused. "Spinosa, old chap," he added with a chuckle that set Rosenberg's skin tingling with fear, "in that case, it's the wall for you. Your belly, flat as it is, will be sticking out in a great round lump. But on the other side of your body, if you know what I mean. It will be a strange sight for me, and quite unhealthy for you." He chuckled at the image so that his own belly jiggled. "I think you'd better sit down and go through that list now," he said sternly, "and with care."

"Yes." The word was without hope. Slowly Carlos sat down at one end of the long table and started to peruse the list. Once he deleted one of the items on it. "I sold that last month," he muttered. Twice he added significant items that had not been included.

For twenty minutes, the tableau in the room remained the same. Carlos, head bowed over the papers, concentrated on correcting the list of his assets. Oliver Chapin, inquisitor, jailor and father confessor as well, remained standing, gun held loosely but competently in the crook of his arm. And Sidney Rosenberg propped himself against the rough but highly polished refectory table, a silent, worried observer.

Eventually, Spinosa looked up. "I'm done," he said like a schoolboy finished with his exam questions. "It's accurate as nearly as I can recall."

"Very good." Oliver Chapin did not even glance at it this time. "I'm sure it is," he agreed. "We'll make it part of our agreement. Later, I'll have it copied for your files." He paused. "Now," he added, "the time's come for implementation. First you sign. Then you use the telephone to issue the orders for transferring the funds. I imagine there are code words and voice prints, all the normal safeguards, that would make it impossible for me to effect the transfers without your help. I know there would be in my case. I imagine that you will not play the game of pretending to make a transfer and then failing to do so. My people will let me know right away if they do not receive confirmation. They are standing by already. Sidney nows who they are and where." Oliver smiled his warmest smile. "Why not just get on with it then," he suggested, "and be sure to get it right the first time."

Carlos Spinosa said nothing. Instead, he twirled in his chair and there was a look of hatred in his eyes. "And if I refuse?"

With barely a movement of his arm, Oliver Chapin swerved the muzzle of the gun, which had been at right angles to Spinosa, more in his victim's direction. Before either of the other men in the room realized what he was doing, there was another thunderous blast. As if by magic, the floor a few feet from where Spinosa sat developed a crater of splintered, gouged wood. And the shoe on Spinosa's previously unharmed leg seemed suddenly to age and wrinkle and fill with blood.

Carlos Spinosa screamed once and fell off his chair, again writhing. There was no sound in the room except his renewed wails of pain. Sidney realized that the room had started to stink from Spinosa's urine, which now stained the front of his trousers right down to the tatters from the first blast. No one said anything as Spinosa's moans gradually lessened to mews of pain and fear.

"Shall we proceed?" Oliver Chapin asked in a perfectly ordinary voice. "You'd better get up off the floor." Carlos Spinosa sat up painfully, and slowly pulled himself back up to the chair. He sank down onto it, exhausted from the effort, his face wet with tears. "Yes," he acquiesced softly. "Okay." It was his final acceptance, and final defeat. Tears started to run down his face copiously. But after a while they stopped and he became still, shuddering only occasionally with dry sobs.

Without another word, Chapin lay down the gun and

walked toward the edge of the room. He made no attempt to look at Spinosa or protect his own back. When he reached the window he pulled the bell-cord hanging there. There seemed to be no sound as a result, but Rosenberg assumed it rang too far away. Then he returned slowly to the center of the room and the gun. Neither Spinosa nor Rosenberg had moved at all. "We'd better get you cleaned up a bit before we proceed," Oliver said kindly. "I've rung for a matron to come in and give you a hand. In an hour or so, we'll reconvene. She'll call me when you're ready."

The door at the far end of the room opened and a middle-aged lady with a bun of white hair on the back of her head and a warm smile on her face entered. "Come with me, dear," she beckoned to Spinosa.

"Where are we going?" Spinosa asked weakly.

"Sorry, dear. I'm afraid I can't hear you. I can see your lips move, and I can read them if you look at me head on. But my hearing's been gone almost seven years now." She smiled warmly at Spinosa, walked over to him and helped him rise. "Dear, dear," she clucked sympathetically.

Painfully, half-supported by the nurse who was evidently stronger than she looked, Spinosa hobbled out of the room.

"Have a good bath," Oliver Chapin called after him, once again jovial, avuncular . . . an altogether charming old fellow.

It was not quite an hour before Carlos Spinosa returned. He was bandaged and clad in pajamas, leather slippers and casual clothes that didn't quite fit. Oliver Chapin welcomed him warmly. "Feeling better, my dear fellow? I do hope so. You looked terrible before."

Spinosa gazed at him with confused and frightened eyes but said nothing.

"Good, good," Chapin continued unabashed, "then we can get on with our work. Why don't we go into the study, the three of us? It's an office, really, telephone, telex, international document transmitter—everything you'll need to communicate. And Sidney here knows how to work them all. Right, Sidney?" Oliver sounded like a proud parent boasting of his son's prowess.

"Yes."

"Good. Then let's get to it. Oh, and I've arranged for a light lunch for you later. Just a little smoked salmon and salad." He led the way into the study. A comfortable two-room suite in total contrast to the ecclesiastical austerity of the dining room, it was furnished in pleasant modern furniture. The sofa and armchairs were covered with a green lattice-and-leaves design. The soft pile carpet was a slightly deeper green, and lots of pillows, some of matching color, others of various shades of brown, were distributed everywhere. "I'll make sure the wine's Brazilian, of course," Oliver said, as he ushered them in. "And Brazilian coffee too." He smiled. "This time I've been able to find some. Now," he added abruptly, "I'll leave you two to get on with your work." He turned without another word and left the room.

All morning, through the lunch that arrived as promised, and throughout the afternoon Spinosa worked, making phone calls overseas, giving Sidney confirmatory telexes to transmit, drawing up powers of attorney, which Sidney typed, notarized on the spot, and promised to have "witnessed" later.

"A lot of work, I must say, transferring assets," Oliver said returning when at last the work was almost complete.

"Yes, it is," Sidney agreed, his own concern muted by the hours of secretarial work.

Spinosa remained silent.

"Is it almost done then, old chap?"

"Yes, it is." Sidney repeated.

"Yes," Spinosa agreed, but the word carried no inflection.

"Very well. I'll wait in the dining room until you are quite finished. Make sure we're fully satisfied, Sidney. Then bring our guest—our new partner, I should say—in to say good-bye before he's on his way." The old man left the room walking slowly, evidently tired out by the long day.

It was another hour before Spinosa was done. And even then Sidney Rosenberg, ever the careful professional accountant, had a number of questions to make sure nothing had been forgotten. But eventually these too were resolved, and Sidney was satisfied. "There," he said at last. "That's it. It's all done."

"Yes," Spinosa said bitterly, treating him almost as if he were his last friend. "A life's work entirely lost."

Sidney clicked his tongue in unconscious sympathy. "It must be hard," he agreed. He could imagine how awful it would feel if he were suddenly to lose his own nest egg. How terrible it would be to be poor again. "Come," he said gently, "Oliver wants to say good-bye."

"All done then?" Oliver asked cheerily as the two men entered the dining room. He was sitting in the corner in one of the wing chairs. The daylight, almost faded into night, was behind him so that he sat in full shadow, a dark figure, dwarfed by the chair, inconsequential in the long, imposing room. "Come to say your good-byes, then?"

"All complete," Sidney repeated. "Some of the papers need your signature, but that can be done later. Everything's in good shape. Carlos has been entirely cooperative."

"Good, good. I'm so glad to hear that. Now I'll be able to rest easy." He sighed in satisfaction. "So it's good-bye, then, I suppose."

"Yes, I suppose," Spinosa agreed. But there was nothing but black despair in his eyes.

As Sidney Rosenberg watched in bewilderment, Oliver

Chapin arose from his armchair. There was a springiness in his movement that belied his age. He seemed no longer in the least tired. He was, Sidney realized with a shock, again holding the shotgun.

Before anyone else could move, Oliver had the gun aimed full at Carlos Spinosa. There was the shattering explosion, even louder, it seemed to Sidney, than it could possibly have been before. And in what seemed like slow motion to the horrified Sidney, the body of Carlos Spinosa disintegrated into a million droplets of liquid, an arc of reds and browns and whites, which eventually splashed against the wall in a large splatter of gore. Then, for a moment, there was silence interrupted only by the sound of dripping.

"Good-bye, old man," Oliver Chapin said in a quiet, sober voice.

"Why did you do that?" Rosenberg croaked, knowing he was about to vomit.

Without answering Oliver Chapin reached for a second gun resting against the other side of his chair. Before Sidney could even move, let alone protect himself, flee, even cry out, it was aimed straight at his own stomach. There was yet another shattering explosion and a new arc of blood. But this one, Sidney Rosenberg could not observe at all.

"Good-bye to you too, old chap," Oliver said softly. He threw the gun that had killed Spinosa down near the remains of Sidney Rosenberg, and tossed the other near to what was left of Spinosa.

"Good-bye to both of youse," he said in the accent of the Boston streets where he had been originally trained. He walked nextdoor to collect the papers that now belonged to him. "Not as much," he muttered. "But better than nothing." He smiled to himself. The good part was that no one had any inkling that this fortune existed. "Sixty-two million dollars," Oliver Chapin said to himself.

"Not as much as the group lost, but a lot more than I did." He finished packing quickly and left the house where, all the evidence would show, two men had quarreled and then killed each other—while Oliver Chapin was far, far away. "And mine alone," Oliver gloated as he drove steadily away.

30

Oliver Chapin kissed his wife good-bye with a feeling of nostalgic sadness rather than real sorrow. She had been a good woman, useful and loyal to him, for almost forty years. And if her reserved Boston breeding had made her hopelessly unresponsive in bed—and his refusal to tell her anything about his wholly preoccupying business activities meant that they had little to talk about—why that was just how marriages were. She had borne his children without fuss, cooked his meals in the early days and later showed the cook how to make what he liked, and adorned his presence at many a social function where wives were de rigueur and she was a particularly appropriate one.

What a shame, he thought, that for such a long time he would have to leave her. It was simply too dangerous to stay. For the moment, he felt safe enough. No one would attack him while the heat was still on from the many slayings of the last few weeks. There were cops everywhere watching, hoping for some lead into the deaths of Spinosa and his chauffeur, Rosenberg and Pollo, and of course the fearful number of unnamed soldiers from the warring factions seeking to take over the lost Chapin empire. All that would calm down after a while. It always did. But then, inevitably, the remnants of the Pollo family—or of the Chapin empire itself, would seek revenge. Limpet might protect him for a while. But to be really safe, a change of name, appearance, habits, and of course abode were essential. Unfortunately, there was no way his wife could possibly learn to change her appearance, or the attitudes and prejudices of a lifetime. Too bad . . .

On the other hand, he reflected with satisfaction, there were lots of pleasant places to live, lots of helpers to care for him, lots of cooks to feed him, and, best of all, lots of attractive women with whom to play his games. And with sixty million dollars, all those things were available to him. Fiction writers liked to pretend that the tentacles of the mafiosi stretched throughout the world. But Oliver Chapin knew better. He feared no enemies in the Peninsular Hotel in Hong Kong, the Okura in Tokyo, the Lancaster in Paris, the Connaught in London or even the Bel Air in Los Angeles. And there was just no need, he decided contentedly, to visit the Beaver Brook Country Club, Chicago's Loop or any of his old haunts . . . not if it meant putting his life in danger.

"See you for dinner, then." His wife called out as he hurried into his bulletproof limousine.

"Perhaps not," he said. "Things are a bit confused. Sorry, old dear. You'll just have to expect me when you see me."

"Yes," she said, far too proud to let on that she guessed he was leaving her for good. Pity, she thought, as she watched his limousine accelerate down the driveway, that he had to leave. If she had a choice . . . but that she'd never had with Oliver, not since that first and only decision to accept his proposal. She could no longer quite remember why she had, except that he was certainly different, unlike anyone she knew, exciting . . .

So now he was going. Well, no doubt she'd survive all

right. At least there seemed to be enough money. Oliver never mentioned it, but he provided everything she could possibly want.

Or could she be wrong? No. He gave every indication that his departure was to be long-term if not permanent. He'd even smuggled out the prescriptions both for his reading glasses and for that special cream he needed to cure the raw patch that sometimes developed on his ear. Was he in trouble with the police? It wouldn't be the first time, she knew. But the less she knew of his affairs—business or otherwise—the better. Perhaps she'd never know why he'd left. "Curiosity killed the cat," she admonished herself.

She turned back from the doorway. There was so much to do today. The roses needed pruning; that gardener really was a lazy fellow.And she had to call Meredith to decide where they'd have lunch. Oh, and there was the Red Cross meeting this afternoon. She'd better make a list. . . .

Sitting in the back of his limousine, Oliver Chapin was as content as he could ever remember being. Considering how very wrong everything had gone, he'd come out on top. His fortune was larger than ever and, if his power base had eroded, why so had the demands and risks he had to live with. No longer would he have to face down the Caro Pollos of the world; nor put up with the aggravation of listening to a man as dreadfully boring as Sidney Rosenberg; nor have to worry day and night where the next shipment was coming from, or which police officer would unexpectedly decide to go straight, or which senator, expensively purchased, would so lose control of his constituency that not even Chapin's money could get him reelected. No, from now on, Oliver decided with a satisfied sigh, he could do just what he wanted.

His fantasies started to rouse and, with them, visions of

the gymnasium. That was one of the few things he would miss. Not that new women would be hard to find, but the facility was almost irreplaceable. What the hell, he'd just decided he could do whatever he wanted, hadn't he?

"Limpet," he said, pushing down the intercom button and speaking into the mouthpiece. "I think I'd like to take a little exercise."

"Yes sir."

"At the gymnasium."

"I understand, sir," Limpet allowed himself no point of view about his employer's activities as long as they didn't affect security. As long as he continued to get paid plenty—and was occasionally allowed to exercise his own talents for mayhem and brutality—why, he would remain utterly loyal to Oliver Chapin. But a dead employer was of no value, so Limpet would see to it that Mr. Chapin remained strictly alive—and would object to anything that made that task more difficult. "I think that might be dangerous, Mr. Chapin. There's no one to protect you."

"No one would know I was there."

"Maybe." Limpet was doubtful. "But—"

"What about an instructor?" Oliver interrupted him. "You know what I want?"

Limpet knew all right. He had been involved often enough in finding the girls . . . and in his own spare time he liked to move in the circles from which some of the toughest ones came. There was one woman, in fact, a bit older than the boss normally liked them, but beautiful and surely hard enough, who'd approached him only a few days ago to see if he could get her onto the old man's list. But, no, he didn't know enough about her. "No, I'm afraid—"

"There'll be a bonus," Oliver interrupted again. "Say a grand if you find an instructor who'll go the distance." Oliver chuckled. "That shouldn't be too hard," he said softly. "I'm a harmless old fellow, now aren't I?"

A thousand bucks. That, Limpet decided, was worth a little extra risk. And the old man was right, no one would expect him to show up at the gymnasium. There probably wasn't much danger. As for going the distance, there was no question in his mind that the lady had what it took. "I'll make a call, sir," he promised.

"Very good. Very good indeed."

Limpet stationed himself outside the solid, soundproofed rear entrance to the gymnasium. From the window he could see both ways down the street. Nothing could happen, now that the boss was inside. A few minutes earlier, he had let the girl in too. God, she was beautiful, that one. And tough. He'd been right. Even the Deacon would be hard put to break her style or spirit. Limpet only hoped that the woman's age would be masked sufficiently by the dimmed lights in the gymnasium. Her body was sinewy and superb, there'd be no problem with that, but there were lines on her face that gave away her age—mid-thirties if she's a day, Limpet decided as she arrived. Twenty years older than the boss preferred, and ten years older than he would normally accept. Still, what choice was there at this little notice? The thousand bucks were as good as his. He started to drift into his own fantasies about spending them.

Inside the gymnasium, Oliver Chapin had dimmed the lights and seated himself on the circular couch in front of the stage. Otherwise, however, he had not had time for preparations. Today's exercise would be spontaneous . . . there was a special excitement in that, he decided. He wondered what sort of instructor Limpet had been able to find. He'd know soon enough. Limpet had telephoned in just a moment ago to say she'd arrived and was changing in the back room.

Next to Oliver lay his favorite three-pronged whip. And under the pillow beside him was hidden a loaded, tiny, but lethal pistol. It was always best to be careful . . .

When the music commenced, Oliver was surprised and pleased. Obviously Limpet had found a resourceful woman; he himself hadn't even known where the tape machines were located. The tape she had chosen was good too, a slow drumbeat, hardly more than a muffled background of rhythm. Oliver settled himself back against the soft, low cushions of the couch and felt himself start to harden.

Suddenly there was the slam of a door, and she was there, tall and dignified, incredibly slim, dressed all in black, as serious as a mourner. Her figure was accentuated by the sheath of black skirt slit on one side up to mid-thigh, and by the exaggerated stiletto heels. The top half of her face was covered with a black veil. Her willowy height was enhanced by her hair, also black, which was piled on top of her head and held there by a tiny black hat and two steel hatpins. Her mouth, just visible, was a scarlet slash of lipstick. In all, she seemed as obvious and excessive as a Parisian apache dancer.

"You look absurd," Oliver Chapin said in disgust, disappointed by the hackneyed symbolism and the exaggeration of her appearance. "Like the start of a third-rate porno scene."

"Fuck you," she said calmly, and walked over to stand in front of him. "For what you are about to receive, may the Lord make you truly thankful." She made the sign of the cross over him.

"Yeah?" He was amused by her blessing. "Who the hell are you then, my dear, to say grace over me? What's your name?"

But the woman turned away without responding. And with a leap she was on the stage. Oliver realized that there was a dancer's strength and litheness about her that he found attractive. She towered over him, one leg demurely in front of the other, a tall figure seeming more likely to burst into a song or lead a musical production than to arouse his sadistic desires.

"So?" he asked. "Are you proposing just to stand there?"

"What do you want then, old man?" she asked scathingly. "This?" She ground her hips and then jammed them forward in the classic erotic dancer's bump and grind. "Or this?" and she turned and sashayed across the stage, keeping time with the drum beat, which had become louder, the globes of her buttocks rolling under the tight skirt. "Or perhaps this?" She returned to stand in front of him and lifted the front of her skirt so that he could see the black garter belt holding up her stockings. "Oooh," she cooed. "Aren't I cute." She dropped her skirt abruptly. "So what is it to be, old man?" she said in her cold, Brooklyn twang.

"Goddamm it." Oliver Chapin's anger was mounting rapidly. "If you don't—"

"Don't what?" she demanded. "Don't pretend to be whipped? Don't suffer for you?" She sneered down at him. "Listen, mister," she said, her accent even more pronounced, "you paid me, so you call the shots. Anything you want, I'll do. Okay? As long as it don't take more than an hour, or mess up my clothes. You do that number, an' you just might find yourself payin' more than you bargained."

"You miserable bitch," Oliver spoke softly. "You're going to get a lesson you won't soon forget."

"Yeah? From who?"

"A lesson in manners, my girl, and in the meaning of respect."

"From you?" She laughed at him. "You gonna shoot me, then?"

"I'll . . ." He reached for the whip beside him. Taking it firmly by the handle, he started to rise. "I'll . . ."

"Do what, darling?" She showed no fear whatsoever. "Hit me with that?" Slowly she turned away from him.

"When you've decided what you want me to do," she said, "let me know." The yawn she stifled was either authentic or a brilliant piece of acting. She seemed utterly bored by Chapin and the whole scene, a Broadway professional forced into amateur theatricals. "You poor old man. I guess you've forgotten what it's all about."

Oliver Chapin, standing beneath her, was so furious now he was trembling from head to toe with his outrage. "Bitch," he cried through clenched teeth. "You bitch!" He raised the whip and brought the cord cracking down with a pistol explosion next to her.

But if he expected a reaction of fear, he was again disappointed. Slowly she turned. "Games?" she asked, lifting up her veil so that he could see her whole face for the first time, coldly beautiful and full of disgust for him. "Very well, little man. If that's what you want, you shall have your games." Her mouth was contorted into the cruelest of smiles. "Oh yes," she repeated, "you shall have your games."

Oliver Chapin had had enough. "You will not think it a game when I'm done," he said softly. She was not young enough, he realized, but there was no doubt she was tougher than any instructor he'd had for a long time. He would enjoy beating up this one. Enjoy wiping that sneering supercilious look off her red-painted lips. He walked deliberately to the side of the room where the great cat-o'-nine-tails, hanging on the wall, had long awaited his pleasure—a lethal instrument, this, with which Jews in Belsen used to be punished and often killed. He had acquired it many years ago from a very specialized collection somewhere in Bavaria. Up to now, he had used it only once before, and the instructor—a five-time veteran of his excesses who thought she could take anything—had howled for mercy within minutes.

"What's your name?" he asked her again in his gentlest voice, walking back with the whip's cords draped delicately over his arm as if he were a waiter about to pour wine.

But again the girl wouldn't answer.

Incensed, Oliver brought the great cat down onto her shoulders with killing force. "Your name?" he demanded through clenched teeth.

She screamed once as the whip ends wrapped themselves around her body, as painful as barbed wire. Then she twisted, throwing her whole body away from the old man. So violent was her wrench that she fell forward halfway across the stage, breaking the heel of one shoe and losing the other shoe entirely. Her hat was jerked loose, and her hair fell out of its arrangement and cascaded onto her shoulders. The two needles holding it slid across the floor.

But she had the whip.

Kicking off her broken shoe, she jumped upright, her banshee wail full of triumph. Long before Oliver Chapin realized the extent of his danger, she had him beaten. The very first slash of the whip drew blood from his cheek and wrist. He staggered back, away from the gun under the pillow, his only hope.

She lashed into him then, coldly and methodically. He started to scream. As her cracking blows continued to cut into his body and face, his clothes became more tattered, his skin more lacerated.

Then, as the flogging continued, his screams lessened until he barely whimpered.

Still she continued to slash the mighty whip at him, each blow landing with a lethal thud, as heavy as a stick, as sharp as a blade. Occasionally, she wiped the sweat from her brow with her free hand. Her chest heaved with her exertion, but the blows did not weaken.

Slowly, Oliver Chapin started to die.

But even through his searing agony, his heart now barely able to sustain him, he knew the fates were somehow just; that his pain was deserved. Yet still he had to know who his tormentor was, to whom his expiation was being paid. Blinded, and his body reduced to raw flesh, he made one final, momentous effort. "Who are you?" he screamed.

As from an infinite distance, like huge bells reverberating in his head, more painfully loud than any noise on earth, the answer came. "My name is Gina Belladonna," the woman cried between her gasps for air. "Carlos used to call me Bella."

They were the last words Oliver Chapin ever heard.

In the heart of New York's financial district, dwarfed by the skyscrapers of Wall Street and the twin towers of the World Trade Center, nestles a tiny church. Usually it is forgotten or ignored amidst the daily rush and struggle to multiply dollars. But today it showed a festive air: a wedding was in progress.

Up the aisle walked the bride, a beautiful young woman, dressed in a traditional white wedding gown. Her mother, who had worn the same gown before her, held her head erect and smiled happily. Why people cried at weddings she couldn't imagine. This was a simply marvelous occasion as far as she was concerned. Considering all that had led up to it, certainly the best day of her life.

Beside the bride walked her obviously prosperous father. He moved with dignity and assurance. Occasionally, he glanced down at his daughter, and the pride and love glowing in his eyes would have astonished those who knew him only as a rather pompous businessman. He felt blessed beyond most men, resurrected, awed by his luck. Like his wife, he was also certain that this was the finest day that his life ever had or ever could bestow.

The service, traditional in every respect, proceeded without a hitch. "Do you, David Fellows, take this woman to be your lawful wedded wife?"

"I do."

"And do you, Susan Bagnew, take this man . . ."

"I do."

Then, the service over, Susan and David kissed. And for both of them too, there could be no doubt that this was by far the best day of their lives.